QUEENMAKER

QUEENMAKER

A Novel of
King David's Queen

India Edghill

Picador
New York

www.picadorusa.com

Picador® is a U.S. registered trademark and is used by St. Martin's Press
under license from Pan Books Limited.

For information on Picador Reading Group Guides, as well as ordering,
please contact the Trade Marketing department at St. Martin's Press.
Phone: 1-800-221-7945 extension 763
Fax: 212-677-7456
E-mail: trademarketing@stmartins.com

ISBN 0-312-28919-7

First published in the United States by Talitho Press, Xlibris

10 9 8 7 6 5 4 3

For Dad (James Henry Wenk, 1925–1989),
who heard the first 150 pages.
For my sister Rosemary, who read those pages to
Dad and then made sure I finished the book.
For Devra, who taught me
to write in the first place.
And for my first agent, Anita Diamant Berke
(1918–1996), who made me feel like a real writer.

ACKNOWLEDGEMENTS

The author wishes to thank those who read *Queenmaker* in its various incarnations and provided invaluable comments and criticism: James Allen, eluki bes shahar, Anne Bushyhead, Jane Butler, Sue Krinard, James Macdonald, Myra Morales, Susan Poirier, Niloufer Reifler, Dora Schisler, Bonnie Wenk Stallone, Muriel Verdibello, Gloria Edghill Wenk, and a very special thanks to Judy York, artist extraordinaire.

The book you now hold in your hands has been many things: a labor of love, to show my father his faith in my writing ability was not misplaced; an attempt to give a voice to a biblical woman long condemned to silence; a proof to my mother that she didn't waste her money when she bought me that new computer; a self-published novel; a St. Martin's hardcover. And now it's a trade paperback! Sometimes *Queenmaker* seems to have as many lives as a cat —a very fortunate cat with a great many friends helping her along her way. This latest incarnation provides me an opportunity to thank *Queenmaker*'s new friends—the ones whose efforts made the book's current life such a thrill to share.

So here I'd like to thank Anna Ghosh, my very special agent, and Russ Galen, who both are not only great agents but great people, always willing to share knowledge and to advise and help. And Danny Baror, my wonderful foreign rights agent, who added a great many foreign languages to *Queenmaker*'s repertoire.

At St. Martin's, there's Matthew Baldacci and his great marketing team, who made sure everyone knew about *Queenmaker*. And there's Nichole Argyres, the world's greatest editorial assistant, who fixes problems I didn't even know I had.

And then—of course—there's the queen of *Queenmaker*'s friends, my amazing and supportive editor, Diane Higgins. No writer could ask for a better editor; to have her guiding my book into its future is an author's dream come true.

So thank you Anna, Danny, Diane, Matthew, Nichole, and Russ, for bringing *Queenmaker* so far and doing so much for the book and for me. I can't wait to see where *Queenmaker* goes next!

—India

PROLOGUE

"What can he have more
but the Kingdom?"
—I Samuel 18:8

There are many who say that David loved me because I resembled
my brother Jonathan. That is not true; David loved no woman,
though he lay with many. Women loved him.

Even I loved him once. When I was young, my very bones
melted for love of David.

Although I was a king's daughter, I did not think he would
ever look at me. David was a hero. A hero should receive great
beauty as his prize, and I was not beautiful. When I was young I
was thin and dun-colored, like the summer hills.

But I looked at him. When he and my brother Jonathan came
riding their chariots through the streets in the pride of their triumphs, I was one of those who waved palms and threw flowers
and cried his name. I had no eyes for my brother, it was all for
David—David, who glowed hot as the sun, and was as far from
my reach.

All the world knows David's story now—he always had a
master's way with words, and always could tell a tale so that men
repeated it to his credit. When I was a child I would sit at my
brother Jonathan's knee and listen while David sang his songs. My
favorite was the tale of the death of the Philistine champion Goliath.
David had to be coaxed to sing that, but he would always laugh
and give in, in the end. "What, that old tune again? Oh, very
well—to please you, Michal."

"Five smooth stones," he would sing then, smiling down at me. "Five smooth stones did Yahweh put into my hand . . . . "

He always gave the credit to Yahweh, but I knew better. In those days, the god I worshipped was David.

CHAPTER 1

*"Let David, I pray thee,
stand before me . . . ."*

—I Samuel 16:22

My father Saul was not born to be a king. He was a farmer, as his father had been before him. He was a good man, too—so men said then.

We were Yahweh's people, and Yahweh's people were not like other nations; we had judges and prophets, not kings, to rule over us. This had always been enough. The priests and prophets said it would always be enough.

But our borders were now hard-pressed by the armies of kings, and our warriors, answerable to no one, scattered before them.

At last our people tired of losses and cried out for a king to lead them. First the people called for a king, and then the judges too thought a king would make us stronger. At last only the prophets spoke against it. And the prophet who spoke loudest was Samuel.

Samuel was the greatest prophet in all the land, and heard Yahweh's voice most clearly. Samuel told the people that a king would bind them and command them, tax them and work them, take their sons for his army and their daughters for his house. But in the end even Samuel saw it was useless. A king the people would have.

And so Samuel agreed to choose a king for them. Who else but Yahweh's most favored prophet should choose Yahweh's king?

~

Samuel was a tall man, and thin, with eyes that glowed with power—and, I think now, with shrewdness and cunning. Samuel's eyes were fearsome things the day he came to tell my father that Yahweh had chosen him—Saul, son of Kish—to be king over the people.

My father was sitting in the kitchen-garden, bouncing me on his knee, when the prophet came to him. I was barely three, but I still remember clearly the heat of the day, and Samuel's eyes, and how my father laughed, holding me tight against his chest so that the noise boomed under my ear.

"Me, king of Israel!" he cried, when he had done laughing. "Samuel, old man, you have been fasting in the desert too long. Come, let me have a place spread for you—fruit and wine, and in the shade. Michal, my little dove, run and get your mother, that we may do honor to the prophet Samuel." He set me down, but to go I would have to run past Samuel, and after I had looked far up at his eyes, I clung to my father's knee and refused to move.

Samuel lifted his heavy wooden staff and set it down with a loud thump. "Do not mock Yahweh or me, Saul son of Kish. You are to be king. Yahweh wills it so."

"Well and well," my father said. "Mind, Samuel, I think a king a good thing, and so I said when the judges asked us all. There must be one man to make the decisions in the field, or the Philistines will be supping in our houses in another year. But it was to be drawn by lot—or so my women tell me they are saying at the well." He patted my head absently. "And now you say Yahweh has chosen me."

Samuel nodded.

"Well and well," my father said again. "But I am only the son of a humble man, and a Benjaminite—from the smallest house of the smallest tribe in all Israel. Why me, Samuel? Because I was once lucky with my spear?" My father Saul was the only man who had won a great victory since the days of the great judges. He had taken up sword and spear and saved the city of Jabesh-Gilead from the Ammonites in the same year that I was born.

"Yahweh's ways are not for us to dispute, Saul."

"I don't dispute them, man—but if the oil's to be on my head there are plenty of men who will!"

A pause. "Send the child away," Samuel said.

My father laughed again and picked me up. I buried my face in his chest, for Samuel was looking at me. "What? My little Michal? Oh, very well. Down you go, my dove, and off to your mother." There was that in his voice that meant no argument, so I ran, to get past the prophet safely.

It meant I heard no more, but I did not care. That summer I was only three, and the word 'king' meant little to me. It meant more to my brother Jonathan, though. I was playing with him when our father came up to the housetop later that morning and told him what had been said.

Jonathan was not our father's oldest son, but he was, I think, his favorite. He was some ten years older than I, broad and brown and solid as Saul was. Jonathan was not quick, or clever, but he was kind and gentle, and we all loved him well.

Now he looked long at Saul. When he finished thinking, he picked me up, and held me close, his cheek against mine. Then he said, "I thought it was to be lots."

"It is to be lots, boy. But who rules the lots, eh? Yahweh."

Jonathan thought again. "You mean Samuel, Father?"

"Now, now, did I say so? But it's only sense for Yahweh to choose a man who's good with a sword, and who knows more of tactics than herding sheep. Sheep won't drive off the Philistines or the Ammonites, eh?"

Jonathan frowned. "But, Father—"

Saul swooped me out of Jonathan's arms and swung me high. "King, by heaven! Now there'll be something done about that miserable excuse for an army—*army* they call it! And Michal here will be a princess with gold to glisten in her hair. Will you like that, my little dove?"

"No!" I did not know what a princess was, but I had learned that 'no' was a safer answer than 'yes', for then I might be agreeing to all sorts of unpleasantnesses, such as baths and braidings.

My father laughed again, long and loud, and thrust me back at Jonathan. "No, is it? You'll sing another tune when you're older, won't she, Jonathan?"

"There's never been a king in Israel before," was all my brother said as he took me into his arms.

My father did not like this. "Well, by Yahweh, there's to be one now!" he bellowed, and stomped off.

Jonathan stared after him so long I became restless, and wriggled and demanded to be put down. I was sorry afterwards, for Jonathan took me off and left me to the care of the maid who was watching my older sister Merab. He didn't even finish making my leaf-and-flower doll for me, and when I complained of this the maid slapped me and bade me hush. The other two serving-maids had just come back from the marketplace and could chatter of nothing but the search for a king, and so no one had time for me. Even Merab, who was six, wished to listen, although it could have meant little to her either.

So I sat under one of the beds and sulked, and no one paid me any heed. A king, it seemed to me, was nothing but trouble for Michal.

~

And so the lots were cast, and Saul was king of Israel. My life was little changed, save that I saw my father and my brothers less. I still lived in my father's house in Gibeah; his two wives and his concubine Rizpah still wove and spun, and taught Merab and me to do the same. But I was called 'Princess Michal' now, which made me think myself of great importance.

For my brothers all was altered. Saul had seven strong sons, and he took them all to live with the army and fight our enemies.

I thought it a fine thing to have brothers who were princes and heroes. I was proud of them, and twice proud of my father.

Everyone was proud of King Saul then—King Saul, who called the men of Israel and Judah to his banner and led them to victory after victory. All men praised the name of Saul in those days. All men save the prophet Samuel. But it did not seem to matter what one sour prophet said—not while King Saul held Yahweh's favor—and the borders.

Jonathan tried to explain matters to me once, when he had come home to visit us. That was when Jonathan told me that he believed Samuel had chosen the best warrior to be king, and now regretted his choice. I could not see why; my father had forged the chaotic hordes of Israel into a true army. When Saul's army fought, it won. Saul had defeated the Philistines, and pushed the Ammonites back and held the borders against them.

Jonathan thought long before he answered, as was his habit. "Because, little sister, our father thinks more of his own way than he does of Samuel's. He says Samuel is a prophet, not a general, and so should tend to the business of Yahweh and leave the ordering of the army to those who know better how to win battles and hold the peace."

That sounded like sense to me, and I said so.

"Yes, but Samuel says that the ordering of the army and the kingdom *is* the business of Yahweh," Jonathan said.

"And Father does not?"

"And Father does not," Jonathan agreed. I looked at him more closely; laughter danced in his eyes like sunlight over a brook, and I laughed too, hardly knowing why.

"It is nothing to laugh at, Michal," he said after a moment. I did not know why, for a moment before he too had thought it funny.

So I tossed my head, and the gold rings in my braids chimed and clashed. "Father is the king. What can an old prophet do to hurt him?"

Jonathan sighed, and put an arm around my shoulders. "That

old prophet made him king, Michal, and now I think he wishes to unmake him."

"He cannot do that! Father is a great king and the people love him!" I was past eight now. I could not imagine a life where my father was not king—and I was not the daughter of a king.

"They do not love him as well as they love their own way, and Samuel loves him not at all. That time last year when Father would not wait, and made the sacrifices himself—you remember?"

I nodded, for all knew the tale. The Philistines had been massed and ready to attack, and Samuel and the priests had not yet arrived for the sacrifices and blessings. To prevent his army from slipping away, fearful of attacking without Yahweh's approval, Saul had made the sacrifices himself. He had won the battle, so his deed must have found favor in Yahweh's eyes—but Samuel had been very angry.

"Well, that was the start of it, I think. I was away with a raiding party, and by the time I returned Samuel was swearing that Yahweh would turn his face from Father for trying to be priest as well as king, and Father was shouting so they could hear him in Ascalon that Samuel—" Jonathan looked down at me and stopped, so I did not hear what Father had called Samuel. Nor would Jonathan tell me, for all my teasing.

He would not talk of his own deeds, either, for Jonathan was a modest man, for all they sang his name in the streets. If I asked, it was always the same; Jonathan would smile and tug one of my braids and shake his head, saying, "It was nothing, little sister. We fought—I lived—others died. I was lucky."

"You were brave!" I cried. "Everyone says you are a great hero, Jonathan, and killed twenty men at a blow!"

"Go listen to 'everyone' then," he would say, and no more.

But there were many others who were happy to gossip before me. Once I knew there were tales to listen for I learned to sit and keep silent, and soon the house women—and the men, too—would forget I was there, and they would talk.

And so I heard, not only of my father's victories over our enemies, but of his bitter quarrels with Samuel. These quarrels grew worse as my father grew older. As he gained more knowledge of kingship, he was less and less willing to let priest or prophet say him nay.

When I was a girl, I thought that my father was a great king. I know better now. Saul was a great warrior, but that is not enough to make a ruler. Saul's way was to fight hard when attacked and beat foes back beyond their borders.

"Hit a man hard enough and he'll stay down. Hit an army hard enough and it'll stay home, eh?" Saul would laugh, and so would his war-captains—all save Abner, his cousin and war-chief, second in command only to Saul himself. But Abner was a man who kept his mouth tight always, and laughed seldom, so no one minded.

I thought it a valiant saying then, and wise. Well, brave my father always was. Wise? I think he was that, too, once. But that was before Samuel poured the sacred oil on his hair and made him king of Israel.

Now when my father was home he smiled less and shouted more, and swore a great deal. This made us all keep well away, when we could. I still remember how sometimes the very stones in the walls seemed to quiver, and people became still as he raged, crying to heaven that he would tolerate Samuel's interference no longer.

"Who is king in Israel, Saul or Samuel? I am, by Yahweh, and if that dusty, dried-up old man thinks he rules here—we shall see what happens in the next battle! If it's kingship he wants, well— let him take the field against Moab and earn it!"

There was always much more of this, for even my quiet brother Jonathan seemed to have lost the trick of calming him.

But it always passed, in the end, and Saul would greet Samuel in peace once more, and the prophet would smile upon him and bless him. Samuel could do little else; Saul's name was still sweet on men's tongues.

But Samuel's smiles were sour things, now, and his blessings sounded grudging.

~

I heard the final quarrel myself. All the household did, and half the town as well, for it took place in the open courtyard, and my father was never one for quiet words.

It had promised to be a day for feasting and finery—my father had won his greatest victory. For this time Saul had taken the Amalekite army, and the Amalekite king as well. The Amalekites were rich in grain and cattle; this time there had been no slaughter. This time there would be talk instead. The Amalekite king was to come home with my father, and sit at his table. A treaty, Jonathan had said. King Agag would pay us well to return his men and land; he would be King Saul's friend and pay him tribute.

I was on the rooftop, having my new-washed hair combed dry under the noonday sun. When the shouting began I ran to the edge and looked down.

Samuel stood in the courtyard below me. He was silent, but my father was not.

"Man, are you mad? Throw over a prize like that? Well, I won't ask my men to do it! Do you hear me, prophet?" My father bellowed like a stalled bull; only the dead could fail to hear.

The prophet flung back his head and pointed his staff. "You mock the words of Yahweh, Saul. Take care." His voice was low, but it carried clearly to the ear.

"Yahweh's word or yours?" My father yanked the staff from Samuel's hand and flung it away. "Who took the Amalekites, eh, you or me? Well, I'll tell you plain, old man—it was me and mine, and I'll be damned if I'll put all our prizes to the sword! I say I won't do it! I say King Agag will be as my brother—are you so blind now you can't see this will bring wealth and peace?"

"I see you take too much upon your shoulders. Who are you to think you know Yahweh's will? I warn you again, Saul—Yahweh demands the extermination of the Amalekites, man and woman, ox and ass, to the last grain and sheaf. Spare Agag and his wealth at your peril."

"And I tell *you* you go too far! Who do you think the people will follow, eh? Their king, who gives them victory and spoils, or you, you canting hypocrite?" This last was shouted louder than all the rest.

There was a silence. Samuel looked a long while at my father. I could hear the sharp buzz of insects in the roof-arbor, and the softer hum of noises from the streets beyond the house.

"Shall we put it to the test, O great King?" the prophet said at last. His voice was a venomous thing, to wither the ear his words fell upon.

Something in those words made my father swallow his anger and pride. I watched him do it, and did not understand. When he spoke again I could not hear him, although I leaned over the wall as far as I dared.

His words seemed to please Samuel. There was no more shouting, and after a few moments they both went away.

Saul bowed to Samuel's will. King Agag was slain by Samuel's own hand, and all the Amalekite wealth in flocks and herds was offered up to Yahweh instead of being given out among Saul's men.

All should have been well, then. But it was not.

Samuel watched all done as he had ordered in Yahweh's name, and then walked away from Saul. We did not learn where he went until long after, and then it was too late.

My father, bitter as tears, nursed his anger until it turned inward, and poisoned him.

And in time, to heal him, came David.

~

I was nearly ten, and growing tall, when I first heard his name.

"King Saul has a harper to give him rest at night," they said. "Jesse of Bethlehem's son David—he makes music sweet and the king calm."

My father was seldom home now, spending all his time with

his army, and I had not seen him for many months. But I could not imagine his angers soothed by any harper, however sweet. I said as much to Jonathan, when he finally came home to visit us.

"And so I said too, little sister, when his servants said that music would ease him when he was troubled. But then they brought David—and his music." Jonathan smiled in a way that made my heart leap, although I could not tell why. I had no interest in harpers. My marriage-dreams were all of heroes mighty in battle, not of men who dealt in music and soft words. I did not know then that words and music are more deadly than any spear.

Perhaps my face showed my thoughts, for Jonathan laughed. "Not all men can be warriors, Michal. No, do not toss your head at me—we have over-many who know nothing but how to hurl a spear and taunt an enemy. A king needs men with many different skills about him. And David—"

"Has many skills?" I was not sure I liked the way Jonathan's voice changed when he spoke of David. It did not alter so for me, or even for his wife, though he loved her as he should.

But Jonathan was never one to be baited with sharp words. He only smiled again and reached to tug my braids. "He can sing words of honey and play music of gold, and speak with wisdom and tact. He can also tend sheep and never lose the smallest lamb." Jonathan's eyes were soft. "Someday, little sister, you may see for yourself."

Then I did toss my head at him, all the king's daughter. "How should I see him? Will the king bring this shepherd's son home from the war-tents to eat at his table?"

"Oh, so high, Princess Michal!"

I scowled and stamped my foot. I had some of our father's temper, and all my own pride. "He will not," I said. "You know he will not!"

"He may yet," said Jonathan, solemn as a new-anointed judge. "David sings songs our father delights to hear—and a king's hall needs a harper, even as it needs a king's haughty daughter!"

Then I knew he teased, and I flung myself at him in mock

rage, to beat at him with gentle fists until he took back his words. But he would not, and called me prideful and vain, and chased me round the pillars of the outer court to tickle me until I begged him to stop.

He did, and then would have told me more about David, but I would not hear. I had more important things to think of than a shepherd's son—"Even if he *has* killed a lion and a bear, which I do not believe! Harper's tales," I said, and thought it keen wit.

"Wait and see," said Jonathan. "Wait and see."

And we spoke no more that day of David and his talents.

~

But David did not remain only my father's harper. He sang so well that he was given the post of the king's armor-bearer. And, so said the gossip, that was not all he had won. For he had found high favor not only with the king, but with the king's son. It was said Prince Jonathan loved David well—some said too well.

Our other brothers were not best pleased, but there was nothing to be done; they even said that, to give him his due, the shepherd's son had sought no advantage. King Saul had raised David up, and that was an end to it. No, the blame was all for King Saul's moods, which grew inconstant as the moon.

But not so inconstant that he failed to keep our enemies at spear's-point. For all the prophet Samuel's complaints, Saul's army had beaten all nations but the Philistines back from our borders, and held them back, too. The Philistines we had always against us; clashes with them were too common to even be worth much mention at the wells.

So when word came that the Philistine troops were mustered for war at Socoh, we paid little heed to the news. Men would fight, some would die, the Philistines would go home for another season. Then a messenger arrived gasping out a tale hard to believe, and the story of that battle was to be on men's lips forever.

The Philistines had taken their stand on one side of a valley, facing my father's camp, and then, rather than do battle, they sent forth a single champion. He was a man called Goliath, and he was a true giant, two heads taller even than my father. The messenger swore by Yahweh that this was true; when our men returned they swore the same, although some would have him three heads taller. This giant challenged all Israel to produce a man to face him in single combat for the victory.

They expected the king himself, of course. In the old days Saul would have moved like a hill lion to face the challenge, and sent a spear through Goliath's heart even as he swaggered and boasted. But Saul was no longer a young man, and his captains feared to let him try his might against a giant. I thought they were wise, then; later I was not so sure. I do not think my father thanked them for their caution, in the end.

The messenger was all smooth words and spoke all around the coal at the story's heart, but even I guessed, from what he did not say, that King Saul had not taken their interference kindly, and had gone into a rage. In such a temper no man would have been able to hold Saul back; he would have flown like a thunderbolt at the giant, had it not been for David.

While others wailed and pleaded with Saul as if they were women and he a wayward child, David acted. No one had noticed until he stood across the valley from Goliath, shouting that he was the king's champion.

"And the Philistine giant looked upon him and laughed," the messenger told us as we all pressed close and stretched our ears to hear. "For David is young, and wore no armor, and carried neither sword nor spear. But the giant did not laugh long, by Yahweh! While he still mocked, David killed him."

He waited the tale there while he drank deep of the good wine my mother had given him with her own hands; I suppose he fancied himself a harper or a bard, and wished to delay until we begged the ending, to show the value of his tale. In truth, he had chosen his words well, for I could not bear to wait another breath or heartbeat for the finish, and would gladly have shaken the rest from him, had I been close enough.

Others were as eager, and many demanded to know how a man might kill another—and that one an armored giant—and yet carry no weapon. When the courtyard echoed as if a flock of starlings chattered there, he was satisfied.

"A stone," he told us. "David killed the giant Goliath with a stone flung from a shepherd's sling. And when the giant fell, the Philistines ran, leaving their camp open to us. We chased them all the way to the gates of Gath, and they left forty times forty dead. David brought the giant's head to King Saul. The king has made him a captain of a thousand, and Prince Jonathan has kissed him before all the army and called him brother, and given him his own robe to wear."

As if all this were not enough to stretch our eyes wide, there was more. For this time the Philistines had been made so low in the sight of all men that they would surely cower in their own cities for many seasons. And so my father was to come home again—and he was to bring David with him, to live in his house and show all Israel how King Saul loved him.

The shepherd's son was to sit at the king's table after all. But now the king's daughter did not toss her head in willful pride, for my heart and mind had been caught in the net woven of David's deeds and the messenger's words. When my father's army came through the gates of Gibeah to march the streets in triumph, I too leaned far over the rooftop wall, calling out and waving flowers. I had done this before, but this time it was not my father and my brothers I looked for. Like all the others, I longed to see David.

I do not remember now what I expected to see. A war-song's hero, I suppose, spear-tall and armor-hard. But he was not like that.

At first I thought that my father had left David behind, for I saw no one who impressed me. Then Jonathan looked up and waved to me, and the man beside him looked up too. Jonathan turned and said something to him, and then the stranger waved at me too, and smiled, and I knew that it was David.

And I knew another thing as well; I would love him until I died. Yes, that is what I knew that day, when David first looked upon me, and smiled. Between one beat and the next my heart was wax to his sun, and I could not bear that he should not know it.

So I called out his name and flung my flowers at his feet. The blossoms did not stay in the hot dust, for David bent and caught some of them up, and waved my flowers back at me, smiling all the while. Then he spoke to Jonathan, and they both laughed, and moved on so that others might see them.

The rest of the women stayed to cheer the other men, but I did not. I wished to be alone, to clutch my new joy close and cherish it, for it was strange, yet already dear to me.

So I ran to sit behind the arbor at the far end of the roof and wait, and count upon my fingers the hours that must pass before I could seek out Jonathan and make him speak to me of David.

~

Of course I was not let to sit and dream as I wished. There was much to be done to make all ready for the men's feasting and comfort, and even a king's daughter must be of use in the house. My sister found me out, and I was sent here and there and back again on this errand and that. I will not say I found much pleasure in it, but it kept my hands and feet and eyes busy and made the time pass. I knew I would not be able to see Jonathan until long after the men's feast was over, and perhaps not even then.

I was fortunate, for much later I slipped away from the women, and when I went to Jonathan's courtyard he was there, and I did not even have to ask his servants to find him. So much was luck, and I would have run to Jonathan—but then I saw that David sat beside him.

It was almost more than I could bear. David's beauty caught and held me fast; I could do nothing but stare and admire from afar. It seemed to me then that I could look forever and never grow tired of his face. I stood in the shadow of the pillars like a ghost until David looked up, as if drawn by my eyes, and set aside his goblet.

"Your sister would speak with you, Jonathan." David had seen me; David had remembered one girl out of all those who had called out to him that day. "I will come again later, if I may."

David's voice was water flowing in the desert, honey dripping golden from the comb, wind sighing through the spring grass. I was lost forever; stones and butterflies filled me and I could not move, or think, or speak.

"No, David, do not go. This is my little sister Michal, of whom I have told you much. Come in, king's daughter, and meet a shepherd's son, if you are not too proud."

Jonathan wished only to tease, but I was too young for such a jest not to slice deep. I grew hot, and said that I would go, as they were busy with men's matters.

Jonathan knew me well, and saw that he had hurt me, and so he rose and came to put an arm about my shoulders. "No, no—I am sorry I teased you. Come and greet David, who is as a brother to me. I would have him dear to you as well."

All words scattered beyond my grasp once more, and so I looked down at the flagstones. I could not bear to look at David, for I knew he must think me a silly and tiresome thing, and wish me gone.

"If you are my brother, Jonathan, then Michal must be my sister, and I will be glad of it—for my father has many sons, but no daughter left at home to tend us." David did not sound as if he mocked, or thought me foolish, or wished me gone. He took me by the hand and made me sit beside him. "Stay with us, and we will talk and laugh together, and you will smile for me. Come, be my obedient sister in this."

"I will be as obedient to you as I am to my true brothers," I vowed. I would have sworn anything, done anything he asked of me. That night I could imagine no greater joy than to have David call me sister.

Jonathan choked on his wine, and laughed. I would have been angry, but then David laughed too. His laughter did not sting, but somehow called mine as well; the three of us sat there laughing until Jonathan's servants came to see what caused the noise. We must have sounded like jackals in the hills.

And when the laughter stopped I stayed with them, and listened as David and Jonathan talked. When I asked questions, I found that David would not speak of himself, any more than Jonathan would do his own boasting. But each would willingly praise the other, and so I heard much to their credit—although each would deny he deserved any; it was all the other. To hear David tell it, he had done nothing in all his life to earn any man's praise.

"What, Michal? Goliath? Oh, that was nothing—a giant is dull-witted, and slow. There was never any danger. I saw no reason for King Saul to waste his time on so unworthy a foe; I was enough."

"You were so clever, to think of the stones and the sling!"

"It was habit, nothing more. A sling is what I used to chase the bears and the wolves when I tended my father's sheep, and so comes readily to my hand. And the giant was no more than another beast to be kept away. Anyone could have done it."

Later still he sang for us, just for Jonathan and me. That was the first time I heard the song he had made about the slaying of the giant Goliath. "From the claw of the lion did Yahweh deliver me; from the paw of the bear did Yahweh deliver me; from the spear of the giant would Yahweh deliver me. My trust did I place in Yahweh; five smooth stones did Yahweh put into my hand . . . . "

David sang that, and he sang other songs, too. The servants came to light the torches before we realized how dark it was, and how late.

Jonathan sent me off before the women came seeking me there. I kissed him, and I kissed David too, as he was my brother now. I was bold enough when I set my lips to his cheek, but then I grew shy again, and ran away before he could say anything.

~

CHAPTER 2

*"And Michal Saul's daughter
loved David . . . ."*

—I Samuel 18:20

That was the start; it sounds little enough, but it was much to me. For I was the youngest child in my father's house, and treated by all but David as if I still must be held by the hand to take my steps. But I would soon be twelve and thought myself nearly a woman, so I found such treatment hard to bear. David knew it and was always kind; he never teased me as if I were a baby, as my brothers did, but spoke to me as if I were grown, and sensible.

He and Jonathan were together always, and often they would let me come too. I rode beside David in his chariot when they raced; I chased them through the rocks to the fishing pool; I sat with them on the rooftop in the long twilights. I was David's beloved little sister, as I was Jonathan's. I had his soft words and his small gifts and his hands tugging my braids.

My sister Merab had his eyes and his heart.

I knew that from the time I came upon them talking alone together in the gallery. I heard David's voice, and Merab's laugh, sounds like soft breeze on hot summer nights. When I ran around the corner I saw that they stood so close they cast only one shadow on the wall.

At my noise one shadow became two. David turned toward me and smiled, and Merab turned away and put her hands to her shoulder-brooches.

I pretended I had seen nothing, but I was not so young as

that, and I knew what it meant. Merab was already a woman to delight men's eyes; even I thought her fair. Of course David would love her.

I did not wonder if she loved him. I knew she must. Everyone loved David.

~

I thought my father loved him too. How could he not? David was the raid-leader who always won; whose victories brought glory to King Saul, and to Israel. There was a new victory-chant sung in the streets now: "Saul has slain his thousands, and David his ten thousands!"

Everyone sang it; I, too, sang—and not once did I think how my father felt, to hear those words even from his daughter's lips.

But David was more than a great warrior. David was the songmaster whose words brought glory to Yahweh. Hymns of praise, tales of love, psalms to Yahweh—nothing was too great or small for David's songs. He was loved as much for his songs as for his victories; people sang them in the streets. David used words as well as he used sword and spear.

And he loved Saul as a son does, plain for all to see. Even when my father fell into the first of his mad frenzies, so that he thought David his enemy, David said no word against him. My father shouted and brandished his spear, and threatened to pin David against the wall, and those who watched thought he would surely kill him.

But David sang his way out of danger that time, and my father was sorry for his unjust anger. It was not long after that he promised David my sister Merab for his wife, when the time was ripe.

It was a promise that drew my father much praise from the people, but some of my brothers did not like it. "Who is this man, to marry our sister—to marry the king's daughter?"

My father would not listen, and shouted them down. If he

was not too proud to own David, they should not be. And he reminded us all that he was king by chance alone, and his father had been a humble man.

"And who is your sister, that David is too low for her to wed? Is this Philistia, then, and she a queen? *I* say David is to have Merab to wife, and there's an end to it! I have my reasons, and they are better than yours! Who is king here, you or I?"

It was how he ended all arguments now; my brothers left him alone after that. Few wished to tempt his mad angers.

It was left so; David was to marry Merab and be my brother in truth. I tried to take some comfort from that. But I was growing too old to love David as a good sister loves her brother.

Still, a brother's love was better than nothing—or so I told myself.

Later I knew that by the time Merab was ripe for marriage our father was ripe for madness. But the summer that I was twelve I only knew that he was breaking his word, and I could see no reason for it. Merab was not to be given to David after all, but to a man named Adriel, of Meholah.

I heard the news as I passed some maidservants gossiping in the kitchen-court. I stopped and made them tell me the tale; they swore that it was true.

"I do not believe it!" I said, and ran to find Merab.

I found Merab in her room, holding a length of cloth up to the sunlight through the window. "Look, little sister," Merab said. "See what our father has given me! The best Egyptian byssus, and not yet sewn upon—I shall be the first to wear it! Only see how fine—and there is enough for my bride-dress, if I am careful with my cutting."

I cared nothing for that. "Oh, Merab, I have just heard such a tale—that you are not to marry David, but some old man no one has ever heard of!"

"Oh, is that all? Why yes, I am to marry Adriel—and many have heard of him, I assure you." Merab stroked the smooth white cloth and smiled.

"But why?" I asked, flinging myself into Merab's arms and weeping for what must be her sorrow. "You are so brave—but O my sister, how can you bear it?"

To my astonishment, she laughed, and pushed me away. "Bear what, little fool? Should I weep because I am to wed a man with many flocks, and many servants, instead of my father's shield-bearer? Now dry your eyes, and help me sort this linen."

I caught up a fold of my skirt and wiped my eyes. "But Merab, Adriel is so old! How can you take him instead of David?"

Merab thrust a pile of folded linens into my arms. "Because our father bids me do so, of course, and because I am not a fool!" Then she looked at me and put her arms around me, heedless of the bundle between us. "It is kind of you to worry over me, little sister, but what is past is past, and I shall be happy enough. Adriel is not so old as all that, and they say he is a good man. And he has paid our father a pretty bride-price for me, and will send him five armed fighting men as well. He will know how to value me when I am in his house."

She looked self-satisfied as a cat in sunlight. I could not believe she cared so little for David. I twisted out of her arms and flung the linens back onto the cedar-wood chest. "Merab! What of David?"

Merab tossed her head; the thin gold leaves shimmered in her hair. "Well, and what of him? Who is he that he should wed the daughter of Saul the king? Adriel is a worthy man—"

"A wealthy one, you mean!" I fancied this an arrow that would sting.

"Oh, hold your tongue!" Merab looked bored and cross, and not stung at all by my words. "Adriel is to have me and there is an end to it. Now look what you have done—half the sheets on the floor and all to be folded again! Really, Michal, you are far too old to run wild as you do—"

But I did not stay to hear the rest. I was out of her room, running through the house in a way that would have brought reproof even from Jonathan, who loved me well. But I did not care for that now. I had to find David.

~

David had gone up to the rooftop, to sit alone under the arbor of vines and play his harp. When I ran up the stairs and stopped to catch my breath at the top, I thought I had never heard sadder notes fall from harp-strings. Then he set the harp aside, and looked at me, and I knew that I would never see anything more beautiful than his face.

"Why, Michal!" he said. "What are you doing here?"

I could not answer, for I did not know.

"Come and sit by me, sister of Jonathan, and rest. You've been running in the house again—but I promise I will not scold. Sit, and I will play for you."

I obeyed, crossing the rooftop to sink down by his feet. "Oh, David," I gasped, "I have just come from Merab. I am so sorry! How could my father do such a thing to you?"

David shrugged, and the dappled light through the grape-vines danced over his skin; shadows pale gold and dark. "Saul is a king, and kings are driven by reasons only Yahweh knows."

"But he promised you Merab!"

"But Adriel promised him five armed men, five talents of silver, and five hundred sheep." David ran his fingers over the strings of his harp. A ripple of music lay between us, then silence, and sun hot on the stones.

"And who am I," he said at last, "to raise my eyes to a king's daughter? I am only the eighth son of a humble man. I am only David, son of Jesse of Bethlehem. I have never pretended otherwise. And I shall serve King Saul well, whether he gives me one of his daughters to wife or reviles me in the marketplace."

His words fell on me like rain in the desert, bringing hidden wonders to life. "David—" There was a band tight about my chest, almost like a pain. "King Saul has two daughters. Merab—and Michal."

David stared at me until I grew hot and looked at my hands— the lattice of vines above me—the hem of my gown—anything but David.

"You, Michal? I had not thought of you. I never thought that you—You are too young." But there was a note of doubt in his voice that gave me hope and the courage to go on.

"I shall soon be thirteen! And I would make you a good wife, David! I will learn to be meek, and biddable, and—and I love you well."

"As a sister loves her brother." Soft words, rueful words. Gentle sorrow rippled under them, or regret.

"No," I said. I wished to say much more, to tell David all my heart felt for him, but I could not find the words. "No," I said again. That was all.

I waited then for his answer, but he did not make one. He put his fingers to his harp once more and looked out over the dusty hills. He seemed to be waiting, perhaps for Yahweh's voice.

"Saul promised you his daughter," I added desperately, when it seemed David would not speak. "David—you would not want him to be forsworn?"

A jangle of notes from the harp. David laughed, and set the harp aside. "You argue like a prophet! But what makes you think Saul will give me Michal if he refused me Merab?"

His eyes were intent on mine, as if willing me to find the answer. And I did. "You will not ask him for me, David, I will!" Saul had many sons, but only two daughters; he was called over-fond of Merab and me, for he could deny us little. "Merab does not love you, but I do—oh, David, I swear I would die for you— my father will surely give me to you, if I ask it!"

David bent and took my face between his hands; strong hands, hardened by spear and harp. "To have you love me so, Michal—

never did I dare dream of such good fortune. I had feared that to you I was a brother only."

I stared up into his eyes and was dazzled by the sun behind him. I closed my eyes against the burning light. David bent closer; a shadow-shift beyond my lashes. And then he kissed me upon the mouth.

It was not a brother's kiss, but a lover's, sweet and deep and strange; the rooftop seemed to wheel about me, leaving me giddy and trembling. I thought I would die of joy.

"Ask, then, daughter of Saul." David smiled, and lightly kissed my forehead. "Ask your father to keep his promise and give me his daughter to wife."

~

I should have gone to my room and combed my hair and changed my gown, and asked if my father would see me. But all that would have meant waiting, and I could not wait. I ran to him as I was and burst into his presence unannounced.

"Father, may I speak?"

It was only then that I saw my father was not alone. Abner was with him—Abner, his war-chief. I wished then that I had come another time, for Abner made me nervous. He was a man all bone and thin muscle; like the prophet Samuel, I never felt Abner saw me truly, but saw only a stone in the path. But he was called the cleverest man with a raiding party in all the tribes of Israel and Judah both. Men admired Abner, but they did not like him.

Now Abner frowned, but my father only laughed and opened his arms to me. I ran to him and he hugged me and rocked me back and forth. "So here you are—I have had half the women in the house complain of you today, little daughter! Well, well, what is it you want?"

My father was a large man, broad and strong as a bear; when he hugged me, my bones creaked. I begged him to put me down, and even remembered to apologize for interrupting him. I spoke properly, with great dignity; in my eyes, I was a woman now. I wondered that my father did not at once see the difference in me.

"Yes, yes, that's all very well, daughter, but I'm very busy, so out with it. That's the best way, eh, Abner?"

"As my lord king says," Abner murmured, rolling his maps so that I could not see them.

I had wished to speak to my father privately; my love for David was a sacred thing. But he was impatient to return to his work, and so I forgot the pretty plea I had rehearsed and blurted it out, bald as rock.

"Father—you promised David should marry your daughter, but you have given Merab to Adriel. Give me to David instead."

He looked at me and his face turned slowly to a dull red. But he might have calmed had Abner not said, in his dry way, "So the son of Jesse had two strings to his bow. Better that, I suppose, than five smooth stones."

Abner somehow made the last three words a mockery of all David's beautiful songs.

"Can no one talk of anything but that damned shepherd's son?" my father bellowed, striking the table. It shook and the rolled maps jumped. "First Jonathan, now you—praise Yahweh that Merab listened to her father—that *one* of my children is free of his spell! Now get out, girl, and go to your room! And I'll tell you when you can leave it!"

Too shattered to move, I managed to say, "But Father—I love David."

He turned on me and for the first time in my life I was afraid of him. "David—David—always David! I swear by Yahweh that the next person who says that name to me shall be—"

Abner coughed. It was a little sound, but it caught my father's attention and he rounded on Abner. I would have fled then, but I could not make my legs obey me.

"Listen to me, cousin," said Abner quietly. "Princess Michal's suggestion has a certain merit." My father glared at him, eyes rolling like a wild bull's. "Yes, a certain merit," Abner repeated. "There is, after all, something owing to David—"

"*Owing*! I'll show that damned upstart who owes—"

"—and there would be the question of the bride-price," Abner finished calmly. "Perhaps even such a price as we were just discussing. You know I felt it was not necessarily wise to deny him Princess Merab—perhaps Princess Michal will serve as well."

The dull red faded from my father's face. His eyes were shrewd once more, the strangeness vanished. "Yes . . . Yes, Abner, you may be right. Michal!" He swooped upon me; I flinched, but he merely flung one massive arm about my shoulders. "So you would marry our fair young hero, eh? Well, well, so it shall be. Now run along, child, run along. We have work to do. Yes. Run to David, Michal, and tell him to come here to me."

He bent and kissed my forehead, just as David had and upon the very spot David's lips had blessed. There was a light in his eyes that made me uneasy, but I could not tell why.

"Go, child," King Saul repeated.

I went, and did not look back.

~

My bride-price was to be one hundred foreskins taken from the Philistines. So my father said to David before the priests and judges in the open court. David and Jonathan came to me with the news, to tell me before others could. It was the first time I heard Jonathan call our father mad. But I do not think King Saul was truly mad—not then.

"But Jonathan—" I was so shocked that I could think of nothing to say. How could anyone pay such a price? One hundred Philistines! David was a great warrior, but even David could not hope to kill one hundred men before I was too old to care whether I married or not. I would not even think that the Philistines might kill David instead.

"If he is not mad, why should he set such a price for you?"

Jonathan demanded. "Who has ever heard of such a thing before in all the land?"

"But—but he said David might have me!"

"And he has not said I may not." David put an arm around me. "Now do not cry, Michal—and Jonathan, do not look as if you already mourned me."

I sniffed, but obeyed, and David smiled. He could always draw back a smile from me; this time my smile was an uncertain thing, but it made him hug me a little. "That is better, Michal. Understand, I still mean to marry you, but you will have to wait longer than we thought before you put on your bride-clothes."

"Where are you going?" said Jonathan. "And what do you mean to do?" He did not sound as if he thought he would like what he would hear in answer.

"Why, I am going to Philistia, to fetch back the price King Saul has set on his daughter—I will hear no words from you, Michal, for I will have you for my wife, and that is a settled thing."

I was afraid for David, but to hear him speak this way was exciting, too. All that had been paid for Merab was silver and sheep and some men for the army. But Merab had not married a hero.

"I will go with you." Jonathan spoke slowly, as he did when he had been thinking deep; I could tell he liked nothing about this.

David laughed and shook his head. "You will not, brother— this is my task, and I alone will set my hand to it. Do not fear for me, for Yahweh will protect me."

"Yahweh will not stand at your back with spear and blade." Jonathan spoke so sharp that my eyes stretched to stare at him. "David, are you mad as well? Do you think the Philistines will lie down for your knife? You know what my father must mean by this!"

"He means that his youngest daughter is of great worth in his eyes," David said, and hugged me again. "And I am but a poor man's son—what else could he ask of me? Gold and spices? I am a simple warrior, so he set a warrior's price. No, no more, Jonathan.

I mean to do this, and I will come back to pay Saul what he asks and claim his daughter as I have said."

"Oh, David," I said, "you will be careful, won't you?"

At that both men laughed, which made me angry. I could not see that I had said anything to mock.

"I will be as careful, Michal, as you are meek and obedient. There, does that satisfy you?" He and Jonathan smiled at each other, and I scowled. "No, do not frown at me, but kiss me farewell. Come, now, smile for me, Michal—and you too, Jonathan. Do not worry if I am gone long without word—and pay no heed to any tales you may hear of me. True news will come only from my lips, so trust no messenger."

So we both kissed David and said farewell. He left that day, taking no men and carrying little. Jonathan and I stood on the wall over the gateway and watched him go until the haze and dust swallowed him into the blue distance.

We did not see David again for half a year. We had no word of him either, until the day he came to Saul's gate at the head of two hundred armed men. They had marched fast and hard from the Philistine border, and no messenger had outdistanced them to warn of their coming.

"Behold, King Saul—David son of Jesse has returned to claim your daughter Michal for his wife, as you promised him." David stood tall before the gate; he did not shout, but his voice somehow carried clear even to the top of the walls where all the city watched.

"Well, well, so you are back," my father called down to him. "You have been a long time about it, boy, but you are welcome. And if you have brought her price, you will have my daughter, as I said before the priests."

"If I am welcome, will not King Saul open his gate to me?"

My father and Abner looked at each other, and Abner spoke

next. "Who are the men, David? Why do you come leading the enemy to our walls?"

David smiled up at those who watched and waited. "They are not the enemy of Israel, Abner."

"They wear Philistine armor. The Philistines are not our friends."

David stepped back and spread his arms wide. "Look, King Saul—you set a price for your daughter's marriage of one hundred Philistine foreskins. I have brought two hundred—for these men who were of Philistia have abandoned their idols and now worship only Yahweh. They were converted and circumcised by the prophet Samuel himself, and have come to serve the King of Israel." Now his voice was raised to shout a triumph. "A great victory for Yahweh and no man lost, but many gained!"

He stood there in the sunlight, and smiled, and the people watching from the walls cheered and called his name; some flung jewelry to him. I saw many gold leaves and silver flowers tossed down from women's hair.

My eyes were all for David, but then there was a sound from my father harsh enough to make even me look away from David for an instant, and so I saw him turn round on Abner. There was such a noise from the people that I could hardly hear, but some words rose too sharp to be lost.

"Samuel—*Samuel*, did you hear, man!"

All the people had heard; I was glad the old prophet had forgiven my father at last.

"Well, Abner, *well*? And what is to be done now, eh?"

Abner looked at me and I looked away, down to where David stood with his men in the bright noon light.

"Plan the wedding, O King," said Abner, and it seemed to me that he wished to make people hear his words plainly. "What else?"

~

My father grudged nothing for my wedding-day—not the bride-clothes, nor the fatted lambs and calves for the feast, nor the honors for my bridegroom. Saul was the open-handed king to all the world, now, to prove his joy. The wedding festival was to last for seven days and seven nights. A king's daughter did not wed a hero every day, Saul said. How could he do less?

Indeed, how could King Saul do less for David? Of myself, I did not think much. I was so enraptured that I saw the world already as through my wedding veil, golden and beautiful.

On my wedding day I awoke at dawn and watched the sun claw its slow way over the hills to spill shadow and light over the land. The day shone like glass, echoing the joy in my heart; I danced around the room in the pale light until the women came in to catch me and make me stand while I was adorned to delight my husband's eyes.

All the women of the house wished to help deck the bride for this wedding. There were so many helping hands that it took half the day to dress me; plaiting my hair alone took all the forenoon. I was little help to them, for I could not be still. They would have been cross with me on any other day, but it was ill luck to scold a bride, and so it was all jests and laughter. Even when I shook my head to hear the coins ring and there was half the braiding to begin anew they only laughed, and slanted their eyes at each other and teased me for being too eager.

Their voices hinted at things I did not yet know, but was hot to learn with David. Still, I was young enough to blush and duck my head, to keep my face from their eyes.

"And wouldn't we all be eager if such a man waited for us on the other side of the veil!" said Rizpah briskly. "Now stand still, do, child, and let me finish with your hair, or you'll be a maid another season!"

"Not she!" another said. They all laughed, and nodded wisely to each other.

I liked to be mocked as little as any girl at such a time; then each experience is new, and some are sacred to your own heart. "It is only proper for a woman to submit to her husband," I said with great dignity, trying to sound more knowing than I was.

That set them off again, their laughter rising like the shrieks of hoopoes, until my face was as hot as the roof-tiles at summer mid-day.

And then I was ready, or so the women said. When they pulled down the veil and tugged at my hands, crying that my bride-groom awaited, there was a moment when I would have died rather than follow.

It passed, of course; bride's fears are well known and there are always many hands to help her along the way. And once I was moving all was well again, and I was as eager as before.

All the long day there was noise; people singing and chanting and playing every kind of instrument that would clash or chime or jingle. I was not allowed to put back my veil, so I saw it all as a yellow haze of sunlight and sweet incense smoke. That is what I remember about my first wedding day—music clanging in my ears and golden mist dazzling my eyes. I do not remember seeing David at all, though we must have met in the public courtyard when he claimed me as his wife before the people.

Later there was much wine and spiced fruit, and more singing and dancing. I was not let to dance; I was the bride—

"And must save your dancing for your husband," my sister Merab whispered into my ear. She was full-round with her first child; now she laughed and patted her belly. "It will be your turn next year if your husband is truly good with his spear!"

Merab's was not the only bride-jest. I sat among a flock of women who all talked and giggled as though my bridal veil made me deaf, or invisible.

Later still it was night at last, and I was taken in a roar of torches and banging of cymbals to the tower room that had been made ready for us. And then it was quiet and dark, and David my husband put back my veil.

I had dreamed of this moment when I thought I would never know it; I had thought of nothing else since my father had prom-ised me to David over half a year ago. David would free me from my veil and I would go to him and we would know great joy together, as all the songs and stories promised. I had now what I had longed for most in all the world. David stood before me as my husband.

I looked at him as if I were a ewe-lamb and he held the slaughter-knife. David did not let me stand there cold afraid, but took me into his arms.

"Poor Michal," he said, and held me close. His heart beat under my ear louder than morning drums. "Yahweh save me from another wedding! Better forty battles! And now you are tired, and afraid."

"I am *not*!" I wished to sound regal, but my mouth was as dry as if I had eaten dust, and I squeaked like a mouse. "But—oh, David—I—I am not beautiful, as Merab is—"

David smiled at me and stroked my hair. "No, you are not beautiful as Merab is. You are beautiful as Michal is. And that beauty is marvelous to my eyes." And then he made a song, and sang it to me, softly, as we lay down together in the thin lamplight.

The song was all of me. He sang of my hair, and my eyes, and my breasts—there was no part of me he did not praise. His words flowed freely as the wedding wine until I was giddy with love, and when he stopped singing and kissed me, I was soft to his hands as spring rain.

And when it was over, I thought myself a woman who knew all there was to know of love.

~

The lamp-flame was long drowned when Jonathan came in thief-footed. I awoke to his touch on my shoulder.

"Wake up, little sister. Wake, my brother. I must talk to you, and now. No, do not light the lamp, David. Those who wait outside think I have come to leave a morning jest-gift. They must not know that we have spoken."

"What is it? What is wrong?"

"Hush, Michal." David's voice was calm in the dark. "Jonathan will tell us. Well, my brother? You did not join us on our wedding-night only for a jest."

"No, no jest, although I told the men who now guard the stair I would oil the floor thickly for your morning rising. They let me pass for that, and because I am the king's son—and because they do not know I know why they are there. David, you must leave, quietly, and at once."

"What?" I clutched at David. "Jonathan, are you mad?"

"No, but I fear our father is. David, he has set armed men to wait for you at the bottom of the stair. A guard of honor, he says. But in the morning—"

"I will go so far, and then no farther?" David sighed, and put his arm about me so that I might cling close. "I was afraid it would be so. I had hoped that it would not. Poor Saul—he must sleep unquiet with such hate tormenting him. You are right, Jonathan. I must go away for a time."

"No—oh, no! Our father would not do such a thing to me!" I knew our father had grown strange—but that he would do this on my wedding night I could not believe.

"Oh, would he not?" Jonathan reached out in the dark and put his hand upon my cheek. "Ask those at whom he has thrown his spear before you say so. Strange angers rule him now, Michal; he shows first one face and then another."

"I have heard men say he is possessed by an evil spirit, but I do not think that is true." David's voice was low and soft, and he stroked my arm to quiet me.

"Then why else should he hate you, who love him as a son and have done nothing but for his glory and his good?" Bitterness sat ill on Jonathan's tongue; he liked to speak only fair words.

"You are wrong—you must be! You saw what he gave for my wedding! He cannot hate you! It is not fair!"

Again David bade me hush. "Be still, Michal. King Saul thinks he has reason, and who am I to say he is wrong?"

"What reason, brother?" Jonathan demanded. "What reason could he possibly have?"

"None," I said. "Oh, he can have none—you are right, Jonathan, he must be mad!"

"He is not mad, he is afraid, although he has no need to be. I would never harm Saul or any of his blood; I love them all too well. Sit here beside us, Jonathan—it is time, I think, that I told you both the tale. It is only right that you should know."

And there in the dark, sitting on our marriage-bed, David told such a tale—well, if it had not been David, I would have laughed. If it had not been David, I would not have believed.

"It was a fine day, and the sheep were quiet. I was sitting on a rock, and restringing my harp, when my father sent for me—one of my brothers, running—I thought some disaster had struck the house. But it was only a guest, and I was bidden come at once, for he wished to see me. I could not think who or why, but I left the sheep under my brother's eye, and went."

The visitor had been the prophet Samuel. He had looked David up and down, and nodded. And then Samuel had told David that Yahweh had chosen him as the next king over Israel, and made him kneel down there before his father and his brothers, and blessed him, and poured the sacred oil upon his hair.

Beside my ear Jonathan drew breath sharply; a snake-hiss in the dark. "Samuel anointed you as king—with the king still living?"

"As the king to come after," said David. "I thought King Saul knew nothing of it, and I swore then that he and his house would take no harm from my hands. And so later when I heard that a man was sought to play sweet songs for our king and ease his mind, I came to serve him. But he has been told, or has guessed, and now he fears me."

Then there was silence between us in the dark room. I did not know what to say, or think, or feel. It seemed only right to me, in my love, that David should be honored above all men—but to let Samuel anoint him while King Saul still lived in the land—! Even I knew that two kings living meant war, and many men dead.

Kings were new to Israel and Judah, but the bloody histories of our neighbors told tales plain and brutal.

"Well," said Jonathan at last, "so that is where Samuel went when he quarreled with our father, and that is what he did."

"Yes, that is what he did. But Saul is still king while he lives—and I have no wish to shorten his days for him. But now it seems he would shorten mine—"

At that I cried out softly. "No! Oh, David—Jonathan is right, you must go—we will run away until it is safe—"

"It is Jonathan who must go, for I think you have already stayed over-long, brother—even for oiling the floor! No, do not argue with me—be easy, I will not stay to be taken like a stalled ox."

"How? This room was well-chosen for a trap, David—there is only the stair and the window. Men watch at the stair, and as for the window—it is very far to the ground, and I could not bring a rope."

"Only a jug of oil?" David laughed; I did not know how he could. Then he leaned across me to clasp Jonathan in his arms. "Do not fear for me, for Yahweh will protect me, and I am fore-warned of what my enemies would have kept secret. For that, and for all the rest, I thank you, brother. Now go, before you come under suspicion as well."

They kissed, and Jonathan went away as quietly as he had come.

I was not quiet; I flung myself weeping into David's arms. "No, no, I do not believe it! Who—who would do such a thing? No one would harm you, David—everyone loves you!"

"No, not everyone—and some fear King Saul more than they love me. There are always men willing to do evil. Why? Why, they may think good will come of it, or they may be paid in one coin or another. Now hush, Michal—weeping and wailing will not help us."

He set me aside and went to the window. I could see him outlined against the dark sky beyond; it was no longer deep night. We had little time left.

"Can you climb down?" It was a foolish question, and I knew it. This was a new tower, built onto the old house only since my father had become king; the stones were smooth-fitted still.

David laughed. "No, Michal, I can not—nor can I fight barehanded past men well-armed, and I will not try. But your father is generous—he has provided the means to my hand. Come, wife, and help me with our bed-linen—and let us trust it is indeed the best!"

I saw then what he would do, and flung myself out of the bed to pull at the linens and blankets. All was new for my marriage-chest, and all of the finest; fit to support a man, if the knots were tight.

"Oh, yes—oh, David, you are so clever! Where shall we go, and what shall we do? Will your parents take us in, or—"

"Be silent, my heart, for this is not a time for talk. We must hurry if the rope is to be ready in time."

I knew he was right, and so I made haste to do as he told me. There would be time enough to talk once we were away and safe.

It was not so easy as all that to make a rope of bedclothes. Knots that seemed tight and fast fell to nothing when I pulled on them; blankets were too thick to tie at all. But at last we had a length that would hold, at least when we pulled at both ends as hard as we could. So David said it was ready.

"I will go first—I am lighter." The danger thrilled my blood as had David's caresses; it was a night of strange excitements and I could not be calm, or think as I ought. I never once dreamed that I would not go with him, away out the window and down the road to meet whatever new joys life sent us. I was young, and so could not believe life would not go all as I would have it; that anything would truly harm me or those I held dear.

"No, Michal. You will stay here, where I can find you, where you will be safe."

"But I wish to go with you!" I could not believe he meant it.

David sighed and took me in his arms and held me close. "Look you, my dear sister, my dear wife—a man may take a road too hard for a woman, and I will not risk you so. You are Saul's daughter, whom he dearly loves—you must stay, and speak kindly of me to your father while I am gone."

"But David—" Surely he could not mean to leave me behind! Not on our wedding night—not when I would bear any hardship gladly, only to be with him!

"No, I will hear no more disobedience from you—and you have not thought, Michal. I must leave here quickly and quietly— if you go too, who will bring up the rope again? And if it stays—"

If it stayed, linen pale against the tower stones, the city watch-men would see it and raise the alarm. David was right; someone must bring up the rope again, to give him time.

I swore I would do it. "I will always do whatever you ask—I love you beyond death!"

We kissed, and held each other close, and said many foolish things—at least, I did. David's words were never foolish, but worked always to an end.

Then he was gone, down the rope we had made together from the linens of our marriage-bed, and I was left alone in the tower room. As he had told me, I drew the rope up again, and then sat and carefully undid our careful knots, and thought of all David had said that night.

It was hard to believe, now that he was gone, just as it was hard to believe that I was now a woman, and so must be wiser than I had been as a child. But this was a night of strangeness, one no more so than the other. Sitting there alone in the dark, I half-thought I might have dreamed it all.

But I had not—and for all my thinking, I had not thought of what was to happen to me when my father Saul found out my husband was gone.

David had needed my help; that was enough.

~

CHAPTER 3

It was not enough the next day, when men ran to my father crying that David had vanished from the guarded tower, leaving no trace. Eager to avoid blame, they told the tale I had hoped for, the tale that would absolve me also. For I knew some such tale would be needed, and so after much thought I had made a figure under the blankets, using a goat-hair pillow, and had feigned sleep beside it. When the men grew tired of waiting and came to take David, I pretended to wake, and be confused, and tried to shake the pillow awake. Then I screamed.

I did not say it was sorcery. But I made my eyes wide, and trembled, and put my hand to my mouth as I stared at the pillow beside me. And as they took me to my father, I asked many times how any man could have slipped past the stairway guards unseen. I thought myself very clever. I planted the seeds; their own fears ripened those seeds to fruit.

So when Saul roared his angry questions, his men stammered of demons and magic. He fell silent at that; his breath rasped loud, echoing from the cool brick walls, making the room itself seem a living thing. His face paled from its mottled crimson, paled until he looked old, and ill.

The time stretched long before he spoke, and I knew that I had lost, for a man who defied prophets would not believe such a tale. I should have thought of some lie; I should have said that David had threatened me, that I had been too afraid to say him nay. Now it was too late.

"Witchcraft is it, you simpleminded fools? Well, I know where stands the witch." His voice was very soft, as I had never heard it, and I trembled now in earnest. "A rope, eh, Michal? Yes, yes, it must have been—a rope you stole and hid, and used to help your father's enemy escape from him? Now why should my daughter— my own little daughter, whom I loved as my own heart—do this thing?"

He looked straight at me. I had never seen anything like his eyes. They were not my father's eyes; if there were demons here, they lived in King Saul.

I had thought I was clever; I had believed I was brave. Now I knew I was neither. I had planned to speak out and defy all the world for David. But David was gone and I was here alone to face King Saul's wrath, and fear was so cold in my blood that I could not even answer my father to defend myself.

Saul came to me, walking stiffly, like an old man. His hands fell heavy on my shoulders. "Michal, my little dove, do you know what you have done? No? Well, child, you have killed your father. Yes, yes, that is it—you have killed him as surely as if you used the spear."

He stroked my hair, and stared at me, and I tried to speak. "Father—"

"No, no. After this you are not my daughter."

I had expected anger, but he sounded only grieved. I would rather he had raged and beaten me until my bones broke.

He patted my head, as he had done when I was small, and backed away. "I must think what is to be done with her. Yes, take her away, until I decide."

He stood there, swaying gently back and forth, as men came forward to put their unwilling hands on me and lead me away. I had not even the spirit to shrug them off and go out with my pride unbroken, as a princess should.

Abner stopped my guards at the painted door. "Take her back to her bridal chamber," he said. "Set a guard to the door." His lean face showed nothing, but then, it rarely did. "And mind she has no ropes to her hand—magical or otherwise."

~

I was kept close confined, as Abner had ordered. The door was barred, and a guard stood without; a bronze grille was bolted over the window. I had light, and air, but could not look out, save through the slits in the bronze. The woman who tended me I had never seen before; she was old, and afraid to be kind. She was silent as she worked, and her eyes slid from side to side so that she need not see me. I saw no one else in all the days I spent locked in the tower room that had been my bridal chamber.

And I knew nothing of what happened beyond that barred door. I told myself brave tales—that David would come back, climb the wall, and take me away with him. I told myself that my father would surely forgive me. He had never been long angry with me; I would ask to see him, and beg his pardon, and explain all to him so that he would kiss me, and send for my husband, and they would be friends once more—Jonathan would intercede for me, and for David—

Well, the last was true enough. But it did no good, as Jonathan told me many long days later.

"He threw his spear at me when I tried, little sister—oh, I think he meant to miss, but all the same, I felt its wind on my cheek." Of course the men who had been meant to kill David had told of Jonathan's visit; Saul could guess what had been said. "He has not forgiven me that, Michal. We must all be careful now, you and I most of all."

After that, Jonathan had gone out into the fields beyond the city. There he had met David, and warned David that he must not come back.

By the time I learned even this much, David was far away in the wilderness—and I, too, was far away, and married to another man.

~

CHAPTER 4

"But Saul had given
his daughter Michal, David's wife,
to Phalti the son of Laish . . . . "

- I Samuel 25:44

I waited alone in my tower room a month and more after my wedding night. Then I thought that endless confinement was to be my punishment; no one told me that a moon's turn would free me of this prison at least. It was only later, when I was older, and wiser in the ways of kings, that I realized that my father wished to know if I carried David's child. I do not know what he would have done then. Perhaps he would have remembered that it was my child, too; blood of his blood, as well as of David's.

But there was no child. There were only slow-winding days of silence and nothing.

At first I thought I would die of fear, then of boredom. When at last Abner came to see me, early one morning, I was unpicking an embroidered cushion to sew anew. It was not how I would have chosen to be found, but Abner paid no heed. He already thought me a silly child, so I suppose it did not surprise him.

I set the cushion aside, its threads half undone and all a-tangle, and looked at him, and waited. I knew Abner's tricks well, after all the years he had been my father's war-chief; he would wait and wait, and soon or late you would say something foolish only to break the silence. Then he held a weapon to twist and turn against you. I had seen him do it often enough to others. So I sat and waited too. I thought my tribulations had taught me some wisdom, which pleased me.

"I see you are happy here, Princess Michal," Abner said. His eyes were keen enough to see through to my pleasure in my own cleverness. Now he used words flint-sharp to pierce it. "You will be happier still to know that you may now leave this place; you go this day to your wedding. Hold yourself ready, for men will soon be sent to fetch you to your bridegroom. Many men," he added, and smiled a little.

My skin turned cold and there was a noise in my ears like a river in spring flood. "No. I am David's wife. You—you are trying to frighten me."

"Then it takes either a great deal to frighten you, Princess, or very little." Abner turned away, as if to go and leave me alone until the men came for me.

I forgot that I had learned wisdom; I jumped up and ran after Abner, clutching at his arm. "No, wait! I am David's wife, he married me before all the people! My father—" Surely my father would not do this; I could not believe that he would. I was his youngest daughter, his little dove Michal. He loved me.

"Your father will not see you, nor will he again call you daughter. As for your marriage to David, that has been set aside."

"He cannot do that!"

"You are in no position, Princess, to say what can be done, and what cannot."

"My brother—I wish to see my brother Jonathan!"

"He is not here, and if he were you would not see him."

Abner would have pulled my hand from his sleeve, but I would not be moved for the new fear his words gave me. "Jonathan—he is not dead? Please tell me!"

I was afraid Abner would shrug me off, but he had kindness enough to answer. "He is not dead. King Saul has sent him away for a time. Now calm yourself, and be thankful for the mercy the king has shown you—both of you."

And then Abner was gone, and the door barred once more,

and I had not even thought to ask who the man was who dared to marry David's wife—for I swore I would never be anything else.

~

Grief and pain hone memory sharper than joy and love. I remember my second wedding day better than my first. Men came as Abner had said they would and took me silently out of the king's house through the pillared gate. There was no music, and no dancing; there was no incense, no waving flowers, no feast spread before guests. I was not bedecked as befitted a bride; I had no veil, no jewels, no gold dusting my hair. I was married outside the gate, before my guards and a few serving-men, and the quiet was ill-omen for a marriage. If any rejoiced, it was not the bride.

I did not know what the bridegroom felt, and I did not care. I looked up once, as I was led to him; my eyes blurred with tears, and I saw only that he was tall and broad and not young. I denied the tears, squeezing my eyes hard-shut against them. I would not weep before these uncaring men.

Each word of this ceremony beat against my ears until I knew I would never be able to forget. It was so that I learned I was marrying Phaltiel of Gallim. I had never heard of the man or the village before. The priest droned his words in haste and the witnessing was a shuffling, muttered thing; no one wished to be there.

And then it was done. I stood and watched as the priest and the witnesses hurried away as if the very air about me carried harm. I stood and watched as the gate of my father's house was closed against me.

I would have stood there until the night fell and the watchmen threw stones at me, but my hand was taken and held fast. His hand was strong and warm; I looked against my will.

I had been right; he was not young. Twice my age, or perhaps three times—surely forty at the least. For that first day I saw only that his hair and beard had some grey, and his face some lines, and so I called him old.

There were many lines around his eyes; he smiled at me and all the lines slanted upwards. "Come, Michal—now we will go home."

I wished to deny him; I wished to be as brave as the great heroines of Israel, to be as Deborah and Jael, who had defied armies. But I was not, and I had nowhere else to go.

Phaltiel did not make me speak; he lifted me in his arms and set me upon the waiting donkey. "Here is a veil against the sun and dust—well, if you will not take it, I must wrap it for you, and I am no master of women's drapings. Are you steady in the saddle? I warn you, my farm is far by foot and donkey-back—you must tell me when you are tired."

I thought again of the heroines of Israel; I thought of David. Surely he knew of this, and somewhere on the long road he would swoop like an eagle out of the hills and take me away with him. He would not leave me in the hands of my enemies.

"I will not be tired," I said, and made my back stiff. And I vowed I would keep it so every step of the way to Gallim.

~

At first I clung to my griefs as to a lover. In my eyes, I was a princess in a harper's tale; though disgrace and revilement were my lot, my bearing would be royal. And someday David, my true husband, would come for me.

So when Phaltiel brought me down the valleys to his house I kept my chin high, and stared straight ahead, and would not speak to him. I wonder now that he did not beat me. Most men would have.

Phaltiel was a farmer, with lands in a fertile valley and in the plains beyond its sheltering hills. When we came over the rise of the last hill before the valley, Phaltiel stopped the donkey.

"This is the valley of Gallim, little princess, and that is the village. I know you will think it humble and quiet, but traders and travelers pass through often enough to bring us news and goods from grander places."

I looked, but said nothing. There was not much to see—a dozen houses dust-gold in the late-day sun; a stone well where the women would gather at dawn and dusk; fields beyond the houses. What was Gallim to me but a small backward village like a hundred others? David's wife had nothing to do with such places.

"Now look there, down the valley past the village—that is my house. And now it is yours as well."

But I did not look at his house, for my eyes burned as tears welled hot. I turned my head away so that he would not see. He did not wait after that, but took us straight down the dusty road past the village. Only when we stopped at the gate did I look for the first time upon the house in which I was now to live.

Phaltiel, or perhaps his father before him, had built the house to press against the rock cliff on the eastern side of the valley. It had the look of a dwelling that had been there long and was settled in its place. There was a stone wall running low around the house, and vines growing over the wall. Poppies splashed bright scarlet between house and wall.

Phaltiel put his hand on the donkey's neck and turned to face me. "Well, Princess Michal, we are home at last. Will you come in with me?" He did not wait for my answer, but put his hands on my waist and swung me down to stand beside him. As he did so a dark-haired girl of my own age came running from the house, holding out her arms and calling out for joy at her father's return.

I stood stiff and cold as Phaltiel caught her and kissed her forehead.

"So, Miriam, you are running out without your veil again." Phaltiel hugged her shoulders and smiled at her. "But I will not scold you—it is your stepmother's place to do that. I refuse to interfere in women's matters."

Phaltiel's daughter paid no heed to this, but turned to me eagerly. "You are Princess Michal!" Her eyes were sloe-dark, and wide with admiration. "Oh, it must be wonderful to be a princess and to have all that you want! Will you tell me what it is like to live in a king's house? Do you wear gold in your hair every day?"

To have all that I wanted—! Miriam's warmth and heartfree words loosened the ice within me until it spilled out as tears. Angry at this betrayal, I turned away and hid my face in my hands. Tears slid between my fingers, trickled down my wrists. I prayed for the earth to open and swallow me up.

It did not, of course. Instead, Miriam flung herself upon me, petting and stroking and indignant. "Oh, do not cry! You are tired—Father, how could you drag her all that way on a donkey!— come indoors, and the maids and I will tend you. We will bathe you in cool water, and comb out your hair, and you will have the best linen, and we will all love you well. Do not cry!"

She hugged me hard, as if that could protect me from all ills. More ice melted; I turned into Miriam's arms and laid my head on her shoulder and let her stroke my hair while I wiped my eyes with my dust-dry veil.

"I see that I am not needed here," Phaltiel said. It seemed to me that he mocked, but when I glared up at him his face was smooth and not even his eyes laughed. "Go with Miriam, wife. She is the daughter of my house, and will take good care of you."

So Miriam brought me into the house. It was a good house, too, built large, with bricks and cedar logs, and painted lintels. There was a pretty court in the women's quarters; it faced upon the cliff wall, where an endless spring bubbled up from a crack in the rock. There was a fountain carved with a basin to catch the water, which spilled over the edge like liquid crystal to vanish into a hole at the base, disappearing back into the rock. Even my sorrow was diverted by this; courtyard wells were common enough, but I had never dreamt of pure running water inside a house.

Miriam saw me staring. "Yes, isn't it wonderful? Do try it, Princess Michal—the water is always cold and sweet."

The water was as she said. I drank and washed the salt-damp dust from my face, taking long over it. Miriam had run off while I was about this, to give orders to the maids, she said. She was back too soon for me, followed by a sour-faced maidservant carrying a laden brass tray. Now that my face was cool, my mind was too, and I dreaded facing the women of Phaltiel's house—my house, now.

But I did not need to fear Miriam. She was plump and friendly as a house-kitten, and bore no grudge that I was her father's wife, no older than she, come to take the ordering of the household from her hands.

Now she stood before me, as the water I had splashed on my face made chill tracings down my neck, and offered me unstinting hospitality. "See, Princess, I have brought pomegranate juice, and wine, and figs, and almond-cakes. You must be thirsty, and hungry as well."

I looked at the tray as the maid set it upon its stand. I could not have eaten all that had I been starving for a week. But I let myself be seated upon a bench that was well-padded with snowy fleeces, and allowed Miriam to press a cake into my hand.

"You must eat something," she told me. She hesitated a moment, then added, "Do not look so sad, Princess. I—I know it must be very hard for you to come here, to such a humble house. But we will make you happy, I promise."

Her anxious eyes promised me sympathy, something I craved more than food or drink or rest. My eyes stung, but I was prepared now, and would not let tears fall again. Instead I said listlessly, "Sit beside me, Miriam. And please, do not call me 'Princess'. My— my father has said I am no longer his daughter, so you see—"

My voice trembled, and I took a quick bite of the cake to hide it just as Miriam, looking indignant, flung her arms about me.

I choked, of course, and coughed until I thought I should die, while Miriam pressed me to drink water or pomegranate juice or wine, and thumped me hard between my shoulders. When finally I could breath again, I leaned weakly against her, and sighed.

"Oh, poor Michal—or should I call you 'stepmother'?" Miriam looked doubtful.

I was certain. Things were bad enough without a girl my own

age calling me 'mother'. I begged her, meaning it with all my heart, to use my name freely.

"Very well, Michal, since you wish it."

Her eyes were full of questions. I knew she must be longing to know all my tale, although she was too soft and kind to ask.

A part of me longed to tell it and relieve the pressure on my heart, which still ached with every beat. But perhaps I was learning wisdom, for I did not speak. It was bad enough that I had wept bitterly on the doorstep of this house; I would not make my love for David into gossip for its women.

This was sheer folly, for the tale had gone from Dan to Beersheba and back twice over by the time I reached Phaltiel's safe house. In time, I was to learn that all Israel knew the story—many better than I.

So I lay quietly on Miriam's breast, and let her say soothing words to me, and pretended I was only weary from the journey. Then we were surrounded by chattering maidservants, and I was taken to be bathed, and combed, and dressed in clean linen. I had not needed to fear the women of this house; no matter what wild tales they might have heard, I was the king's daughter. They were all as admiring as Miriam—although it was a disappointment to them that I had not arrived in a gilded litter decked with carvings and fringes, and that I wore no crown of silver flowers on my head.

It was very pleasant to be made much of, and petted. So I let them do as they would, for now I was weary in truth, and hardly cared that I was being adorned to please a man I had sworn I would never acknowledge as husband.

I cared later, when the sky was dark and the torches bright, and I stood waiting for Phaltiel. The maids had taken long over me, anxious that the king's daughter should find no fault in their care. At last, when even my bones felt polished clean, they had draped me in a thin robe that smelled of sun and spices, and brought me to the bedchamber. That room had been readied as lovingly as I. Even the small lamp that kept watch in the wall niche had been filled with a scented oil. The smell made me feel sick.

The maids withdrew, with much giggling, but Miriam remained behind. She put her arms around me and kissed my cheek. "I am so glad you have come to us, Michal. And—and I wish you joy."

I could not answer, but she herself was blushing and looking away from me, and so the moment passed. It was just as well, for Miriam had been good to me today, and I did not wish to hurt her by telling her the truth—that I would never find joy with her father, nor he with me.

"There is wine," Miriam said, and kissed me once more. Then she was gone, and I was left alone to wait.

I had expected Phaltiel to come to me at once, but he did not. I grew restive, and found that it was hard to remain a graven image long. So I roamed about the chamber, keeping my ears pricked for any sound. I did not want Phaltiel to find me prying like a weasel, as if I had a true interest in his house.

Phaltiel was a quiet man; I had warning enough to close the olive-wood chest into which I peered, but not enough for dignity. So he came in to find me scrambling to my feet and clutching the thin sliding robe the maids had giggled over so as they pinned it upon me. I settled the robe and faced him tall and silent.

"It was kind of you to wait for me," Phaltiel said, dropping the curtain over the doorway. "But it is late; you should have been asleep long ago. Go to bed now, child."

"I will not," I said. "You are not my true husband, and I will never share your bed." I held my chin high, to show I meant what I said.

Phaltiel looked at me, and sighed, and then came to stand before me. "I think it is time we had plain words between us, so stop your sulking and listen to me."

He took my hand; I tried to pull away, but he was a man, and stronger. He drew me over and made me sit beside him on the bed and held my hand so that I could not run away. "Do not look at me like that, Michal. I will not touch you as my wife if you do not wish it."

"I will never wish it!"

"Never is a long time, child, and until it comes you and I will sleep peacefully in the same bed. I am neither so young nor so old that your body alone is enough to tempt me."

"No," I said. "I—I do not want to sleep here."

"Little princess, what you want and do not want is not so important as you like to think it. Now listen to me and use the mind that lies behind those pretty eyes. I agreed to marry you because I was sorry for you, and because your brother Jonathan asked it of me. No one else dared, and Jonathan feared King Saul would kill you or send you to a far country if no man could be found who would take you disgraced and dowerless. It is a hard thing for a young girl to be betrayed by those she loves, and harder still to be cast out by her family to go among strangers. I knew that we at least would be kind to you."

"No one has betrayed me! David loves me and will come for me and put all here to the sword and take me back again and I will not listen to you!"

"Speak softly, Michal—unless you wish to bring the servants to the door. I am not so old a man as you think, but I am old enough to like peace, at least in my own house. If you are wise, you will forget about David and live here happily and quietly— and do nothing to remind your father the king that you still breathe. Now dry your eyes and we will sleep. The day and the way were long, and I am tired, even if you are not."

~

I was not unhappy in Phaltiel's house. At first, I was a princess wronged; I was young enough to find some solace in that. When you are fourteen, even grief can be a kind of joy.

Phaltiel had children older than I; two sons and a daughter, all well-married and in their own houses elsewhere in the valley. The eldest, a man nearing twenty, had a son of his own, a babe still in swaddling bands. Then there was Miriam, and Caleb, who was too young to remember his own mother, but was old enough to know that I was not. He looked at me as sullenly as I looked at his father.

The running of the house I left in Miriam's hands. It was not my house and Phaltiel was not my husband. I told him so when I had not yet been there a week. I stood stiff and tall, glorying in defiance, but he only said calmly that I was doubtless too young, and should run along and play until I was ready for a woman's work.

"I *am* a woman!" I thought to sound proud and royal, but even to my own ears my voice was only that of a sulky child.

Phaltiel had laughed and left me standing there in my false pride. My cheeks burned; I went and complained bitterly to Miriam of the hardness of my lot. That was not well done of me, for she cannot have liked to hear her father so spoken of. But she was always a good girl, and understood more than I thought. She knew I still grieved for David, and so was kind to me—kinder than I deserved.

Nor was I lonely in Phaltiel's house, for I had Miriam and the other girls of the village for my companions. None of them had ever gone farther from home than the sheep could wander in a morning, and they liked nothing better than to hear of the glories to be found in the world beyond. They had no experience of great ladies, and thought me impressive. I drooped, and smiled wistfully, and told them I was nothing to my sister Merab. This only made them press me harder for tales of life in the king's house. Admiration is balm to smarting feelings; I took great pleasure in being what they wished to see.

And they loved to hear of David. I was not unwilling to spin them tales—when I found they knew the story already, I could not see that it did any harm. So I talked more than was prudent; it is always wiser to say little and smile much than to proclaim your ills throughout the land.

So time passed, and days became weeks, and I still heard no word from my true husband. He neither came to take me away with him, nor sent a message, not even so much as one word.

I longed for news, but there was none. Jonathan, alone of all my family, came once to visit me. That was when he told me what had happened while I was prisoned in my tower. That was when I heard how Saul had raged against David, and called Jonathan traitor, and hurled his spear at Jonathan as if he would slay his own son. Then Saul had sent Jonathan away, and even now would not speak to him unless he must.

Jonathan told me also that he had spoken once with David, warning him against returning while Saul's madness ruled. And that was all I learned, although I pressed Jonathan hard for fresh news of David. Jonathan kept his mouth tight, saying only that David was in the hills.

"And he has not forgotten me? He will come?" Already it had been long, and overlong, I thought; in those days I did not find waiting easy. I had already been in Phaltiel's house many weeks.

Jonathan hugged me tight. "Oh, Michal, how could any man forget you?" Then he kissed me, and went away again. And I cherished Jonathan's words, thinking they held the meaning I wished them to have.

CHAPTER 5

*"Now there was long war
between the House of Saul
and the House of David . . . . "*

—II Samuel 3:1

When the weeks had grown into months there were tales told that
spread even to villages as small as that in which I now dwelt. A
light such as that cast by David cannot be long hidden. His fire
had been banked, hidden in the hills. Now he came forth to blaze
for all men to see, and to make King Saul look old and weak as a
toothless lion—in the tales men told.

David had fled to Philistia, and been captured there. No, he
had escaped the Philistine king as easily as he had escaped King
Saul.

David had taken two hundred of King Saul's own men and
raised the east against him. No, it was the north. No, he had
forbidden any man to lift a hand against Saul.

David had gone to Gath. To Moab. Foreign kings did him
honor. The king of Moab had given sanctuary to David's mother
and father.

Some of these were nothing but tales sown by the wind; others were true, and no man could tell one from the other. Tale and
truth sounded the same.

So when the news came that King Saul had massacred the
priests at Nob, and all the town as well, I refused to believe. All
slain, from the tallest man down to the smallest babe, only be-

cause they had given bread to David and his men—that was what was said.

"A tale for fools," I said when I heard. "My father would never do such a thing!" My father had treated me cruelly—but still I could not think that even he would act as men said he had at Nob.

But the slaughter at Nob was truth—and it turned men against Saul and toward David.

The prophet Samuel strode through the land once more, calling down curses upon King Saul and blessings upon the hero David. Men who were discontent with Saul rallied now to David's camp in the wilderness of Ziph. Saul tried to take David by force, and then by guile, but it was too late. David knew the wilderness and the mountains, and his men danced circles about Saul's army.

Saul could catch him as little as he could catch a flame, or a ray of sun. Saul could stop him as little as he could stop time, or men's tongues.

David was praised by all for his wisdom, his courage, his strength. He had come upon King Saul in a cave, it was said, and done him no harm, but only cut off the hem of his cloak. This proved he meant no treason or malice to King Saul; this proved David a good man.

Perhaps it did. But it made King Saul look foolish in addition to all else. I sometimes think that Samuel held to life as long as he did only to see my father brought low, for the old prophet died not long after men began to say "King Saul" and laugh.

The war that was no war was all that women chattered of at the well and all men talked of in the street. Even children's games were all of David and his men. I stood at the gate one evening and listened as the small boys ran by, quarreling over who would have to be Saul's men in their play. No one wished to take Saul's part; they were all for David. Well, and so was I—but the boys' thoughtless words made my heart hurt for my father, for all of that.

But my head was high, and my heart full of love and pride for David. I still thought us pledged until death; every man of Saul's who fell brought David one step nearer to my arms.

But other arms had been outstretched to David, and he went to them, not to me. Jonathan came to tell me the news himself, running light and swift to reach me before it was women's noise at every well in Israel and Judah. It was kind of him to do so. Even when he told me, and something died in my heart, I knew he had been kind.

I had greeted Jonathan joyfully; he had kissed me and taken me out of Phaltiel's house, out beyond the gate, to tell me what he had come to say—that David had married again.

"Her name is Abigail, and she came to David a widow. Her husband Nabal refused to aid David, but she gave David food and drink for his men. She must have been right to defy her husband for David's sake, for when she told Nabal what she had done, they say he fell as if Yahweh himself had struck him down, and became as one turned to stone until he died."

I stood as if I too had been struck to stone. Jonathan put his arms around me; I did not feel them. He spoke more, telling how David had sent an offer of marriage to Abigail, and how she hastened to accept and bring him all she had. Nabal had been a wealthy man; his sheep were fat, his lands rich, and his servants many.

"This woman Abigail—" The words echoed cold in my ears, as if a stranger spoke; Michal stood far away.

I did not have to finish, for Jonathan knew what I would ask. "She is still young and unblemished, or so I have heard. But I have not seen her, Michal, and they say all rich widows are good to look upon."

"She has brought him much," I said. "More than Michal, who is no longer called daughter by Saul the king."

Jonathan stroked my hair and said words he thought it would ease my heart to hear. "Do not weep, little sister. A man must do things a woman does not understand. This does not mean that David loves you not. He will come for you when the time is right." He held me tight for comfort, but I would not yield to it.

And I did not weep. Not then. I kissed my brother's cheek and stepped back to stand with my head high. "David may come if he likes. The wife of Phaltiel knows how to welcome guests to her husband's house."

Proud words. Jonathan was not deceived. But he granted me my right to them, and let me act the lady of the household for his benefit. As I have said, my brother was always kind.

I walked back through the gate and into Phaltiel's house. I called for the maidservants, and ordered a bath for Jonathan, and food, and wine, and all things done that were proper for an honored guest and a king's son. And when all had been done, I told Miriam that I had looked too long into the sun and my head hurt me, and that I would go to lie upon my bed.

"Oh, poor Michal! No wonder you look so pale—here, lean upon me—and you, Beka, go and soak a cloth in the cold spring for your mistress's head—hurry!" Miriam fussed like a nesting hen, chivvying maidservants and coaxing me. "Would you like to drink some bryony—no, some willow-bark water would be better—"

I had been proud and dry-eyed for Jonathan. Suddenly I was frozen stone no longer. "No!" I flung off Miriam's tender hands; their gentle touch would drive me mad.

"Why, Michal, what is the matter?"

"You will know soon enough!" I cried. "Go away!" When she stood there gaping at me, I snatched up a pillow from the bed and flung it at her. I wished it were a stone; I wished it were something that would hurt. "Leave me alone!"

Miriam reached out to me; I turned and threw myself down onto the bed to hide my face. After a moment I heard her run out of the room, and I was able to wail and weep as I pleased. My tears were hot and hard, not the easy grief of childhood, and there was a dull ache in my throat that made it hard to breathe.

David had not waited; David had not come. He had forgotten me in half a year and married a rich widow before her husband had lain forty days dead. He did not want me any more, and all his words of honey had been lies.

And under all my pain was the knowledge, sharp as a serpent's tooth, that I would look a fool to all the world. Too many knew my tale. I had told them myself.

I wailed again and beat my fist against the pillows. I could see nothing but grief and shame ahead, and I could not bear it.

"Well, my wife, is this a proper way for you to behave with your brother a guest in the house?" Phaltiel came and sat down beside me on the bed. "Come now, stop your weeping—do you wish him to think I beat you?"

I did not look up. "My brother will know why I weep, and he will not blame you for it, if that is what you fear." My voice was tear-thick and sullen. "You do not understand—everyone will know—I wish I were dead!"

Phaltiel was a good man; he neither laughed nor beat me senseless. "Yes, everyone will know that David has married Nabal's widow," he said, and stroked me as if I were a kitten. "Come, daughter of Saul, would you have it said at the well and in the village that you lie weeping for David, who has abandoned you?"

I sat up. "I hate David! May Yahweh strike him dead!"

"You and Yahweh need not concern yourselves, Michal. Men like David will always make their own problems." He put an arm around my shoulders. "Now dry your eyes or they will be redder than poppies. You are too pretty a girl to weep for any man. Make them weep for you."

His voice was rough, his words blunt-edged, not supple and sweet as David's were. Yet they made me turn to him; I hid my face against his chest and wept again. "They will laugh at me in the street! How can I go to the fields, or the well, or—"

"They will not laugh if you laugh first." Phaltiel set me back and took my chin in his hand to make me look at him. "Laugh, little princess, and hold your head high, and make it a joke before the world does."

His words warmed me and gave me some hope. I sniffled, and let him wipe my face, and hold me, while I thought. Everyone would know the tale; that could not be helped now. But the blow to my heart no one could see, if I did not choose to show it. If David cared nothing for me, then the world should see I cared nothing for David.

And David should see and hear that Michal was happy without him. I would not let David think I went with dust on my hair and tears in my gown for love of him.

I looked through my lashes at Phaltiel. It was true that he was not young, and not handsome, and not a hero. But he was a good man, and had been kind to me. Now I would be kind to him, and David would know that Michal preferred her second husband to her first.

And so I flung my arms around Phaltiel's neck and kissed him as I had learned to kiss a man on my first wedding night. I must have surprised Phaltiel indeed, for he did not kiss me back. I opened my eyes, puzzled and indignant. Phaltiel looked at me and began to laugh. I suppose I deserved it.

But I was young and still raw from David's betrayal, and I did not think it was funny then. I would have struck Phaltiel, but he did not let me. I was all stiff with anger, but he held me close and kissed me on the brow, and then on the tip of my nose, and then on my mouth.

I stopped saying no, then.

It was no proper wedding night; it was not even dark enough to light the lamps. The chamber was not prepared with fine linen, sweet herbs, and scented oils. The bride had not been bathed and perfumed, nor had the bridegroom.

I had always thought those things important. But I was wrong.

They did not matter.

~

The next morning Jonathan left again. He had come only for love of me, to tell me of David's marriage; he was needed with the army to keep King Saul content with prudence. Saul had forgotten, now, that he did not trust Jonathan. Or at least, so Jonathan told me. I do not know if it was true. Perhaps it was, and all Saul's hate was kept hot for David.

I walked hand-in-hand with my brother to the first turn in the road, loath to part with him so soon. When we had to say good-bye, I said, "I have a message for David, brother, if ever you should meet with him."

"You know that I do." Jonathan did not look happy; he was a good man, loyal and kind and loving. To be torn between Saul's love and David's was not easy. "What is your message, little sister?"

"Tell David—" I had had the words well-prepared, bitter, clever words, I thought them; words that would eat into David's heart like poison. But something in my brother's face made me stop. I kissed him and said instead, "When you see David give him that from me, and say that Michal wishes him well. And tell him—tell him that my husband and I are happy."

And when I said it, the words were true.

Jonathan smiled and some of the trouble left his eyes. He kissed me back warmly. "David will be glad of it, Michal. He never wished to hurt you, that I know. Please Yahweh, this senseless war will soon be over, and we will all be friends again."

"Yes," I said, and knew we both were thinking of what David had once told us. The oil was on his head as well as on Saul's. There could not be two kings in the land.

But this was a thing neither of us wished to say.

~

From that day I lived quietly in my husband's house in the valley of Gallim. Time flowed by, the days all smooth as pebbles in a stream-bed, as sweet to me as apples in wine. My father had cast me out, my first husband had abandoned me. My second husband cherished me, and kept me close, and I loved him for it.

Men might fight and die; it was far now from me and mine. We heard that David took service with King Achish of Philistia, who gave him lands in Ziklag. Then it was said that David's men raided for the Philistines in Yahweh's name, and all men looked on this with wonder and horror. To me it was more that Phaltiel's youngest son Caleb learned to call me 'Mother', and more still that the name came easily to his tongue.

Men said that my father Saul grew ever stranger, until no man dared cross him. They said Saul's army spent itself chasing David's men through the wastelands, until Saul's soldiers grumbled and began to desert. In Phaltiel's house we dressed Miriam for her wedding, and the folds of her veil, and how her bracelets settled upon her round arms, were matters real and urgent.

David's songs were sung from Dan to Beersheba; no one else had his easy way with words. All men said so, and all women too. A harper had only to say a new tune was from David's lips to be sure of a warm welcome and a good meal at least. There were many new songs to sing in those days—and as Phaltiel once said, perhaps some of them indeed were David's.

I heard that David had married again—and again. I told the teller of the tale that I wished David joy. "Only think of roaming the hills with so many wives! David is a hero indeed!" I laughed, and meant it. David's wives were nothing to me now. I was Phaltiel's wife; that was enough.

Even when I heard that David had married another king's daughter I only marveled as any might that David the rebel had wed Princess Maachah, freely given by her father Talmai, King of Geshur. It was another and clearer sign that David's star rose ever higher.

And because I was happy with my husband and my lot, I did not even wonder that David now took so many wives into his life of strife and danger, when once he would not risk even one. Those who live content do not ask such questions, even when they should. And I was full content.

I do not say I was happy and heedless as I had been with David, for he had made time shine like glass at noon. But I was content—and useful, which I learned to value more. With Miriam gone the household was mine to order as I thought fit, and to do so gave me more pleasure than I had expected to find in such work.

I had the raising of young Caleb as well; he was a good boy, and caused me little grief, for I was still young enough only to think it a good joke when he danced upon the rooftops after wild rock doves, or came home well-bitten by a fox-cub he had somehow caught in the fields.

"But Mother, it followed me home!" He was panting and dirty and clinging tight to the small furious thing he had wrapped in his tunic for safekeeping. The cub growled and sank sharp white teeth into Caleb's thumb; Caleb yelped, the maids shrieked, and I laughed until tears dropped off my cheeks to make holes in the dust.

"You may keep it if it will stay of its own wish," I said at last. Released, the fox-cub ran off as if its tail were afire. I laughed again, and this time the maids laughed with me. Caleb stopped sulking when I recklessly promised him a spotted hound puppy in the fox-cub's stead, for I could not bear to see him sad.

Phaltiel, when I explained and begged his aid, agreed to procure the dog for his son, and praised my womanly wisdom. I knew he laughed at me as well as at Caleb, but this I no longer minded.

I became friends with the village women, for their joys and griefs were those of all women and I shared them too. I was no longer 'Princess Michal'; I was Michal, the wife of Phaltiel. I was another woman to talk with at the well, or to call upon for aid when a woman was in hard labor. I was often called for by women in childbed, once they knew I was not too proud to help. I had good hands, they said—but in truth, children birth themselves if they are but let.

One thing only fretted me as my time in Phaltiel's house steadily lengthened into a well-woven strand of years. I had all my rights of Phaltiel, and he his of me. He came in to me often, and our nights pleased us both, for he was patient and loving and I young and curious. But no matter how often we lay together, no child quickened my womb.

At first I did not worry. I was young, I told myself. Children would come. I had only to wait.

I waited, but full moon after full moon shone over the valley and still I was not with child.

"Be patient," my husband told me. "All things come in their own season, and you are not so very old yourself."

But I still had not truly learned to wait. I had been Phaltiel's wife over five years, after all; I wished to give my husband the sons that were his right. I wished to hold my child in my arms—Phaltiel's child.

Anxious, I consulted the other women in the village. They had many suggestions to make and remedies to offer: prayers and charms and herbs. I even, against all warnings, consulted Hastar, a hot-eyed foreigner who was said to have come from a land beyond Moab, where she had learned many strange and useful things.

Hastar listened, and then said frankly that many would pay well for the barrenness I wept over. "Your husband has sons of his first wife, has he not? Well then—why quarrel with your luck? Better to be an old man's darling, they say—"

"My husband is not old!"

Hastar smiled, and the long lines painted past her slanting eyes wavered and wrinkled. "No husband is old to a loving wife. Well, you are a good girl, Michal, and as you wish it for yourself I will tell you what I can. But it may not work, and if it does not, do not complain of me to all the village."

I swore I would not, and listened well. But it did me no good, for her advice proved as worthless as the prayers and charms and potions of the others. The best that could be said for Hastar's foreign wisdom was that it found more favor with my husband than did that of the good wives.

At last his patience with my folly ended, and Phaltiel made me throw away the charms and amulets, and pour the herbal potions on the midden. "Wife of my bosom, I and my children love you and you make me laugh, and I care not if you ever risk yourself in childbed. I lost my first wife so, when Caleb was born—your sister Merab died giving a fifth son to a man to whom she had already given four. I have sons and daughters a-plenty, so let me hear no more of this."

But he agreed that there was no harm in what Hastar had told me, and each new moon we tried once more. It did not work. I remained barren.

Sometimes I wondered if it was my father's curse that kept me childless. Later I knew it had been his blessing.

~

It was beautiful, that last day I ever saw my brother Jonathan. As beautiful as one of Jonathan's smiles.

Sweet spring would soon be hot summer; the air was soft as lovers' hands. I was lazy, that day; I sat beside the courtyard spring, and let the water run winter-cold over my fingers, and counted over my little joys like jewels.

Once I had run hot after David; now that I had been eight years married to Phaltiel I knew how foolish I had been. What would there have been for me with David? Nothing but weariness and loneliness and grief; going from wilderness to foreign court and back again, always knowing that of my father and my husband, only one could live if there were ever to be peace.

No, this was better—this warm content. I thought I knew now what love was, and peace. I thought I knew how to value them both.

But I had not truly learned that harsh lesson. Not yet.

And so I played the water sparkling from my fingers, and laughed, and rose easy in my mind when a maid came to tell me there was a man striding down the road that led only to Phaltiel's house.

The man at the gate was dust-covered and road-weary, but I

knew him at once and ran to him with my arms outstretched. "Jonathan! Oh, my brother, be welcome!"

He let me clasp him close, and I was startled by his thinness. It seemed my arms circled bone. Frightened, I began to scold him.

"Jonathan, what have you been about? You will be ill if you keep this road! Come into the house and let me feed you! And you will bathe, and rest, and I will not have you say me nay!"

"What, is this proper goodwife my little sister Michal? Country life has changed you, Princess." It was meant for a jest, I think, but his words fell flat and heavy on the ear, as his arm lay heavy on my shoulders.

"I am no longer a fool for temper and pride, if that is what you mean—now do as I say, brother, and save your news for later. I will listen to nothing until you have eaten and rested."

"You are still as stubborn as a rock in the road." Jonathan smiled a little, but he was too tired to argue, and so did as I bade him.

I had meant my words, too, and so it was not until well into the day, when the shadows began to reach out across the valley, that I heard what had brought Jonathan to see us now.

We sat in my little courtyard where the spring welled endless from the rock—Phaltiel, and Jonathan, and I. Jonathan was clean now, his hair combed and oiled, his clothing fresh from a cedar-wood chest. He had slept; I had sat beside his bed myself to make sure. It had made no difference. He still looked like a man whose wound is mortal, and who knows it and does not care.

I pretended I did not notice, and chattered on like a silly squirrel about this and that—my new gown, a recipe for stewed dates in cream that no one had liked, how much Caleb had grown—until Phaltiel put his hand over mine and bade me cease.

"Boys of his age grow, and always have and always will. This is not why Jonathan has come to us now."

"Let my sister speak, Phaltiel. It has been too long since I have had time to listen to house-talk. I am tired of war and fighting men. Caleb looks to be tall, you say? I would see him, before I go—my boy Meribaal is nearing five, and I think of him as still clinging to his nurse's hand. I have not seen him since the winter." It was late spring now.

"Oh, Jonathan—is it so bad then?" I knew it for a fool's question before the words left my lips, and could have cried.

He did not seem to hear. "I do not know why I came, save that it has been long since we met and I would see you once more. I have seen David, and now I have seen you, Michal." He smiled at me and held out his arms. "Come and kiss me, little sister, and then I would talk with your husband."

Phaltiel looked at me in the way that meant I was to be biddable and obedient, and Jonathan looked so tired I did not argue, but kissed him and went away. I knew he must be troubled in his mind indeed to speak as he had done; David's name was not often spoken in Phaltiel's house.

~

It was not until Jonathan was gone that I learned what he had said to Phaltiel that day. He had made Phaltiel swear not to tell me sooner.

"He would have it that you should not know at all, but that I would not promise. Put that distaff down, Michal, and come and sit with me, and I will tell you."

As Phaltiel told it to me, the tale was simple; he did not try to wrap it in sweet words, but told me plainly.

During the years King Saul had hunted David through the land, we had been fortunate beyond measure; the Philistines had not attacked. But now King Saul was known to be mad in truth, and the kingdom divided against itself. And now the Philistines had declared open war on Israel. The Philistine army was massing near the plain of Jezreel.

"David is not there—the Philistine leaders do not trust him overmuch, it seems. Well, I would not." It was the harshest thing

I had ever heard Phaltiel say of David. "Jonathan will not have to face David across a spear, at least."

I was glad of that, for both their sakes. But there was more, and worse. Jonathan had not come all this way only to tell us that. He had come to say good-bye.

My father had never before feared battle—mad or not, he still knew how to fight—but this time he had grown uneasy in his mind. He had gone to consult a necromancer, a woman who lived at En-dor. Saul wished to speak to Samuel; the mad consulting the dead.

This had caused great wonder and talk, for Saul himself had ordered all witches and necromancers and oracles banished from his kingdom long since. Yahweh would no longer come to Saul in dreams, or answer his prayers, or speak to him through prophets—and so no one in all the land might seek solace or wisdom through those means.

But now Saul himself had need of counsel; well, he was given it freely enough. Samuel appeared to him and told him what many living could have told as well, had they dared, with no need for sorcery: Yahweh had abandoned Saul long since, and the prize was David's now.

"That would not have brought Jonathan so far, only to stay a day and a night. What else, Phaltiel?"

He held my hands tight while he told me. Samuel had indeed had more to say; in death as in life, the prophet Samuel must always have the last word. Because Saul had disobeyed Yahweh, he had already suffered much, and now would lose what he had left to him. In the coming battle the Philistines would conquer; Saul and his sons would die.

Is it better to have warning of the blow, when it cannot be halted, or to walk serene and unheeding until the knife cuts deep? I have suffered both; I still have no answer.

"No! My father is mad—all men say so—this is one of his ravings." But I had seen Jonathan's face, and my words did not comfort me.

"Whether King Saul spoke with Samuel or only with his own fears I do not know, Michal. But Jonathan says that Saul believes, and the men believe. And that is half the Philistines' work done for them."

"And Jonathan went—you let Jonathan go to be killed—why did you not stop him? I will send after him—no, I will go myself and bring him here, where he will be safe—" Now I raved, and knew it, and could not stop myself.

"Yes, he went to fight beside your father—to save him if he can, to help win the battle if it can be won. Who is to say if Samuel's ghost spoke truth or lies? Jonathan is a warrior; he might have lain dead after any battle, and with no help from prophecy. When all men fight, some men die. Can you guard a man from the future?"

I shook my head, knowing that was the answer the wise would give. Then I went trembling into his arms. "Then why did he come, if he does not believe?"

Phaltiel held me close, and stroked my hair. "To see you once more if it should chance to be his last battle, which is by no means certain. Come, tell me—did Samuel love Saul so well he would give him true prophecies for nothing but the asking?"

I smiled for him a little, and let him coax and pet me until I could smile more. But my heart was not eased, nor my mind. In the night, when I closed my eyes for sleep, I saw red splashed across the black; blood and death to come, I thought.

And in the day, when I sat and spun our best wool beside the courtyard spring, I heard again the sound of men's voices murmuring through the water. Here Phaltiel and Jonathan had sat and talked an evening into a night. It seemed long, only to tell of Saul's vision at En-dor. I would have given much to know what else they had spoken of. But Phaltiel did not tell me, and so I did not ask.

I told myself it was because he refused me so little that I did not wish to ask what he plainly did not wish to grant. But I think now that I was afraid of what I might hear.

~

All men know what happened on Mount Gilboa, where the army of Israel fell.

Saul was dead; Jonathan was dead, and many of my father's other sons—less dear to me than Jonathan, but no less my brothers for that. Half the army was slaughtered by the Philistines; the other half fled, leaving the towns beyond the battlefield open to the enemy.

The Philistines looted the towns and stripped the dead. They took my father's armor and set it up in the temple of Ashtoreth. They took my father's body, and my brothers', and nailed them to the wall of the city of Beth-shan.

All happened as Samuel's spirit had foretold.

~

I was a woman, and so thought only of my grief. I wept for all my brothers who lay dead; for Jonathan I pulled off my bracelets and tore my gown. As for my father—he had cast me off long ago, and I had thought I cared nothing for him now. But I found tears to honor him as well.

Men had other ways to heal their hearts.

Abner, who had been my father's war-chief since men could remember, consoled himself by making my half-brother Ishbaal king over all the north, over the lands of Israel. I found it hard to think of Ishbaal in King Saul's place; Ishbaal had never looked past his flocks and his fields. Still, men called Ishbaal king now—at least the men of Israel called him so. The men of Judah swore that Saul's son was nothing to them, and looked now to their own concerns; the south would rule itself.

But Ishbaal was called a king, if only in Israel, and he had Abner to lead his army. Perhaps he would do well enough.

We were not well-known to each other, but there were few of Saul's children left, now—only Ishbaal, and the concubine Rizpah's two sons, and me. And so I sent a sister's message to Ishbaal, to wish him well.

David consoled himself by making the deaths of Saul and Jonathan a song to haunt men's ears forever. "The beauty of Israel is slain upon thy high places; how are the mighty fallen..."

It was David's greatest song; men remembered the song when they had long forgotten Jonathan and Saul. They sang it in all the villages of Israel, and even in the villages of Judah. Even I wept when I heard it, and by then I had thought I had no tears left and must bear my grief dry-eyed.

". . . How are the mighty fallen, and the weapons of war perished!"

CHAPTER 6

". . . first bring Michal Saul's daughter . . . ."
—II Samuel 3:13

But David made more than a song after Gilboa. He broke with the Philistine king and moved south with all his people to Hebron, the largest city in Judah. And soon there came word that David had sung so well to the men of Hebron that they had lifted him in their arms and anointed him as king of Judah.

"Well," I said to my husband when we heard the news, "so the shepherd's son is a king in the land, and Samuel has had his will at last. But Saul's son is king of Israel. So much for prophets."

Phaltiel said nothing. I had been combing out my hair; now I set aside my wooden comb and turned to him. He looked troubled, and I rose and went to him. "You know it is nothing to me. And David and Judah are far away."

"Nothing is far away when men fight for kingdoms," Phaltiel said, and put his arms around me. "So keep close to the house, Michal, and when you go to the village take some of the menservants with you."

"With my veil well pulled down, too, lest my face drive men mad with lust?" I meant it as a jest, to make him laugh, but he did not. "Phaltiel, what is wrong?"

"Perhaps only that I am an old man besotted with a young wife," he said, and kissed my brow. "You will do as I say, even if you think me a fool. King Saul is dead, but you are still the daughter of Saul."

I could not see that King Saul's daughter had anything to do with kings and armies. Oh, I had been a king's daughter once; now I was a woman in her husband's house, important only in his eyes. But that importance was all I asked for now, and so I kissed Phaltiel, and denied that he was old, or foolish, and promised I would do as he wished.

It did no good in the end, of course. Phaltiel was a wise man; he must have known that it would not. But even a wise man may have foolish hopes. Phaltiel hoped to keep me safe.

But I was one of Saul's children, and there was now no safety for us anywhere in the land.

Ishbaal was king in Israel, David was king in Judah. So matters stood, even-balanced, after the battle at Gilboa.

But David soon tipped the balance in his favor. Hebron was far to the south—too far for King David. And so he found a city that was neither north nor south, and took it for his own.

Jerusalem.

Jerusalem had belonged always to the Jebusites; it could not be taken from them. So men had always said. For not only did the city crown a rocky hill high above a fertile plain, but it had fresh water always, for it was blessed with a secret well. Jerusalem sat complacent in the midst of Israel and Judah, for a babe could defend it and no host could take it.

But David found a way. He found the well.

And so David's men, led by his war-chief Joab, crept up the well-shaft by night and took the city. David lost not one man in the taking; he walked triumphant through the great gate of Jerusalem the next day and claimed the city as his own. Yahweh had delivered Jerusalem into his hand; here, so David said, he would build his king's house.

It was the greatest tale since David had slain Goliath, or since King Saul had been slain upon the slopes of Mount Gilboa. David and Jerusalem—it was all men talked of when they came through our village. A true king, they called David. The beloved of Yahweh.

Now Jerusalem was King David's city—and Jerusalem guarded the ways both north and south, east and west, from the mountains to the sea.

But David was still king only in Judah. In Israel Ishbaal had Abner, who had been my father's war-chief, to stand at his back. With Abner, Ishbaal had what was left of King Saul's army. The army was loyal to Abner now, not to Ishbaal.

So when the tale ran round that Ishbaal had quarreled with Abner—and over a woman, so men said—I laughed. I could not believe that Abner would ever look hot at any woman—or that any man would be such a fool as Ishbaal would be to deny Abner anything he asked.

But I was wrong. Ishbaal had been just such a fool, and had reviled Abner publicly.

Perhaps it was true that madness ran in the blood of Saul. I could think of no other reason for Ishbaal to treat Abner like a dog, when it was Abner who had made him king, and who could un-make him again with a word to the army. And over what? Abner asking to take my father's concubine Rizpah into his own house!

A common enough thing; Saul had been Abner's own cousin after all. But Ishbaal had called it treason and betrayal; had ac-cused Abner of wishing to claim the last king's crown by claiming the last king's woman. Folly piled upon folly, like stones piled high to build a wall of anger between good neighbors. When had Abner been other than faithful?

Yes, I had laughed when first I heard the tale of Ishbaal's quar-rel with Abner. But I did not laugh the day that I looked out my front door and saw soldiers standing in the road, and Abner stand-ing at my gate.

~

Abner was no fool, and he was a careful man. He had many men at his back when he came to Phaltiel's house to take me away. I came to the gate to speak with Abner, as he asked; I saw no reason, at first, why I should not. It would have made no difference, of course, if I had refused, save that things would have gone harder than they did.

So I went to the gate. I was surprised; he must have brought a full fifty men. I was not sure we could feed and house so many, even for one night. But I greeted him, and offered him all that was his due as a guest. And I thought how little Abner had altered since the day I had last seen him, when he had come to my tower prison to tell me I was to marry Phaltiel. But Abner had been a man grown while I had been only a child; of course he seemed changeless to my eyes.

"You are Michal, daughter of Saul?" He sounded unsure, which was odd in Abner. But he had seen me last when I was fourteen, and I had changed much in the ten years since.

"I am Michal, wife of Phaltiel," I said. "Be welcome in his house, Abner. I will send Caleb to fetch Phaltiel from the fields."

Caleb had come running and now stood under my arm, his eyes all wide for the sight of well-armed and armored men. He was past twelve, growing fast, and was straight and tall for his age, nearly as tall as I. He was a good boy, and a good son to me. Now, of course, he did not wish to heed me, and protested. "Oh, Mother, why can not a servant go? I can help you here!"

Abner looked at him as a man looks at a stone set in his path. "Your son, Princess Michal?"

There was nothing in Abner's words to frighten me. Yet my skin grew cold, and I seemed to stand before a deep pit into which I would fall if my words were wrong. I knew this was foolishness; I had never liked Abner overmuch, and so let my dislike rule me.

I looked into Caleb's eager eyes, and laughed. "I am not so old as that! This is Phaltiel's son, and he is usually obedient to his stepmother. Caleb, go and fetch your father as I bid you!" My voice came out flint-sharp, and Caleb ran, startled.

Now Abner and I faced each other across the soft hot dust of the path. "You have changed, daughter of Saul."

"You have not. What do you want of me, war-chief of Ishbaal?"

"War-chief of David," he said. I stared, and Abner smiled with his mouth, but not his eyes. "Ishbaal is a fool and worse than a fool. David is the man for Israel as well as Judah."

"If you can say that, then David must be the anointed of the Lord indeed. But this is nothing to do with me."

"He is the man the prophet Samuel chose—did you know that, Princess?"

"Yes." I thought of a tower room, and David's voice low in the dark.

"I can bring him Gilead, and Jezreel, and Ephraim, and Benjamin, and all the armed men of Israel. You can bring him the blood of Saul, who was king before him. Between us we can set the seal of Yahweh over all the land from Dan to Beersheba. David wants you back, and I have come to take you to him."

It seemed to me that a long time passed before I spoke. "No," I said.

"You are his wife, Princess," Abner said, and I found that the title I once had cherished now made ill hearing.

"That marriage was set aside long ago," I said. "I have another husband—and David has other wives."

"You are his first wife. He would see you again and honor you before all the people."

"Tell him it is too late," I said, and turned away.

Abner caught my arm to make me stay. "For kings it is never too late. Be wise, Michal. Come willingly, and smile upon him, and David will set you up as queen over Israel and Judah both."

"No," I said again, and twisted out of his hands and pulled my veil close. But I already knew I would have no choice. A man who will take a 'no' and turn away smiling does not come with fifty armed men to ask his favor.

And then there was an arm about my shoulders, and strength to lean upon. Caleb must have run like a fox, and Phaltiel too, who never went in haste.

"I see we have many guests kept standing at our gate." Phaltiel's words were unhurried, but as he held me I could feel the way his heart beat against his chest. "Michal, go into the house and see that all is prepared for them."

"No need," Abner said. "We have come only for the wife of King David."

"She is not here," said Phaltiel.

Abner stepped close and spoke low. "You are called a wise man, Phaltiel. You know what King David wishes, and what he will do. Help him, and he will reward you. Hinder him—" Abner stopped, as if he had said enough.

"The way of kings is always clear to those with eyes to see," Phaltiel said. "Samuel warned the people long ago what harvest a king would bring to the land, but they would not listen. Now the reaping begins."

"Then we understand one another, as wise men do. Give us Michal, Phaltiel, and we will leave your house in peace."

"Michal goes or stays as she wills. What is your will, Michal?"

"I am Phaltiel's wife, and have been many years." I closed my hand over Phaltiel's; although the day was hot, his fingers were cold under mine. "I do not wish to see David again. He is nothing to me."

"There is your answer, Abner. She will not go."

"We all know that she will." Abner did not speak as a man angered; he patiently instructed stubborn children. "Women are fools, but men should not rejoice in folly. I remember when she swore she would die without David—you see that she has not. She will forget you as easily. Now tell her women to pack whatever she would take with her. We will wait." Abner was not unkind, when kindness cost him nothing.

Phaltiel turned away from him, so that his body hid me from Abner's eyes. He put my veil back from my face. "Well, Michal?"

I looked up at him, and for the first time in many years truly saw the lines by his eyes and mouth, and the grey in his dark hair. He was a good man growing old, who deserved peace. I could not bear to bring trouble to his house. And in the road stood fifty strong men with clubs and spears.

"They will take me anyway," I said, and held my head high. "But do not worry, husband—I swear I shall not betray you with David."

Phaltiel smiled. "You are still so young, Michal. Do not swear to me, and do not be afraid. Go and tell your maids to pack what you would have."

~

Abner had brought a litter to carry me back to David; a thing carved of heavy wood and painted blue and gold. It was worthy of a queen; all the women of Gallim, and the men too, ran to the side of the road and stared as we passed by. My face grew hot as I thought of what they all would say of me now. I was glad of the crimson leather curtains that hid me from my neighbors' wide eyes.

Phaltiel walked beside the litter as we went along the road through the village of Gallim. He stayed beside me until we had reached the top of the long hill that led from our valley to the world beyond. There Abner told him that he must leave me.

"Set her aside, for David, King of Judah, says she is no longer your wife. Say farewell as you please, and then go back home and forget her."

Phaltiel did not answer, but put back the leather curtains and lifted me out of the litter to stand beside him on the road. We stood almost on the spot where I first had looked down the valley to Phaltiel's house, when I had come here as his unhappy bride.

I put my arms around him and clung, and would have wept, but Phaltiel bade me dry my eyes. "You have no reason to fear. Let David say what he likes, you are my wife, and I do not think he will lay his hands on you."

"He does not want me. He wants to make a show with King Saul's daughter."

Phaltiel looked at me for the space of a dozen heartbeats, while I heard how my words must have sounded in his ears. Bitter words, said by a woman who found them bitter still. Then he sighed and held me close. "Be calm," he said. "Be wise. And do not break your heart over this. It will pass. See David again, and then send to me and say whether Michal is still the wife of Phaltiel."

"And if I am?" I said.

"Then I will come, and bring you home again. Even King David is not above the Law; he cannot keep a man's wife against his will and hers."

And then Phaltiel kissed me, there on the road before Abner and all the soldiers. That was how we said good-bye.

CHAPTER 7

"So David dwelt in the fort,
and called it the city of David."
—II Samuel 5:9

It had been long since I traveled far, and never had I done so in great state. I learned now how a gilded litter swayed and dipped; how crimson leather curtains cut off light and air. I would rather have walked in the sun and the dust. And I told Abner so.

"Let me walk," I said when we at last stopped to rest. I was so hot and giddy I feared I would be ill. "I am a farmer's wife, and used to work—I can keep your pace."

"You are a queen now," Abner said. "David's queen does not walk in the dust for all to gaze upon."

"Oh, so high! My father's wives walked to the river with the other women—yes, and did the washing, too. So do not be so foolish, Abner. I would rather walk."

"You will ride," Abner said, and nothing I could say would move him from that.

And so I rode in the swaying queen's litter, lying upon embroidered and tasseled cushions. The colors were bright as butterfly wings, the cloth so smooth it caught on my fingers when I stroked it. I looked at the pulled threads now marring the fine pattern; threads caught and broken by my touch. Then I looked at my hands.

I had always tended them well enough, rubbing goose fat on them in the winter. But even so they were roughened by woman's work, by spinning and sewing and weaving. A woman's hands.

Not a queen's. I looked at my housewife's hands, and at the queen's cushions, and suddenly I knew all would be well.

David had not seen me in ten years; he did not know how I had changed—and that I was truly happy with Phaltiel. When last David had seen me I had been sick with love of him; I was cured of that illness now. I had been cured long since. David had never come for me, or sent word; well, Jonathan had always said David must have his reasons. But I no longer cared what those reasons were.

David had last seen an overproud little princess; King Saul's daughter. That girl was forever gone, and only Phaltiel's wife remained. King David would not want Phaltiel's wife.

And so I smiled and stroked the embroidered cushion—carefully, so that I would break no more threads. Yes, I had changed with the turning years; David must have been changed by time as much as I. Phaltiel was right, I had only to be calm, and wise. I had only to wait, and talk once more with David.

We would meet one last time, and perhaps we could speak of Jonathan, and I would tell David that I heard his songs even in the village of Gallim. And I would tell him of how I now loved Phaltiel. Yes, David and I would talk, and laugh at how foolish I had been when I was young.

And then all would be well. David would send me home, and we would part as friends.

It was a comforting thought to hold as talisman against the jolting of the litter and the closeness of the dim air trapped by the leather curtains. I think I even thought that it was true.

~

And so I was brought as a queen through the land. When we went by a farmstead, or through a village, women and children, and even many men, ran to watch wide-eyed as we passed. Such a show was a new thing in our land.

A man ran ahead to cry out that all should *"Make way for the*

war-chief Abner and Queen Michal, make way for King David's men."
When first I heard that I thought of how my father King Saul had
walked with his men as a comrade, and of how David had dwelt
with his in caves in the wilderness, and I laughed. It seemed that
Abner kept greater state for David than David did.

So I thought until I saw Jerusalem.

Abner stopped the men at the crest of the ridge north of the
city and held back the curtains himself so that I might see. "There,"
Abner said. "There is Jerusalem. King David's city. The city where
you will be queen."

The twin walls of Jerusalem circled the city like bracelets on a
bride. Behind them the city flaunted itself upon its hills; pro-
tected by such guardians without it could afford to be careless
within. Even so far away the city's riches flashed and caught the
eye—pillars green and crimson and blue, flowers bright upon rooftops, market awnings striped white and yellow.

"That is the king's house," said Abner. "There, on the far hill,
beyond the second wall."

I did not answer Abner, but I looked. The king's house stretched
my eyes; I had never seen anything like it. Walls white and gold in
the sun, galleries with columns of purple and scarlet—so much I
could see through the dust and distance. That, and the way the
dwelling crowned its hill and surveyed all the shining city below
like a queen.

My father had lived all his life in the house his father had
given him as a wedding-gift. When he needed more room, he had
built a new courtyard, a new tower. Saul's house had been like any
man's, even when he had been a king for many years.

It was only two years since the battle at Mount Gilboa; two
years that David had been called king in Judah. What had David
become, that he built himself such a house?

"You see before you King David's city, you can guess his power.
What do you think now, Princess?" Abner smiled, a snake sure of
its bird.

I looked at him, and looked again across the roofs of Jerusalem to where the king's house waited for me on the highest hill. "I think," I said at last, "that King David has a great house—and that he spends too much on paint and gilt."

It was not what Abner wished to hear, so he pretended he had not and gave the order to move on. It was a small victory, without meaning—but I now had need of even small comforts, and so it pleased me a little. And Abner did not speak to me again, which pleased me more.

~

It took the rest of the forenoon to reach the gates of Jerusalem and then to climb its crowded streets to the upper city where the king's house crowned all. There was much stopping and waiting, for the marketplaces were full, and the streets also. Sheep and donkeys and old women hauling water from the well move at their own pace, and even the king's name will not hasten them. Delay did not trouble me, for I was in no hurry.

The crimson leather curtains were drawn tight closed; I could not see Jerusalem. But I could hear it, city noises louder and more varied than anything I remembered from my father's city of Gibeah. And when we stopped, I could hear the street-talk clearly—one's own name will always catch the ear.

"It is the Princess Michal," they told one another. "Mad Saul's daughter. King David's queen." They sounded pleased and proud, as if David, or they, had done something clever or had a debt well paid.

I wondered what tale David had spun that my coming seemed to bring the people pleasure. I heard more and more talk of me as I was borne through the streets. "David's wife, returned to him at last." "She saved his life, they say." "Her father was mad; what of the daughter?" Once again I was thankful that heavy curtains veiled me from curious eyes.

At last we were at the gates of the king's house on the hill;

soon I would see David. And I wondered now what tale David would weave for me.

It did not matter; I did not care. So I told myself, as I had all the long way from Gallim—but now my blood beat hard and thick and slow under my skin; a serpent tempted to rouse from a winter's long sleep.

Through gates and through courtyards, until at last my litter was set down and the curtains pulled back. My journey was over. I stepped out into a quiet courtyard and a horde of chattering maidservants. Giggling all the while, they bustled me in through a wide doorway before I could even look about me and draw a deep breath.

No one came forward to say that she was David's wife, and bid me welcome as a guest should be. That was ill done; David had half a dozen wives now, and more concubines. Someone should have been here to greet me properly, and see to my comfort.

Oh, I stood in a fine room, that I would grant. On the walls new-painted swallows flashed bright among poppies and wheat. Carved cedar shutters were hooked back from two large windows; the room was full of light. But painted walls and wide windows, however fine, are not food or drink or rest.

The maids who surrounded me seemed to have no proper notions at all; they tugged at my gown and urged me to hurry, hurry, for the king would see me. The serpent under my skin slid cold beneath my heart and coiled there, and waited to see what Michal would do.

I counted three, and breathed deep and slow, and then I flung back my veil and spoke sharp words. "See King David like this, with dust up to my eyes and my hair a nest for bees? Is that a fit way for him to welcome the daughter of Saul—or for her to greet the king of Judah?"

They stood all round-eyed; I stamped my foot. "Fools, do you truly not know how to serve a woman weary with travel? I will see the king, but not until I have washed my body and oiled my hair and changed my linen. Now go and ready a bath, that I may prepare myself to receive King David."

I clapped my hands hard and the silly girls scattered, noisy as partridges, to do my bidding. For all its fine scarlet columns and gilded lintels and purple curtains over doors, it was not a good house; I did not think overmuch of the way David's wives kept his state. I did better for Phaltiel with less—and my handmaids did not gape and giggle at visitors.

Still, the maids did well enough, though it took them their own good time to bring the brightly painted bath and fill it with water. I had no wish to hurry, so I smiled upon them and spoke as a foolish woman will, worrying over what I should use and wear and say, and then changing my mind and asking what they thought. They were most willing to advise me, and happy to quarrel with each other. It was another sign of an ill-run house, but the manners of these maids were no concern of mine.

At last the bath was readied to their liking. They drew out the pins from my travel-used gown and took it away; I stepped into scented water. Water that tasted of roses and lilies was poured, and ran cool over my hot skin.

Water spilling over me, and women's talk. I closed my ears to the idle chatter and my eyes to the light. I would not think now. I would only rest, and wait.

Water poured, and silence. Water that slid over my body like oiled silk. Silence of breaths drawn deep and held, movement quickly stopped.

I did not have to open my eyes. I knew.

"Leave us, all of you," I said, and listened behind my lids as the maids went from the room on soft-padding feet. There was little sound from them now; a skirt rustled, a bangle chimed. The heavy curtain flapped and sighed; it fell with a final thud across the doorway and they were gone.

I opened my eyes and looked into David's.

"You have not changed, Michal. I would have known you anywhere." He was older. There were thin lines around his eyes and mouth that had not been there when I last had looked upon his face—well, that had been ten years ago; he was near thirty now. But his voice was still as beautiful as harp-song, warm as love in winter dark.

"How, among so many others?" I said the words as if what I most wished were true, and I cared nothing for David or for what he might do. But it did not matter what I said, or how; David smiled, and my heart twisted in my breast.

"By this," he said, "and this, and this." His hands were soft and free as water on my wet skin. "We had only our wedding night, Michal, but it would take forty times forty women to make a man forget you."

My skin trembled under his touch as the serpent woke full and sank its fangs deep. I could hardly breathe; I could not move. I was no unripe girl now. My body knew what it would have, for my loving husband had taught it well—

"No!" I cried, and turned away, pulling my hair around me. It stuck and clung wet, and did not cover much. But I tried.

David laughed. I had forgotten how he laughed; rain after summer heat, spring leaves in the wind.

"May a man not touch his wife, Michal?" His hands slid over my shoulders, lifted my hair damp from my neck. "It has been too long since you looked at me with love in your eyes, sister of Jonathan. I have missed you as I miss him. He is gone, but you are still here to walk and talk with me. Turn your eyes on me again, and we will start anew."

Sweet words. But David's song came too late; I was wiser now, and would not be drawn to that lure. I swore I would not. "No," I said again.

This time I moved farther, out of reach of his hands. I stepped out of the bath and caught up a length of drying-linen to wrap and shield me. "You do me too much honor, great king. But I am another man's wife. Would you see me stoned at the wall?"

"You were mine first."

"And I am Phaltiel's now."

"There are no children; he is old; you were not willing. Such a marriage can be set aside."

"I have been married ten years," I said.

We faced each other across the now-still water in the painted bath. Once, long ago, I had been a princess and he a shepherd's son. Now I was a farmer's wife and he was a king; a lion to do as he willed. And he willed me to bend freely, for love of him, and so he smiled, and held out his hands.

"Ten years is nothing to the heart. Come back to me, Michal. As I loved your father Saul and your brother Jonathan, so and more do I love you. Whatever you wish, that you shall have—you are my first wife, and I will put aside all others if you ask it. Come, and I will set a crown upon your head and you will walk first among all the women of Israel and Judah."

I stood there in my linen sheet, the scented water drying from my skin. I looked on him, and listened to words like honey from the heart. David had always had a way with pretty words. But I had learned that love was not made of soft hands and pretty words.

"Ten years is much to a woman, David. Let me go back to my husband, who is a good man, and loves me."

"And do you love him, Michal?"

"Yes," I said.

"As you did me?" David came to me again, walking slowly around the bath of cooling water. I watched him come and could not move, even when he stood behind me and put his arms around me to hold me close against him. "Do you love this old man as you did me, when we both were young?"

I would not struggle against David as if I feared his touch had power over me still. "No," I said. "I love him better. He took me in when no other would, and was kind. I loved you long ago, and you love many others now. Be content with them, and let me go home. You may be king of all the world with my good will, and I will tell all men so from the marketplace if you ask it."

"I ask only you," he said, and set his lips against my neck.

"No." My skin chilled, burned. "No. It is too late, David."

"How too late, when we both are here and your heart still beats hard for me? See here, under the skin, how your blood leaps to meet my hand—"

I knew I had no choice; it was my mind only that would deny him. The body and the heart are stronger.

CHAPTER 8

". . . who clothed you in scarlet,
with other delights . . . . "
—II Samuel 1:24

David was right; my body and my heart were still hot for him. But I was right too; it was too late for us. And when we came together, our bodies twining and clinging in the semblance of love, I knew it, even if he did not. He seemed pleased enough, after. But I had lain ten years with a husband whose caresses were for Michal; David's hands and lips and body were for pleasing any woman.

And so afterwards, when we rested beside one another on the damp linen sheet and David asked again, sure of my answer, I still said no. That did not please him at all, though he tried to hide it, and laughed, and stroked my body anew to show me that I must bend soft to his touch.

"No, again? You do not mean that, my Michal, and it is unkind to torment me after so many years."

I lay quiet under his hand; he could set my body alight, as he said, but he could no longer content Michal. On our wedding night David had taught me love; today he had taught me lust. Phaltiel had taught me to know the difference.

"The years were not my doing, and you have found many other consolations."

"What, are you jealous? You need never be that; I have told you that you will be first, and only, if you ask it of me. You may have anything you desire, my queen, if only you will come to me and take it."

I turned my head to look at him, and he smiled, and took up my hair to twine in his fingers. "Your hair is a skein of silk, it is wheat in the wind. See, the king is caught in its net. What jewels can he give that will not be lost in its glory?"

Once, long ago, I had been called a princess. Now, if I chose, I could be that again—more, I could be a queen. David offered all a man thinks a woman could desire; he was cleverer than most men, for he promised love, too.

But I knew better, now, than to cry after the moon, for David himself had shown me what the moon's cold love was worth. I would happily thank David on my knees for the lesson if only I might then go home to my husband Phaltiel and never more look back.

"Come, do not be silent—you have only to speak and whatever you wish for will be granted."

"Send me home. Send me home to my husband."

David laughed again. "And would he take you back, after this?"

I thought of Phaltiel, and how he had looked at me when we said farewell. "Yes," I said. "Yes, he would take me back."

"Even if all the land knew his wife had lain with the king?" The lion showed claws now, and fangs: *see what I could do, if I would.*

"Even so," I said.

"Then he is a fool, and you are a greater one." David's voice wooed no longer; kings have no great store of patience with denial.

"Perhaps I am, but not such a fool as to think ten years can be wiped out with a word."

"A king's word," David said. "A king's wishes. Who are you to set yourself against the king?"

"A woman," I said. "A woman with her rights under the Law. I am another man's wife and I do not come to you willingly, nor does my husband set me aside. You have no right to keep me here. Even the king is not above the Law, David."

"The king is the Law, Michal."

"Did Yahweh tell you that?"

I thought he would be angry, but he only laughed. "No, it was Samuel and Saul between them who taught me that lesson." David took up my hair again, smoothing it between his hands, and twined its length twice around my throat. "You must learn it too, Michal, and then we will be happy together."

~

David was clever. I had always known that. But now he was cunning as well—and that I only learned when it was too late. And so when I would ask only to be sent back to Phaltiel, David did not rant, and rage, and swear I should do his will or have all my bones broken, as my father would have done. No, David was all soft smiles and sweet words and lavish gifts.

That day I was given rooms with cool tiled floors and walls painted with birds and flowers and monkeys in yellow and red and blue. The rooms were full of riches hoarded against my pleasure. Sandalwood and cedar chests held gowns of scarlet and purple. Ivory boxes held rings for my ears and fingers. Glass vials held gold dust for my hair.

Everywhere I looked I saw more wealth than I had ever heard of, save in harper's tales. I remembered my father's house, and how large and grand we had all thought it because it had two courtyards and a tower three rooms high.

I was still stretching my eyes wide at my rooms when David's wives came to me and gave me more to wonder at.

~

I heard them before I saw them; a noise like winter branches in the wind. Then half a dozen women burst upon me in a jangle of bells and bracelets and gold-fringed skirts. They stared at me as if David had never before brought home a woman.

I had more cause to stare than they. I had heard of them all, from one tale-teller or another. Abigail, Ahinoam, Eglah, Haggith,

Abital, Maachah—David's wives; the mothers of his sons. Farmers' daughters, merchants' daughters—all save Maachah, daughter of the king of Geshur. These women had followed David through the wilderness, had kept his tents in the desert. To see them now, you would think them all Egyptian harlots.

Eyelids were painted green as beetle-wings; eyes were ringed dark and heavy with kohl; lips and fingers were stained with red henna. Wrists and ankles were heavy-laded with gold and silver. And they wore clothes my father's women would have thought almost too fine for a king's marriage-feast; stiff-pleated gowns bright with dye and heavy with gold fringe and tassels.

Gaudy as jays, they were. With the same manners, too, I thought then, and I never afterwards had cause to change my mind. Perhaps they had been good enough women when David was only a great warrior in the hills. But being a king's women had spoiled them. They wanted now what they once could not even have dreamed existed.

"King David sent us to make you welcome," one said at last—a comely enough woman, but no longer truly young. Discontent lined her face; this woman desired what she could not have.

"That is kind," I said. "I am Michal, wife of Phaltiel of Gallim."

They stared again; one laughed; one whispered to another. The woman who had spoken to me tossed her head, making her earrings dance hard against her cheeks. "I am Abigail, wife of King David—we are all David's wives here—"

"—and Abigail does not speak for us!" snapped another.

"I have been longest married to King David, Eglah." Abigail turned her shoulder to Eglah.

"Not so long as Michal." That was the tall dark one; Maachah, I learned later.

"I am not married to King David," I told them patiently. "I am the wife of Phaltiel, as I have said."

"Oh, yes, we all know the tale," said Abigail. Her red-dyed mouth was pinched at the corners, as if she had bitten too hard into an unripe quince.

"We all know many tales," Maachah said, and looked hard at Abigail. "It is better not to tell them, lest another know even more."

I did not know then what Maachah hinted at; I thought that she at least had no love for tale-bearing and gossip. So I smiled at Maachah, and would have spoken to her, but Abigail pushed herself forward again.

"Who has dressed you? That is no gown for King David's queen—and where are your bracelets, your jewels?" Abigail frowned and clapped her hands. "Where are the maids? They are a flock of useless, lazy girls—you must not let them be idle, Queen Michal." She spoke as if the words were dust thick enough to choke her.

"They dressed me as I bade them, and I sent them away. I am a farmer's wife. I am not used to such fine things."

Maachah laughed; she had fine teeth that gleamed white against her painted lips. "You will be. David has said--"

"King David," Abigail corrected her.

"I can speak for myself, Abigail!" Maachah turned back to me. "David has said that you are to be called queen, and we are all to bow to you and do as you bid us. What is your bidding, O Queen?"

They all stared at me like angry cats. They were united at least in this—they hated me. I could not blame them. David should not have spoken so; it made them as nothing.

"Shall we deck you with gold and gems? Shall we comb your hair, or wash your feet?" Maachah now spoke for all of them in her hurt pride.

I shook my head and spoke calmly, as if I did not hear the vinegar in Maachah's words. "I thank you for your welcome, but I need nothing—except perhaps some goose-fat for my hands." I held my hands out, palms up. "You see how they are."

"They will not be so long. Tell your maids to tend them." Maachah tossed her head; her braids moved on her shoulders like dark snakes.

"Then your hands will be soft for King David," Abigail snapped.

"I do not need soft hands for the king," I said. "I need strong hands to do the work in my husband's house. I am Phaltiel's wife, not David's. Soon I will be gone again, and you may all live in peace without me."

I could not say it plainer. But they did not believe me.

"If the queen does not need us, then she should give us leave to go," said Maachah.

"I do not need you," I said. "And I tell you again, I am no wife of David's—and no queen."

They turned their backs upon me then and went away, all stiff with malice and injured pride. David should not have shamed them to honor me. I stood in the doorway and watched them go rustling and chiming down the smooth-tiled hall.

It was plain that Abigail and Maachah fought for pride of place; only Eglah had tried to assert her own right to speak as well, and she had been quickly pushed aside. The other three—Ahinoam, Haggith, and Abital—had only whispered among themselves. But their eyes had been as flat against me as those of the ones who spoke. I would find no friends among David's wives.

And I did not think they were friends to each other. Now that I had met David's wives I knew why his king's house was kept no better than a jackdaw's nest. When he had been a rebel warrior, each wife had her own tent to queen it over; now there was only one king's house. No wife could take its rule firmly into her own hands, nor would any grant her rights to another. They were all against each other, and for nothing else.

And now David had said that I was to come and be queen over them all. I watched as Abigail rounded the corner out of my sight. The thick gold fringe edging her skirts slid over the bright wall like clutching fingers.

I listened to the faint sounds of their passage echoing back along the empty tiled halls. I wondered if they knew that David had sworn to put them all aside, if only I asked it of him. I wondered, too, if he would do it, if I chose to ask.

But it did not matter, for I would not stay here to choose or to ask anything. My future did not lie here, in this house of kings and quarreling women. I was going to go back to the little village of Gallim, to Phaltiel and to my home.

And nothing David gave or said could change my mind; I knew that in my bones and heart. And so I listened after David's wives, and was sorry for them. And when I could hear them no longer, I went back into the queen's rooms that had been given to me. I thought I would be left there in peace for a time. I was wrong again.

There was a sound from the doorway; soft, a ripple of water over white pebbles. A pretty sound. I looked, and saw a girl standing there, dark and beautiful as honey. Her hair was not woven into braids, but fell in long curls to her hips; it flamed crimson as sunset, hot as the heart of fire. I had never seen such a color before.

When I looked she smiled and spread her hands; when she twisted her wrists her bracelets jingled once.

"O Queen, live forever—" she began. Her words were slurred; an accent I did not know.

"I am not the queen." It seemed I had been saying the words endlessly.

She stretched her eyes wide. The bright-painted lids flashed like dragonflies in sunlight. Then she laughed. It seemed honest enough; I heard no malice in it, as I had in Abigail's laughter.

"But whether I am queen or not, I will be glad of your company," I told her, and smiled in my turn. "Will you come and talk with me?"

"Of course I will, O Queen—and those who are lazy as men and spineless as oysters may envy me all they please!" The girl came toward me. She took small steps, gliding over the smooth-tiled floor; her hips swayed as she walked, the long crimson curls of her hair did not. She was graceful as a palm tree rocked by wind. And she knew how to walk silent. Her gilded fringes did not clash, her jewelry did not clatter.

"Be welcome," I said, and invited her to sit beside me on the padded bench. She seemed surprised, but pleased; she smiled again.

"You do me great honor, O Queen." She sat beside me and folded her hands in her lap, where they lay quiet as fallen leaves.

Her hands too were painted; ruddy circles and rippling lines adorned their cream-smooth skin. Henna, I thought; henna on her hands—and on her hair, too.

"I am Zhurleen." An odd name, I thought, but sweet-sounding, like a silver bell. She touched the edge of her teeth to her lower lip. "I am one of King David's concubines." She looked at me slant-wise; her eyes were rich and dark as sloes. Now that she was close to me, I saw that Zhurleen was no girl. Now I thought she must be almost as old as I. But her honey skin was smooth as butter; under that skin her flesh was round and firm.

"I suppose that is a great honor," I said. "You are very beautiful; you must please the king greatly." I thought flattery could do no harm; besides, I thought it must be true.

"The queen is most gracious. But the king has many women . . ." She shrugged, and coiled one long sleek ringlet in her hand. Dark-fire hair slid over honey skin; turn and turn about her patterned fingers. Waiting. Then she looked at me again with that slanting cat-gaze, as if she wanted something from me.

I did not know what it was; I had nothing. And so I asked. I saw no reason, that first day in King David's house, that I should not speak plain and free.

"What is it you want of me? I am only a farmer's wife—come to my husband's farm, and I can make you welcome, but here—" I stopped, for Zhurleen laughed.

"O Queen, you are as clever as the serpent! Yes, I want something of you, if you will grant it. I would be your friend. You will find me useful, I swear it."

"I am always glad of friends," I said. "But I will not be here. I must go back to Gallim, and my husband."

She laughed again. "King David's queen, to dwell in farmyard dust!"

I did not laugh, but looked at her straight. "I am not King David's queen."

"The king says you are, and we all know the king's word makes truth."

"I care nothing for the king's words. My marriage to David was set aside long ago—and set aside by a king, too, my father King Saul."

"What kings make, kings break," Zhurleen said, and shrugged, and spread her painted hands. "And so here you are at last, the king's first love and first wife—wise enough to wait and take care, while the others grew old before their time." She smiled, as if we shared a precious secret. "Now you come back to King David fair and straight, and still young enough to give him a son of the royal line."

"Royal line?" I stared at her, and then laughed. "Where do you come from, that you speak so? It is Yahweh who chooses our kings."

A pause; Zhurleen's eyelids flickered, flashed jewelfire. "Ascalon," she said at last. "My home is Ascalon, O Queen."

Ascalon, queen of the sea-cities of Philistia. So that was why there were henna waves upon her smooth hands, and why her very words held the rhythms of sea upon shore. The great cities of the Philistines were guardians of the sea-coast.

Zhurleen waited as I stared, curious. A Philistine concubine—how did David's so-proud wives like that? I thought of Abigail's sour face and smiled; I could not help it.

Zhurleen laughed again, soft. "Yes, I am a Philistine; in our land we know how to value kings—and queens."

"And so do we here in Israel and Judah." I did not truly understand Zhurleen, nor she me. That day knowledge lay hidden between us, and we each thought our wisdoms spread plain before the other's eyes.

Zhurleen coiled her ringlet once more about her supple fingers, and smiled again. "Yes. How long was it, O Queen? Ten years married to a farmer, and yet no child?"

"That is true; it is a grief to me." I kept my words sweet; Zhurleen was a Philistine, after all, and her ways were not mine. "But children do not come only because they are wished for."

"Wise women know that. But I am sure a king will give you

sons, O Queen." Zhurleen leaned forward, close to me; I smelled spikenard upon her crimson hair. "And so because I am wise, and can see my future, I would be your friend, if you will let me. A queen needs eyes and ears, and mine are keen and sharp."

"I do not understand," I said.

"I will be your faithful friend from this moment on," Zhurleen said. "I swear I will serve you well. I ask only that you take me into your household. The king will forget me one day; I know the queen will not."

I stared at her; she sat back and lowered her glittering dragon-fly lids. She waited, but I could think of nothing to say.

"Tell me how I may serve you, O Queen. I can braid your hair with pearls or paint your nails with gold—King David has said you are to have whatever you desire—and I can make those fish-brained maids behave as they should! I can tell you what you should wear, and how—you are wise, to dress simply until you have the best—"

She plainly meant each word; I was sorry that I could do nothing for her. But there was something she could do for me, if she would. I held my hand out to her. "Zhurleen, do you truly wish to be my friend?"

"Of course. Only a fool would not."

"There is something I would have done, and I do not know who else to ask. It is a great favor, but it will bring you no reward."

"Serving the queen will be my reward." Zhurleen spread her hands and bowed; I could not see her eyes. "What would you have me do, O Queen?"

"I wish a message sent." Suddenly I was weary even in my bones; it was hard to find the right words. "A message to Phaltiel of Gallim. Tell him—tell him his wife awaits him. Tell him to come to Jerusalem and take me home."

Zhurleen sat quiet, then, and looked at me, her painted face smooth as a temple-carving. A graven image. Then her heavy lashes quivered; there was comprehension in her eyes, and pity.

She took my hand in both of hers and touched it to her forehead. "Live forever, O Queen. I will do as you ask. But I tell you now, it will not work."

~

That night I could not sleep; neither my mind nor my body would let me rest. I lay upon the queen's wide bed and heard again the day's voices, an endless hissing, like sand in the wind. I felt again David's hands upon my wet hair as he made me want him; I saw again that odd pity in Zhurleen's black eyes.

I tried to think of homely things: the spinning I had left undone; how many baskets of figs I must dry after harvest; whether the rent in Caleb's almost-new tunic could ever be properly mended. I tried to count the stitches that must be set. But what I told over to close the gap were the days that must pass before I saw Caleb again; the hours that must be counted before Phaltiel again held me close, and laughed.

At last I rose and went to the window. The opening was shuttered against the night by ivory carved until it was fragile as old bones. I set the ivory screen aside and looked out over Jerusalem.

The moon sailed high, just past full, spilling light pale over the city. From my window, housetops were flat shadows; streets wove between, dark as the bottom of a well. Even so late I saw lamps still lit. Far away, at the city gates, torches blazed high. I could see the torch-fires dance even from my distant window.

Jerusalem. King David's prize.

King David's city, calm and powerful as a lion asleep under the dreaming moon.

I stood at the window and watched the moon's shadows grow long. The small bright flames of lamps went out, one by one. At last all that was left of light was the torches at the great gates, flaring harsh yellow against the night like wild eyes.

When all the city lay dark within its walls, I set the ivory screen back in its place, and went to lie once more upon the bed. I did not think I would ever sleep, not this night, in this room.

But I did, of course. And if I dreamed, I did not remember my dreams in the bright morning when David came to me again.

~

I was still sleeping when David came to wake me with a kiss, as if he were an ardent bridegroom. He was not pleased when I called him by Phaltiel's name before I truly woke; but it was his own fault and I told him so.

"I am not yours, David, I am Phaltiel's. Did you think I had lain these ten years in his arms thinking of you?"

His eyes flickered; I thought suddenly of my father. I did not know why, for David was nothing like Saul. But then David smiled; he had set aside anger.

"I have lain ten years thinking of you, Michal." He reached out to stroke my hair.

I sat up, wrapping the linen sheet close around me. I was still half-drugged with sleep. The light through the carven screens fell in bright hot patterns; it must be nearly midday.

David smiled and leaned closer, into the window's path; sun and shadow slid over him. He caught a strand of my hair up in his fingers and wove it through them, back and forth. "Ten years since our wedding night, and now at last we have our honey morning."

I moved away. "Yes—ten years since you left me because you needed someone to raise the rope again so that you would not be caught. I wanted to go with you, David. I loved you then."

"And now you hate me for leaving you." His voice was slow hot honey pouring through the warm air between us.

I laughed and shook my head. That bright morning I thought myself much wiser than he. "No, but I do not love you for it either. Oh, David, all that was long ago—let us forget it now."

"Yes, let us forget it now." He smiled in the way that once had made my bones melt with love, and lifted my hair to his lips. "Now that your patience and faith have been rewarded, and we are together once more. As we should be, Michal. Now we shall found a house of kings to rule over Israel and Judah both."

"My brother Ishbaal is still king in Israel," I said. "As for your house of kings—I have been ten years married and have no child. I cannot give you what you want, and you have a dozen sons already. Do not be foolish, David."

"You will get sons with me. Yahweh has given me so much, he will not withhold that."

"Has Yahweh given you a sign to say so?"

"Everything I have done is a sign of Yahweh's favor," David said. "See, I am king in Judah—I, who was born the last son of a humble man, am king. I have risen high when others who were greater are brought low."

He moved again, closer still, and put his arm around me. I sat very quiet, like a bird before a snake. "I have Jerusalem, and I have you, King Saul's daughter, and soon I will have the sacred Ark as well. Is that not sign enough for any man?"

"The Ark?" I stared; I could not believe it. The Ark held graven in stone the words Yahweh had given long ago to seal the covenant the god had made with our people. But the Ark had not been seen since before my grandfather's time. The Philistines had won it away during a long-ago battle; no living man knew where it now lay.

"Yes, even the Ark of the Lord will be mine, to rest here in Jerusalem in all honor. Yahweh has revealed it to me. At the right moment it will be revealed to all the people. Who could ask for a greater sign of favor?"

David waited, smiling, but I could think of nothing to say. That would be a wonder indeed, to see the holy Ark. At last I said, "Yahweh indeed loves you, David. When will you bring the Ark to Jerusalem?"

"Oh, when the time is ripe." He said the words carelessly, as if the Ark of Yahweh's covenant were no more than a cartload of melons to be brought to market. He shifted his arm, stroked my shoulder. "So you see, I will have all—with Yahweh's blessing."

I would not move under his hand; that he would not have of

me again. "If you have all that," I said, "what do you need with me? You have wives aplenty."

"But none of them are King Saul's daughter," David said. "None of them are the princess I loved so dear. None of them are the woman I waited ten years to hold again within my empty arms."

I thought about what David had said, but his words only sounded like foolishness to me then. And we both knew he had not waited even one year with empty arms, let alone ten.

"Oh, David, you believe your own songs now! This is not Moab, or Egypt—any man can be king here, if Yahweh wills it. Look at me—I am a farmer's wife, and no princess. Who in all Israel or Judah now cares that I was once a king's daughter?"

"I care," said David. "You will be queen of my house and my heart for the love I bore you, and Jonathan—yes, and even for King Saul." He leaned to kiss me; I drew back.

"No," I said. "I am married, and not to you. Do not touch me, David. It means nothing to me but pain, and I know how much it means to you. Go to your own wives, if you lust. You have women enough without me."

For a heartbeat I thought he might force me, to have his way. But he did not.

"This is all new to you, and strange," he told me at last. "You must have time to become accustomed; you shall have time. You shall have whatever you wish, my queen. You have the king's word on it."

"Truly?" I said.

"Have I not said it?"

"Then I wish you to send me home," I said. "Send me home to my husband."

For a moment David did not speak; I sat and waited while the sunlight danced hot upon his hair.

"I am your husband," he said at last. "You have waited long and patient for me, and now you will be rewarded, as I promised you. Now you will see what it is, to be King David's queen."

And then he went away, before I could deny him again.

It did not matter, I thought. Words did not change what was. I thought I had only to be patient and virtuous and all would be as I wished it.

I thought I knew all of what David was, but I was wrong. I knew nothing, then.

~

David sent me even more gifts that day. More jewels; more brace-lets, veils, earrings; finer cloth than I had ever before seen. The maidservants held each thing high so that I might see it and ad-mire.

I fingered a bolt of some thin stuff that was yellow as saffron and wondered at the color; I could not believe, then, that anyone could afford to use saffron only to color cloth. I thought of my sister Merab, and how pleased she had been with a length of Egyp-tian byssus. Enough for her wedding-dress, if she cut carefully— what would Merab have thought of this?

"My sister should have been his queen," I said. Beautiful clever Merab, who had married rich Adriel and given him five sons in six years, and died of it. Yes, Merab should have been David's queen; how she would have loved his gifts and her crown....

"Do not weep," said one of the maids. "If you do not like this, there is more, and better too."

"Better?" I said, and laughed. "Nothing could be better, and it does not matter. These things are for a queen—do I look like a queen?"

"Yes," they said, and looked back and forth among themselves. Yes, a queen, a true queen—and if only I would let them paint my eyelids green and my mouth red—and oil my skin so that it would be soft and rinse my hair with lemon-water so that it would shine—

I laughed again; I could not help it. They sounded like a covey of quail trilling and cooing over a berry bush. They looked as much alike as a quail's brood, too; like David's wives, they were all eye-paint and bright cloth.

See, they went on, see the cloth, the jewels—see how fine, how rare—see how the king delights in you—

"They are not for me," I said. I turned my eyes away from the riches they thrust upon me, and saw the concubine Zhurleen standing just inside the doorway.

There was a hissing sound from the maids. One, braver and louder than the others, stepped forward. "How dare you come before the queen? Go back to your own place, Philistine!"

"Oh, do not be so silly." I smiled and held out my hand. Philistine or not, Zhurleen was the only one under David's roof who had been kind. "Be welcome, Zhurleen—and help me tell these foolish girls I am no idol to deck in scarlet." I smiled, because the over-fine clothes were no fault of theirs, but I meant my words, too. It would be easy to let them have their way—but I did not want to taste what I would not keep. And I did not want David to think he could win me with such gifts.

"O Queen, live forever." Zhurleen bowed and walked past the maids as if they were not there. She looked at the gifts from David; lifted the necklace of gold and amber, touched the shining cloth of saffron. Then she looked at me, and then at the maidservants.

"Is this the way you serve the queen? Idling and chattering like sparrows in the street? Look at her hands—you, get the almond-cream for her skin! And her hair—who braided it? An ox? Undo it at once—where is the comb? Give it to me; I will do it myself, if you cannot!"

They moved for Zhurleen as they had not for me. I was not surprised; the way she spoke made me want to do her bidding at once myself before I was well-slapped.

"And what would you have me do?" I asked her, making my voice meek as a dove's.

"Why, nothing—save sit upon this chair and hold yourself still." Zhurleen's voice was once again the lazy slur of waves upon the sand. "I told you I would serve you well. You need do nothing, my queen—nothing at all."

One maid brought a pot of dark red clay, another an ivory comb, a third a thin alabaster vial. Zhurleen stood behind me and began to unbraid my hair.

"It is a fine color," she told me as she worked, "and will be finer still when it is cared for."

I began to protest, saying yet again that I was no queen and would go back to my husband's farm—"and all your work will go for nothing, Zhurleen."

"Nothing? Will it be nothing to go back to your Phaltiel with your skin soft as water and your hair sweet as spring grass?" Now Zhurleen's voice was low, soothing as dark wine, a comfort to the ear. "The king has given all this for your use—use it as *you* will."

When she spoke like that, it seemed wisdom. What harm could it do, after all? So I sat there quiet.

One maid rubbed my hands with thick cream that smelled sweet of crushed almonds. Another combed light pale oil through my hair; when she was done my hair was scented with spikenard and cinnamon and shone like glass. Zhurleen herself braided my hair into a dozen strands, and wove those dozen strands into one, binding them with ribbons of silver.

It was Zhurleen who chose what I should wear. "No, not that—the green, and the blue over it. And then the ivory girdle, and that is all."

And when they protested, saying it was not fine enough, Zhurleen looked them up and down and called them fools, and blind as well. "For the queen wears the clothes, not the clothes the queen! Now do as I say!" And into my ear alone, she whispered, "Do not worry, you will look as you should; I will not make you look a prideful fool."

She began to paint my mouth with carmine, red as blood; I sat quiet and considered her words. I had not thought of that—that she might dress me as she pleased, and I would not know if her choices were malice or mockery.

It seemed to take hours to dress me as they all thought fitting.

But at last Zhurleen took the girdle of carved ivory hinged with gold and clasped it about my waist, and called me ready. Then she held a mirror up so that I might see myself.

The mirror was silver polished so smooth I saw myself almost as clearly as I was; so large I could see all my face and neck at once.

"Is the queen pleased?" Zhurleen smiled, a worker sure of praise.

I did not know what to say. I looked very fine; perhaps I even looked like a queen. I did not know. But I did not look like Michal. The malachite and kohl hooded my eyes; the carmine hid my mouth; the silver ribbons in my hair, the golden chains about my throat, caught the eye and drew it from my face.

Michal was hidden away, veiled behind jewels and paint. I looked now like all the other women dwelling in King David's house.

They all watched me, to see if Zhurleen had pleased. To see if the Philistine woman would be rebuked and scorned. Even I could see they hoped for that. But Zhurleen's smile was steady as she waited for my answer.

"Yes," I said, and watched my red lips move, mirrored on silver. "You are very skilled, Zhurleen."

She handed the mirror away; I was no longer forced to watch myself a stranger.

"The queen is kind," Zhurleen said. She did not look at the maidservants. "Now if the queen pleases, let her come and I will show her the queen's domain. And the queen's women will care for her rooms—and they may start by sorting that cloth and folding it as it should be done!"

~

CHAPTER 9

"See, now, I dwell
in an house of cedar . . . . "
—II Samuel 7:2

And so that was how I first saw the women's quarters of the king's great house in Jerusalem. I walked with Zhurleen through long hallways, upon floors of bright-glazed tile, past walls adorned with painted flowers that would never wilt beneath hot sun. I looked into rooms large and small; rooms dark and private; rooms with windows wide to the sun and the wind.

I saw courtyards open to the sky and courtyards roofed over against the cold rain of winter and the harsh light of summer. I saw fountains spilling water, dazzling as crystals in the sunlight; water splashed over carven stone as freely as if it cost no effort to bring pure water up here; as if water, too, were a king's lavish toy.

I saw lemon trees in painted pots. I saw gardens laced with paths that wove aimless through roses and lilies.

And everywhere, I saw walls. Walls around the gardens; walls around the courtyards; walls around the whole women's quarters too high for even a giant to look over. And set into the walls were gates, to admit or deny.

"Each of the king's wives has her own courtyard and her own servants—that is the gate to the lady Eglah's court." Zhurleen was a good guide; it seemed to me that she knew everything and everyone within the women's walls.

I looked and saw a gate of cedarwood smooth-carved in a pattern of vines. The gate was closed; there was no welcome there.

"But yours is the finest court, my queen, and your rooms are the best." Zhurleen spoke as smoothly as she glided over the tiled floors, her voice pleasant as summer breeze.

"It does not matter," I said. "I will not be here to dwell among these women and cut their peace. I told them so, but they would not listen to me."

"If not you, it would be another. With a man like King David there will always be a woman—if they were wise, his wives would be your friends." Zhurleen cast a disdainful glance at Eglah's closed gate as we passed by. "Since they are fools, they will be ever unhappy. And no man likes a jealous woman, or a weeping one—or one who shows him a face like a sour quince!"

I smiled, for I thought I knew who she meant. "Like Abigail?" Yes, that was how Abigail had looked.

"Ah, you are sharp-eyed as a hawk! Yes, like Abigail, who is twice a fool. She likes to think herself the king's first wife, and first in all things as well. But she is no longer young; she had nothing but her looks and her wealth, and King David has had both already."

"What of her children? Does she not find joy in them?" I had no son born of my body, but I had a boy who filled a son's place in my heart. Children paid for much.

Zhurleen shook her head. "No, for that one finds no joy in anything save dreams. Oh, she has a son—Prince Chileab—but he is only the king's second-born, and he has not the gift of winning hearts. It is Prince Amnon, the eldest-born, and Prince Absalom, who are King David's darlings."

"Is that what Abigail wishes? Her son as king?"

"What mother would not? But the next king will not be Abigail's son—and she is not wise enough to see that, and to make other alliances." Zhurleen looked at me sideways, tilting her head; the gesture made her eyes look even longer. "Prince Absalom is his father born again—or so I have been told by those who saw King David when he was a boy. And Prince Amnon is a good child, and is very much loved. It is easy to be kind to Prince Amnon."

"You sound like his mother," I said, smiling and thinking of Caleb. "I have a boy at home—no, he is not my own, but I love him as if he were." And then I told her about Caleb; if she listened she learned much of his virtues and a little of his faults. Like all mothers, I would speak long of my child, if I were only let.

At last I laughed, and shook my head. "But I am telling you more than you wish to know! It is good of you to listen, Zhurleen, and I thank you for it."

"Only a fool does not listen when the queen speaks," she said.

I sighed. "Zhurleen, I am not the queen. I am only a woman, and I am not here of my own will."

Zhurleen looked at me, but said nothing then. We walked silent through the light and shadow of halls and courts until we stood at last before a gate made of ebony. Upon the ebony were set straight rows of ivory plaques, polished fangs against dark wood. Beyond that gate lay the queen's courtyard; beyond that courtyard lay the queen's rooms. The rooms I had been given by David.

Zhurleen set her hand upon the ebony gate. "This is the queen's gate—you have only to walk through it to be in your proper place."

I smiled, for I knew my proper place; it was not here, in this maze of walls within walls. I thanked Zhurleen again for her kindness.

"It is easy to be kind when kindness is wise as well," she said, and laid a hand upon my arm. "And I will tell you this, which is both wise and kind—do not deny the king too loud and long, Michal."

I smiled, unworried, for I thought I knew better than she. Zhurleen was a Philistine, after all—what should she know of Israel and Judah? "Your land is different, Zhurleen, so you do not understand our ways. I know other lands worship kings—but here a king is only a man."

Only a man, even if a king. I thought of my father Saul. King, yes—but Saul still tended his fields and obeyed the Law like any other man, until his madness took him.

Zhurleen's face showed nothing, not even that she heard my

words. She bowed, as if I had dismissed her, and then turned away. And suddenly my heart pounded hard and I called her back, my voice sharp.

"Zhurleen—the message to my husband Phaltiel—it was sent to him?"

She stopped and turned back, and bowed again, graceful as a willow branch. "It was sent, O Queen. My own lips told your words to the messenger. Each word, O Queen, just as you asked."

And then she went away, walking supple and gentle upon the sunlit tiles. Silver bells chimed sweet and clear about her ankles. Long oiled ringlets swayed across her back like slow dancing serpents, rich and shining as dark blood.

~

When I walked through the ebony gate into the queen's courtyard, I saw David waiting for me beside the singing fountain. He stood looking into the water as if he saw the future there; he was smiling as a man smiles who has won a bargain hard-driven.

I looked at him, then, as if my eyes were new. Like his wives, David wore scarlet and gold—but his fine clothes did not dazzle more than he. As Zhurleen would have said, he wore the clothes; that made them a king's. Yes, a king's finery, such as I had heard foreign kings wore daily; there was even a circlet of gold about David's head, metal shining pure against his hair.

I stood, and looked, and thought of my father King Saul, whose best robe had been made of wool from his own sheep, woven by his wives and sewn by his daughters. *"If it's good enough for my men, by Yahweh, it's good enough for me!"*

And then I looked about the queen's courtyard with my clear new eyes. Smooth cedar columns, a gallery full of flowers in hanging pots. Paving stones of marble, white and green. A fountain of some stone so pale and smooth it was almost as transparent as the water that fell endlessly over it. Water and wealth, both free-flowing—such a house was made of dreams.

David's dreams. How had he made them real?

I walked across the courtyard to the fountain, to King David. I thought of all I had seen that day, and of all I saw now, and weighed what I would say to him. Careful words, carefully chosen, to show him how far we had come from what we once had been together. Surely David must see it as clearly as I. The water sang loudly in its pale prison; David did not hear me until I was beside him, and spoke.

"O King," I said, "live forever." And I touched my forehead with my hand, as I had seen Zhurleen do.

He turned to me as easily as if he had watched me come; he did not laugh at my greeting. To David my words were no jest. He smiled instead as if I had given him an unexpected gift.

"Michal, my love—I was waiting for you."

He held out his hands, but I did not raise mine. "There was no need. You are the king, as you have said. If you wanted me, you had only to send for me."

"I asked after you and was told you had deigned to inspect your kingdom, my queen. I was content to wait until you had seen what is now yours." He reached and took my hands, willing to pretend that I had given them into his. "Tell me plain, my heart— is all as you would have it? Or shall I tear it to the ground and build again nearer to your wish?"

"You have a great house indeed, David. I could never have imagined such riches." I did not pull away; my hands lay cool and unmoving in David's grasp. "But I do not understand how all this is possible—that you are king, yes—but this is a house fit for the king of Egypt himself. How was it done, and so quickly?"

David laughed, a sound rich against the endless noise of falling water. "My clever Michal, always so practical! But this is nothing, truly—the least Philistine noble lives as well. And my people love me, and that made all work easy. You will see how easy, how sweet—you have suffered for me, my queen, but now all will be soft as feathers beneath your feet. Look at you now, fair as a rose at dawn."

"A painted rose," I said. "A false rose. Oh, David, can you not see that all is changed? I am no girl now—"

"Your eyes dim jewels; they are brighter and more precious." He let my hands go free and touched the golden chains about my neck. "You adorn jewels; they shall adorn you; you shall have gems beyond counting. You wear a token only, that you may see how King David keeps his word."

"Yes," I said. "I see. And you shall see how I keep mine, David. I will not break faith with my husband."

"You already have," he said, and took me into his arms, fast and rough, as if we both were young and hot and could not wait. "Look into your heart, Michal; you know it is true."

He would have kissed me then, but I held him off.

"No," I said. "Not now—or there will be carmine-paste and kohl and I know not what else all over your beard, and you will look a fool. I told you this face was not my own."

"I care nothing for that," he swore, "only for you." But he contented himself with a kiss upon my lips only; a chaste kiss, such as I might have taken from my own brother.

I smiled, for I prided myself that I was learning, and learning quickly. We both sat upon a padded bench, after that, and I listened as David talked of the days when we were young. I needed only to smile, and to nod; it was no hardship, for I liked to hear of Jonathan. Such talk did not give me pain, as I told David.

"Jonathan is dead now, but he lived once. I would not forget him, and how he loved me, and I him. Now all that is left is his son Meribaal—and I have not seen him since he lay in swaddling." Meribaal was with my brother Ishbaal now; I wondered if I would ever see him. Perhaps he looked like Jonathan. I did not know.

"Yes, his son Meribaal, whom I too have not seen since we all were young and happy together." David laid his hand over mine; his rings clashed against those on my own fingers. "I have heard Meribaal is a sickly boy; it is a grief when I think of it. I wish he were here, so that I might tend Jonathan's son myself."

"You are wrong, so be comforted," I said. "I never heard that

Meribaal was less than any other boy—and more than some!"
Jonathan and I had shared the same mother; Meribaal was my
nephew. If Meribaal were ill, there would have been a message
from Ishbaal, if only for duty's sake.

"That is good hearing," David said, and smiled. "I hope you
are right, Michal, for I had heard—well, it is nothing after all, and
we see how rumor misleads us into grief. If it is not so I am glad,
for the love I bore Jonathan. The boy must be a great joy to your
brother Ishbaal; does he mean to make Meribaal the next king in
Israel?"

I stared hard at David, and then laughed when I saw that he
was not jesting. "Oh, David, I do not know! I have told you before, I am only a farm-wife, and know less of kings and courts than
that fountain does. I have not seen my brother Ishbaal since before
my father banished me from his sight. Why would King Ishbaal
tell me such things? Ask him yourself, if you would know."

David laughed too. Light flowed over the gold circlet about
his hair as he shook his head. "You do right to rebuke me; I know
it was hard for you. But your path will be smooth for the rest of
your days."

"I know my path," I said. "It will be as smooth or as harsh as
the world makes it. Do not worry yourself over me, for I shall be
well cared for." I might as well have saved my words. It was as if I
were dumb, and could make no sound; as if I said nothing unless
David liked my words and so chose to hear.

"As for Meribaal, and your brother Ishbaal—you are right, I
will send a message. There are so few of Saul's kin left, it hurts my
heart when I think of it. Perhaps Ishbaal will be generous, and give
me Jonathan's son to raise as my own."

"Perhaps," I said. "But Ishbaal has no child of his own, and
you have many sons, David."

"And will have more, Yahweh willing!" He was all boy, then;
reaching out, eager.

I leapt to my feet and backed away. "But you will not have
them with me."

"Do not be unkind; I know you are the gentlest of women. Show me your sweetness, honey-heart; make us both as happy as stars."

"How happy are the stars, David? Are they as happy as a king? No, do not—I beg you, listen to me."

He stood back then, all tolerance. "You command and even a king must obey. Speak, my love; give me your wisdom."

"You jest with me, but it *is* wisdom I speak. I have been here two days, and I have looked and listened, as you bade me. And I have learned, as you also bade me."

"And what have you learned?" David's face was smooth as swept sand.

"When we were young together we all sat upon the roof at night and spoke of dreams—do you remember?"

"You, and I, and Jonathan. Yes, Michal. I remember us all together in the summer nights."

I drew a long breath, and chose my words with as much care as if each must be paid for in coins of gold. "I know your true dream now, David. You wanted to be king. You must always have wanted it, even when you lived beneath my father's roof and ate his bread. It was why you married me, because I was King Saul's daughter—oh, do not deny it! I am no fool, and you are not either."

He made no more denials. He said nothing, but stood quiet, pulling the end of his sash through his hand. It slid through his fingers like a crimson snake, endlessly circling, as I spoke.

"Now you have your dream—you are king. I rejoice for you; live forever, O King, in your house of wonders. But I am no part of that dream, David. You cannot hold all the world in your hand; you must let me go."

David stood quite still, then. The end of the sash lay motionless in his hand. At last he said, "And if I say I need you, Michal? That I must have you for my true queen, to keep this great house and all you have seen within it? If I beg you to stay with me, and to take all that I have offered you?"

For a moment my blood ran hard; later I knew that throb of blood had been a warning. But that day, when David spoke so soft and quiet, I only feared his words had tempted me against my will. And so I clung to virtue, and laughed.

"Oh, David, do not make a song of everything! You have shown me what you have, and I have said it is not enough. There is no bargain. Send me home to my husband."

CHAPTER 10

"Behold, the king hath
delight in thee . . . . "
—I Samuel 18:22

Yes, I was a fool, and worse than a fool. I thought David had heeded my words at last, for he left me alone after that. I saw him neither by day nor by night, although he sent me gifts enough to make my maidservants coo like setting doves. I did not want the gifts, and so I let the women take what they liked for themselves; it was nothing to me.

Now I let the maidservants dress me and jewel me and paint me as they wished. My gown did not truly matter, after all. To garb me finely pleased them—and there was nothing for me to wear, save what David had given.

I also ceased to protest when they called me queen. For each time I did, each time I denied the tale that made me David's wife, his queen, his dearest love, there would be a pause, and they would all look at each other, sharp and sly. And then there would be a quick bright torrent of words as if I were a nervous ewe that must be soothed.

And there would be eyes looking at me, slantwise and uneasy. I did not like those cautious eyes, and so I stopped speaking of Phaltiel. I ceased denying David. Silence was easier, and seemed safe enough. For now I need not see his face, or hear his voice, or feel his hands upon my body. And I grew tired of saying words that were never heeded.

So I let the queen's women do as they would with me, and smiled, and waited in peace for Phaltiel to come. I knew I would not wait for him long. Phaltiel would come as soon as he had my words in his ears.

And the waiting was not unpleasant, now that David no longer came to trouble me. Well, what woman would find it unpleasant to be petted, and tended, and spoiled as if she were an only daughter and everyone's darling?

So I waited, and idled the days away. It was no more and no less than the other women did; there were so many servants underfoot that King David's wives and concubines spent their time with games and gossip, and not with the work of their husband's house. It had not been so in the house of King Saul, and I did not think it a wise way to order a household. An idle house lacked peace and purpose. David's wives were all quarrelsome as sparrows, and David's concubines were no better. They quarreled over everything, and over nothing; Zhurleen told me that no day went by without harsh words.

"But they are many, and even the king is only one man—he has a fine eye, but it roves." David's faithlessness did not seem to trouble Zhurleen as it did his other women.

"It is folly," I said, righteous where I did not understand. "And you are right, there are too many of them for any man. How many women can even a strong man desire?"

"Why, all of them!" Zhurleen laughed, and made her hands dance desire through the air. All her moves were supple as the water she had once dwelt beside. I wondered if Zhurleen longed for the sea; if she did, she never said so. She had always a jest ready to fling out, or a laugh as easy and practiced as her swaying walk.

But I had looked upon David's house and upon David's women, and I thought I was right, and Zhurleen wrong. There were too many women. There was too much of everything. I could not imagine what reckoning paid for all that I saw. I might only be a farmer's wife, ignorant of kings and courts—but I knew that what was bought must be paid for, in coin or in kind. Who knew that better than a farmer's wife?

Still, King David's follies were nothing to me. That was what I told myself, all those days that I dwelt in idleness and in comfort. The only thing I was denied was freedom; I might roam the women's quarters as I pleased, but I might not set my feet beyond the brass-bound gate that led to the world beyond. I had tried, once, and been turned back by armed men—guardians of the women's gate, they said. They bowed low, and they too called me "great queen", but they would not let me pass.

I was sorry, for I would have liked to see the famous city. Still, perhaps Phaltiel and I would walk Jerusalem's wide streets before we left David's city together. But seeing the city was not important. Soon I would be home, and this half-life in the king's house would be nothing more than a glittering memory to recall on a dull winter's night.

And so my days slid by, easy as pleasant dreams, each slipping away into the next like oil pouring from a jar. A dream means an awakening. But as I waited through my days in David's house, I did not even know I slept.

~

My waking was cold and harsh. One evening after my maids had undressed me and combed out my hair for the night I went to my window and watched the moon rise pale and smooth over the hills beyond the city. Moonlight washed silver over the day's dust-gold; the moon was just past full.

Just as it had been the first night I had spent beneath this roof, within these walls.

A month. I had been here a month—how could I have stayed so long content? A month since I had come here; a month since I had sent word to Phaltiel.

A month since Zhurleen had sworn she had sent that word.

Anger filled my throat; I turned away from the window and

caught up a veil to fling about me. At the door out to my courtyard one of my maids barred my way.

"What troubles you, Queen Michal? Where do you go so late?"

"Let me pass," I said. I had no time now for the maidservant
and the airs she gave herself.

"No, no," she said, patting my arm. "It is late—you must
sleep now, O Queen." Others of my women, hearing her noise,
came hastening out of the shadowlight to bar my way. They murmured soft words, urging me back to my proper place.

"I do not care what hour it is," I told them, and sharply, for I
had lost all patience with them. "I am going to see the Lady
Zhurleen. Oh, do not be sillier than you must—no harm will
come to me within the women's quarters! Now let me by!"

"Be calm, Queen Michal." It was Chuldah who spoke; a woman
older than I, with eyes as sly as the weasel she was named for. "If
you wish to speak to the concubine Zhurleen, she shall be brought
to you."

"Now," I said. My anger choked me; I could not wait. "Bring
her to me *now.*"

"Yes, of course. Now." Chuldah's voice was butter-smooth.
"Go, someone, and fetch the Lady Zhurleen, as the queen bids.
And tell the Philistine woman to make haste."

~

I stood by my window and watched the telltale moon as I waited
for Zhurleen to come to me. I did not wait long; the moon still
hung low and golden over the eastern hills when I heard her step
into the room behind me.

"O Queen, live forever. You wished to see me?"

I turned away from the window. Zhurleen bowed before me.
"Yes," I said, and my voice sounded thick and ugly in my ears. "I
wished to see you. You swore you would be my friend, and you
have betrayed me."

Zhurleen straightened. "How have I betrayed you, my queen?

And who is it who says so?"

"You did not send my message to my husband Phaltiel—and it is the moon that tells me so. It has been a month, and he has not come. A full month." My throat ached with my anger at my own betrayal as well; I had not noticed as time bore me gently on, away from Phaltiel and toward David.

"Ah." Zhurleen's eyelids lowered over her long eyes. Then she lifted her head and looked at me straight. She too was ready for night and for sleep; her face was washed clean. For the first time I saw her plain, without her mask of paint.

"Will the queen let me speak?" Zhurleen's voice was as soft as I had always heard it.

"What can you say? I know the truth now. You did not send my message." And Phaltiel would think I had chosen a king's riches over my life in his good plain house in Gallim.

"Please, Michal. You must let me speak—yes, and you must listen, too." Zhurleen had never spoken so before; I was always the queen to her.

"Very well," I said grudgingly. "Speak, and I will listen." But I did not sit, nor did I bid Zhurleen to do so.

She stepped forward, close to me. "I sent your message, each word, the day you asked it of me."

"You did not," I said. "If you had, Phaltiel would have come. The road to Jerusalem is not so long as that!"

"I spoke your words to the messenger myself, and heard them back from him three times. Michal, did you truly think such a message would be carried any farther than from the women's gate to the king's ear?"

I stared at her; my blood pounded hard behind my ears and in my throat. "Do you mean that David—"

"Will hear all your messages and send only those that please him? Of course; he is the king."

I believed Zhurleen; she might have lied, but I did not think that she did. "I do not care what David is. I am not his wife and I have told him so." When anger goes it leaves weariness in trade; I sat down upon my bed. "But it does no good—I told him no, and no again, and he would not hear."

I thought of another thing; I had not seen David since the first days I was in his house. I told this to Zhurleen, although she must know it as well as any in that house of tale-bearers. "Now I cannot even deny him, for he will not come to hear me. What am I to do?"

"When a woman speaks, men hear only those words they wish. And never will they heed denial." Zhurleen sat beside me and took my hands between hers. "It is plain that your mother never taught you wisdom, Michal—will you learn it from me?"

It was the first time she had spoken as if we were only two women together, not queen and concubine. I was glad, for she was the one who kept distance between us; Zhurleen never presumed upon the friendship she had asked of me.

And so I nodded, and asked her what it was that she would tell me. "For I have sore need of advice now—yes, and of your friendship."

"You will have both," Zhurleen said, and smiled. "It is simple, truly—you have only to remember that your David is both man and king. If he will not let you go—well, one man is much like another, save that some are rich and generous, and some are not! King David is both; you may have all you ask for—"

"I have asked to go home," I said. "If he will not grant that, I care for nothing else."

"Are you dead, then, that you have no other desires? All that you ask, I tell you, if only you will choose carefully what you ask of him, and how. He will be a great king, your David, all men say so—yes, even the kings of Philistia. He will have power, great power—but it will be a man's power." Zhurleen stroked my hands, and smiled in a way that made me remember my first wedding day, the day that I had married David. It was the way all the women had smiled at me as I sat behind my bridal veil. As if they knew a secret that I did not.

"You have a woman's power, Michal. Only find what David wants of you, and give it to him—and it will be some easy thing, for men think women have nothing, and so they ask for little when they could have much. And when you know what the king desires from you, why, make it a gift to him, and give it graciously. Then he will spread the world before your feet for you to tread upon."

I stared at her, for I did not understand her at all. I had thought Zhurleen would help me; she had said she was my friend.

At last I said, "But David has nothing that I want, Zhurleen. I love my husband Phaltiel, and he loves me. That love is what I want; if the king gives me that, I shall be content."

Zhurleen stared back at me and for a moment her eyes were dark pools; unreadable. Then she smiled again, her eyes alight once more. "Think what you can do for your Phaltiel, then. He is a farmer? Well, then—ask the king to reward him finely for the loss of you. More land, more sheep, more of whatever a farmer needs—and fewer taxes!"

"Taxes?" It was my turn to smile. "This is not Philistia, Zhurleen—our people do not tithe to kings, only to the priests."

She did not argue that; she was right, of course, but that too I only learned later. Well, had not Samuel himself warned our people long ago what harvest a king would reap? Zhurleen had never known Samuel, but she knew what the prophet had known: kings demanded payment.

And so I went on, "And what Phaltiel needs is me. I am his wife, I keep his house for him. He has no one else; even his youngest daughter is married now—Miriam, I have told you of her."

"The one who will bear her next child at harvest-time? Yes, you have told me. You could do much for her—you could make all easy for all those you love. And as for your Phaltiel—" Zhurleen paused, as if she thought, and then laughed.

"Oh, yes, that will do very well! Now see, Michal, you must send word to King David and say that you would see him—David will come, for you have never asked before. And when the king comes to you, you will beg a favor—"

"What favor? David will not send me home, and that is all I want of him." But I hoped in spite of myself, for Zhurleen's voice was rich with happiness now, as if she had at last unknotted a badly-tangled thread.

"Yes, and you have said so loud and often; no one can say Queen Michal is not virtuous and law-abiding, even your sour-faced priests! Now they will say she is generous as well—no, listen to me! You will beg the king's favor, and when he asks what you desire, you will say to him that the man Phaltiel deserves much for having kept you safe all these years."

Zhurleen squeezed my hands, then released them and spread her own hands wide. "You may then ask whatever you wish for Phaltiel and his family, and King David will grant it gladly. And if you worry that Phaltiel will be lonely—why, send him a good woman to tend his house and a pretty girl to warm his bed! Choose her yourself, if you would be sure of pleasing him—you will know just what he likes, after all!"

She said more, after that, but I scarcely heard her. I had thought myself angry before, when I had first sent for Zhurleen. But now I knew true anger, hot anger; anger ate my very bones.

"No!" I rose up to my feet; my hand ached to strike Zhurleen, to make her unsay those words. "Be silent, I will not listen! I am Phaltiel's wife—I will never say I am not! The Law says I am his wife!"

Zhurleen sat and looked up at me; the lamp's small flame flashed in her black eyes. "If one marriage can be set aside, so can another."

"The first was one night! The second has lasted ten years! For ten years Phaltiel and I have lain together as man and wife. Only my husband can set me aside and he will never do that! And if he does not, all King David can have of me will be adultery. And the penalty for that is the stones—for the man and the woman both!"

Zhurleen sat so still she did not seem even to blink. "Say you never lay with Phaltiel," she said. "Say that all these years you lay chaste beside him, waiting for David."

"No one will believe that!"

"If you say it is true, Phaltiel will not deny it if he loves you as you say. And then your marriage to him will be no marriage, and between you and the king there will be no adultery. And if there are those who do not believe—well, they will not say so," said Zhurleen. "Not where the king's men can hear."

Anger still ruled me, its grip so strong it forced all else from my mind. Anger tore away the accusations and the harsh words I wished to fling at Zhurleen and devoured them until I could say nothing at all.

"I thought," I said at last, "that you were my friend."

Zhurleen stood to face me. "I am your friend. And because I am, I will risk much and speak freely. Now listen to me, Michal, for what I say is worth hearing.

"You are not happy here—or you think you are not. I do not believe, when you speak wildly, that it is a sign of madness. But they say your father was mad. I do not know whether that is true. But do not give King David that whip to rule you."

Each word she spoke rang strangely clear against my ears, like a bell chiming on a frosty morning.

"You are the queen," Zhurleen said. "If you would have happiness and power, do as I have told you."

"Leave me," I said, and my voice was cold as winter dawn.

Zhurleen bowed. "O Queen, live forever," she murmured, and was gone.

When I was alone I sank back down upon my bed and gave myself to my anger. *Never*, I thought. Never, never would I become like Zhurleen. She had no heart; none. Send a girl to warm my Phaltiel's bed—

I laid my shaking hand upon a embroidered cushion; I traced its patterns, hoping to calm myself.

My trembling fingers slipped easily across the fine threadwork, smooth as oil sliding over water.

~

CHAPTER 11

"This will be the manner
of the king that shall reign . . . . "
—I Samuel 8:11

The next morning anger still ruled me; I would allow none of my maids to tend me. "I am neither old nor ill," I told them. "I will wash myself—yes, and dress myself, too! Go, and leave me in peace."

It was a battle I could not win; I might be neither old nor ill, but I had only two hands and no talent for donning finery. I found that a queen's clothes need a queen's maids to wrap them and to fasten them. And so in the end I must call back my maidservants, if I would dress.

And when I had been forced to that I was twice angered, and so nothing pleased me. At first my women tried fair words and a new veil, a new girdle, a new necklace, hoping with such honey to sweeten my temper. Then they worked silent, with careful hands and downcast eyes.

When I was ready they stepped back, and bowed, and I thought of the day that stretched before me with nothing to fill its hours. *No*, I thought then. No, I would no longer sit with empty hands, pretending to be what I was not.

"A spindle," I said. "Bring me a spindle, and some wool." And when they stared, round-eyed as sheep, I stamped my foot, as unruly as if I were a wild girl again. "Are you deaf? You may idle all the day away, but I will not! Fetch me what I asked for, and quickly! Do not tell me that in all this great house there is not one spindle, not one handful of wool fit for spinning!"

~

The spindle they found for me was formed of ivory, its whirl of amber; pretty as if it were a toy. Still, it spun well enough. An ivory spindle still could serve an honest purpose.

My skin was soft, and so the new-washed fleece seemed harsh. I had done no work in too long; my fingers reddened as I twirled and drew thread. But I would not stop. I swore that there would be at least one task well done in the king's house this day.

And so I was spinning in the queen's courtyard, diligent as a spider, when Abigail came upon me. She spied me from the gallery, for I did not keep my gate closed against the world. When she saw what I was about, she came into the courtyard in a clash of anklets and a cloud of musk.

"Fine work for a lady's fine hands!" Abigail said. "You are not living in a farmhouse now—why not leave such work to the maids?"

"Because they are useless as weeds in the road!" Then I heard how my voice sounded, shrill as Abigail's own. And so I gentled it; what I suffered was no fault of Abigail's. "Such work passes the time," I said. "Here I find time lies heavy in the hand. Do you not find it so?"

Abigail stared at me; even the paint she wore thick upon eyes and cheeks and mouth could not hide her surprise. "The queen is bored?" Abigail made a queen sound lower in her eyes than a village harlot.

"I am not a queen." I said it firm, and set my mouth tight, and watched my thread. It was easy to tangle, and difficult to unknot after.

Abigail spoke on as if she had not heard. "If you are bored now, when the king smiles upon you, what will you do when the king turns away? Oh, he sends you gifts, but he does not come to you—we all know that. You cannot hold him—I have been married to David these ten years, and he always comes back to me, in the end. What is a crown worth, compared to that?"

Sour words, spoken by a woman jealous as a cat of its place in the sun. Words that told wishes, not truth. And when I heard them, I was sorry for Abigail, for I remembered what Zhurleen had said of her. Abigail fought a battle already lost, and lost through no fault of hers.

Oh, Abigail was still comely enough, and must have been pretty when she was younger, and a wealthy widow. But as Zhurleen had rightly said, Abigail was no longer young, and no longer had anything with which to bargain against her rivals. No wonder Abigail hated me; my coming had wounded an already sore heart—

That was when my own heart seemed to cease beating and then leap up again for sheer joy. At last I saw before me my true deliverance from this place; I must have been blind, that I had not seen this path before. My hands were no longer steady; I stopped spinning thread and laid the ivory spindle in my lap.

"Abigail, let us speak plainly—I do not want your husband. I have a better one of my own, and no matter what King David says, I am not his queen and not his wife."

"You spin thread better than tales! David is the sun for beauty and the moon for love, and king besides—and you would rather have an old farmer who cannot even give you sons?" She glared at me, angry as if David were her first-born son and I a rich bride spurning him at the very moment of wedding.

I laughed; I could not help it. Abigail stared at me as if I were mad. Perhaps she thought I was—I was Mad Saul's daughter, after all.

"Yes," I said at last. "I would rather have my old farmer. But he is not so old as that, and he gave his first wife sons enough."

"Then why do you stay here?"

"Find me a way to send word to my husband Phaltiel." My blood beat hard as I said his name. "Find me a way, and he will come and I will go, and trouble you no more."

"Do you swear that is true? Your husband will take you back?"

"Yes. Yes, he will take me back. And I will go gladly. But I must be able to send true word—I sent a message once, and was betrayed. I have no one I can trust. Abigail, will you help me?"

She embraced me, then, and swore that she would. Tears welled in her eyes; wet kohl streaked her reddened cheeks. "I will bless you all the days of my life," Abigail said, and kissed my cheek before she hurried away, all jangle and flash.

Poor Abigail, I thought, and smiled. My anger was gone, turned all to pleasure in my own cleverness. I picked up the pretty spindle and set it spinning again; I hummed softly as thread formed and lengthened between my busy fingers.

~

Abigail was swift and clever; it was how she had won marriage from David all those years ago, after all. She did well for me and for herself, and sent me the prophet Nathan.

It was a wise choice. David might keep me behind the women's walls and stop my words at his gates—but prophets went where and how they would, and obeyed only Yahweh. Even a king could not say them nay.

I had heard of Nathan even before I had been brought to Jerusalem; he was the first great prophet in the land since Samuel died. The priests, who had spent the years since Samuel's death quarreling among themselves, agreed now that Nathan spoke with the true voice of Yahweh.

And as proof of his worth and power, Nathan carried Samuel's own staff. Before Samuel died, it was said that he had given his staff to David; David had placed the great prophet's legacy into Nathan's hands. Yes, even King David bowed humble before Nathan and gave him all honor.

That was all I knew of Nathan, then: that he was a prophet, a truth-sayer, a pillar upholding Yahweh's Law. Later I learned to know Nathan for myself, and to value him at his true worth.

The first time I saw Nathan he seemed to me an unlikely prophet, but no law decrees prophets must be tall and lean and dry as bone, after all. Nathan came, round and red, puffing from the heat; when he listened to my words, his face grew even redder.

"This is a disgrace to the land and to the king," Nathan said sternly, and took my hand. Nathan was the only prophet I ever knew who did not seem to dislike all women. "Come, we will go now and speak to him."

"I cannot. David will not let me set foot beyond the women's gate."

This meant nothing to Nathan, and so he did not listen. He simply led me along and waved his staff at any who barred our way until we came into the king's great courtyard, where David sat at judgment.

Nathan strode up to the king's chair and pulled my veil from my hair to show me plain to all men in the court. "This woman says you keep her here for your own pleasure, against her will and while she has a husband elsewhere. Is this true, O King?"

David's face was smooth as fresh butter; he even smiled. "It is not. All men know that Princess Michal was my wife first—it is only right that I take her back under my roof."

"She has a husband still living who has not set her aside. If he will not, you must send her back to him."

I was glad we stood in open court before many witnesses; David's eyes did not make for pleasant thoughts. I had seen my father's eyes like that. King's eyes.

But David spoke softly enough, for all the look in his eyes; my father would not have done that. "Very well, Nathan—come aside, and I will speak with you privately on this matter."

"Kings have no private matters," Nathan said. But he went aside with David, and they spoke together while I stood unveiled and held my head proud and my mouth tight.

At last Nathan came back to me, smiling and nodding. "I have made the king see his error—for he is truly a good man—and he has promised to amend it as best he may. Be no more troubled in spirit, daughter—give me the message for your husband and I myself will carry your words."

"And I," David told Nathan, "will send the king's best men to escort you in all honor, to show how I atone for my sin and folly.

And I will send servants and fine gifts to this woman's husband, and I will beg his forgiveness."

"If you send all that," I said, "send me as well." *Home*, I thought. Soon I would look down the long valley of Gallim, and see Phaltiel's house basking in the sun—

David shook his head. "Ah, Michal—you are a good woman, and forgiving, but you were right, and I wrong. I have sinned against you, and against Phaltiel. I must show all men that I acknowledge my sin, and make amends."

A show for men's eyes. I should have known; always David thought of that. But I did not protest again. This was the last time I must bow meekly to David's wishes, after all. I had won; I could wait a little longer.

"Yahweh has shown me the wrong I have done," said David, smiling at all the world, "and now he has shown me how I may right it."

~

David was as good as his word in open court. He would not let Nathan go alone with my message to Phaltiel; no, the prophet Nathan must be sent on his way with as many men and servants and baggage mules as if Nathan himself were king. It took time to make all ready for such a grand journey, and so Nathan did not leave Jerusalem that day, or the next. I wished he would go quickly and at once, but I understood that David wished to stand well with Yahweh's prophet.

But on the third day I stood beside David upon the wall above the high gate to the king's house and watched as Nathan's procession marched out. The cavalcade would make a great show for all Jerusalem before it reached the city gate. Armed men marched before Nathan; plump servants and laden mules followed him. Nathan fit oddly between glory and riches, for he was only a small round man in a coarse robe. But Nathan walked proud, as Samuel once had—and Nathan smiled wide, as if life pleased him. I did not think life had ever pleased Samuel.

"There, you see, Michal? Nathan goes to Gallim, as you asked. You see how I keep my word." David's eyes were clear and bright in the sunlight, like a child's.

"Yes," I said. "I see." I watched, and I smiled, and I wondered what Phaltiel would think, when next he saw me. I would show him Michal the queen, I thought. I would ask Zhurleen to dress me finely, and perhaps to curl my hair as she did hers. And Phaltiel would come into the queen's courtyard and see me sitting there with my eyelids painted glitter-green and my hair oiled ringlets and a dozen copper butterflies pinning my gown—

—and he would laugh. I could hear him now. Phaltiel would laugh, and catch me up into his arms, and so much for the eye-paint and the hair-oil and the copper pins—

"Ah, that is better," David said, and put his hand over mine. "I like to see you smiling, Michal."

I looked sideways at David, and smiled wider. "The king is kind," I said, and bit my lip so that I would not laugh outright. No man likes to be laughed at by a woman—least of all a man who has been forced to admit a fault. So I only smiled, and turned away.

Oh, I thought myself clever as a vixen, subtle as a serpent. I thought I had bested David at his own game.

I knew nothing. I was awake, now—but I was still blind.

~

Late the next morning I was tossing white pebbles into the fountain in my courtyard. I had my waiting days counted out as pebbles: so many for Nathan to reach Gallim; so many for Phaltiel to reach Jerusalem. I counted and threw carefully, telling over each twist and rise in the road between.

Seven, I counted. No more than seven days left to wait, for

Phaltiel would not march slowly with banners, or linger upon the road. Once he heard my message, he would come swift and sure.

But I was wrong; I had no longer to wait.

I heard footsteps upon the paving-stones, and when I looked up, I saw Caleb standing within my gate. I flung all the stones at once into the fountain and ran toward him, holding out my arms. Then I saw Caleb's face.

I think I knew then, for I stopped and put out my hands as if to ward off the words that he must speak. "No," I said.

Then Zhurleen stepped into the courtyard and closed the ebony gate behind her. "Tell her, boy, and quickly—I have risked much to bring you here. Remember that, Queen Michal, when you number your friends."

"Caleb," I said, and tried to put my arms about him, to clasp him to my breast. But Caleb would not let me; he made himself stiff and straight.

"Greetings, Queen Michal," Caleb said. "I bring you news of Phaltiel son of Laish, who was your husband. Will you hear it?"

I saw he struggled to keep his dignity, and hold aloof from me to speak as a man even though he was only a boy still. It hurt, but I let him have it; I let him go. This time I could not take Caleb in my arms and comfort him as a child.

"Yes," I said. "I will hear it."

And so I listened as Caleb told me how Phaltiel had gone to visit Miriam and her husband and their children. No one had been surprised when Phaltiel did not return that night, for he was a fond parent, and they did not doubt that Miriam had pressed him to stay. It was unlike him not to send word, but they thought nothing of it until late the next day, when a boy from Miriam's house had arrived bearing a well-memorized scolding from her for Phaltiel's forgetfulness, demanding he come to them at once as he had promised.

"We worried then," Caleb said, "and I ran to Miriam's myself. My father was not there, and nowhere on the road between, and no one could be found who had seen him." His mouth trembled then and he made it thin, to keep from crying.

"Do not make a long tale," Zhurleen said, and her voice was thorn-sharp. "Quickly, I told you."

"Yes," I said. "Tell me quickly." I stood like a pillar, listening as Caleb told me how all the men of two households had searched, and found Phaltiel at last. His body had been hidden, but not well, in a fall of rock not far from the road.

"By the bend past the village, where the stones are red," Caleb said.

I knew the place; a pretty spot, with flowers wild in all the cracks of the rock. Miriam and I had stopped there often on our way to the river with the clothes for washing-day, letting the maid-servants go on ahead while we braided poppy-crowns for our hair.

"I know the spot. Is there more?"

Zhurleen came forward then, reaching out as if she would seize Caleb. "There, you have told her. Come away now."

"No." My voice came from far, and hard. "Leave him, Zhurleen. I would hear the rest."

There were not many wounds upon the body; Phaltiel had been killed by a man who knew how to make a blow count. No one could understand the murder, for Phaltiel was a good man, and had no enemies—and it was not done as robbers would have done it.

"For they killed his donkey too," Caleb cried, boy again now that the worst was told. "They slit Dove's throat and left her lying there—robbers would not have done that, would they, Mother?" Then he came at last into my arms, to weep while I held him close.

I tried to weep too, to find ease, but I could not. And Zhurleen hovered like a hawk, seeking to drag Caleb from my arms. So I put Caleb from me and stroked his wet cheeks. "Tell me, my darling, when this happened. What day was it?"

It had been two days ago. Two days after Nathan had spoken to King David, and King David had agreed that he had been wrong, and that I might go home to Phaltiel.

"Caleb," I said, and held him close against my body; he was

hot, and still dusty from hard travel.

"And so I came to tell you, Mother, and—and to bring you home." Caleb shoved his chin forward. "That is why I am here. My brothers say you will not come, that you would rather live with the king, but I know that is not true, and so I came by myself!" He looked at me, pleading. "It is not true, is it?"

"Tell him the right truth, O Queen," said Zhurleen softly. "Be wise, and speak carefully. The boy came all this way alone to find you—it is only because I had gone out to the bird-market and chanced to pass by while he argued at the king's gate that he is safe here now. I told you I risked much—but not as much as he did."

She put a hand upon Caleb's shoulder as if to draw him away; Caleb shook Zhurleen's hand off and stared at me. I looked at Zhurleen, and I knew at last what I should have known the moment I had seen Abner at the gate with his fifty armed men: that never again could I know peace, except at King David's bidding.

"Come with me," Caleb demanded. "I will take you away, Mother. I will protect you—I do not care what Ezra says—he is a coward and no man! You are our father's wife, we must take care of you!"

He tugged at my hand, as he had long ago when he was still only a babe, and I only a young girl playing mother. His fingers clung to mine as they had when he was small. But Caleb was no longer a little boy; he was almost thirteen, almost as tall as I; some might see him as a man. Some might see him as a threat.

Suddenly Caleb's fingers seemed to clutch my heart as well. For a moment I stood frozen still with fear, as if I had almost trodden upon a viper. Clear in my head I heard Phaltiel's voice counseling me to lie quiet in his house—"—and do not remind the king that you still breathe." Do not remind the king. . . .

"Mother!" Another tug at my hand, a plucking at my sleeve. Come, Mother, come and see, you must look—

I put my arms tight around Caleb, who was once my own boy.

A son to me. David had so many sons. Why must he deny me mine?

"O Queen, you must make haste now. He must not be found here—go, boy, and take care. Here, you may carry this—" Zhurleen unclasped a necklace, twisted it hard between her fingers, and held it out to Caleb. "Tell them you are taking it to the goldsmith's for mending, if you are stopped and questioned. Tell them the Lady Zhurleen sends it."

Caleb glared at her with the fierce sullen anger I remembered from our first days together, when I had only just come to dwell in Phaltiel's house. "I will not go! She is my father's widow and it is my duty to tend her! I will slay anyone who tries to stop me!"

Zhurleen looked from me to Caleb, and back again. "Are you both mad? If you care for him at all, O Queen, you must send him away, and now. Say farewell, quickly!"

She was right; I knew she was right. So I took Caleb's face between my hands, and kissed him, and told him he must go. He did not wish to leave me; he was only a boy still, and so thought right must win over all.

"No," he said. "I will protect you—Father would want me to, and it is the law."

"Come away, boy!" Zhurleen begged. "It is over, and this does no good to you or to the queen. Come, now."

Caleb set his mouth, stubborn as a badger. As stubborn as Princess Michal had once been, when she was almost thirteen, and still thought the world would spin obedient to her wishes.

And so I did what I must. I stepped back, away from Caleb, and spoke. "You must go now, Caleb. She is right; it is over now, and I am the queen. If you wish to please me, you will go."

Caleb stared at me, eyes blank as stones. "Do you mean," he asked, "that you want to stay here—with *him*?" His voice wavered, begged me to deny it.

I would not; I must not.

"Yes," I said. "Yes, I wish to stay here. Now do as the Lady Zhurleen bids you, Caleb! Go home, and tell Miriam--"

"I will tell her nothing! My brothers were right, you wish to be the king's harlot because he gives you jewels! I hate you!" Caleb's voice rose high and broke. He turned and ran, away from me, toward the gate.

His words tore my heart like saw-blades; still worse was the pain and betrayal in his eyes. I could not bear it.

"Caleb!" I started after him, but Zhurleen barred my way.

"No," she said. "Let him go, Michal. Let him go free of love for you, if you would keep him safe."

I stopped, then, and stood silent, watching as Zhurleen padded swiftly after Caleb. Her flounced skirt swung wide in her haste, and her bare belled feet made harsh music against the paving-stones.

~

Phaltiel was dead and would never come now to put his arms around me and take me home. Phaltiel was dead, no man knew how or why, and his loving wife dwelt in fine gowns and rich gems in the king's house and did not shed one tear for him. I could not cry; the blow had driven too deep.

But mourning there must be, to ease my husband's spirit, even though my eyes were dry sand and my heart a stone for silence.

The bracelets from my arms made little splashing noises as they dropped into the shining fountain. The gold falling from my hair made no sound at all; false leaves glinted and spun on the water's surface as I dragged my fingers through my hair, ripping free the narrow twisted braids. My fingers caught, yanked; I welcomed the little hurt.

Phaltiel was dead, dead—and he had never heard my message. He had died knowing only that I had sent no word; that I had chosen the king's house over his.

My courtyard was smooth-swept stone; there was no dust for my face. But I had nails, long and well-tended, as befit a queen's soft hands. I could rip my fine gown to rags, and my skin to blood.

And I did, until my maids came running up to me crying out in horror and hung upon my arms to make me stop.

"Leave me. My husband is dead, and I must mourn for him."

They all looked at me, and then sideways at each other, and then all spoke at once. "No, no, the king is well—he sits in the great hall even now—come, come to the women's gallery and you may see him with your own eyes—"

"Be silent!" I pressed my hands over my ears, but it did not help. They chirped and chattered at me until the noise rang inside my head as well as out. More slanting looks, some knowing and some of pity, and then many vows to be silent as a mouse's shadow if only I would come inside with them.

It was easier to go than to stay, and so I went.

In my rooms there was another uproar, for I would not let them wash or comb or dress me, and called for ashes from the kitchen hearth. "Now, I tell you! Go—go at once!"

They stared at me, round-mouthed as a flock of ewe-lambs, and did not move until I threw a lamp at them. I did not fling it in hot rage; I wanted them to go, and the lamp was handy to my hand. The clay lamp cracked to pieces against the painted lintel; oil spread, marring the pattern of lotus flowers.

The maids ran away, after that, and my room was quiet for a time. And then David came to me.

"Why, Michal, what is this? Look, the sun is bright and the birds sing for joy—come, do not sit alone on such a day." David would have raised me up, but I made myself a heavy burden.

"My husband is dead. Let me be, that I may mourn him in peace."

"No, Michal, I live. See, here I am before you, well and whole." David knelt before me, and took my hands. "Only look, and be comforted."

"You know I speak of Phaltiel. He is dead. Did you think no one would tell me?"

There was silence before David spoke. "If that is so, I am sorry for it. I am told Phaltiel was a good man. But a man's death—even a good man's death—is no reason for the queen of my house and heart to claw her face and rend her garments."

He stroked my face, tracing the scratches I had gouged into my cheeks. "You cannot grieve like this for every man slain by robbers on the road—or struck down by illness. And Phaltiel was an old man, after all."

"Phaltiel was my husband. You swore you would send me back to him!"

"I swore to send Nathan with your message, and that promise I kept. All Jerusalem saw me keep my word. But who is to say that Phaltiel would have wished you back?"

"He would," I said. "He would. He loved me."

David set his hand upon my hair. "I did what you asked of me, Michal. Now you see it is Yahweh's will that you stay with me. Come, now, and let your maids tend you."

His voice was smooth and soft as warm butter; his hands were gentle and kind. His eyes showed nothing, neither joy nor triumph. But I knew. Phaltiel had been slain by a thief indeed—a royal thief, who would own what Phaltiel possessed, and had killed him for it. For me.

"My bride-prices are high." I drew away, slowly, and rose to my feet. "Once it was a hundred foreskins taken from the Philistines. This time it was my husband's life."

David stayed on his knees and looked up at me with eyes like pools in the salt desert, bright surface hiding deep poison. "You rave, Michal. Perhaps madness does run in the blood of Saul. Do not fear; no one will harm you."

"Now I understand—Nathan was only the second messenger from the king. Who was the first, the one who ran before Nathan in secret to strike Phaltiel down?"

David did not move. "This is not wise, Michal. This is no way for a queen to act." His voice told nothing at all, as if I had never spoken of King David and murder within one breath.

"It is the way for a widow to act. I have a widow's rights, now, and a widow's duties. Leave me in peace with them."

"Enough of this folly." David arose, now, and came to put an arm around my shoulders, and would not let me move away. "If Phaltiel is dead, as you say, then Yahweh's will is clear—you are my wife, and the queen. I will not have the people see you weeping and wailing for another man. Come, now, you have been content enough here all this month past—be content now."

I said nothing, and David stroked me, caressing now he thought he had won. "You are too fair, beloved, to use yourself so." The day was hot, and his hands slid damp on my skin. He was smiling, now.

Even his eyes smiled, his beautiful eyes in his beautiful face. Phaltiel's eyes had been beautiful once, before he had lain two days as pleasure for the jackals and the crows.

"I will send your maids to you again, Michal, and now you will let them bathe you, and anoint you, and dress you as befits David's queen."

King David, the sun for beauty—I would have marred that beauty if I could, but David held me close and hard and I could not move. So I smiled, and spat in his face.

"Give me a dress befitting David's harlot," I said, thinking of Caleb's last words to me, "and I will wear that."

Most men, guilty or not, would have broken my bones in payment for those words. But David was always smooth as sand and water, swallowing up what was meant to hurt and keeping it buried to repay later. He lifted one of my loosened braids and wiped his face with my hair.

"Your father was a king, Michal—and he was a madman as well. All the land knows that. Now your women tell me you talk wildly, and demand odd things. So be calm, or you will be queen of silence, and see no one who will excite you to these strange fits."

He did not say more than that; he did not need to say more. The bargain was as plain as any carved in the market clay-boards. The king's house was large, and held many, many rooms within its walls, and not all of them were spacious, painted things. If I were not docile and obedient now, I would leave the light and the air and the companionship of my women, and be kept alone in the darkness known to soothe the mad. And all men would bless David's charity in keeping his poor mad wife locked safe away, when other men would have put her aside and cared nothing for her.

I was still young; I might live so twenty years, or thirty—I trembled, and sour liquid welled up and burned in my mouth.

"You see? You are tired, you must rest," said David, as if my comfort were his only care and delight under the sky.

"Yes," I said, and did not look at him. "Yes, I am tired. I will rest."

"Good. I will send your maids." He kissed my forehead, and made me lift my head. "Be content and happy, and you may ask anything of me and I will grant it. Now smile for me, Michal— our people like to see their king and queen smiling. Smile."

I made some movement with my mouth; the scratches I had scored in my cheeks for Phaltiel stung and cracked.

"There, you see? It is easy and simple. I will come to you tonight, Michal, and you will smile for me then. You are lovely as lilies when you smile."

CHAPTER 12

"Is there yet any that is
left of the house of Saul . . . ?"
—II Samuel 9:1

After David had gone I went up the shallow steps to my balcony, to the air and the sun's light. My body was stiff, and hard to move; I knew now how my bones would feel when I was old.

My mind also would not obey. My thoughts pulled always back to one thing, like a wheel dragged into the deep rut made by others in the summer earth. And that thing was not Phaltiel's death, but David's eyes when he had spoken of it.

I stood in the hot light, stared unseeing across the heat-shimmered roofs of Jerusalem. He would come to me tonight, David had said. Did he think I would lie willing?

No, I told myself. *I will not. Never.*

So said my heart. But my rebellious mind knew better. If David came to me I would lie with him; yes, lie as if I loved him dear. I would be as meek and docile as a pet lamb, as he had told me I must be, lest I be called mad.

But I was not mad; my mind was clear as well-water now that I no longer must look into David's eyes. Now I saw the path I might tread to safety, and to David's undoing.

Nathan, I thought, and stared out and past the city walls to the road that led over the hills to Gallim. Nathan the prophet, the upholder of Yahweh's Law.

In our land, a prophet held in his hands more power than a

king. Had not Samuel raised my father high, only to bring him down to dust and give his kingdom to another? To David—

Oh, yes, I would speak to Nathan. And when Nathan had heard what I now would tell him, David would have no power over me. Yahweh's king was not held above Yahweh's Law; Yahweh's Law did not condone lustful murder. Phaltiel would be avenged.

But first I must wait yet again, wait for Nathan to return from Gallim. When he did, surely he must come to me, to tell the sad news.

First I must live through the days, and the nights. I thought of David, and of the coming night, and clenched my fingers hard on the burning stones of the balcony wall. I swore to myself that I would lie beneath David meek and obedient; that David would not know I was other than that.

That night David demanded smiles, and kisses, and caresses, as if nothing but love had ever been spoken between us. I was wise, and remembered my vow. I smiled, and kissed him, and did all as he would have it done.

I was rewarded; I felt nothing, and gave nothing. And I thought of nothing, not even of Phaltiel.

When it was over, David lay beside me and stroked my hair, and smiled upon me, and promised me whatever I wished for pleasing him so.

"You see, Michal? You are mine, and mine alone—your body tells me so. There is no other woman like you for pride and passion. Yahweh has blessed our union with joy, and it will bear royal fruit."

No, I thought. *I am mine, and mine alone, and Yahweh has blessed me.* For I knew now that I could endure and wait; David could not touch me. David would take the surface, and think me loving. He would not know I gave only shadow.

He would never know, until I stood before him with Nathan

at my side and accused him of his crime before all the people. Nothing would bring Phaltiel back from the land of ghosts and shadows, not even justice. But justice would mean Phaltiel slept there in peace.

"Do not look so solemn—see, I will give anything for a smile from your lips," said David, begging me like a true lover. "Come, now, ask and it shall be granted, if only you will grant me a smile. Let me show you how I love you, queen of my heart."

"You have shown me already," I told him. My voice was steady, gentle as a dove's. "And there is nothing I want more than what you have just given me."

And then I smiled at David, just as he had asked. It was easy to smile, then. It was only later, when David had gone at last, that I wept, and could not stop.

⁓

I was calm, as David had ordered that I be, as I waited for Nathan to return to Jerusalem. I asked for nothing, I wished to see no one. By day I sat upon my balcony and watched the road to the city; by night I wept into my pillow so that no one would hear.

Four days after Caleb had come to me to tell me that his father was dead, Nathan returned to the city. I suppose he thought there was no need for haste with the news he carried. And as I had known he would, Nathan came. David himself brought the prophet to me.

It was close to midday; I had been staring out over the city since dawn, watching through the hours as the sunlight changed and shadows slid over the walls and houses like oil. I rose to my feet when I saw the two men standing there, David tall and beautiful, Nathan round and plain.

"I bear unhappy news," Nathan said, and his eyes were kind. He was not one who took joy in bad tidings.

"I know your news already," I told him. "Phaltiel lies dead."

Nathan stared at my words. "That is true, but how can you

know that, daughter?"

David answered before me. "You know her father King Saul once fell down and prophesied. Perhaps that is how Michal knows what she has neither heard nor seen."

I smiled; this time it did not make my face ache. "No, I am not mad. But I must speak to the prophet Nathan."

"Speak, then," said David. And smiled.

"Alone," I said, and waited for David's smile to change, for his eyes to warn.

"Speak alone, then," said David, and his expression did not alter; there was no warning there. There was nothing but kindness and forbearance. "I will await you here."

David sat upon the bench where I had spent so many hours watching for Nathan's return. He looked out over the city below, all his city now. I led Nathan to the far end of the balcony; no one would overhear us there, and I could watch David as I spoke.

"Someone came before you, and so I know your news already," I said, before Nathan could speak. "And there is something you must know—it was King David who slew Phaltiel."

Nathan looked kindly upon me and took my hand. "No, no," he said. "The king was here, you know that. It was robbers who fell upon Phaltiel. The king has ordered men to search for them, that they may be punished."

"Tell the men to search here, in the king's house, then! For it was David—he sent someone to kill my husband, that he might keep me. You know I am here against my will."

I still spoke calm and firm, but my bones were chill; they knew already what I still could not bear to know. Nathan did not believe. Nathan would not believe. I could tell it from his eyes, and from the slow sad way he shook his head at my words.

"You are a good woman, Michal, and you grieve rightly for Phaltiel." Nathan patted my hand, as if I were a small child. "But you are wrong. King David did all as he should—why, he even sent me with rich gifts for Phaltiel and all his family, to show that he bore no ill will."

"Kings give easy gifts," I said. "Nathan, you must listen—"

"No, you must listen," Nathan said, and his voice was gentle. "You must not say such things about King David, Michal."

"They are true!"

Nathan shook his head. "Look into your heart, daughter, and you will know that it is only your grief that speaks. When you are calmer, you will regret your hasty words."

"I am calm, and I have given much thought to my words," I said. "David wanted me, and Phaltiel would not give me up. That is why he was killed."

Nathan looked sad. "What is your proof, child?"

I was silent; there was no proof, only my heart's wisdom. But I had thought that Nathan would know truth when he heard it, and believe me. Samuel would have believed.

"You see? There is none. And you do not know that Phaltiel would not have given you up. For I will tell you a thing that the king would not—he also sent a message to Phaltiel, to ask if he would consent to give you to the king. And King David offered him much if he would do this, for David loves you well. So you see, there was no need for the king to slay Phaltiel—no need at all."

"No." I was numb, as if I had drunk too much wine. "No. Phaltiel would not have done that. He would have taken me back. He swore it."

Nathan patted my hand again. "David is a great man, Michal— and greatly loved by Yahweh. Such a man is born but seldom. Only see what he has already done for our people—why, even the Philistine kings do him honor. David will bring glory to Yahweh, glory to Yahweh's people. No longer will we be weak, but strong— yes, stronger than all our enemies."

I stepped back, away from Nathan. "You will not help me," I said. "You will let David do this thing. Are you blind, Nathan? Can you not see what David is?"

But Nathan's eyes glowed now as if he saw bright visions. "David honors Yahweh and walks meek before him. David honors Yahweh's priests and prophets. David is Yahweh's beloved and

Yahweh will raise him up, and all his people with him, until his kingdom covers half the earth."

I looked past Nathan. David sat still upon the bench, watching us. He still smiled. When he saw me looking, he rose to his feet.

He walked across the balcony to me, slow and confident, like a lion advancing upon a fallen lamb. I thought I stood there proud and waiting; I did not know I had moved until I felt the stones of the balcony wall hard against my back.

David stopped before me. "You have spoken alone with Nathan, as you wished," he said. "Now can you rest content, my love?"

"I have told her the truth, O King." Nathan seemed to take pride in calling David so.

My mouth was dry and my skin cold, but I spoke. "So now kings buy truth in the marketplace. What does truth cost you, David?"

Nathan looked upon me and spoke again, soft and kind. "The sun is hot, and you have had ill news, daughter. You should rest quiet inside, where the air is cooler."

It was useless; I looked away, but saw nothing save hot bright light. I heard Nathan go, his sandals brisk against the stones. Then I looked back at David, the golden king shimmering before my eyes in the cruel sun.

"You see?" David said. "You rave, Michal."

And still he smiled. I closed my eyes and bowed my head; when I looked again, David was gone. But my women were there— there to tend me gently, and to make me lie down quiet inside, in the cool shadowed rooms.

I let them do with me as they would, as if I were a child's doll, with no more will than that toy possessed. And when I lay upon my bed and they had closed the ivory shutters, I asked for Zhurleen to be brought to me. I had not seen Zhurleen since she had come to tell me Caleb was safe away from Jerusalem. Now I wished to see her once more, to speak with one who saw the world clearly.

One who did not lie to me and slant her eyes away. One who was my friend.

So I roused myself enough to ask for her.

"Zhurleen?" said Chuldah, with her sideways look. "The Philistine concubine? Why, she is gone, O Queen."

"Gone?" I stared, my mind blank as new parchment. "Where has she gone? I wish to see her."

"I do not know. I know only that she no longer dwells under the king's roof. But she was only a Philistine harlot, not worthy of your notice." Chuldah smoothed the linen sheet over me and nodded at the others. "Now you will rest, and Keziah will fan you. Do not trouble yourself, O Queen—we will take great care of you, for you are precious to us."

It was useless; David had reached out his hand and all was bone and ash. I turned my face away and closed my eyes.

~

I thought I never again would care for anything, after that. I lay upon my bed weak and silent, as if I were ill. But I was not ill; at least my body was not. I think now it was my mind that sickened.

It was my mind that would not let me truly rest, or sleep. When I closed my eyes I saw Phaltiel's face, saw him smiling at me in love and trust. Trust that I had betrayed, thinking myself faithful.

When I stopped my ears, I heard again Zhurleen's words; she had warned me, but I had been both blind and deaf. Zhurleen, my wise friend—why had I not heard or understood? If I had bowed to David's wishes, Phaltiel would live today.

Now that it was too late, I knew that David had won even before the battle. But I did not yet know how complete was his victory, how tight-closed his trap. That was left for Abigail to show me.

~

When I had lain three days upon my bed, Abigail came to see me. She came in malice, and not for kindness's sake; her first words told that plain.

"The queen is bored again, I see." Abigail's lips were pinched thin; the lines around her red mouth cut deep.

Abigail's woes were no fault of mine. I looked at her once, and then closed my eyes. It was easiest, I had found, to let people speak over me as they would. I need not listen, or heed.

"Perhaps the queen will not be so bored when she hears what I next will tell the king." Abigail had bent over me, her voice hissed close to my ear.

I did not look at her. "Tell him what you please. I do not care."

"Will you care when I tell him how you tricked me? How you begged me to send a messenger to the man you called husband, so that you would seem innocent? The man who now lies dead, struck down by robbers—or so they say. But I know better, O Queen."

I opened my eyes and looked into Abigail's. They were flat with malice, like an adder's. She waited, poised above me, while I pondered her words. They seemed empty noise, meaningless to me. At last I said, "I never tricked you, Abigail. Now go, and leave me to my grief."

She laughed, short and harsh. "I know how much you grieve, Queen Michal! And soon others will know too."

My heart was ice and my blood ran thick with sorrow, but I was not yet dead. Abigail's words pricked deep, as they were meant to; anger woke in me, sharp as thorn.

I sat up then. "I do not know what you mean, Abigail. I have spoken only truth to you; it is not my fault if you do not believe me."

"Oh, you were clever—but not so clever as I!" Abigail tossed her head. "But I am a good woman; how could I know what you would do, to be queen?"

Yes, I thought, as anger's thorn bit deep. *Yes, I still live.* Perhaps

I should have thanked Abigail, for showing me that. But I did not.

Instead, I swung my legs over the side of the bed and stood. I had lain abed too long, and so was weak as a new-born lamb. When I first stood, blood pounded behind my eyes and lights flashed and danced like torches, blurring my sight.

"And what is it I have done, Abigail?" My voice came from far away, as if it were not my own. "Tell me, for I do not know."

"You are shameless," Abigail said. "Shameless, and heartless, and no true woman. No one else dares to say so, but I do!"

"If you dare so much," I said, "then say the rest plain." If only Zhurleen had spoken plain, I would have known the truth. If only Zhurleen had spoken plain—would I have believed?

Abigail began to speak, but I had thought of something that she might know, and so I held up my hand to stoop her. "You say you know everything, Abigail—tell me, then, do you know what became of Zhurleen? My women tell me she has gone."

Abigail started as if I indeed raved. "Zhurleen? That Philistine slut? What was she to you, that you care what became of her?"

"My friend," I said. I thought of Zhurleen's dancing hands and cautious eyes. Perhaps Zhurleen had been sent back to Philistia. Back to her home in Ascalon, where the sea whispered and sighed beneath her windows. . . .

"A Philistine whore! A fine friend!" Abigail's eyes narrowed. "Now I see—she was the one who helped you. She was always a sly, sneaking thing, I knew she could not be trusted! But do not look for her to aid you now—she is gone. David tired of her, as we all knew he would, and sold her—to a slave-dealer going north, or so I heard. He is better rid of her than he knew!"

I did not act in hot rage; I thought quiet for a moment, and then I raised my hand and slapped Abigail hard across her cheek. "She was the only true woman under this roof," I said. "King David cannot tell gold from dross."

I thought Abigail might try to strike me in turn; I would not have blamed her if she had. But Abigail only gaped at me, and took a step backward.

"Now," I said to her calmly, as if we talked only of the weather, "tell me why you came here to torment me. What have I done to you, Abigail, that you should hate me so?"

Then Abigail's truth was spoken, spat out like a cobra's poison. I had taken her place in David's heart; I had stolen what was hers. I had told her I had no wish to be queen— "—yet your husband—or so you called him—lies dead! No one knows who slew him, but I do! Who else had cause to wish him dead but you?"

She backed away as she spoke, as if fearing I would strike her again. But I did not, for I could not deny her words.

I was guilty. I had struck Phaltiel down as surely as if my own hand had dealt the blow.

"And do not think you shall escape justice, for I shall tell King David what manner of woman you are," Abigail said. "He would never dream such evil—he thinks only good of everyone. But he must know this, lest you bring shame and dishonor to him, as you did to that man Phaltiel!"

"Go and tell him, then," I said.

After Abigail had gone—quickly, as if she feared I might somehow stop her—I sat down again upon my bed. I saw at last how cunning David had been; how closely he held me in his net. Now, when I looked through Abigail's eyes, I saw what others would see. What David had meant them to see.

Who had more to gain than I from killing Phaltiel? *To become King David's queen, she bought her husband's death.* That was what men would say, if that death were brought to judgment.

It was not David who would stand accused of Phaltiel's murder. It was I.

⁓

I do not know what David said to Abigail, when she accused me to him. But she never afterwards spoke a word to me, save at his command.

I cannot say her silence grieved me overmuch.

The days were long, after that. And the nights were longer.

By day I walked queenly and obedient, as I had been bidden. By night I lay in David's arms and let him have his will of my docile body.

By day my hair and wrists and ankles glittered with gold, with carnelian, with lapis and fine silver. I had new robes, more than any woman could wear; robes stiff with embroidery and heavy with tassels. I had necklaces and earrings of crystal, coral, chalcedony. I had gold dust on my hair and mirrored sandals on my feet.

By day, I had all a man thinks a woman dreams of.

By night, I had David.

I had thought I knew what grief, and anger, and bitterness were. Now I learned them anew each time I held out my arms to David as if he were my heart's delight. I dared do nothing else, even as I called myself coward and harlot.

Only one risk did I take, and that was to speak of Phaltiel's family, that had once been mine. I could not bear not knowing, but I knew I dared not send a message to them; no, not so much as one word. And so I did what I had sworn I never would. I begged a favor of David.

I wished to make it a simple thing, but it came hard. I hated the asking, and I feared what I might hear; my face was hot and my fingers trembled as I spoke the words.

"Phaltiel's family? Oh, yes—he had three sons, and two daughters as well, did he not? And grandchildren, too?" It was strange knowledge to have so ready to his tongue; King David showing me the lion's paw held heavy over those I loved.

"Yes. I—I would know if they are well. I was fond of them, when I dwelt among them." I heard the pleading in my voice, and was afraid to say more.

David slid my hair through his fingers; he liked to weave it into chains, as if he would bind me with them. "They are well, Michal—even the boy Caleb. The king is shepherd to his people;

I sent them gifts to ease their loss. Do not trouble yourself over them; they are nothing to us now."

And then David smiled upon me, and spread my braided hair across my breast. "There, you see? My loving wife has only to ask, and it is granted."

He was pleased I had come to him for even so small a thing. So pleased that he did not even demand I smile.

~

That summer, there was much to please King David. It seemed he had only to stretch out his hand and whatever he wished fell into it like ripe fruit.

He already held all the south; I knew Abner had promised to bring him the north as well. Abner, once war-chief of King Saul, then war-chief of King Ishbaal. Abner, who had been rewarded well for bringing me to Jerusalem, and better for abandoning my brother Ishbaal. Without Abner, King Ishbaal's warriors scattered to their homes. Without Abner, Ishbaal's crown was David's for the asking.

So now—Abner, war-chief of King David.

The title had a fine ring to it. And as King David's star rose daily higher, Abner had reason to think himself both clever and fortunate. King David gave with lavish hands.

But Abner did not enjoy his triumph long. For King David had a war-chief before Abner—Joab.

Joab was a mighty warrior and a proud man. And he was David's nephew, being the son of David's sister Zeruiah. Joab had fought at David's left hand since David had first taunted King Saul in the wilderness. Joab had been the first man up the well to take Jerusalem by cunning and force.

Joab, war-chief of David—who knew David's mind without need of words.

So when Abner went away from Jerusalem on some business of King David's, Joab sent after him and called him back—in David's name. Abner was no fool; he would never have heeded a message from Joab.

When Abner came inside the city gate, Joab killed him. For vengeance, Joab said. Because Abner had slain Joab's brother Asahel in some forgotten battle. Blood called for blood.

King David made a great noise of mourning for Abner, and buried Abner with as many honors as if he loved him well. King David publicly reviled Joab and all his family for the dishonor they had brought to David's name. And all men saw King David turn his face from Joab, and weep for Abner.

And Joab did penance for his crime; David forced him to walk behind Abner's bier, wailing and rending his garments. But nothing else was done, for all that Abner had been slaughtered like a sheep within the gates of David's own city.

Harsh words were heaped upon Joab's head, and Joab bowed down under them; when he rose again, he held Abner's honors in his own hands.

And so—Joab, once more war-chief of King David.

I heard all the story from my women. They knew every tale told at the well, and retold all of them to each other. It did not seem to matter to the women whether or not I attended to them as they chattered. Often I did not, for listening tired me.

But I listened well to the tale of Abner and Joab, and of King David's grief and horror. And I thought, and counted time upon my fingers.

It was only forty days since Abner had taken me from Phaltiel and brought me to King David's court, a seal upon Abner's bargain with King David. Now Abner had his reward.

I suppose I should have rejoiced to hear of Abner's death. But I could not; I could think only of how Abner had stood faithful at my father Saul's side through all those years.

"It is wise to know the measure of a king's memory," I said. My women asked me what I meant, what I wished, what I would have; I turned away and did not answer.

Death fed upon death; David still mourned Abner when men brought him my brother Ishbaal's head. Brave men who had slain Ishbaal as he slept in his bed; men who came to King David proud of their bloody deed, sure he would reward them well.

They were wrong. King David wept instead for Saul's son Ishbaal—"My brother in kingship, and in marriage." Ishbaal's murderers were put to death.

"They slew a king, so their crime is twice sin," David said, when he came to tell me what had happened.

I had been already told of Ishbaal's death, of course. And I had tried to mourn him as was proper, even though I was only Ishbaal's half-sister, and had never known him well. But I had no tears left; when David came to me—to comfort me, he said—I was sitting in my courtyard. My eyes were dry; the queen's fountain must weep for me.

"Is a king twice a man?" I looked at David; his eyes were red with his tears for Ishbaal.

"But you may rest content, your brother's murderers have been punished as the Law demands. And Joab has taken half the army north to your brother's city, to keep the peace there."

And to make sure there was no other king in the north but David. Even I knew that.

Ishbaal had never wished to be a king; it was Abner who had placed him upon an unsteady throne. Now Abner was dead, and Ishbaal too, and David would have Israel as well as Judah. North and south, both held in King David's hands. And Jerusalem to stand guard over both King David's kingdoms.

David waited, but I said nothing. There was nothing I need say; David himself had said it all already.

Then he smiled. "But I have brought glad news as well. Joab will bring Jonathan's son Meribaal back with him. Now Meribaal will make his home here, with us. That will please you, will it not?"

"Yes," I said. "That will please me, David." I remembered
Jonathan talking of his sturdy little son; I tried to reckon the time
passed since then. Meribaal must be nearly ten now. Jonathan's
boy; my nephew. Perhaps there would be some love for me here,
after all.

Hope is hard to kill.

~

David made Meribaal's coming a great day in Jerusalem. The streets
were decked with palms and flowers, as for a festival. All for
Jonathan's son—and for the peace David had brought to the land,
now that he was king indeed.

Yes, it was a great day for King David, to have Jonathan's son
come to him. That was the day King David spread all his prizes
before the people, that men might look upon them and marvel.
And this time I saw all for myself, for I was there. I was King Saul's
daughter.

I, too, was a prize.

~

Once more I saw the king's great courtyard, where he sat to pass
judgment. Now David sat there to show his power and his mercy.
The king's chair was set before a glazed garden of lilies and reeds
and lotus-flowers; tiles brought from Egypt for David's hall. A
wild cat hunted birds among the painted reeds.

I sat upon a leather-padded stool by David's feet. I wore scarlet, and gold, and a circlet of sea-pearls about my head; a queen's
image gracing King David's rich court. I did not like to show myself so, before so many men's eyes. But David wished it, and my
life now was lived at David's bidding.

Nathan stood beside David's chair; Yahweh's blessing upon
King David's handiwork. I looked at Nathan once, and then away.
Nathan had not listened to me; he had not known truth. Samuel

would have listened, and known. But Samuel had not taken gifts and honors from the king's hands. Samuel had not dreamed of glory.

David had the day as closely planned as a wedding of twin brothers to twin sisters.

First came men of Israel, men to beg King David of Judah to wear the crown of Israel also. They had brought a crown with them; a thin circle of gold. They knelt before David and held the crown out to him, pleading as if he might choose not to take it.

David sat quiet as they spoke, and then he rose to his feet. The king's chair sat upon a slab of marble a span higher than the floor; when David stood, even those placed far away could see him.

"It is a hard thing, to be a king," David said, "and a harder thing to hear of a brother's death. King Ishbaal was my brother, as his sister is my wife. You all know how I care for her, and how I punished Ishbaal's murderers. Before I take his crown from your hands, I would know if it was King Ishbaal's wish that I be his heir."

"It was King Ishbaal's wish," said the man who held the crown of Israel in his hands. His head was bent; he looked at the floor, and not at David.

"Are you sure it is so?" David asked, and his voice rang sweet as springtime through the great court. "For my brother Ishbaal had no living sons, but his brother Jonathan had a boy with a better claim to Ishbaal's crown than I."

"We are sure," said the man, and the others with him all agreed. They all nodded their heads; yes, yes, it was King Ishbaal's wish; it was so.

David stood silent for the time it took to draw three long breaths. "I would not take what is Meribaal's. Meribaal is only a child, but he is the son of Prince Jonathan and the grandson of King Saul. Are you sure it is not Meribaal you would have for your king in Israel?"

"Yes," said the man, and for the third time swore it was David they would have as king. "For Meribaal is not fit to rule over us.

You are king of Judah, King Saul's daughter is your wife. You are the man chosen by Yahweh and by King Ishbaal to follow after him. You are the king we would have in Israel. You and no other."

It sounded like a lesson the man had learned to recite, each word clear and perfect. David bowed his head.

"I am humble before the Lord. If it is Yahweh's will, I must obey, for I am only his servant."

"Yahweh's will be done," Nathan said, and David turned to the prophet and knelt while Nathan poured oil on David's hair. Nathan smiled wide; I think he was truly happy that day. Well, as I later learned, Nathan believed that day brought peace to the land. "Yahweh's blessing is upon this act."

David rose to his feet; I thought he smiled. The man who held the crown of Israel rose and came forward. I thought that Nathan would place the crown upon David's head, as Samuel had once placed a crown upon my father's. But David took the crown into his own hands.

"This crown does me honor," David said, "but I will not wear it."

He waited for the exclamations to cease, and then he smiled, broad, for all to see. "This is the crown of Israel," he said, and held it high above his head in both his hands. "I wear already the crown of Judah. Two crowns—but now I shall wear only one. For I shall take them both, and they shall be melted down and recast into one—one crown and one king, for one people. For Yahweh's people!"

Even David could not stop the shouting, after that. It was the first time I had heard such a noise confined by walls; waves of sound beat against me like eager hands. But for all his fine words, David set the crown of Israel firm upon his own head before he sat in the king's chair once more.

I alone neither moved nor praised. I sat quiet upon my stool at David's feet; I must have looked proud, or lifeless.

At last the noise became less; before it ceased David raised his hand and waved them all to silence. "This is indeed a day for all men to rejoice. And today I too rejoice—for Jonathan's son has come to me, that I may love him as I loved his father."

And then David motioned with his hand and Meribaal was brought before him. That was the moment I learned what hate truly was. That moment in King David's great court when first I saw Jonathan's son Meribaal.

A sound rose from the assembled people, a murmur, low but swelling, like wind before the rain. A sound of grief, or of pity. At first I did not understand, and then Meribaal's litter was carried into my sight, and laid down on the floor before the king.

Meribaal lay almost at my feet, and so I saw all clearly. His feet were thickly bandaged; even so, it was clear they were twisted and broken. Meribaal would never run free. It would be a wonder if he could walk.

That was bad, but it was not the sight of those broken feet that pierced me, and made me bleed once more when I had thought myself all unfeeling stone. It was Meribaal's eyes.

They must have looked like Jonathan's eyes, once. They must have held light, and love, and happiness. Now they held nothing. Meribaal was not blind, but he did not see. His eyes stared or wandered, aimless as air.

I thought of Jonathan sitting beside me when I had dwelt in Phaltiel's house, speaking of his boy. "He runs so swift his nurse can hardly catch him, and he is clever as a little mouse!" Jonathan had laughed, then, and so had I.

The murmur of sound ceased; there was a hush, silence before a storm. David looked upon Meribaal, and put his hands over his face. "Is this all that is left of my beloved Jonathan? Is this to be his only legacy?"

Then David looked at Joab and demanded to know what had happened to cause this sorrow. "Who is to blame? How did Jonathan's son come to this?"

Joab stood straight before David's throne and neither smiled nor blinked. "It was no one's fault." Joab had a voice like stone, yielding to nothing.

"When we marched into Ishbaal's city there was great alarm, and no one watched the boy. He ran up to the rooftop to see what was happening. He must have leaned too far, for he fell to the street below. We called Ishbaal's own physician, but there was nothing to be done. Now the boy is as you see him."

David wept, then. He sat still upon his throne, and wept.

While all men watched the king's grief I alone dared to move, and to speak. I slid forward off my stool, to rest upon my knees beside my brother's son. "Meribaal," I said. "Meribaal, I am your father's sister. I am your Aunt Michal."

Meribaal did not answer; I do not know if he even heard. And if he had, my words would have meant nothing to him. He was crippled now, in mind as well as body. Meribaal would never know me or anyone else.

I stroked Meribaal's hair; it was soft and brown like Jonathan's. And when I pushed his hair gently back, I saw the bruise upon his temple. A mark the size of a fist, or of a sword-hilt; dark purple at the center, paling to greenish yellow as it spread away.

Boys run and jump—and fall. Caleb had often done so; I had tended his cuts and bruises. I knew the look of a fall's injuries. And I had been a warrior's daughter, a warrior's sister. I knew the look of a blow.

I looked up, then. Joab was not looking at me or at Meribaal; he looked only at David. Joab's face showed nothing, neither sorrow nor triumph. Joab's eyes were flat and keen as the sword-blade he carried at his side.

My body froze, my flesh cool and unfeeling as marble, while my blood rushed and beat under my skin like a river in full flood. *Joab*, I thought.

It had been Joab. Joab who had struck down Phaltiel. Joab who had slain Abner. Joab who had crippled Meribaal.

Joab—David's sword, striking at David's bidding.

There was a rustle beside me; David had stepped down from his throne. He bent and took my hand; he lifted me up.

"Do not grieve, my queen. For Meribaal will dwell in peace

beneath my roof, and never shall he want for anything. All men will see how I do him honor, for his father's sake." That is what David said.

But I did not grieve; I had gone far beyond sorrow. *Learn,* David had told me. *You must learn, Michal.* Now I had.

I had learned hate, and hate was stronger than grief. Hate flowed over my skin; hate coiled in my loins and around my heart. Hate strong enough to topple kingdoms, cold enough to turn blood to ice.

Hate almost too great for me to bear, for there was nothing to ease its press upon my bones.

I stood free before all the chief men of David's stolen kingdom—the judges, the priests, the warriors. I could cry out the truth now, quick and loud, before even David could silence me. But I did not, for no one would believe me. David had seen to that.

Men would not draw back from David in horror. Men would call me mad, and murderess. And then for me it would be the stones, or the endless dark. And King David would still reign free, beloved. That was useless to me; that would not slake my new hunger.

"I am glad that Jonathan did not live to see this day," David said, as he looked down at Meribaal.

I too was glad; David's evil would have broken Jonathan's loving heart.

"Do you remember how happy we all were together, when your father King Saul still lived?" It was not said in quiet sorrow for my ears only. David's voice was a weapon, casting words as once his sling had cast stones. Words that rang clear through the great court, drew tears from those who heard them.

Then David reached out his hand to me, as if we shared our joys and our sorrows. "Do you remember, Michal?"

"Yes," I said, and my voice told nothing, smooth as a bowl of milk. "Once we all were happy."

To bring down David's happiness as he had brought down

mine—I felt his fingers close over my hand and I trembled with the strength of my new desire, as I once had trembled in Phaltiel's arms—and in David's.

I thought again of words, and of stones. Five smooth stones, so David's song ran. Once Yahweh had put five smooth stones into David's smooth hand. With them David had brought down a giant—and won a kingdom.

Five smooth stones—ah, if only Yahweh would put into *my* hand five smooth stones....

I looked again at David. His head was bent once more; tears flowed free upon his cheeks. His sweet-oiled beard shed the teardrops as easily as David shed guilt.

Give me vengeance against David, I begged of Yahweh. *Let me bring him down to tears and sorrow as he has brought me and mine.*

That is all I ask.

CHAPTER 13

"Michal...despised him in her heart."
—II Samuel 6:16

My hate pressed always against my skin, behind my eyes, so that I could not find true rest until that pressure was eased. I must murder David's heart as he had mine; all the people must see him as he really was; he must be reviled and spat upon and stoned in the marketplace. Nothing less, I swore at first. Nothing less will satisfy me. Nothing less will bring me peace.

David had everything, now. But I swore I would find a weapon to use against him. I did not know what that weapon might be; I knew only that I must find it. Perhaps I would chance upon my weapon as once David had chanced upon his five smooth stones.

The moon changed three times; I walked and slept always with my hatred as if it were a twin sister. Hatred ate at my stomach like bad wine; filled me like stones so that I could barely eat or drink.

And Yahweh sent nothing—save a sign that King David was Yahweh's best beloved, dearer to him than all the world. David brought the Ark into Jerusalem. The Philistines, who had held it captive for so many years, had surrendered the Ark into King David's hands. Because Yahweh had set terror into the Philistines' hearts and made them humble, David told the people. Perhaps Yahweh had.

Others saw only the Ark; heard only Nathan's voice shouting praises in the gates. I saw sun on David's hair; heard David's voice as he boasted of his treasures. *"I have Jerusalem, and I have King Saul's daughter; and soon will have the sacred Ark as well. . . ."*

King David, and the sacred Ark of Yahweh's covenant. What sign could be clearer, or easier for all to read?

I read that sign of favor clearer than most; my hate had given me a seer's crystal eyes.

~

The sun was a golden apple; the sky a perfect azure bowl behind it. A cloudless sky, a flawless day. Even the heavens smiled upon King David when he took the Ark from the Philistines and brought it to rest safe within the walls of his city.

Men and women too, had come from all the land around to see the Ark as it traveled up the road to Jerusalem and passed through the streets of the city. No one had seen the Ark in two men's lifetimes; they would tell their children of this, and their children's children.

David had set up a tent of purple and scarlet for the Ark on a hill at the far end of the city for all to see; the tent stood higher than the king's house. It blazed brilliant in the sun, like a beacon-fire.

All the world rejoiced, that day, and none more wildly than David. He seemed to forget he was the king, and threw aside his royal robes to dance through the streets of Jerusalem, naked before the Ark and all the people.

He had oiled his body; his skin shone brighter than sun on water. I was on the palace rooftop with all his other women to see his triumph. I saw how he caught and kept all men's eyes on him; the women's eyes he had already.

That was how it was; David danced first, and the Ark followed behind him. David danced, and sang, and clapped his hands, and made all the watchers clap and sing as well. He led the Ark into Jerusalem, through the streets, up the long hill to the glorious tent he had built to enclose it.

I stood silent on the palace rooftop and watched David dance. His other wives and his concubines all made a great noise, crying praises and flinging flowers down upon his head. David looked up once, as he danced on past the palace wall; he looked straight at me, the only one who neither moved nor called.

I remembered the day David had first come through my father's gate, walking close beside Jonathan, covered in dust and glory. David had looked up at me that long-ago day; he had smiled, and I had thrown fresh-picked flowers at his feet.

David looked up and smiled now; I looked down with my crystal eyes.

Ghosts danced before him in the dust. Saul, Jonathan. Ishbaal and Abner. The son's love Caleb once had given me. The Meribaal who might have walked, and run, and laughed. Phaltiel.

I had no flowers for King David. I put my hands to my head and lifted the broad circlet of gold from my close-braided hair. A queen's diadem, David had called it when he had placed the circlet there. *"The people like to see us so, Michal. You will wear it, to please them and me."*

I held the golden circle in my hands; I held my queen's crown out, over the waist-high wall; I opened my hands and let it fall. The golden crown glittered as it spiraled down through the clear air. There was no noise when it hit the stones by David's feet. There was too much rejoicing for so small a sound to be heard.

David saw, but his mad dance never faltered. He only clapped his hands harder and danced on, leading the Ark away, toward the high hill. It had been only a moment, after all; a few heartbeats between one turn of his dance and the next. No one had noticed. Only Michal, and David, and the ghosts who went before him, clearing the path for David's dancing feet.

~

David came to me afterwards, swollen with pride and demanding my praises, as if he had no other wives to flatter him. As if only my admiration would content him.

"This day went well, my queen—you saw how the people loved me."

"Yes, I saw."

He took up a braid of my hair, his fingers working it free of the woven knot my maids had taken so much trouble over that morning. "And they saw how you loved me, Michal. How you took the very crown from your head and cast it before me, that I might tread upon it as if it were less than the dust beneath my feet. That the good people might take its gold up for themselves, a gift from my generous queen."

Once again he shaped truth with false words. I said nothing. David toyed with my braid, began to unweave my close-twined hair. I did not move. "But was it a wise gift, Michal?"

He did not say more; he did not need to. I knew what he meant. David could make my act a proof of my love for him—or only another proof of madness.

"No," I said, past pain that I thought would rip my throat open; words were tearing teeth. "No, it was not wise."

My braid was now only a loose skein; David let my hair fall and smoothed it over my breast. "Do not let it trouble you, my love. It was unwise, but wisdom can be learned. And you will learn it, as I did."

Never, cried my heart. Never would I learn David's wisdom. But there was another voice within me. A voice that whispered soft, like silk being drawn through rough fingers, like an adder sliding over sand. *You must.*

Bow before him, that soft voice told me. *Give him what he wants now, and wait. Someday*, it hissed. *Someday.*

But to obey that command I needed skills I did not own; I thought of Zhurleen, of how she had walked to silent music. Yes, Zhurleen's skills were what I now must have. I slanted my eyes down, and then up. I smiled.

"How glorious was the king this day! Surely there is no dancer like the king in all the land." I made my voice sweet as poppy-syrup. I raised my hand and placed it over David's where his fingers lay heavy upon my breast. "But was it wise of *you*, O King, to show yourself so before all the maids of Jerusalem?"

David laughed, and turned his hand under mine to catch and hold it. "What, are you jealous? But yes, it was wise, Queen Michal— to dance before all the people, for the glory of Yahweh—"

"And for the glory of his king?" It was easy to shape words to please David. Phaltiel had liked me to speak my mind; David liked me to speak his.

"You are still clever, Michal." He pulled me close, to hold me beside him as if we were loving man and wife. "Yes, the people must see how great the king is as well, and how Yahweh smiles upon him."

I looked sideways through my lashes, in the way that shows a woman thinks a man handsome as well as wise. "Surely all can see David's greatness, lord?"

"Not everyone," David said. "Not yet. But they will, for I have right and might on my side—and the Ark within the walls of Jerusalem."

"With the city you hold the land, and with the Ark you hold the people. You have good reason to be pleased—all my father ever won were battles." And even those words fell pleasant from my lips.

"King Saul did well enough for his day, but I mean to do better for mine, and leave a true kingdom for my son and my son's sons. Now come, let the king and queen dance their own dance to the glory of the Lord. If ever there were a day for the king to beget a king, it is this."

And I smiled again, and turned within the circle of David's arms. I reached up, and cradled his face between my hands. I thought again of Zhurleen, whose hands had been bird's wings, and waves. Zhurleen, who had tried to teach me, and now was gone.

"Yes, this is a great day, David. Let us see if Yahweh loves you as much as I."

I was not cold when we lay together; I was not quiet and accepting. That day my blood ran hot, as if I were a warrior whose enemy fled close before him. Hot for victory, and the kill. That day I learned that hate, too, is passion.

Hate drove me harder than love ever had. I was fierce and wild as a wounded leopardess; I marked David as a hunter marks prey. I let him have nothing from me that he could not earn. And that was nothing at all, in the end.

It was a battle between us—and David never knew he fought it, or what he had lost. He could not tell love's fire from hate's. That was when I first wondered if David knew the difference between them.

In that raging hour, I held power David did not. In the end, I was stronger than he.

~

David got no son upon me that day, either. I had prayed daily that he would not; I took joy in telling him as soon as I was sure. The news hurt him, as if he had been denied a gift his by all right.

"Perhaps Yahweh did not care overmuch for your dancing, my lord king." I rejoiced too much; my voice betrayed me.

That was the only time David ever struck me. I deserved the blow, if only for my sheer folly.

I remembered Zhurleen; I wept, and flung my arms around his knees, and blamed the words on my own sorrow at not giving him what he most would have. It was no more than any proper wife would say and feel; David forgave me easily, for he liked always to be the granter of favors.

I was not so foolish a second time. *Wait*, my hate told me. *Watch, and wait*. And I obeyed that inner voice.

Long days slid by, and hate walked with me always. A silent companion, a cruel one. Love feeds the heart; hate poisons it, and leaves it still empty.

Long days, and then long months, and the hate that had seemed so strong, that had promised so much, proved itself as faithless as David himself. For as slow time passed and still it seemed I could do nothing, I began to wish for less.

Autumn passed, and winter, and then spring again. And all the while King David basked in the sun of the people's love, the priests' approval.

I watched, and waited—and the hate that I had cherished so dear grew weary. It forsook me, sliding away to coil beneath my heart, a viper sleeping beneath a rock.

Slow time; full moon after full moon, until a year had passed since Phaltiel's death. My grief was a poisoned sore that would not heal; hatred had betrayed and abandoned me. Without its power, I was too weary to do more than lie upon my bed, or to sit upon my balcony.

Once I had wished to see David stoned to death at noon before the city wall. Once I had wished to sharpen the stones myself until they would slice his flesh like razors. Now even a pebble to bruise his foot would have pleased me, and made me smile.

And that was when Yahweh granted my prayers at last, when I had ceased to pray. But he did not send stones to my hand.

He sent Bathsheba.

~

King David did not sit idle upon his throne while I waited a year away. He had told me he wished to leave a true kingdom to his sons; during that year I learned what that meant, and so did all Israel. A true kingdom meant war.

Oh, my father King Saul had waged war, and almost every season, too—but only when we were threatened. In my father's time, we had waited to be attacked before striking.

Now all that was changed. Enemies surrounded his kingdom, King David said. If they had not yet attacked, they soon would. Israel, said King David, must strike first.

And so King David raised up an army. And he called to him not only our own people, but foreigners. Any man who could

fight hard was welcome to King David, whether he was a follower
of Yahweh or not. Any man who brought his own weapons was
twice welcome. And a man such as Uriah the Hittite, who came to
King David with ten well-armed fighting men at his back, was
embraced and kissed as a son, and given high rank in the hosts of
Israel.

Now no nearby land was safe. Aram, Edom, Moab, Zobah—
David swooped down upon them and made them a high road for
his chariot wheels. Already his kingdom was twice that of Saul's,
and still David was not satisfied.

"I have much," he told me once—David liked to come and
spread his triumphs before me, like a trader displaying goods for
sale, "and Yahweh will give me more."

"What more?" I was a dutiful wife to David; I asked the right
questions. "You hold all the land from Dan to Beersheba now."

"Ah, but our land is not all the land there is, Michal. Your
dreams are too narrow; mine spread wings as the eagle's."

You know nothing of my dreams, I thought, and kept my face
smooth. "You fly high, David—do you never fear to fall?"

"Yahweh is my strength," said David, and smiled, and stroked
his beard. His eyes seemed to slant; cunning, like a fox's.

"Pious words—but will words breed warriors? Will words hold
back the Philistines?" I made my words light; baubles for his pleasure.

David only laughed. "There are warriors a-plenty, more each
day—and the Philistines will not attack, my queen—not this season!"

"Did Yahweh say so?"

"I have his word on it," said David, laughing and careless, like
a boy. "It is not the Philistines who threaten us. Victory breeds
victory—and peace. Already the Moabites and the Aramites send
tribute to my court. You have seen this for yourself."

"Yes, I have seen." Sometimes I stood in the new gallery that
overlooked the king's great hall and watched as men came, and
went, obedient to a wave of David's hand. Sometimes, too, words

floated upward to my ears from those who waited. Not all such wayward words spoke of meek obedience. But that I did not tell King David.

"A great kingdom." David's eyes were half-closed, like a sated lion's. "Tell me what trinkets you would have, my queen, and they shall be brought to you—yea, though they come from the world's end."

I shook my head. "Nothing, lord king. I am content only to see how all men honor you." And I smiled, and smoothed the folds of my gold-fringed girdle, and thought myself patient and cunning. I did not know, then, what a fool I still was.

~

A great kingdom, bought at great price. That was what David forged from the union of Israel and Judah that second summer. I thought David's conquests nothing to me; I waited veiled and silent, a queen's image. But I wondered, sometimes, when David came to me with tales of new glories, what would satisfy David's lusts.

Gold, land, women—all these he had in plenty, and still it seemed he must have more, and more. He had taken a fine fertile land to rule—now that was not enough, it must be a vast kingdom, it must stretch from Egypt to Tyre. He had a fine king's house—now it was called a palace, and the roof must be gilded to be fire in the sun and make all men marvel. He had six wives, who had given him strong sons—that had not been enough. He must have a queen; what other kings had, so must King David also have.

~

King David was taking another wife; her father ruled two villages and a lake somewhere—a treaty-bride, poor girl. The women slid their eyes about a great deal when they told me, as if afraid that I would strike them for their news.

"The bride is to be wed from the women's quarters here," Chuldah told me. "King David wishes you to greet her kindly, for his sake." She bowed her head, as if she brought news of a funeral, and not of a wedding.

"Someone must," I said. "And the king knows what I will do for his sake." And then I laughed; well, they all looked so like dying sheep that I could not help it. "Do not believe each song you sing," I told them, and turned away. I heard them whisper behind me as I walked out into my garden. They sounded like mice in the eaves.

~

King David's wedding was an affair of royal state, with as much gold and purple and scarlet as if such riches cost nothing in money or blood. There were guests enough to make Jerusalem a city twice again as large. There was no room for them all even in the king's great house, and so gilded and silvered tents spread all down the hills and through the valley below the walls of Jerusalem.

When the bride arrived, I did my part to make her welcome, as David had ordered. I greeted her as sister, and kissed her mouth. I did my best to be kind, for I felt sorry for her. She was plain and over-proud; I did not think she would be happy.

But my kindness went for nothing. I saw Abigail take the girl aside—and later, when I smiled at the girl and spoke some pleasantry, she tossed her head and turned away. I shrugged, and let Abigail and the others escort the new bride to her new rooms. And I told myself I did not care; I lied, and knew I lied. The slight had hurt me.

I went to my balcony and stared out over the rooftops of King David's city. The air above the city roofs shimmered in the sun; it was early summer again. I looked, and counted back over the seasons.

Even slow time passes; the year had spun full round, and half again, since Phaltiel's death. A year, and more, and I had done nothing to avenge my dead—for there was nothing I could do. I could only walk quiet and grow old in this house that I hated, and that hated me.

And I was weary of hate, weary of bored women and their venom-dipped tongues. David's new bride would be no better than the others; she was neither sweet nor clever. She might learn softer ways, no doubt, but the lesson would not come from me. Who was I to teach lessons, after all?

That was when I looked down from my queen's balcony and saw that the house on the hill below was no longer empty. There was a woman, young and fair, who sat upon the rooftop. I watched her comb her rippling hair; it shone dark as wine in the noon sun, and fell below the bench where she sat.

"Whose house is that?" I asked one of the maids. "Who is the woman?"

My waiting-maid did not know; plainly, she did not care. Her shrug and outspread hands angered me, made me thorn sharp. "You are Hageet, are you not? Well then, go, Hageet, and find out what I wish to know," I told her. "Yes, go now!"

She went wide-eyed, in haste; I rarely asked or ordered. My servants treated me as if I were a woman of glass and ivory—with care, lest I shatter and they be blamed for the mishap.

Hageet was soon back to tell me well-gossip and street-news. I soon learned that Hageet was glad enough to chatter to the queen, if only the queen would listen.

The house below was now the house of Uriah; the woman was Bathsheba, his wife. Uriah was a foreigner, a Hittite who had come to serve the King of Israel and Judah. Uriah was a mighty warrior; Uriah was the captain of ten men, his own men; Uriah was seldom home. His wife was young.

"And so must be close-watched by her neighbors who are not?" I said, and laughed. "Poor girl! Take her a basket of oranges, and say that Michal the queen greets her and wishes her well in her new home."

"Oranges?" Hageet was scandalized; oranges were a new thing

then, and rare, and even King David had only half a dozen trees of them. "I will ask Chuldah if it may be done."

This time my anger flared high, scorching as fire. "Is Chuldah queen now? You will do as I tell you, and you will do it quickly."

She gasped, and backed away. "Yes, O Queen. It shall be done."

"And I will know if it is not," I said, and now my voice was cold, like stone in winter.

"Yes, O Queen!" Hageet bowed, and ran off like a frightened cat. She must have believed me; I do not know why. I knew only what David or my women chose to tell me.

I thought I did it for kindness. But I did it for anger, for loneliness, for spite. For no good reason, save that a maidservant had said that I might not.

That was why I sent oranges to Bathsheba.

CHAPTER 14

"Is this not Bath-sheba...
the wife of Uriah the Hittite?"

—II Samuel 11:3

She was married to a foreigner, and she was very pleasing to men's eyes, and so she was not well-liked by women. Her husband was with the army in the field; she was alone in a city strange to her; the little kindness called her to my hand as easily as honey brings the bee. Well, she was a friendly thing—and I was the queen, after all.

Bathsheba sent me back her thanks, and begged me to accept her favorite wrist-bangle as a token of her gratitude. The bracelet was a common thing, brass chains and river-crystals—her husband was either poor or ungenerous, if this was her best. And she would have sent nothing less, though even she must have thought proud Queen Michal would only toss this cherished treasure to the nearest serving-girl. *Poor thing,* I thought.

Then I looked at the bangle lying in my soft jeweled hand. No, not poor. Bathsheba's message—Hageet swore it had been retold to me faithfully, each word the same—had called the bracelet her favorite...a love-token, perhaps, given when her husband could afford that only, and so worth more than gold itself. I could almost see Uriah clasping the cheap trinket about Bathsheba's wrist. My throat ached; tears stung my eyes.

"I have grown too proud," I said. "I will wear this to remind me of that."

I clasped the brass bangle about my own wrist and sent

Bathsheba a spangled girdle in return. And when next I saw her on her rooftop, I waved, and the cheap crystals flashed oil-bright in the sun. Bathsheba smiled, and waved back, and it all began as simply as that.

I should have kept my heart cold as rock and hard as law, but I was lonely too. We waved to each other, and smiled across the air between my balcony and her roof. And so we became friends.

For almost a week I saw Bathsheba daily; she came to her rooftop each morning, each afternoon. She would look up, and if I waved she would smile and wave her hand in return. A smile, a wave of the hand; little things, but I came to look forward to seeing her there on the roof below.

The day she did not appear I nearly wept. I had so little to cheer me, and today not even that. Yes, I nearly flung myself weeping upon my rich bed—and then I thought, *Michal, you are a fool. Send a message to her, see if she is well.*

Then I had another thought, a better. "Fool indeed—the very queen of fools," I said aloud, and clapped my hands. And when a maid came in, I told her to go and ask if Bathsheba would come and visit with me.

She stared, and went away, and then half a dozen of my women came in all at once. Never before had I asked such a thing; was it wise; what did I mean by it? To hear them exclaim and protest, you would think I had told them to bring in a she-bear taken from her cubs.

"What I mean is what I said," I told them. "Go and ask if the woman Bathsheba will come and talk with me." I was angry, and with myself, for I knew it was my own fault if my servants were insolent. I had let them act so, I, who had prided myself on keeping a smooth house for Phaltiel. I thought about how best to mend my folly, and stamped my foot, hard. "Go, I said—or I will tell the king I am ill-served!"

That sent them. And that was the first time I knew how power felt. Such a small thing, at first; only an itch under the skin. Such a small thing, to make silly women do my will. Such a small thing, to send for Bathsheba.

~

It was not a small thing to Bathsheba. She came in her best gown and veil—I knew they must be her finest, although they looked rough and plain to my eyes. The girdle I had sent her was tied about her hips, oddly brilliant against her gown's good solid country-cloth. She had tried to weave her hair into the new Jerusalem fashion, and had reddened her lips and put kohl heavy about her round brown eyes.

I greeted her on my balcony, where we first had seen each other. She bowed to me, and stammered out a greeting.

"Queen Michal—live forever."

I smiled, and reached out to take her hands; I was as excited as she. "Do not be so silly—I am Michal, and you are Bathsheba. And none of us will live forever!"

"Oh—but they said—your servants—" She stopped and looked down, and her cheeks grew pinker. She was soft and round as a rabbit, and as timid.

"Do not trouble yourself; I will speak to them. We two are friends, are we not?"

Bathsheba looked up at me then. She smiled, and sunlight danced in the dark pools of her eyes. "Oh, yes! That is, I shall always be your friend, O my queen. It is a great honor."

"Honor is a game for men; I would rather have a friend who loved me."

"But you are the queen! Everyone must love you."

I laughed, then; I could not help it. Bathsheba was so young, and her paint and spangled veil only made her look younger still. "I am no queen," I said. "I am only a woman, as you are. Come and sit beside me, and let us talk."

We sat upon the padded bench; Bathsheba folded her hands in her lap and stared at me round-eyed. At first she could not believe I wished to hear what she might say. Well, I was almost a dozen years older than she—and, as she kept telling me, the queen. I do not know what she thought that made me other than a woman; my mother's neighbors had never gone wide-eyed in awe of her, when my father Saul was king.

But I had been right, Bathsheba was alone and lonely in Jerusalem. She was pleased enough to talk freely, once she lost her shyness. And that first day, I learned almost all there was to know about Bathsheba, and her husband Uriah.

Bathsheba was from the hill country to the north and east; she had been married at fourteen.

"But that was last harvest—and this summer I shall be fifteen."

"I, too was married at fourteen," I said. "Twice."

"Oh, yes—I have heard the songs—Michal." She still thought it vast daring to say my name.

"Do not believe every tune you hear sung by the wind."

Bathsheba looked at me like a startled doe, and I heard myself as I must sound to her ears. Harsh and bitter. Soon I would have lines around my mouth like Abigail's, drawing down—Phaltiel's face was suddenly clear before me. A face whose lines were etched by smiles, a face that was never still and cold—

And then I saw myself mirrored against the sunlight in Bathsheba's eyes. The painted queen, with gems upon her arms and gold upon her forehead.

"I have tired you," said Bathsheba hastily. "I have talked too long—Uriah always tells me I chatter so! I am sorry; I will go." There were tears welling up in her eyes; already the kohl was streaking down her lower lids.

"No," I said, and put out my hand to clasp hers. On my wrist the brass bangle she had sent me caught fire from the sun, blazing like true gold. "No, you have not tired me, truly you have not. It was only the sun in my eyes that made me look so."

She was willing to accept that excuse, of course. She blinked back her tears and saw the bangle. For a moment I thought she would weep again for sheer delight. "Why, you still wear it!"

"Yes," I said. "It is my favorite jewel, for I know it is the most precious. Now tell me how you came to have it."

Bathsheba told me eagerly, and when she had done so, I understood much.

About Uriah I had been twice wrong. Uriah was neither poor, nor ungenerous—but he was ambitious. The bangle had been a token, of a sort. But not as I had dreamed; out of my own need, I had spun tales as if I were David. The truth was that Uriah had staked all on one throw.

"When he heard that King David needed men, he thought he could do better here, in Jerusalem. But Uriah has always been very clever—" Bathsheba sounded proud, yet puzzled; she was not clever, only good. "He said that if he brought men and arms of his own he would rise quickly, and then we would be rich and I would have everything I wanted. So he took my dowry-gold and gave me that in token." She pointed at my wrist. "He said he would change it for true gold and rock-crystal when he made his fortune with the king."

"And did Uriah say when that might be?" I was careful to speak light, and smile. So Uriah would make his fortune with Bathsheba's dowry-gold; with what was to be hers and her daughter's after her! Yes, and if Uriah made only bones upon a battlefield, his widow would have nothing but the gown she stood in.

"I do not know. Uriah said I must be good and patient, and wait. But we have been married almost a year, now."

She did not think to ask me if I would speak for Uriah to the king. Bathsheba was too innocent for that, and still young enough to think merit counted for all in the king's court.

"A year! Then I am sure Uriah's fortune will be made soon," I said, and smiled again. I rose to my feet. "The sun is setting, and so I must let you go."

"Oh, I am sorry," said Bathsheba. She jumped up quickly, and bowed. "It has been a great—"

I held up my hand and shook my head. Bathsheba blushed, and smiled, and finished shyly, "You have been very kind, Michal."

"You are easy to be kind to, Bathsheba. Will you come again, to keep me company?"

"Oh, yes!" Bathsheba's eyes glowed in the slanting evening light. "And—perhaps—if the queen would honor me—if you would care to visit my house—but it is not what you are accustomed to, and—"

"Accustomed to!" I laughed, and could not stop until I saw Bathsheba was about to cry, poor girl. Then I put my arms around her. "Do you think I was born with a crown upon my head and gems upon my feet? My father was a farmer first and a king next, and I have lived all my life in farmer's houses. I will visit you if I may, and gladly, and will only hope you will not be too grand for me!"

I did not know if David would let me go outside the palace walls; I would not think of that now. I kissed Bathsheba's cheek before she went away. When she had gone my rooms were empty; lifeless. Even my women seemed false, like dolls.

"Bring me a mirror," I said. And when my mirror was brought, I held the ivory handle in my hand and stared for long minutes into the polished silver. Of all the grief and pain and anger I suffered, I saw nothing yet. And I saw again myself mirrored in Bathsheba's wide eyes. *The queen in all her glory.* I wondered what Zhurleen had seen, when she had looked into my face. I wondered what Phaltiel would see, if he looked upon me now.

After a moment, I set the mirror aside. I turned, and looked at my maids. I did not even know all their names. It had not seemed important.

"You," I said to the nearest. I had to point at her; I did not know her, although she had served me many months. For the first time I felt shame. It was not their fault I was here. "What is your name?"

"Narkis, O Queen." Narkis looked wary, as if she feared I might strike out, as if I were a beast only half-tame.

"Narkis." I studied her, matching name to face to know again. She had a closed face; watchful. "I wish to send Bathsheba a jug of wine—good wine, well seasoned. See to it."

"Now, O Queen?" Narkis had testing eyes. She would be cautious before she was proud.

"Yes," I said, and smiled at her. "Do it now, Narkis. And you, Chuldah—"

There was such a stone in my throat I could hardly say the words; Chuldah watched me, waiting. *That one,* I thought. *That one must go. I will not have her serve me.*

"Yes, O Queen?" Chuldah sounded like a mother impatient with a backward child.

I swallowed, hard, and spoke. "Go," I said. "Go and tell King David that Queen Michal would speak with him. Tell him—tell the king there is a favor that his queen would ask."

CHAPTER 15

"And David sent and
inquired after the woman."

—II SAMUEL 11:3

I do not think that anything else I ever did pleased David as much as did that message. He did not come to me himself, or send for me, which was all I had asked or expected. But then, David was always one to make a great show even of small things. So now he sent a servant to me to say that whatsoever I desired, that I should be granted, even unto half his kingdom.

The man knelt at my feet before the gateway to my own courtyard and spoke David's words loud and clear, a clanging bell that all must heed. Women came to their own gates to listen, and to look sharp at me.

A tiny harp upon a chain hung about the man's neck. King David's badge. A little thing of carved and gilded wood, to remind all men of how King David had been raised up from lowliness. I looked at the gilded token, not at the man's face.

"That is good of the king, and generous," I said. "But it is only a small thing I would ask. Something between a wife and husband only. Thank the king, and tell him I—tell him that his queen asks him to come to her."

The man bowed his head low over his knee and went away again, obedient to my command. I turned slowly and walked back through the gate of ebony and ivory that guarded my courtyard. I did not look around to see which women had watched, and which had whispered. It did not matter; they all would know David's message and my answer by day's end. It was what David had intended, after all.

"Close the gate," I said, and walked on, into my rooms, to prepare myself for David's coming.

~

"A captain! Uriah is to be a captain in the king's host—captain of full fifty men! He sent me word, and this!" Bathsheba held out her left hand; silver chains circled her wrist. Then she looked at me, and blushed, and pulled back her hand. "But I am foolish—Uriah always calls me so—this bracelet is nothing, only—"

"Only a sign of your husband's regard, which makes dross gold," I said, and smiled at her. I did not deny that she was foolish, for she was. But there are far worse faults than loving folly. And I thought Uriah might have sent his wife a finer gift than a few silver chains.

"Uriah was right," she went on, excited as if it were her wedding day. "The king himself must have seen him fight—or perhaps Joab did, he commands the host, you know—"

"Yes, I know." I did not check her, only listened, smiling, as she chattered on. While she talked, I absently whirled my ivory spindle, drawing thread I knew I would never use. Still, I found the motion soothing; I had spun a league's length since Phaltiel's death.

I had known Bathsheba less than a month, and already she was dear to me. I watched her now, content in her happiness. Never would it occur to Bathsheba that my interest, and not Uriah's merit, had earned her husband this honor. David had kept his word. I wondered, as I idly spun, what else I might ask, and be granted.

It took so little to please Bathsheba that I would do much for her. To come to the palace, to walk through its tiled halls and fragrant gardens, to run my jewels through her plump fingers as if gems were precious water—this was joy to her, and Bathsheba made no pretense that it was not. She walked into my life all wide-eyed and trusting, like a kitten new-come into a house.

A maidservant paused in the doorway, waiting. I shook my head, and the maid went away again. My servants walked meeker now that I watched their steps.

Bathsheba had not even noticed the maid; she was too proud of Uriah and what he had achieved. "And the king—King David himself, Michal!—spoke to Uriah, and told him he had heard great things of him. The king himself!"

David had gone to the army in the field soon after I had asked my favor of him; he had not been back to Jerusalem since. I was glad of it. If David stayed always with his army, it would please me well. Then I would not have to face him, and see him smile at me, and know he thought that he had won.

"Well," I said, when at last Bathsheba stopped to take a sip of cooled wine, "that is great news indeed."

"Oh, you are laughing at me now. But yes, it is great news. Now—"

"Now you shall have everything you were promised," I said, and laid aside my spindle and thread. "Come, and I will show you some new cloth I have—it is from a land far to the east, and never have I seen anything like it—it is like woven firelight. No, leave the spindle as it lies—I prefer tangles to be of my own making!" And I laughed as I said it; it was only a jest, and a small one. I forgot the words as soon as they were spoken. I did not know that our thread was already knotted past unraveling.

~

The summer that I first saw Bathsheba sitting on her housetop King David's army was besieging Rabbah, chief city of the Ammonites. Another war—hardly worth a mention at the well. Bathsheba and I spoke of it only when we spoke of her husband Uriah, which was not often. He rarely sent her messages, and she seemed content enough without him.

"Oh, he is a good enough man, I suppose, Michal—but—"

"But not what you dreamed of as a maiden in your father's house?"

She shook her head. "I know he is a good man, but he never talks of love, only of war, and of the future. Always it is wait, and later it will be better, and then I shall have fine gowns and maids to wait upon me. But that is not what I want—well, of course it would be very pleasant to have such things too. But he is always away, always fighting—and of course he always wins, but—" She stopped, and for a moment she would not look up at me.

But suppose he does not? Suppose he is injured, suppose he dies? That was what Bathsheba feared, and would not say. *Yes*, I thought, *and Uriah has spent the gold that was hers, gold meant to keep her all the days after her husband was dead. And she does not even think of that!*

And then a thought flashed through my mind like crystal through water. *You are queen, Michal. If Uriah falls in battle, take Bathsheba into your own household. Does not David always swear he will give whatsoever you ask?* The thought flared swift and bright; it startled me.

At last Bathsheba looked up, and her eyes were very bright. And what she said was, "But why can he never speak to me of love?"

"I do not know." To tell truth, I was still turning that new thought over in my mind, judging its merit as I would judge a melon in the market. "Who can say why men act as they do?"

Then she looked at me, full of hope. "Perhaps you can tell me what I should do, to make Uriah love me. Everyone says that King David kisses the dust beneath your sandals. I have heard the songs about him and you." She said this last almost in a whisper, as if the songs were secrets that I might not have heard.

"Everyone is wrong," I said. "That is not what life is like, Bathsheba. And from all you have said, Uriah loves you well enough. Hot love makes cold marriage, in the end. Uriah is kind to you, is he not?" At least, from all I had heard, Uriah was not cruel—I thought it would be hard to be cruel to Bathsheba.

"Oh, yes, he is kind enough. But he is so *dull*." Bathsheba sighed and her mouth drooped, and I laughed. Bathsheba was so young—no older than I had been when I first had married David.

"Easy for you to laugh," she said, hurt. "You, who are married to King David!"

"Yes," I said. "You are right—that is nothing to laugh at."

She looked at me with eyes like a startled dove. She was sweet as spring-water; bitterness frightened her. So I smiled, and then we talked of other things. I had learned long ago that a kind heart is better than a clever tongue.

~

Bathsheba eased my heart more than she knew, or would have believed. She liked to hear palace-talk and bright tales—well, I told her what I could, and one day I spoke of Zhurleen. A Philistine concubine, I said, liking to see Bathsheba's eyes grow round and eager.

"A clever woman who was kind to me when—when I was new-come to Jerusalem. She gave me much wise advice." It was not Zhurleen's fault that I had been too frightened and angry to heed her. Yes, and too foolish as well.

"A Philistine concubine—oh, Michal—what was she like? I— I have never seen one," Bathsheba confided, as if such lack were a shame to her.

"All paint and silver bells—and she did not wear her hair braided, but in long curls falling down her back, like this." I traced a ringlet down the air, spiral upon spiral. "And she dyed her hair with henna leaves so that it was red as pomegranate seeds, and when she walked her curls danced like snakes."

"And did she worship strange gods?"

"I do not know, Bathsheba. We never spoke of gods, only of men." I thought of Zhurleen laughing, and of Abigail's sour triumph when she had told me how Zhurleen was gone, and where. "But she is gone, now."

"Gone? Where?"

I stared at my hands. "I do not know." Nor did I know why I had spoken of Zhurleen at all; I could not tell sweet Bathsheba the truth.

"To another king?"

"Yes. Perhaps to another king."

Bathsheba sighed happily. "So beautiful and so clever—and so wicked," she added hastily. "Oh, Michal—I wish *I* might turn life about my fingers as I wished!"

And as I stared at Bathsheba, one of the weights pressing upon my heart eased. *So beautiful, and so clever*—for an instant I saw Zhurleen shape the air with her swaying hips and serpent hair. Yes, if any woman could twist life and men round her rosy fingers, it was Zhurleen.

Perhaps she now belonged to another king, as Bathsheba had said; perhaps she had found a better friend than I to aid her. *Perhaps*—hope only, but hope is better than despair, a lamp lit against darkness.

I smiled, and put my hands on Bathsheba's shoulders, and kissed her. "You are better than wine for joy, Bathsheba. I swear I could not live content without you near to teach me wisdom."

Bathsheba blushed, and stammered, and begged me not to be foolish—"For I am *not* clever, Michal—I have always known that. Why, even my husband says so. It is you who are as wise as you are beautiful."

"No," I told her. "I am a fool and a coward—and it is the malachite and kohl and lapis-dust that are beautiful. What you possess is worth twice all I have."

Bathsheba did not believe me, of course. But she was pleased. So she laughed, and blushed, and promised to come every day, since I asked it.

Yes, it was very pleasant to have once more a woman whom I could call friend.

And it was twice pleasant to walk freely once more. That, too, I owed to Bathsheba.

"Come with me to the market—there is a new spice merchant selling the oddest things! Come see the new gate—there is a statue of a winged bull sent all the way from Asshur and the priests say it is idolatrous and so everyone has come to gaze upon it."

But I would not; I did not wish to ask any more favors of David. Not for my own sake.

"Come to my house—it is a humble place, but you said you would come gladly—"

Ah, that was harder to refuse. What could I say? "I am the queen, but I may not walk where I wish." "I am the queen, and a prisoner." "No, Bathsheba, I cannot come to your house."

I looked at Bathsheba and said none of those things. "Yes, I will come, and gladly, if I may. I will tell you tomorrow—and do not ask me any questions now."

I had thought it would be hard, to ask David for anything. But I had done so twice already: once for Caleb's sake, and once again for Bathsheba's. The third time was almost easy. I did not even need to look into David's eyes.

For when I summoned my courage and sent a message to David, David sent back a man bearing a fine jasper ring and the words that the king was too busy to see the queen. Perhaps that night—but today the Ammonite war ate the king's time—the king knew the queen would understand, and forgive—

"—and if you would send the king words now, O Queen, I can repeat them just as they fall from your lips. Each word, not one forgotten."

I slid the jasper ring upon my finger without looking at the jewel. "Thank the king for his gift. And tell him that the queen would visit the house of the woman Bathsheba. That is all."

And the king's words came back to me from David, each word, not one forgotten.

"David's queen may walk where she pleases within the city. Only ask, O Queen, and have it granted to you."

~

Everyone is a little mad when the summer wind blows fire across the land. Then even air cannot be still and dances hot before the eyes. The summer wind had lasted a week, the last time it burned across Jerusalem. This time—who could say? It had begun three days ago, and even talk of wars and weddings bowed aside to give the weather pride of place.

I had gone to sit on Bathsheba's housetop, hoping it might be cooler than my own. It was not, but at least *her* roof was shaded by the palace, and we had done what we could. We had piled our hair high and I had brought peacock-feather fans as wide as a cart-wheel. They did little good, for the air was thick and damp as a bath sponge. Sweat ran down our faces and backs and breasts until our thin linen gowns clung wet to skin.

"Oh, Michal, it is so hot!" Bathsheba's lament was almost con-stant—she was a hill girl from beyond Lake Kinneret, and this was her first city summer. "Why, the women at the well told me that if you leave a shield or a mirror in the sun for an hour at noon you can fry meat on it after, and that the soldiers always cook their food so in summer. Is it true?"

I laughed and shook my head. "They say so every summer—but the only thing that will fry is your hand when you take up your mirror again." I waved the peacock fan again, slowly, and the royal feathers glittered. "And they say every summer that it is the hottest that even their grandfather can remember, but that is not true either."

Bathsheba stared at me round-eyed. "Do you mean it can grow hotter than this?"

"Oh, yes—but the heat does not last forever. Take heart, in another month at most you will sleep cool at night."

"A month? Another month of this? Oh, I shall die of it!"

I thought the poor girl would burst into tears for fear of roasting to death on the spot. I could think of nothing that would ease her, and then I looked at the cistern in the corner of the roof. The stone vessel was deep, still full from the last rains; the water stored within would be cool—or at least cooler than the air. I set down my fan and took Bathsheba's from her hot damp fingers.

"Come," I said, and pointed to the cistern. "It is too hot for talk—and there is cool water. I will pour for you, and you for me."

Bathsheba hesitated, and looked up across the way to the palace. I laughed and began to unpin my gown. "Do not worry, no one will see. That is my balcony, and mine alone, and I am here."

I looked up, then; high stone walls hid what lay behind them from prying eyes below. Sun-glare on stone dazzled the eye and hid still more. The queen's balcony was far away from the world of women's housetops. My skin was suddenly chill under the sweat.

"But—your serving-women—"

When Bathsheba spoke the chill vanished; I laughed again. "Have seen women before, and often. We are all alike in the bath. Oh, come—if I am not too proud to serve as your bath-maid, are you too proud to serve as mine?"

She came, then. She truly did not wish to fight the water's cool lure any more than I—and she was still young enough to wish to be thought more worldly than she was.

~

After that Bathsheba bathed often on her housetop when the wind was hot and the sun cruel. I warned her it was folly to use cistern water so freely, but she was young enough to still think the moment everything. So I held my tongue; the summer was hard on her, and I could order her house given water, if it came to that.

Was I not the queen, after all?

And so I wove disaster, all unknowing. I liked to go to Bathsheba's house; the dwelling was small and full of homely comforts, and what I thought myself used to. Bathsheba was my friend, as Miriam had once been, and Zhurleen. I should have remembered, and taken greater care; I drew eyes to Bathsheba. David's eyes. And I think, now, that David knew what he would do long before the day he came to my balcony and saw Bathsheba bathing there below, with her dark hair piled upon her head and all her skin bright with water in the harsh white sun.

~

The day burned hotter even than all those searing days before it; the sky was a glowing bronze cauldron over the city trapped beneath. I had gone to Bathsheba and we did nothing but stand naked and pour water over each other. The cistern water was warm as blood now, but we cherished it as if the liquid were melted snow fresh from the high hills.

I was trickling the precious water down Bathsheba's back when she squeaked and jumped like a trapped mouse. "Michal—a man watches us—see, on your balcony!"

I knew before I turned and looked; it was David, of course. No other man would stand on the queen's balcony. Even through the heat-hazy air I could feel his eyes upon us.

Bathsheba stood as if struck to stone. "Oh, Michal—is that the king?"

"Yes," I said, and stood between Bathsheba and David's eyes. "I am sorry, Bathsheba—I thought him still at Rabbah."

"He is gone. Oh, but he is beautiful, Michal—he was golden as glass in the sun. You are the most fortunate of women, to be queen to such a king!"

"Bathsheba, listen to me. Do not bathe here during the day until I send you word your roof is safe from prying eyes once more."

"Do not worry. The king will not look at me, when he has you." Her dove's eyes were soft as morning mist.

I wanted to slap sense into her foolish pretty head. Once I might have, but I was older now, and knew it would do no good. Bathsheba was blinded by David's glory, as I once had been. So I kissed her instead, before I went back to the palace, and told myself it could do Bathsheba little harm to dream of David.

And that much was true enough; the harm would come if David dreamed of her. A king's dreams need not cease with waking. It worried me, that thought. Then I thought of the good captain Uriah, who had brought King David ten well-armed men, and now captained fifty.

David was not a fool. Never would he risk anything for a woman. No, not even though, as Zhurleen had once laughingly told me, he had a taste for them. Well, and so did all men; what was that, after all, but the way a man was made?

You fret over nothing, Michal, I told myself. *Nothing. David looked upon her, that is all.*

But still I was uneasy. And I wished with all my heart that I had been close enough to see David's eyes when he had looked upon Bathsheba.

⁓

David came to me that night. He could not keep away, he said. "When a man has been in battle, he thinks of his wife."

"And when he is with his wife, he thinks of battle? Then he will never be satisfied."

"Oh, I am well content. You have made me so." He lay there beside me, with his hands upon my body, and asked, as I had feared he would. "Who is the woman I saw you with today? Is that your Bathsheba?"

"The wife of Uriah the Hittite," I said. "Yes, that is Bathsheba."

"I had not heard she was so beautiful. She is like a dove of the rocks." He stroked my breast; I lay quiet.

"Yes, she is beautiful," I said. "But take care how you praise her—I do not think Uriah would like to know his king had looked so upon his wife." I kept my voice light, to show I knew David's words were no more than idle talk, leaves blown by the wind.

David smiled as if he knew more than I. "If Uriah's wife did not wish to be looked upon, she would not bathe naked in the sunlight."

"I, too, bathed naked in the sun. Would you say the same of me?"

"You? A man would be too dazzled to lift his eyes to you. You are an idol to worship, all gold and honey in the sun—"

But when David wove words into pretty patterns, I no longer listened. "Bathsheba is a good country girl, chaste and modest. She followed only where I led her, safe on her own housetop where no man could see."

"No man save the king."

"No," I said. "No man save the king."

"Well, the king's eyes alone will not ravish her—a royal look, they say, brings luck."

David's eyes were hot; something seemed to lurk there. Something that hungered. I looked into those eyes, and hoped he lusted only for Bathsheba. That was a clean lust, a man's lust. That, at least, was something I could understand.

"Do you go back soon to Rabbah, to the siege?" I was so eager to turn his mind from Bathsheba that I hardly knew what I said.

"No," he said. "No, not soon. Joab can do all that is needful there, for a time."

~

I had been right to fear; I had not dreamed David would truly be so foolish. But he was. All his own women—his queen, his wives, his concubines, his handmaidens—all these women were not enough. No, David must have Bathsheba.

He sent for her; he lay with her; he could not sleep for love of her. He burned hot for her; hotter than the summer wind. So hissed palace whispers. Kings with many servants have few secrets.

I learned of his new folly from David himself. He came to me late one night and I smelled chypre and sweet spice when he embraced me. A perfume that had not suited me; I had given the perfume to Bathsheba and combed it into her long dark hair myself. She had been pleased with the scent and twice pleased because it was my gift. She always wore it now.

So I knew, then, but said nothing to David. And I knew, too, why Bathsheba's cheeks had burned red as country poppies when I last spoke to her; why her eyes had not met mine; why I had seen her so little for the past two weeks.

Why today she had sent to say she could not come to me at all, and that I must not go to her.

Ill; Bathsheba had said she was ill. Now I called her illness by its true name: David.

～

The next morning I questioned my maids. They had heard, they told me. But rumors only, O Queen! They had not dared to tell me.

"To spare me pain? How much more pain for me when others can mock my blindness?" I looked at them all, and knew true obedience now lay in the balance. After today either I ruled them or they me. I stood quiet a moment and then slapped Narkis.

She wept, though the blow had been light, and swore they had kept silent only for love of me.

"Fine love, that leaves me naked to scorn and laughter! Did you think I did not know, or would not find out? Now go, and remember you serve a queen, not some sniveling village wife!"

They fled away like deer, all but Narkis, whom I called back. My blow had smeared the paint upon her cheek; I held out my hand so that she might wipe away the carmine from my fingers. She did so carefully; I watched her, and waited until she had done.

Then I said, "Chuldah no longer serves me. Do you know why?"

"Because she displeased you, O Queen." Narkis bowed her head, meek at last.

"No," I said. "That is not the reason. Chuldah no longer serves me because she was foolish, and thought the crown the woman. Do you understand?"

Narkis eyed me straight. Pale eyes, like a hawk's; proud but cautious. At last she said, "Someone who would serve Michal, and not the queen's crown . . ."

"Would be rewarded," I said.

Still Narkis waited, eyes downcast and hooded now. What had I ever done, that Narkis should believe me? I turned the memories of my life here in the king's house over in my mind, like pebbles in the hand. Most were dull and ugly things, harsh to touch even now. But here and there among them were some that shone white; gleams of alabaster, smooth and pleasing.

"Do you remember a woman called Zhurleen?" I asked at last. "A dark woman, comely, from Philistia?"

Narkis looked up quickly; the caution was back. Well, it was an odd question, from a woman Narkis already thought half-mad. She nodded. "Yes. I remember her."

"And so do I." I paused. "But the king does not. My memory is longer than his."

And then we both looked at each other, plainly, like two housewives judging pigeons for the stew-pot. I smiled.

"Oh, I do not go against the king," I said. "But the king is far away from the women's quarters; I am here. You know what trust the king places in me—and so I do not wish always to be running after him, whining and beseeching, like the Lady Abigail."

I looked sharp as I said that; Narkis looked down again, tapped the silver bracelets upon her slender wrist. The bangles rang together, small sweet noise. "The Lady Abigail speaks against you."

"Yes." Even I knew that, and I had gone half-blind and half-deaf this last year. And then I tried to think what next to say.

Never before had I tried to win someone like this; a task as delicate as bringing a wild bird to hand. I did not know how it might be done, save to speak frank truth, as Zhurleen had once spoken to me. But Zhurleen had spoken truth, and still I had not believed. I had not wished to. I must make Narkis wish to believe;

I despaired, for I did not know how. I was tired; I could not do this; I nearly shrugged and turned away from Narkis. And then I found words sliding unbidden from my lips.

"Abigail is not important. She is neither good nor wise—and her son Chileab is a lazy fool, too easy content. Chileab will not be the next king." It was as if another spoke for me, answering my need.

Narkis was listening now, head tilted, hand closed over the silver bracelets to silence them. I smiled, and spoke on.

"David is king now, and that is a wonder and a glory to our people. But who will follow him?" Until I asked, I myself had never wondered; I had not cared.

But now I knew it was a question that many must ask, including David himself. Yahweh had chosen King Saul—so the prophet Samuel had said; Yahweh had chosen King David—so David had said. Would King David sit idle on his throne and let Yahweh choose a third time? I heard Zhurleen's laughter in my ears, low and throaty; I heard her soft voice that sounded of wave and ocean saying, *"With NATHAN for his prophet? O Queen, live forever—and do not be a fool!"*

Do not be a fool. A man does not build up a fine house—or a great kingdom—only to fling his prize to owls and wolves. No, men build for their sons, and their sons' sons.

And King David had many sons; one of them would rule after him. But which? They were all only boys still, unformed; Amnon, the eldest, not yet twelve. But boys became men; if the choice were equal between them all, what then?

The answer slid into my mind smooth and brilliant as a little viper. I smiled.

"To serve the queen is much," I said to Narkis. "And how much more to serve the mother of the next king? A woman must think of her future. Do you wish to serve the future, or the past?"

As I spoke, I laid both my hands flat upon my stomach, and I smiled. I did not say I was with child; I was not so foolish. But I meant to make her think of that, and she did.

Now she bowed. "How may I serve you, O Queen?"

"Bring me words, Narkis. Bring me the well-talk and the market gossip. I would know what men say in the streets, and women on their housetops." I had been blind, and deaf; now I wished to see and hear. I would try Narkis, and see if she might be trusted. "Tell me what they say of the king, and Bathsheba—but tell no one what I know. And twice do not tell Bathsheba."

Narkis regarded me steadily and swore that she would do as I bade her. "All that you ask, O Queen—and I do not see why the king must turn to that woman when he has you to comfort him. She is only a silly girl, and everyone knows her husband is a Hittite!"

"That is no secret, and not Bathsheba's fault. Now go, and remember, when you think to serve me, that Bathsheba is my friend, and that I love her dearly." And I gave Narkis a brooch, hammered gold set with turquoise, to seal our bargain.

When Narkis had gone and I was alone, one thought beat in my mind, hard and steady as a smith beating out a new-forged blade. There was one son of King David's who would surely be the king who came after. *Must* be king after; the king David had schemed for, had murdered for. My son.

The son David would never have.

I had told him, when first he had brought me here. *I am barren*, I had said. *You will get no son on me.* But David would listen only to himself and his desires. And for all his demands to Yahweh, my body remained as flat and barren as it had all the years I lay with my husband Phaltiel.

No, David would never hold up my son and claim him for his own. That at least Yahweh denied to the great King David.

"Ten years married and no child," I told the air, as I had once told David; the air listened as well as he. "So much, David, for your house of kings!"

~

I was not the first to know of King David's latest folly, but neither was I the last. David never cared to hide his light under a bushel, as they say on the farms—

"—and the woman Bathsheba's eyes show all. She might as well embroider her secret upon her veil in scarlet and hang it from her house wall. A silly little girl playing at—" Narkis looked at me and shut her mouth over her next words.

I looked steadily at Narkis for a heartbeat, then smiled—but only a little. "So it is known."

"And well known, O Queen—at least among her neighbors. But they will not speak—"

"Against the king," I finished for her. No one would ever speak against David; all the world saw was the golden king. Yahweh's beloved. "And I suppose half the palace knows as well."

Narkis grew cautious. "He sends for her, O Queen. And she is brought to him."

There was nothing else to say, then; I smiled upon Narkis, and thanked her, and sent her away again. And when Narkis had gone, I picked up my ivory spindle and twirled it. The soft rush and whirl soothed me and aided thought.

I could not stop David; I knew that. And I did not blame Bathsheba; she was young and he was the king, after all. I knew the silly girl was dazzled as if David were the sun, and she thought him all the world and all her heart. And I knew she was afraid that I would guess her secret; I could not tell her that I knew, and did not care. Bathsheba was too innocent of all that could be between a man and a woman to believe that truth.

Neither could I warn her against David. I had once been that young and hot for love, and would listen to no one. Words from me now would do no good, and much harm. For King David would tire of her, and her husband would return; then Bathsheba would need the queen's friendship. I did not want her to be afraid to come to me and ask it.

~

CHAPTER 16

". . . and the woman said,
I am with child."

—II Samuel 11:4-5

Narkis did all I asked of her, and more. She brought me the street-news and the well-gossip, as I had asked her; she also brought me the whispers and slanders of the women's quarters. That was when I learned how Queen Michal was seen through the eyes of others.

"They say you are proud, and cold as ice, and hold the king's heart by sorcery."

"Who says so?"

Narkis lowered her eyes. "Need the queen ask?"

"Abigail," I said. "She should know better; that will not please the king, should he hear of it."

"Shall he hear of it, O Queen?"

I shook my head. "No; Abigail is unhappy, that is all, and through no fault of mine."

"Perhaps he should hear, O Queen. Abigail says also that you keep the king's desire hot by unnatural arts. That—"

I laughed. "Unnatural arts! What are they?"

"Abigail does not say."

"Because she does not know, any more than I! This is not Egypt! What else does Abigail say?" I was angry, but I would not let Narkis see that I cared. Abigail did not speak to me; David had seen to that. But he had not stopped her venomous tongue.

"She says also that you procured the woman Bathsheba to

serve his lusts, flaunting her at him as a gift. And that you use unnatural means to deny the king a son." Narkis twirled her bracelets; she was still uneasy with me, and thought to hide it so. "Abigail hints at other things as well."

"Abigail seems to know overmuch of the unnatural for a good woman! I will not even ask what those means are, for fear she will tell me." I smiled, and kept my voice even, like poured cream. I was two women now, as David had made me; one Michal lived fever-hot within the second Michal's thick skin of ice. It was the second Michal that Narkis saw. It was the second Michal who laughed, and turned away, careless.

"Abigail says so-and-such! Well, and you may tell any who care that I spend half my days begging Yahweh to grant me the king's son for my own!" I laughed and sent Narkis away, and then I sat upon my balcony and stared out, down at Bathsheba's housetop. Bathsheba was not there; I had not expected to see her.

Abigail's hissing was nothing; if others believed her, that belief was much. I was alone in this house, alone save for Bathsheba. And I did not see Bathsheba now; I knew she was ashamed to face me, and so I did not ask her to come to me. It would have been cruel. But I longed to see her, for I was lonely—

Do not be a fool. How many women dwelt beneath King David's roof? How many wives, concubines, handmaids? They were not all my enemies—and I was the queen. If I sat here alone it was by my own choice, not theirs.

If the palace women knew me only by the lies Abigail chose to scatter—well, that too had been my own doing. What else did they know of me, after all? King Saul's daughter, King David's queen, who for pride kept to her own courtyard and never spoke.

And so I left my balcony and went to sit beside the fountain in my courtyard. I had the ebony gate thrown wide to the open hall beyond. And when a woman passed by the gate, walking slowly and slanting her eyes to see in, I raised my hand and called to her, and asked her to come and bear me company.

~

Abigail stayed away from my courtyard, as did some of David's other wives, out of spite and jealousy. But others did not. I was the queen, King David flung jewels before my feet. That was enough to bring some to me; others came because the gate to my courtyard now stood open. Some were curious, some were friendly. Some wished favors of David and hoped that I would speak in their favor. All were only women, no different from my friends in the little village of Gallim.

I invited them to my courtyard; I went to theirs. Their world was mine, now, and I must learn its ways as I once had learned Gallim's.

And so I began, a stitch at a time, to mend the rent I had torn between myself and the other women. Visits and gifts and gossip. Little things, women's things.

I did not suddenly beam upon them and chatter, and press gems into their hands. I went slowly; I was the newcomer still, though I had spent two years within these walls; I must take care. But I learned their names, and their joys and sorrows, and I taught them that I was not too proud to share in them. It was hard, at first—but then one of the concubines who was with child was brought early to childbed.

Narkis had brought me word, and I had gone to the woman. I did not listen to those who cried out in horror when I appeared; I had delivered babies enough in Gallim to be a comfort to those who labored in childbed. My hands had cradled a dozen children into the world. Now they once more held and urged and comforted; the child was safe born and the mother lived.

"Do not be foolish," I said after, when I was praised as much as if I had raised the woman from the dead to breathe again. "In Gallim my neighbors said that I had good strong hands, and that is all birthing takes!"

That, and a calm voice, which many do not have.

"But you are the queen," one protested.

"Does a queen not breathe and bleed? If ever any woman needs me, she has only to send word. Children are more important than crowns!"

~

The summer dragged on, hot long days and hotter nights. The war too waged on, and on, and David came and went between Rabbah and Jerusalem, balancing battle and passion.

I smiled, and kept my own council on both. I knew nothing of war, save how my father had fought it, hard and clean. I could not imagine Saul laying siege to a city that had never done him any harm, as David was doing at Rabbah.

Nor could I imagine my father risking all to lie with another man's wife. As once Zhurleen had said, with a man like David there would always be a woman—but David had wives and con-cubines a-plenty. And if those did not satisfy him, well, there were always new brides to seal treaties, new pretty girls as gifts to seal favors.

Sometimes I wondered why David must have Bathsheba; I dared not ask. I thought perhaps it was the forbidden that first lured David that summer; perhaps it was the risk. Perhaps it was the pure worship in innocent eyes, as once, long years ago, the girl Michal had worshipped the shining youth who slew the Philistine giant Goliath. I was wrong. David had another use for Bathsheba's love.

~

But it seemed that even risk and worship could not hold David long; as the summer waned, so did King David's passion for Bathsheba. He loved her less, and less still, and one day Narkis murmured into my ear that it had been a week since he had gone to her. That Bathsheba wept, and waited for the king in vain.

The king's lust for Uriah's wife had ended, it seemed. David left Jerusalem again, going to Rabbah, to the war that seemed endless as the summer heat.

And when King David returned from Rabbah, angry at that city's long defiance, he came to me and never once thought of Bathsheba, who loved him with all her foolish heart. But while I stroked David's pride with soft words and his body with soft hands, I thought of her, and rejoiced, for Bathsheba had come safe from the lion's paw, with a wounded heart the only price paid.

I, too, had once been as wounded as she, and by the same man. I knew no words could heal that pain; even the kindliest eyes seemed harsh and uncaring. I remembered my cry to Phaltiel when he had sought to give me wisdom and comfort. *You do not understand!*

Perhaps Bathsheba would fling those words at me; she would be as wrong as I had been. But I would do my best to spare her more pain. I would give her time to grieve alone—and then I would go to her and tell her that I knew all, and loved her still. I knew Bathsheba; she would weep rivers upon my shoulder, and then her grief would all be over.

And then I would have back what David had stolen from me; Bathsheba and I would be friends once more. I had missed her sorely all these weeks that shame had kept her away.

~

The lady Teshura was one of King David's concubines; pretty enough, pliant enough, passionate enough to have pleased him for a time. She had asked for me, and so I had been there to hold her hand and wrap her child in fine linen. Now Teshura begged me to tell the king of his new daughter.

"Please, O Queen. Ask him only to look upon her. See—see how she resembles him. Do you see, the eyes?"

The baby was as any newborn, a miracle to its mother, small and wrinkled to the eyes of others. But I admired the child, and promised to tell the king. "And surely he will see her—as soon as he has the time, he will come."

"Yes—yes, when he can, he is very busy with the war, but he will come—" Teshura's eyes pleaded with me, but I could not reassure her. We both knew David had forgotten her almost before her waist had thickened with his child.

"I will tell him. Now rest."

I went away, more tired than I should have been from attending such an easy childbed. It was late morning, and I had been awake more than half the night. I wanted wine, and rest, and so when Narkis told me the lady Bathsheba wished to see me I was almost tempted to say that she was to go away again and come back another time.

But I did not; I said that she might come to me. And I was glad I had been kind instead of sensible, for when Bathsheba saw me she flung herself weeping at my feet. I could not understand a word she wailed, until at last I shook her hard and made her drink a cup of cooled wine.

"Now tell me, Bathsheba—and calmly—what troubles you, and I will help you."

"Oh, Michal—I am with child."

"And it is the king's."

She gaped at me as if I had turned into the Wise Serpent before her eyes. Bathsheba was good, not clever, and too frightened now to think at all. Of course half Jerusalem knew the king had gone to her by night—and by day, too, for a time.

"But no one knows—no one knew, save only you, now."

"Does the king know?"

Bathsheba shook her head. "I have sent messages, but he does not come to me—he is the king, and he has much to do, I know, but—but soon it will be too late. My husband has been gone—"

"—too long," I finished for her. "Yes, and even the dullest can count to nine!"

She flung herself down before me and clung to my knees. "And I can hardly clasp my girdles round my waist and my servant will guess and then everyone will know and then—my husband will throw me out and they will *stone* me, Michal! Please, I must talk to the king! Hate me if you like, but please, please help me!"

I could not speak, for I could not draw a full breath. Nor could I move, even to touch her hair in comfort, for I saw now how Yahweh answered a woman's prayers.

A stone to bring down King David. At last Yahweh had sent me what I had once prayed for—what I had demanded. A stone to my hand.

A stone for vengeance. With this I could bring David down as I had once sworn to do. The great king, the beloved of Yahweh, the keeper of the Law, seducing a humble soldier's wife and getting her with child while her husband fought in the king's war—oh, yes, that would make fine hearing at any time.

And such a tale would make better hearing now; it had been long months since King David had given the people a glorious victory to repay the blood and money spent on the Rabbah siege. Let the people see him as a despoiler of his neighbor's flock, a thief who let other men fight and die while he stayed safe and lay soft behind Jerusalem's walls—yes, let the people see David not as a great king but as a man who should be judged like other men, according to the Law he had so often broken.

Adultery, proven. Too many already knew of this sin. Neighbors, servants—too many for David to sing his way clear of this. The Law was clear: adultery meant stoning at the city wall for the guilty woman—and the guilty man. Ah, yes—King David could be brought lower than a dog in the gutter.

I could avenge my husband Phaltiel. I could avenge my brothers Jonathan and Ishbaal, and my father Saul. Yahweh had delivered the weapon I had sought into my hand; Yahweh's weapon lay weeping and trembling at my feet.

The weapon was Bathsheba.

I need do nothing; I need only turn away. Bathsheba's guilt would soon be plain—and David's guilt plainer. Too many people knew, and Bathsheba would name David in all innocence, trusting the king to save her.

Turn away, and all would be avenged, and vengeance would cost me nothing. All my ghosts would sleep quiet in their caves, blood-price paid at last. . . .

"I am sorry," I said, and the words were not said to Bathsheba.

For my prayer had been answered too late; I could not do it. I could not sacrifice Bathsheba. No, not even for Phaltiel's memory could I give her into the hands of the judges and the priests. *I am sorry. Forgive me, I cannot.* I knew there would be no answer; the dead are not generous.

But I was wrong.

"You are too warm for such a cold dish as that, my little princess. You are alive—choose life!" I could hear the words as plainly as if Phaltiel stood behind me and spoke them.

I bent and drew Bathsheba to her feet and wiped her face with my own veil. "I do not hate you, and no stone will ever touch you, I swear it. I will speak to King David myself. Now be calm, and smile—the king may come to see you here, and he has never liked a weeping woman. No, do not kneel and thank me—what is the use of being queen if I cannot even help my dearest friend?"

~

Bathsheba was a foolish cloud-dreamer. But David was not, and I was not, and so I thought before I ran to him. And then I called for my women and was bathed, and rubbed with oil scented with spikenard. Then I dressed as David liked to see me, as a queen, choosing what I knew would make me fair to his eyes. My robe was colored with Tyrian dye, tasseled with gold and embroidered with silver. I painted my eyes with kohl and my mouth with carmine, and my maids braided my hair with scarlet cords and crystal disks. To save Bathsheba, I must please David. And over the past two years I had learned well how to do that.

I did not think Bathsheba's life would be a hard boon to win; I did not think Bathsheba's husband valued her beyond a price the king could pay. And even if David had tired of her, why should

King David not pay whatever Uriah asked? David had a dozen wives and twice a dozen concubines; one more woman under his roof would be nothing to him.

~

The heart of the king's house was the great center court. Here David sat upon his throne of carved and gilded cedar and heard all who came before him to praise, or complain, or ask for justice. Here the work of the kingdom was done, in plain sight of all men— or at least, so all men thought. I knew better; the true work of kings and kingdoms is done in darkness and in secret, and in death.

I might have sent a messenger before me, but I knew David, and what he liked. And so I made a great show of going to him, a queenly sight to stretch men's eyes wide, and make them envy King David his wealth, and power, and his beautiful women.

I came to the great court with my head high and walked the tiles of marble and jasper that led from the doorway to the throne. There I knelt, and smiled, and begged that King David would come to Queen Michal when the court was ended, that she might speak with him upon a private matter.

All this fine show pleased David, as I had known it would. The House of Saul bowed willing to King David; that would always please him.

"The king will come," David said. I thanked him, and would have risen; David leaned forward and caught my hands and spoke low and laughing, to my ears alone. "What is this private matter, Michal?"

"If I tell it in open court the matter will no longer be private, my lord king. It will be for all men's eyes and ears soon enough." I bent my head, as if I kissed his hands. "Come to me later, that I may beg a boon of you."

That pleased him still more; David liked me to turn to him for favors. "Whatever you ask, I will grant—have I not sworn so to you often enough? Whatever will please my queen, that shall she have. Nor shall you wait upon my pleasure, or that of any man's— they shall be gone, beyond the pillars, so that you may speak."

I swore I would happily await the king's pleasure, but David would not have it so. A padded stool was brought for me; the court was cleared, with much pushing and shouting, to make way for the queen to speak with the king. All this was what David liked—it was the great king stooping to humor a woman's whim. The gesture would sing well, and David liked life to be a song, with King David plucking the strings to set the tune.

And when at last the people were back past the pillars, and the court stretched barren and empty around us, David smiled and caught up my hand like an eager lover.

"Your private matter, Michal—shall I guess it? You are with child at last!" He seemed very sure, as if he had planned it this way. "Oh, Yahweh is good—"

"No," I said. "Not I. It is Bathsheba who is with child."

For a moment David did not answer, as if I had sung a line from a different song, one he did not know. "Bathsheba?"

"Bathsheba, the wife of Uriah. It is only a month last you went to lie with her—even you must still recall her face." I made it a jest; praise for his manly prowess.

He did not try to deny his fault. "That is true—but I swear, my queen and my heart, that she is nothing to me now."

"I care nothing for what she is to you, but she is dear to me. She carries your child, lord king. She weeps her eyes out for love of you. I told you I craved a boon of you—give your captain Uriah whatever he asks, but take Bathsheba from her husband and bring her to your house."

Again David did not answer quickly. There was a moment when all I heard was the murmur of men's voices from beyond the pillars that ringed the court. Then David said, "Even if the woman is with child, who is to say it is not her husband's?"

"All Jerusalem, for he has been gone half the year at the siege with his men—" And then I stopped, for I knew David; I saw his mind now as plain as a snake-trail through thick dust. Uriah the Hittite had come to him with ten well-armed men, and fought well for David the king. Uriah was of more importance to the king than a woman he had already possessed and tired of. But that I had known already; David cared nothing for Bathsheba. It was not the proof of that carelessness that made my skin cold.

Forty times forty David had sworn he would give me anything I asked, so long as I walked queenly and obedient. *"Anything, Michal; you have only to ask, ask, and it will be granted. The king's word on it."* I had kept my part of that bargain; why did David now seem to set his vow aside?

Was Uriah worth more to David than I? I looked into David's face; his eyes slid away and would not meet mine.

I did not weep or wail or revile him; I tried to think as David might. David had not yet said he would not grant this. Why, then, had he spoken so? Why hint that he might deny me what I had asked?

Think as David might—Even if Uriah did not value Bathsheba for herself, no man wished to be dishonored in his own house; Uriah might give Bathsheba to David, but the hurt to Uriah's pride would fester. Uriah was a good soldier, worthy of the captaincy he had been given. David would not risk losing Uriah's goodwill— and his well-armed men—over Bathsheba.

And there was another thing: if the king were known to set his hands upon his soldier's women while they went out to fight and die, who would serve him? Yes, that was what David must be thinking now. It was a great pity he had not thought of that before he had broken Bathsheba's foolish loving heart.

But Uriah's goodwill would be lost once the Law took Bathsheba and she named her child's father. Then all Jerusalem would know, and soon all Israel and Judah. And men forgave David much; I had seen that many times. But this they would not forget. Sn1ear Bathsheba's good name with mud and David too would be besmirched.

The cold lifted from my skin; I had been wrong, I thought. David would not deny me this—but this time even David had been caught in his own coils. No man likes to look a fool, even to himself. Yes, I thought David would do as I wished after all. But what I asked must be done without hurt to Uriah's pride; I remembered that Uriah was ambitious.

I smiled, and put my hand on David's. "We are not children, David—you are the king, and all eyes follow your deeds."

He knew what I meant; I saw his eyes flicker. There was no way that Uriah would not know that David had lain with Bathsheba; Uriah had eyes and ears—and Bathsheba's neighbors had eyes and tongues.

"Great deeds," I added with a sidelong glance. "Bathsheba was married more than a year to Uriah with no sign of a child—until you went to her."

David smiled again; that is one flattery all men swallow easily. I only told truth, after all—David got sons as easily as songs, except on me. Then I laughed, and slanted my painted eyes at him, and told him of his fine new daughter, the Lady Teshura's child.

That pleased him too—a lusty man, as well as a great king. I knew how David liked to see himself. I had held up the mirror; now I had only to let him shine upon himself. For a heartbeat I saw myself too in that mirror. David's harlot begging gifts from him, as he once had sworn I would—was anything worth granting David that?

But I already knew the answer. And so I praised David's prowess, his kindness, his wisdom—and then I spoke again of Bathsheba.

"Poor girl," David said. But it fed his pride to think of her sick with love for him. "But what can I do? She is married to one of my good captains—a man who has fought well for me, and shed his blood for Yahweh's cause—"

I longed to say that he might have thought of that before he lay with his good captain's pretty wife, but I did not. "I beg of you, lord—can you think of nothing for poor Bathsheba? Once she is known to be with child she will be dragged before the judges and questioned in the marketplace—"

And she would name the king, and she would be believed. David knew that; I could see the knowledge in his eyes. So I waited.

"I cannot take another man's wife from his house—"

I kept my lips closed over the words I wished to spit at him.

David's scruples were like his songs; written anew for each occasion. I looked away, past him, so that he would see nothing in my eyes. Behind the gilded throne, the cat still hunted birds through painted reeds.

"All I ask, lord, is that she be safe from the Law. Her husband has been gone so long even the kindest could not think the child his."

"And well-side gossip is not kind. Tell me, how many months gone is she?"

"No more than two—perhaps a little less."

David was silent a moment; then he smiled, all kind indulgence. "Then I will send for her husband. I need fresh news from Rabbah, and Uriah is a good soldier, deserving of time spent in the comfort of his own house—and bed."

An ardent soldier stopping even one night at home with his young wife—who then could say for certain that a child, however early come, was not truly of that house and lineage? Uriah would almost surely know the truth later; ill news always spills, and Uriah, too, could reckon nine moons upon his fingers.

But I thought Uriah would hold his tongue; Uriah was an ambitious man. If the scandal could be made uncertain, be made all a matter of gossip and guesses, if his wife were known still to be Queen Michal's dearest friend—why, who else would believe the whispers, after a time? Thanks to David, all the kingdom knew I loved the king to the point of madness; would I welcome Bathsheba in my courtyard if she had been loved by David?

Yes, the scheme would work; once again David's own tale-spinning would provide proof of what had never been. It was like biting into an unhoneyed lemon to grant that, and use it.

But *this* false song would save Bathsheba from the judges and the stones. I was content with that; I praised David once again for his mercy and wisdom; I kissed his hands.

"No, it is you who are merciful, Michal." David smiled, and put his hands upon my shoulders, and kissed me upon the mouth. "You say there is still no sign *you* are with child?"

My mouth was thick-painted with carmine; I barely felt his

lips on mine. I shook my head. "No. Not yet. But do not despair, David. Yahweh will give me your son. I know it."

David smiled, all kingly confidence, and kissed me again. "I know you pray for my son nightly—and we both know Yahweh answers prayers. We will have this, too."

And then I went away. Behind me I heard a rush and clamor as the men who had waited upon the queen's pleasure surged back to their places. I did not look back; I thought of David believing I longed to hold his son cradled within my arms, and I smiled. *Yes, David, you are king indeed. But you cannot see what lies behind my eyes.*

In my own courtyard, Bathsheba was sitting as I had left her; her veil was damp with tearstains and the fringed end of her sash was twisted into knots. "Michal! Is—is the king—?"

I took her hands and spoke briskly. "No, he is not coming— not now, and just as well; he must not see you like this. You have been weeping and rubbing your eyes until they are red as—no, do not cry again, my love, all is well. Come into the garden with me, and we will talk there."

Like my courtyard, my garden too had a fountain; unlike my courtyard, my garden was quiet, away from prying eyes. Anyone who entered must come through the garden gate; anyone who sat beside the fountain must see whoever came. A quiet place, a safe place. What was said among the lilies and roses of the queen's garden could not be overheard.

When Bathsheba and I sat shielded by falling water, I told her I had gone to the king. I did not tell her all that had been said.

"Was he—was the king pleased?" Bathsheba's eyes begged for comfort; I smiled.

"What man would not be pleased? And David is fond of all his children." That was true enough—an easy fondness, as if they were pets. A large, loving family, such as King David liked to see about him; did he never think that boys became men, and girls women?

"And—oh, Michal, what did he say? Please, please tell me, or I shall die."

"Of course I shall tell you, if only you will be silent and listen." I smiled at her, and put the end of my own veil into the water filling the fountain's basin. I squeezed the wet cloth until it did not drip, and wiped Bathsheba's hot face. "Now, this is what the king said—"

I told her that David would send for her husband; I told her that she need only lie once with Uriah. "A simple thing, and then all will be well."

I thought Bathsheba would see all as easily as I did; she did not. "But Michal—I do not love Uriah, and it is the king's child. I could not do it! And Uriah would not believe it," she added.

"No, of course he will not—but the Law will be satisfied, and so will Uriah."

"But Michal, he will beat me!"

Better beating than stoning—but I did not say that to Bathsheba. "Not if he knows it is the king's child—oh, come, Uriah is not a fool. He knows the king will not forget him, if he holds his hand and his tongue. And I will stand your friend—then no one will believe evil of you."

Bathsheba stared at me, her eyes dark moons. "But the king loves me—he swore it—" Then she turned red and put a hand over her mouth. "Oh, Michal, I am sorry—I did not mean—"

"Do not be sorry. David loves you as well as he does me." I smiled, although it was hard; I did not like to see Bathsheba so hurt.

"And you do not understand—you must not be jealous—it was not like that. Why, you are the queen, and tall and beautiful, and—" She stopped, her words as tangled as the fringe of her sash.

"To David we are all beautiful." I remembered what David had said to me, long ago on our wedding night. "Why, to him you are beautiful as Bathsheba is, and not as Michal is—"

Bathsheba gasped, and tears spilled down her cheeks. She put her hands over her face and would not look at me.

I put my arms around her and rocked her as if she were my

daughter. "Bathsheba, do not cry—see, I love you still, I do not care—David has many women—he did not mean to hurt you—"

At last Bathsheba let me hold her hands and look into her face. Her eyes were swollen and red; tendrils of dark hair clung tear-wet to her neck and cheeks.

"All will come clean," I said. "Let me wash your face—see, the water is cool." Once again I used my veil to wash Bathsheba's face. "There, my love. All will be well, I swear it. Do not cry again."

"You do not understand, Michal. That is what he said to me, the first time—That I was not beautiful as you were, but—" Her lips quivered; she pressed her fingers to her mouth.

If David had been standing before me then I would have clawed his bright eyes out. My fingers clutched for something to hurt; I clenched them into my skirt. After a moment I found my voice. "He said that because it is true, Bathsheba. Do not think of David now. It is time to think of your husband. When Uriah comes, you must greet him loving, as you always did before. That is all."

I thought such counsel nothing; I did not see then how far I had come from Gallim. David and I between us had made a tangle of court cleverness and lies. But Bathsheba was sweet and simple; life had not pierced her heart and bled it dry. Even now, Bathsheba still believed in David, and in harper's tales, and in true love.

And even now, I still did not know how truly cunning David was, or how cleverly he could twist life to his bidding. I should have thought of the words of one of David's own songs: he had sharpened his tongue like a serpent; the poison of asps was under his lips.

I had thought I had learned all my lessons hard and well. But David had one lesson still left to teach.

For when I had refused Yahweh's weapon, I gave it into David's own hand. And the stone I had laid down for love David caught up again, and hurled back to strike my heart.

~

CHAPTER 17

"Send me Uriah the Hittite."

—II SAMUEL 11:6

"I could not, Michal—I could not! How could I let Uriah touch me when I love the king and carry his child beneath my heart? I tried, truly I did, but he—he sickened me. I love the king—I would rather die than let any other man touch me!"

Once again Bathsheba lay weeping in my arms. David had kept his word and sent for her husband Uriah, and Bathsheba herself had unraveled all our careful weaving. Uriah had gone to her, and she had sent him away. Uriah had not set foot into his bedroom or hand upon his wife—and Bathsheba's servant would be able to swear to it.

I listened, and could not even be angry at her folly. Once I had been as young as she; once I too had loved David and sworn I would die rather than know another man's touch.

I sighed, and stroked her hair. "Well, it is done now. So dry your eyes and tell me how you convinced your husband that he would not lie soft with you last night. When the king spoke to me, he said Uriah was hot for you—well, he had not seen you or a clean bed since the siege began, and that is some months now!"

"I—I told him he was still as a warrior in the field and he would be unclean for battle if he came to me. And I told him it was my woman's time besides, so he went down to the soldiers' tents beyond the city wall to sleep there."

"And that your head ached, too, I suppose. What a tangle!" I laughed; I could not help it. But I wondered who had told

Bathsheba of the Law for soldiers; she knew nothing of warriors and their ways. Nor did I understand why a Hittite captain should care for Yahweh's Laws. "Oh, Bathsheba—"

She began to weep again. "Do not scold me, Michal—please do not! I tried, I truly did—but I could not. Not when I saw the king again—"

David. My blood beat slow and cold, warning of danger. Do not move, it warned. Do not move lest you fall.

"—and he kissed me and told me how much he loved me—that he could not bear to think of me with another—oh, Michal, you are too good, I have sinned against you, but I never meant to—"

"Be silent," I said. "Bathsheba, what else did you tell your husband, when you sent him away from you?"

She hung her head. "I—"

"Tell me."

"I told him that the king would not like it, if he took me." Bathsheba whispered so low I could hardly hear her. "Oh, Michal—I could not lie with Uriah, loving the king. I knew the king could not truly mean to ask it of me. Please forgive me—I do not know why you are so good to me, when I have betrayed you so—"

No, I thought. *No, he cannot mean to take Bathsheba from me too.*

Bathsheba flung herself to her knees and went on begging my pardon; I was too frightened to pay her any heed. I wanted to shake Bathsheba, to slap her, to hurt her to ease my own sick fear.

At last I could speak again. "Bathsheba." I touched her hair. "Do not cry anymore, you will make yourself ill. Now be silent, and let me think."

But there was only one answer, and I knew it. Whether he wished to or no, David must now take Bathsheba into his house. It was the only thing that would save her. Somehow I must make David do so, whatever cruel game he played. I cared nothing for what it might cost David.

I did not know what it was to cost me.

~

CHAPTER 18

"Set ye Uriah in the forefront
of the hottest battle...
that he may be smitten, and die."
—II Samuel 11:15

If my rooms were a queen's, David's were twice a king's. David liked to think himself a lion, strong and bold; in his rooms wooden lions guarded doorways, painted lions prowled walls. Even his bed had a lion's paws, gold-painted. Ivory claws were set into the painted wood. Many men would be diminished by such rooms; David outshone them—so men said.

I went to David as I was, my gown still blotched dark with Bathsheba's tears. David was having his beard trimmed and curled, as if he were a Philistine prince. When he saw me, David sent the barber away to wait in the outer room.

"So you have come to me, Michal. Is this another private matter?" And then he smiled, and I thought, *He knows already why I have come.*

But I made myself smile back, as if it were all a fine jest, and told David what Bathsheba had confessed. That she had sent Uriah away.

"I am sorry, Michal—but if the woman is such a fool as to refuse her own husband when she is in such a case, what can I do?" David stroked his new-curled beard, and smiled again—the smile of a man who has won.

"You are the king. Surely you have the power to save one woman whose only fault is that she loved you too well? Take her from her husband into your own house—as you promised her you would. You have done as much before, after all."

"It is not so simple, Michal. I need Uriah, and his men—and my other foreign warriors too. It is not an easy thing to have foreigners in my army—you know the priests do not like it—"

I cared nothing for all that. "Surely Yahweh smiles upon you, O King, and the priests know it."

David smiled again. "It means much to me to hear you say that. But as for Uriah's wife—"

"Bathsheba," I said, as if he had forgotten. David had forgotten nothing. He toyed with me as a sated lion might toy with a wounded deer. A blow of the lion's paw, and all would be over. But while the deer lived and struggled, the lion was amused.

"If I take Uriah's wife, my warriors will say 'King David does as he pleases, and has no care for us or his words to us.'"

"You knew that when you went to Bathsheba."

"I did not know I would get her with child," David said. "I did not know she would refuse her husband after." He paused, and smiled, and said, "I did not know the woman was such a fool, Michal. Did you?"

I could not answer.

"But you are not a fool, Michal—I have always known that. Now you will ask what it is men will say when Bathsheba is accused as an adulteress, and names me. But you know what they will say, because you are not a fool. They will say she was an unchaste wife. They will say that a woman who opened her arms so freely to me would do as much for any man."

It was the same beautiful voice that sang his lying songs. It rang in my ears as if I had struck my head, leaving me sick and dizzy.

"I am king, Michal. And I am not like Saul—I will not let the priests use me for their own ends. Yahweh loves *me,* not the priests. No man will use the Law against me. Do you remember what I once told you, when first you came back to me?"

I remembered. "The king is the Law. But David, I care noth-

ing for that—do as you please with the priests! I care only for
Bathsheba."

I sank down upon my knees and clutched at his hands. "David,
you have always sworn before Yahweh that you would grant whatever I asked. You know I have asked for little, when I could have
asked for much." Little, and that little to please Bathsheba. But
now I knew the asking had spread my heart open before David's
eyes. "Now I ask you to save Bathsheba. I beg of you, David."

"And if I do not? You ask much of me, Michal."

I would have risen, then, but he turned his hands to press
down on mine. I stayed on my knees before him; I looked up, and
when I spoke I hardly knew my own voice.

"If you do not, I will stand before your throne and tell all men
what you have done, and I will charge you before the priests and
the prophet Nathan. If David's own queen tells the same tale as
Bathsheba—well, it is such a tale as men are always happy to believe."

"More mad ravings from my poor queen?"

"Are all the women in Jerusalem mad, that they tell the same
tale? Call me mad if you like, I do not care. You will have to kill me
to keep me silent."

"Speak then—but Bathsheba is still guilty, and still will die.
That will not change."

"I beg of you, David. See, I will kiss your feet and beg, if it will
please you. Give me Bathsheba's life. You are the king—surely it
can be done, if you will it! There must be a way."

David smiled, then; he drew me to my feet. "Oh, yes, Michal.
There is a way. A royal way. It is rough and harsh, and paved with
stones like blades to cut you. But it will save Bathsheba, if that is
your choice."

I was shaking so I could barely stand, or speak. "I will take it,"
I said. "Anything, if it will save Bathsheba."

Again David smiled. His face was beautiful as an idol's face is
beautiful, a king's image formed from flesh and blood. He slid his

arm about my shoulders and led me to the window that overlooked the city and the rich hills beyond.

"Look to the east, Michal. That is where Rabbah lies, and the
fighting there is hot. Battles are hard, the warrior's life an uncertain thing, easy to lose as a lamb in the mountains. And if a king's
brave soldier should chance to die in the king's service, would it
not be a worthy act to cherish his grieving widow, for his sake?"

"Yes." My mouth was dry as summer dust. "That would be an
act worthy of a king."

"Uriah is a valiant captain. Such men do not often live to see
their son's sons on their knee. They seek the forefront of the fighting, for honor and glory's sake. A word sent to Joab would ensure
Uriah's destiny—and Bathsheba's."

The snare had been set before my feet, the trap-string ready to
my hand. I had only to choose to take it up. An act worthy of a
king—or a queen.

This was what David had planned for me; this was why he
had gone to Bathsheba and ensured she would reject her husband.
But no one could say he had told Bathsheba to deny Uriah. No
one could say that.

David had not spoken to Bathsheba of denial. Only of love.
"*—he swore he could not bear to think of me with another—*" And
Bathsheba had faced Uriah with David's lying kisses still sweet
upon her lips.

This was what David had planned since I had first gone to
him and told him that Bathsheba was with child. Each step since
that day had led here, to this choice.

I knew I held Bathsheba's life within my hands. Sweet, fool-
ish, trusting Bathsheba—and her child. David's child, for whom
David cared less than nothing. Against those two lives I must weigh
Uriah's.

I had never seen Uriah. I knew of him only as a good enough
man, an ambitious man. I did not know Uriah....

"Well, Michal? Shall I send to Joab? Uriah returns today to
Rabbah—he will be honored to carry the king's letters to his

war-chief." David was all smiles and honey, now. His arm coiled heavy about my shoulders. I had thought I hated him before; now I knew that hate had still been only a child's thing, next to this.

I thought of Uriah, and of Phaltiel. I thought of Bathsheba naked to sharp stones.

"Yes," I said. I closed my eyes and turned away from the open window. "Send word to Joab."

CHAPTER 19

"And Nathan said to David,
Thou art the man."

—II Samuel 12:7

That night I lay awake; through my window I watched the sky grow dark and darker still, and then pale again, until it was dawn at last. I told over all that had happened since first David watched Bathsheba bathing in the sunlight. Now I saw how, and where, David had caught life's thread into his own hands, twisting events into a knot he alone could undo. That night I did not wonder why he had done it. I thought only of David, and of what he had made me do, to save Bathsheba.

Time is long, and women weak, and I might have come to forgive even Phaltiel's death, or forget. But now David had forced me to be no better than he, to buy Bathsheba's life at the price of a man's death.

For that, I never forgave him.

The next seven days were hard to bear. I kept Bathsheba with me as much as I could, and tried to reassure her while telling neither truth nor lies. "Do not weep, all will be well. Do not weep, the king has promised to come and see you today—tomorrow—soon."

I tried to think only of Bathsheba; I did not want to think of Uriah. An ambitious man, but good enough to his wife, in his way—no, I would not think of Uriah. Only of Bathsheba, and of the child.

David did not come to see Bathsheba—"He told me it would not be wise, just now. He said you are to wait, to be patient. You must trust him, Bathsheba. There is still time enough."

And so I soothed and cozened and tried not to think of the message that had gone out to Joab. Soon word must come of Uriah's death—unless David had tricked me once again. That thought tormented me; I could barely eat or sleep; my face grew pale and my eyes bruised with fear. Then I would cling to Bathsheba, and say only that I was weary, that I was ill. Then she would try to comfort me.

But Bathsheba could not ease my mind or heart; she could not banish my terrors. Bathsheba did not know what I knew, or what I feared. And I loved her too well to wish her ever to understand.

~

David brought me the news of Uriah's death himself: a gift set before his queen. David liked to be the bestower of gifts.

Bathsheba was with me, helping me sort my bracelets; I hoped the task would keep her hands busy for a time. It was the sort of work that pleased her, after all. But it was growing harder to find such tasks. "Wait", I had said—but soon Bathsheba could not wait. She was past two months gone with child—

I handed her a pair of bracelets all glitter and flash; gold and pure rock-crystal. "Here," I said. "These are for you, to show how I love you." My voice sounded strange, even to my own ears; even to Bathsheba's.

"Michal?" She did not take the bracelets; she touched my cheek. "Are you ill again? Shall I call for Narkis?"

I shook my head, and tried to think of a pretty lie—and then I saw David.

He stood tall in the doorway, waiting for us to see and wonder at him. Beyond him I could see my maids stretching their eyes, all admiration for the great king. Bathsheba gasped; her cheeks flushed bright dawn-roses. She took a step toward David, then stopped.

I did not move. "We are honored," I said, and still my voice was not my own. "How can we make the king welcome here?"

"I come not for honor, but for duty," David said, and went to stand before Bathsheba. "I bring sad tidings to Uriah's wife."

Bathsheba stared up at him; I saw that she trembled. I knew it was with love of King David. "Sad tidings?" she said, puzzled. "I—I do not understand, my lord king."

David took her hands. I knew how David saw it: he was a shepherd gentling a timid lamb. I knew how Bathsheba saw it: the king loved her still.

"There has been a great battle at Rabbah—we have won the city, but we have lost many good men." David sighed, bowed down by kingly grief. "War is hard, but your husband died as a man."

"Uriah is dead?" Bathsheba only sounded surprised; then her eyes widened. "Dead? Oh, no, no!" And then she burst into tears, weeping for Uriah as if she had loved him well.

"Do not weep so," said David quickly. "Uriah was a fine man, a true warrior—and I have vowed to care for my soldier's families as if they were my own. So the king will care for you, Bathsheba—you have his word on it."

Then David set Bathsheba aside to weep or not, as she chose, and came to me. "Does that please you, my gracious queen? Shall I take this woman into my house, and marry her?"

"That is more than you promised." My mouth was dry, my face hot. Words came hard. "Yes, that pleases me. I am fond of Uriah's wife."

"That is good hearing," David said. "I would have my women dwell together in peace under my roof. Come to me tonight, my love, and we will share joy between us." And he kissed me upon the mouth.

Then he went away again, with only a pat upon her shoulder

for Bathsheba, as if she were a puppy. I took her into my arms and let her weep upon my breast. Nor did I try to stop her and make her dry her eyes. She had much to grieve over; more than she knew.

But Uriah was dead and David would marry Bathsheba. And David and Bathsheba's child would come early into the world, and that was all anyone could ever openly say. Bathsheba was safe; I did not wish to know more.

I did not wish to know if the blow that killed Uriah came from before him—or from behind.

~

So David wept over the loss of his brave captain Uriah, and took Uriah's widow into his own house, and married her. *See what care the king takes for his people; a shepherd indeed. Even the meekest lies safe under the king's hand.* That was what David showed the world.

Of course there was talk; Narkis brought me news from well and market. But no one spoke against him. What would have been scandal in any other man became virtue in David the king.

The women whispered at the well. *Of course the Lady Bathsheba's child is the king's, what can you expect from a hill-girl, and her husband gone. Of course she dropped her veil for the king's eyes—ah, if the king would only cast his eyes upon me—*

Yes, that was what was whispered among the women.

The men whispered too. *Look at our King David! Still a lusty man, for all he's a great king. Another child, too! Ah, that I were king, and could do as well.*

Envy, and pride. That was all. Perhaps if Uriah had not been a foreigner, a Hittite, there would have been blame, even for King David. But there was not. No one thought of Uriah, save me.

The siege at Rabbah ended; a great victory at last. Once more David's star shone bright, and people forgot what the city of Rabbah had cost in men and blood.

No one fretted over the loss of one Hittite captain. No one

questioned what the king chose to do.

No one save the prophet Nathan.

~

Then I thought only of Bathsheba, and of myself. And so I did not wonder why Nathan chose to rant at David over this sin when he had ignored so many others. In truth, I did not care; I thought Nathan a blind fool. He had done nothing when I had become a sudden widow, nothing when I had told him plain that David had killed my husband. I knew Nathan would hear no word against David.

And that was not strange. David had long bowed humble before Nathan, and given the prophet all honor. Nathan, like so many others, was loyal to the David he saw.

But now Nathan spoke out and chastised David, and harshly too. I heard it all, and Bathsheba with me, and did not need to rely on rumor for Nathan's words.

Bathsheba had wished to see David act the king in his court; to please her I had taken her and shown her a king's secret— "And a queen's," I said, and smiled.

The secret was a small dark room set deep into the wall behind the throne; here one might stand and spy upon the daylight court. From the court below, one saw only the glazed garden of lilies and reeds and lotus-flowers behind the king's throne. From where Bathsheba and I stood, all that went on before that throne could be seen and heard through cunning lattice-work.

Bathsheba was delighted with the secret room, of course. "Oh, how clever!" she breathed, and touched the screen-work with cautious fingers. "And no one knows we are here?"

"No one. See, I have set cushions for us so we may sit in comfort—and I warn you, Bathsheba, court business is long and dull. You must tell me when you grow bored."

"How could I be bored when I watch the king?" Then Bathsheba frowned in thought. "But Michal, who sits here? Not the king—he is there—" She pointed; thin streams of light pressing through the lattice danced splashes of gold and silver over her wide bracelets.

"Why, no one—save those who dally here with a sweetheart, or seek to evade a task. David heard of an eastern king with such a spy-room as this, and so he must have one as well. But of what use it is to the king, I do not know. Nothing said in the court can be private—only see how many men stand there to listen."

"And—and I suppose the workmen all know it is here, unless they worked blindfolded!" Bathsheba laughed, and put a guilty hand to her mouth.

"Well, this room is not a *great* secret." I smiled, pleased to see her happy, which she often was not. Oh, she tried to hide her pain, but I had once suffered from her illness, and so what she might conceal from others was plain enough to my eyes. Bathsheba was still sick with love for David; she could not yet believe that David's love was gone. Had he not married her, after all—and yet he never came to her, or saw her unless she was with me—Oh, yes, I knew what Bathsheba suffered.

And so we sat hidden there when Nathan came before David's throne and spoke. Nathan strode through the waiting men; he pushed aside those who bowed low before David and spoke of trade with Tyre. Then the prophet stood there, and thumped the marble floor with his wooden staff, and demanded justice.

David's boast was that no one asked the king for that in vain, and so he begged Nathan speak. In truth, he could not have stopped him.

There were two men, Nathan said, one with many sheep and one with only one ewe; the rich man prepared a feast and slaughtered the poor man's ewe instead of one of the many he himself possessed—what should be done with such a man?

"Why, the answer is simple. He is a thief, and must make fourfold restitution for the ewe he stole." David spoke firmly; he liked to be seen as just and fair in his judgments. This would show that even the simplest matter was not too lowly for King David to see to.

"You are the man! You are the thief, O King! You took another man's wife in secret, you who have many women of your own, and stole her away and sent him to die in battle. You have sinned greatly, and Yahweh will strike you for your crime!"

There was silence in the great court; all men waited to see what the king would do. David did nothing. He sat cold upon his throne and did not move.

I did not move, or breathe; I could not. *Uriah*, I thought. *Nathan knows.*

"Do you speak of the wife of Uriah?" David's voice was calm enough. "Why, that is no sin—and no secret either. All men know how I took her into my house. A king cares for his people, as a shepherd tends his flock."

There was a murmur from the watching men; agreement. Nathan drew a deep breath and stood as tall as he could. But prophet or no, Nathan was not impressive; he was still a short man, and now he was rounder than ever. King David kept a lavish table.

"Do not mock, O King. This is a grievous thing that you have done. You have broken Yahweh's sacred Law."

David spread his hands wide. "I am humble before the Lord. Show me the sign of Yahweh's anger, Nathan. I have done nothing but what I must and should." David raised his voice; his words echoed among the pillars of the court. "And you all have seen how I have been rewarded. Rabbah is ours now, and there is peace in the east. The Ammonites send us talents of silver and bushels of wheat in tribute to Yahweh's greatness."

Bathsheba and I sat hidden behind the throne; I could not see David's face. But I saw Nathan's. The prophet looked stubborn and desperate, like a boar facing dogs and spears. Now, I thought, now Nathan believes; now, when it is too late.

I knew Nathan's next words must be of Phaltiel, and of me, and then Bathsheba and I would stand accused before the priests.

Murder and harlotry, and both crimes called for death. I knew better now than to think David would stand beside us; we would be sacrificed to purify David's name. Abigail would happily bear witness against us—

"The sword will dwell in your own house and you shall find no peace therein!" Nathan did not answer David, but raged on as if he had not heard. "The child of sin will perish! Yahweh will not be mocked by one whom he has set up, and can as easily cast down below the worms in the dirt!"

Bathsheba cried out in distress. I put my arms around her; her belly was moon-round now with the child. "Hush, Bathsheba. Nathan raves—he says nothing, nothing. Do not cry—" I held and rocked her, and listened hard, fearing the next words would destroy us.

But I was wrong; Nathan knew nothing. Only pride and anger fed his words.

"I say you mock Yahweh and me!" Nathan was red-faced and panting, as if he had run far and hard. He pointed his staff at David. "Heed well my words, O King!"

For a moment David said nothing. Men began to turn to one another, and whisper, and look to see what the king would do now. Never before had the prophet spoken loud against the king—what did this mean?

"If I have sinned, I am heartily sorry for it," David said. I knew his voice too well; I knew he smiled, even if no man could tell it. "Come, Nathan, sit beside me until I have finished here—then you must tell me how I may make amends. Bring a stool for the prophet; make haste, do not keep him standing here."

A man ran to bring a stool and set it beside the throne. David held out his hand, showing Nathan where he might sit.

Nathan hesitated, then walked toward the throne. "No. I will stand, upright in Yahweh's eyes."

"Stand, then," said David. "But when you tire, you must sit beside me, as I said." Then David lifted his head, and spoke to the assembled men once more. "Now come, who speaks next?"

"You see?" I said, and clenched my hands to stop their trembling. "It is nothing, Bathsheba—"

"My child—the prophet said my child will die. Oh, Michal—"

"Your child will not die. Dry your eyes, Bathsheba, and do not think of it. Come, and I will give you wine and fruit, and we will forget this. It is nothing, nothing—only empty words."

I rose then, and made Bathsheba come away with me. I looked back, once, at the throne below us. David sat tall upon his throne, giving justice. Beside the king's throne stood the prophet Nathan, waiting at the king's command.

⁓

Later I saw that day for what it truly was: the day power slid from prophet's hand to king's, a harlot spurning a good man for a wealthy one.

For it was not the priests and the prophets who had brought riches and power to Israel—it was King David. It was David who had brought back the Ark; it was David who had captured fields and cities. It was David who bestowed gifts upon the priests, and gave them a place at the king's table. It was David the priests praised, and the people followed.

Nathan had wished to warn David that he was king only by Yahweh's will, and could still be brought low if he offended. Samuel had brought King Saul down for lesser crimes.

But Nathan was not Samuel—and King David was not King Saul. Samuel had chosen Saul as king. David had chosen Nathan as chief prophet. David with his own hands had given Samuel's staff into Nathan's keeping.

King David had given Nathan honor. Great honor. But honor was not power.

How it had happened I did not know—and I think Nathan knew no more than I. But now it was King David who held power over the people and the kingdom.

Now the king ruled; ruled as Samuel had long ago foretold.

The prophet Nathan was left with only empty words.

⁓

But Nathan's words did not seem so empty some months later, on the night Bathsheba labored to bring David's child into the world. That night Nathan's words were nearly cruel truth.

The birthing room was crowded with sweating bodies; the air swayed with heat, cloyed with burning oils and incense. I could scarcely draw breath; Bathsheba, who labored on the birthing chair, suffered even more.

I sat beside her and held her hand. Her skin was cold, for all the room's oppressive heat. "Soon," I said. "It will not be long now. Hageet, give her more wine—a mouthful only."

Bathsheba looked at me with the fearful, hoping eyes of one who labors for the first time to bring forth a child. "Oh, Michal— I shall die. I know I shall die."

"You will not," I said firmly.

She clung to me. "I, and the child—the prophet Nathan said— you remember—"

"Nathan is no midwife. I tell you all is well; you will have an easy birth and a fine child." I wiped her forehead with a damp cloth. "Remember what I told you, and do not worry—fretting only makes birth harder for you and the babe. It will soon be over, and then you will care nothing for all this."

I did not lie to her; I had seldom seen an easier labor. All was as it should be and all went as it should, until the child was born. Easy born, too, as I had promised—though I knew Bathsheba would not believe that.

The child was a boy, and perfectly formed. But he was white and still; his lips and tiny fingers tinged with dusky blue. Death-shadowed.

The midwife showed him and the other women drew away, cautious. Bathsheba was the king's newest wife and the queen's dearest friend; no one wished it said she or her child had come to harm under their hands. And there was the prophet Nathan's curse upon this birth as well—causes enough for them to slide away, and leave the work and blame to others.

So they began to wail, enjoying their lamentations too much. "Dead—born dead, as Nathan foretold—oh, who will tell the king?"

"Be silent! Give him to me!" I had seen this before; perhaps the child could be saved, if I were quick.

Once I had the child in my own hands I held him by his heels and shook him hard, as if he were a chicken to be plucked. The women gasped and looked at me like sheep, with the same stupid malice. It would make a fine tale if the Lady Bathsheba's son died of Queen Michal's tending.

But I cared nothing for whispers, and much for Bathsheba. A son would give her standing in the king's house, even if she were not loved. David would not set aside the mother of his son.

"Stop your wailing—bring a basin of cold water, and some hot wine—quickly, before I throw you all to the guard for flogging! And someone tend to the Lady Bathsheba!"

I rubbed the child's arms and legs with my bare hands, blew into his cool mouth, willing the maids to hasten with what I needed. The basin was brought, and the wine; I set the babe into the cold water for a moment. "Soak a cloth in the wine."

I lifted him out of the water and laid him upon my lap. I took the dripping cloth and squeezed hot wine between his lips.

I was not sure; I had seen a child saved this way, once. I had seen more who were not. But then his still body grew warm under my hands, and moved as he drew his first breath.

"He is not dead," I said, and knew triumph as I heard him cry, a triumph as hot and heady as any victorious warrior's. "Rejoice; King David has a fine new son."

As I spoke I rubbed the child softly to bring the blood to his hands and feet. He was small, and wriggled and mewed in my arms like a hungry kitten.

My heart beat hard swan's-wings in my breast; I held him to my cheek and brushed my lips over his soft damp hair. It was pale, and framed his head with sun as it dried. He opened his eyes; they were like cloudy milk, as babes' are, but still it seemed as if he looked, and knew me.

And then Bathsheba called for him. She was his mother; I set the child naked in her arms. She smiled and cooed like a setting dove, but I do not think she had the same fierce desire to keep him against her heart that made my arms ache.

He is mine, I thought. *But for me, he would never have been born, or drawn a breath. He is mine, not hers.*

~

CHAPTER 20

". . . and she bare a son,
and he called his name Solomon . . . . "
—II Samuel 12:24

Nathan salved his honor as a prophet by proclaiming that Yahweh had softened toward David, and that the child should be known as Jedidiah, as Yahweh loved him well. Too late; the child had already been named Solomon—peace. The choice was David's public defiance of Nathan's curse.

"For see, the babe lives, in spite of Nathan's words. If the rest of his words fall out as true, then I and mine shall dwell in peace and riches all the rest of our days." David looked upon his newest son, and smiled. Solomon was a quiet and pretty child, and did not wail in his father's face, so David was well pleased with him, and promised Bathsheba new bracelets of amber and coral, and whatever else she might desire.

"I desire only that my lord should look upon me with favor," Bathsheba told him. She meant those words with all her heart, but David held such gifts as hearts careless in his keeping.

"A very proper speech, Bathsheba, but women always want some new bauble or other and you must not be shy of asking— none of my other women are, save only my modest clever queen."

"Wisdom is better than rubies," I said sharply, for I knew his words had hurt Bathsheba. "But the king is right, Bathsheba—he should reward you for the gift of peace you have brought his house." I took Solomon from David's arms and cradled him close to my heart, while his father and mother laughed at my small jest upon the child's name.

Solomon's eyes were clear and round as a little owl's as he stared at me. He did not seem puzzled by life, as other babes did. I put my finger to his small soft mouth; he sucked at it.

"He wants the breast, Michal—give him here, to me." Bathsheba took Solomon from me and made a fuss over unpinning her clothing and putting the child to suck. "See how strongly he pulls, lord—"

"Yes, yes, he is a wonder. Each son is like the first, a sign of Yahweh's grace," said David. But he was not looking at Bathsheba or the child, and did not stay long after. He had seen many of his sons take their mother's milk, after all.

Bathsheba's eyes filled with tears; a well that did not quite overflow. I stroked the top of Solomon's head where the bones were still soft to the hand, and bade her look at how lustily he clutched her gown.

"And do not trouble yourself over David—he did not mean to cause you pain." I knew this was true; King David no longer thought of Bathsheba, save as another woman in his house—no less and no more than that. Bathsheba was wise enough to know it, and foolish enough to deny cold truth to herself.

"He is the king—he is busy, and much troubled. But he is pleased with Solomon—with our son."

I answered the plea behind her words. "Who would not be pleased with Solomon? He is worth all David's other sons together, as you are worth all his other wives. David is no fool; he will know this. Ah, look, our Solomon has finished—give him to me and I will rub his back, or he will be colicky, and not sleep."

And look to your son for your heart's comfort, Bathsheba, I thought as Solomon's small head lay heavy on my shoulder, and he slept. *Look to your son for love, for you will never have it from his father.*

But I knew Bathsheba still grieved for the days when she had only to lift her veil to bring King David to his knees. Her pain would pass; I knew it would pass. But I knew, too, that she would not listen to me yet.

And so I said nothing.

~

Long after, when I was old and thought back upon those years when Solomon was young, I did not see them as a whole. They were like beads strung upon golden thread. The thread was my life in King David's house; some of the beads gleamed jewel bright— Solomon smiled upon me, and reached out his small plump hand.

Some of the beads were coarse and dull—King David smiled upon me, and poured words into my ears that I wished I did not hear. But a bargain had been struck; I was his now, or so he thought.

Once again David spoke to me in darkened rooms, by night. On and on, all the words he dared not speak by day.

All the words he would never sing: betrayal, and lies, and murder.

How a crown had been won, and a city, and a kingdom.

And I would lie there beside him, watching the little lamp flames dance shadows across painted walls, and listen.

~

"Once you asked how I—I, David of Bethlehem—did all this." David flung his arm wide, offering all the wonders of Jerusalem and the land beyond.

Once; I no longer cared. "Yes. Once I asked."

"A locked riddle; I will show you the key." He leaned close, to speak low into my ear. "Why labor with your own hands when others will labor in your stead?"

"Why indeed?" And then, when I saw he desired more, "What others, David?"

David kissed my hair and touched my breast, coaxing. "Can you not guess? Come, try."

I shook my head. "I cannot."

"Well, then, I will tell you, since you ask it." David pressed close against me and spoke soft into my hair. "The Philistines. Ah, you see?—you still are not so cunning as I."

I stared at him; in the lamplight his face was dark fire. "The Philistines?"

"Yes, my queen. The Philistines gave all this into my hands as a gift. Did you think my army so strong then that the Philistines could not destroy it if they chose?"

"But why?"

"Perhaps because they loved me well—who can say?" David toyed with my hair and looked slantwise at me. "Ah, Michal—did you think two hundred Philistines marched to Gibeah with me for the love of my bright eyes—or yours?"

"Two hundred Philistines . . . ." My bride-price. David standing tall before the gate of Saul's little city, calling up to him . . . .

David stroked my hair again. "There are great empires to the east; the Philistines press against the sea. A king set between—a friendly king, to keep the peace between, as Saul did not—"

As Saul could not, because of Samuel.

Yes, that would be worth much to the Philistines. A king set like a painted doll upon a gilded throne. "So King David dances to Philistine tunes?"

"While Philistine music pleases him," David said, and laughed, and kissed me.

I closed my eyes and thought of two hundred Philistine warriors set within Saul's army, and of David tuning his songs for Philistine ears. In the dark behind my eyelids King David danced again before the Ark.

Yahweh's Ark, which the Philistines had given into King David's hands.

~

"Look, Michal—see how strongly Solomon grasps the harp. No, no, my love—see, you must touch the strings so, to make music."

Bathsheba pulled Solomon's tiny fingers across the strings of the child's harp David had given. Olive-wood set with amber; no one could call King David a miserly father. "There! Music!"

"Music as fine as King David's," I said. I looked at Bathsheba's dark head bent over Solomon's bright one. Solomon would not grow to be like David; that I swore. I smiled. "And he will make finer yet, when he is grown. What was David thinking of, to give him a harp now? He is not yet half a year old!"

Bathsheba protested. "It was kind of the king to send him so fine a present. See, Solomon wishes to sing and play, like his father."

Solomon smiled happily and yowled like a wild cat, and hit the harp-strings, hard.

"Yes," I said. "As fine a harper as his father."

Bathsheba laughed, then, and took the little harp away. "You are right—I will set this aside until Solomon is older. No, no, my love—you may not have it now."

"You must learn to wait for what you desire," I told Solomon, and scooped him up into my arms and kissed his soft sweet cheek. And Bathsheba gave him a coral to chew on instead of the king's gift, and so he was satisfied.

~

"The king of Ascalon has asked for one of my daughters for his son. What do you think of that, my queen?" David smiled; lamp-lit shadows flickered across his mouth like serpent tongues.

"That it is a great honor. Which daughter?"

"Why, do you think he cares? Any king's daughter will do to seal a bargain. Come near to me, my queen; winter nights are chill."

"I am not cold."

"Ah, Michal—did you think I saw *you* so? Never. You are a jewel past price."

"Not past price." I rose up upon my elbow to stare down at

him. "I know what you paid for me. What price did the Philistines set upon Saul's daughter, David?"

David smiled again and took my chin into his fingers. "You are a king's daughter indeed, Michal. You know."

"I know more than I once did." I knew what Zhurleen had told me in an idle moment—that the Philistines counted the mother's blood as great as the father's. If there were no son to mount the throne, the last king's daughter held the crown in her own hands; a bride-gift to her husband.

"Then you know how you are valued, Michal. You are more to me than rubies. Much more."

I knew, now. I was more than rubies; I was the crown. Sacred oil and a prophet's blessing were good; a king's daughter and Philistine gold were better. *Two strings to his bow, always. . . .*

"Yes," I said. "I know how much I am to you, David. I will never forget how much; that I swear to you." And I drew back, out of the lamp's light, hiding my eyes behind my lashes.

~

"See what I have for you, my heart—see, here is a new ball for you to play with." And I held out a globe of scarlet leather painted with golden stars.

Solomon sat propped upon cushions; I tended him while Bathsheba bathed in her own rooms. Now he watched the ball, his solemn eyes stretched wide. "Yes, my love, all for you—here, take it."

I set the ball into Solomon's chubby hands; he stared at the toy and then tried to stuff it into his mouth. The ball was too large; he chewed upon its bright leather, and then spat it away.

"You do not like it? No? Then come to me, my love—come to Michal." And I sat beside him upon the cushions, and took him onto my lap. "I will sing you a song about a little bear-cub—how will you like that?"

Solomon smiled and grasped my hands with strong little fists;

as I sang and rocked him in my arms, he sucked happily upon my fingers.

~

"Hiram of Tyre built this king's house for me—did you know that, Michal?"

"Yes, I knew."

"Do you know why? Do you know why the king of Tyre did this thing for me?"

"No. Why did the king of Tyre do this thing for you?"

David stroked my arm. "Because he had the Philistines at his back, and would put me at theirs. I am in high favor with the Philistine kings, you know." He paused, to let me marvel.

"Yes, I know."

"And Hiram is almost as shrewd as I; he suspected what I might become. And so he built me this fine house—as fine as his own. A gift, from one great king to another." Again he waited.

After a moment, I said, "And now you are as great as the king of Tyre."

"Greater," David said, embracing me as loving as if I were the throne itself. "Much greater, as the lion is greater than the peacock."

Obedient, I put my arms around him. On the walls beyond the bed, painted lions paced among endless shadows.

~

My garden, too, held shadows; sun-shadows for a boy to play with. Sunlight through leaves danced shadow-leaves upon the grass. Solomon crawled after them, patting at the moving shapes.

"Look, Michal—see how fast and strong he is! No, no, Solomon—you must not put that in your mouth, my love, it is dirty—"

"Do not tell him so, Bathsheba—take it from him." And I

swooped Solomon up and plucked the pebble from his small mouth. His face puckered up; I kissed his neck, and blew upon his warm skin, and he laughed instead.

"Ma!" he said, and wriggled like an eel to be set free again.

"Listen!" Bathsheba caught him from my arms. "A word! Say it again, Solomon—come, speak for your mother—"

And Solomon smiled sweetly, and pressed his mouth closed, and would not utter another sound for all our coaxing. At last I laughed and bade Bathsheba set him down again. "He will speak in his own good time—and perhaps it was not a word at all."

"It was," Bathsheba insisted. "He called you 'mother'—I heard it clearly. Oh, he is so very clever!"

"No," I said, cold beneath my skin. "You are wrong; it was baby-noise only." For no matter how I loved him, Solomon was Bathsheba's son, and not truly mine. His love belonged to her, and not to me.

Bathsheba set Solomon down upon the grass again; he crawled off hastily, busy as an ant. Bathsheba slid her soft hand into mine. "He knows you love him as much as I, Michal. He knows he has two mothers."

And then Bathsheba stretched to kiss me upon the cheek, and smiled. Her eyes were bright as crystal in the sun.

~

In the king's bedroom, David dropped secrets into my ears like jewels into a well, knowing the jewels would be forever lost in darkness.

~

In the queen's garden Solomon clasped Bathsheba's forefinger in his left hand, and mine in his right, and took his first unsteady steps, balanced safe between love and love.

~

Beads upon a golden thread; a necklace of life. I dwelt behind walls of stone and silence, and for a time the world beyond seemed far away.

And so I cherished Solomon as if he were my son, and Bathsheba as if she were my sister. And for a sweet span of years, while Solomon grew from babe to boy, there was the peace his naming had promised.

~

Yes, a sweet span of peace—but a brief one. As Nathan had prophesied before Solomon was born, trouble was bred within David's own house. King David had too many wives, and they had too many children, and David was too soft with them all. His sons had too much freedom, and his daughters also, and they were all hot-headed and hot-blooded.

But who could have foreseen how it would happen, or what grief it would cause? Before it was over, many good men lay dead in battle, and David lost two sons, and a daughter too. And for no good cause, save that King David would not heed the whisper of the passing years.

~

The seasons had turned once more to harvest-time, rounding a year that had brought a full harvest of power to King David. The summer that Solomon was seven King David had called up his army, well-honed by years of smaller victories, and turned it at last against the Philistines. David's folly, some had called it before the battle; Yahweh's will, they called it after. Yahweh's vengeance upon the Philistines for the slaughter upon Mount Gilboa a dozen years before, when King Saul and his sons had perished.

I called it nothing; I only smiled, when David was praised

before me, and said that I had never doubted. That was true: I had known David would defeat the Philistines. The Philistines had trusted David, and paid the price of that trust.

King David laid all credit at Yahweh's feet. It was Yahweh, King David said, who had won this great victory. It was Yahweh who was honored with the great feast and festival that was held in Jerusalem. A great day, and greatness to honor Yahweh.

But it was not Yahweh who walked the streets of Jerusalem with a golden crown upon his head and scarlet boots upon his feet. It was David. An image flashed behind my eyes; David the king dancing before the sacred Ark, a flame in sunlight. But that had been long years ago, before Solomon was born. Today the king did not share glory.

Today King David led a procession through the city in solemn majesty. He was all dignity, all a king; that day David did not dance. He led, and his sons followed, glittering princes all. Even Solomon wore a circlet of gold about his head and walked with the other princes. The youngest, and so least in precedence, but he walked beside King David, and the king clasped Solomon's hand in his. David knew what men and women liked to see.

Yes, the king first, and the princes next. And then came the prophet Nathan, and the high priests Zadok and Abiathar.

I watched all this from the palace roof with the other women. The king's women made as fine a show as the princes; scarlet and purple swirled about our bodies, jewels hung heavy about our throats. Any who raised his eyes from the king would see the king's women, and the king's wealth.

"Look," said Bathsheba. "See how straight Solomon walks! Oh, he is the best boy in all the world!"

"But he is the youngest," Abigail said. "Solomon will never be king." Abigail would not speak to me, but she would torment Bathsheba, if she could.

Bathsheba would not be drawn; she looked puzzled. "But Solomon is much too young to be king, Abigail—why, he is only a little boy!"

I laughed, and set my hand over Bathsheba's. "Of course Solomon is the youngest—all men know the king could never look at another woman, once he had seen Bathsheba's face!"

"Oh, Michal, you know that is not true!" Bathsheba blushed, and I smiled and kissed her cheek. Abigail flushed and turned away, to Eglah and Abital. I laughed again, and saw Abigail's shoulders tense.

"Ah, Bathsheba, you are too good. You should not let her speak so to you." I stood back from the wall; I had seen David's pride before.

Bathsheba's eyes were soft. "But I am so sorry for her—her son dead, and she cares nothing for her girls—I do not understand why she does not—" Abigail's son Chileab had been killed in battle two summers ago; David lauded him a hero, and praised him now as he never had while Chileab lived.

"You are right to reprove me; I should be kinder to her." I thought of Abigail, aging now, and with neither husband nor son to comfort her. David had little time for her, and her son was dead. Did she wish now that she had stayed with her first husband Nabal, honored in his house? But David had wanted her husband's wealth, and Abigail had wanted David, and so Nabal died. Now Abigail grew old in the king's house, no more to him than any other woman.

"Oh, no—I did not mean—"

"Of course you did not, my love. But you are right." I stepped forward again, watching David's procession wind away from the palace, into the city streets below.

David the king, holding Prince Solomon's small hand. Solomon flushed with boy's pride, walking straight and trying to be solemn and manly. Men called David's name; women smiled and called Solomon's, to be kind.

Prince Amnon, the eldest, drew cheers from men and women both; Amnon smiled, and waved back, and bent to catch up the flowers tossed before his feet. *"Amnon!"* The call came high and clear from Amnon's little half-sister Tamar, who pressed against the wall a dozen paces from me. *"Amnon!"* I do not know if Amnon heard or if he only chanced to look up; he smiled, and blew a kiss from his fingertips up to Tamar.

Tamar flushed, and called his name louder. *"Amnon!"* And she pulled copper bangles from her wrist to fling them down before him; her mother Maachah caught her hand and the bangles fell instead to the stones at Tamar's feet. I could not hear what Maachah said to Tamar; the noise from the street below was too great.

Beside Amnon strode Prince Absalom, the second son—also straight and beautiful. But his pace was measured, haughty as a peacock. Absalom was as proud as his mother Maachah, who was the King of Geshur's daughter—and had never forgotten it. Tamar did not call out Absalom's name, although he was her full brother.

And then Adonijah, and Ithream, and all the rest of the princes. A dozen fine sons still left to King David, even after all the years of war.

And after all the princes of the House of David came the prophet, and the priests. Once Nathan would have led the victory procession. Now the prophet followed after the king. *Does that mean much, or little?* Nathan still stood beside David's throne; the king still gave up sacrifices to the priests and bowed low before them. *Does Nathan smile today, as he swallows dust from David's feet?*

"How things change." Bathsheba leaned over the wall to watch Solomon out of sight. "Why, it seems only yesterday that I first held Solomon in my arms. Look at him now—why, he is past seven!"

"Time passing; a marvel indeed."

Following Yahweh's men, Joab's. Joab, who was to King David what Abner had been to King Saul. Joab paced the streets as if they were a battlefield; behind him came his captains carrying iron swords taken from the Philistines. The captains waved the Philistine swords high so that all might see what had been won. The captured blades glinted sullen in the sun.

I drew back again, lest Joab look up; I could never bear to look into his eyes. I feared what I might see there—or not see. For battles are uncertain, and in them many men die. And so I wondered, sometimes, if David had ever sent Joab a message concerning the Hittite captain Uriah, who was husband to the woman Bathsheba. Perhaps Uriah had died clean in battle, as any man might. Perhaps if I looked into Joab's eyes, I would see nothing.

"Look, Michal—see how the Philistine blades flash in the sunlight! How terrible they look—I could never be a warrior, never. I would die of fright. They are so brave, our men!"

"Yes, they are brave—and foolish too."

"Fools?" Bathsheba was shocked, of course. "Our good brave men?"

"Yes, fools—what does it buy men in the end, all that blood they spill so easily?"

Bathsheba looked down at David's soldiers, and frowned. "I—well, I do not know. But men must be soldiers."

"Of course. And the blood makes the crops grow thick."

"Michal, you cannot mean that. That is what idolaters think!"

"And they are right," I said. "Look at the farms in the vale of Gilboa now, and on the plains of Hebron. Men say such a rich harvest has not been seen since their grandfathers' times."

Bathsheba looked at me, and then away. "Well, if that is true—then at least the dead warriors still feed their children."

"Bathsheba!" I stared, and then laughed. "Well, and so they do. You see? You are always cleverer than I."

"No, no—I only try to think and speak as you do, Michal."

I was silent a moment. "Never do that, Bathsheba. It is you I love, not my mirror."

She did not understand, and only smiled. "You have no reason to fear, Michal. They say you are still as beautiful as you were when you were a girl."

I laughed. "I was the plainest maiden in all Israel, and I remember that well, even if 'they' do not! Tell another!"

"Well, then—that you are still as beautiful as when you first came to Jerusalem. As if it were yesterday." Bathsheba leaned out farther. "Oh, I cannot see the princes anymore. Do you think Solomon will be all right?"

"He will be fine; you must not over-coddle him, my love." My face was smooth as my silver mirror, and told as little to the watcher. Bathsheba's careless words coiled themselves into my mind. *"As if it were yesterday . . . . "*

"It was not yesterday," I said.

"What was not?" Bathsheba was not attending; she always loved a fine show. "Oh, look—Philistine chariots—see, Michal—"

And so I spoke only to myself. "It has been ten years."

~

Yes, it had been ten years since King David sent Abner to take King Saul's daughter from her husband and bring her to Jerusalem. David liked to think himself always the young hero, the beloved. But David was past forty, an aging man; his sons were the young heroes now. Amnon, Absalom, Adonijah—they were his captains; they rode through the streets in their chariots and the people praised them as they had once praised David when he was a war-captain for my father King Saul.

I thought of that, later. Many years have passed since that day; I still wonder, sometimes, if King David suspected Amnon of playing young David's own game. A young hero; a king's daughter—did David think the next move was a prince's rebellion?

Well, and David was right, after all. But Amnon was innocent of anything but unwise love.

It was Absalom whose heart was rotted through with ambition.

~

CHAPTER 21

"Absalom the son of David had a fair sister, whose name was Tamar; and Amnon the son of David loved her."

—II Samuel 13:1

Amnon was tall and strong, like all of David's sons, but far more beautiful than the rest. And Tamar, Amnon's sister—well, she was young, and he dazzled her eyes like sun on a mountain lake.

So when Prince Amnon returned from the battles he fought and won for King David, Tamar was there to call his name and garland his neck with flower-chains woven with her own hands. And she would cling to him and kiss him on the mouth. Amnon took the kisses and laughed, and called Tamar his dearest little sister.

"See how fond Amnon and Tamar are," David said, smiling upon them. "Why cannot all my children live in peace together as they do?"

I could have told David that he himself ensured he had no peace under his own roof. David thought he loved his children— yes, so long as they were beautiful and perfect, like painted princes and princesses upon a palace wall. And so he sometimes petted and spoiled them, and sometimes curbed them sharp. They never knew, when they ran to him, if they would be greeted by the father or the king. Uncertainty made them quarrel over his favor, vying for a place in the sunlight of his smile. David liked to be the sun. But too much sunlight, or too little, and the crop withers and dies in the field.

So David smiled upon Amnon and Tamar, and encouraged the

girl to run to her brother. "Go—greet our conquering hero. A boy needs to know he has done well in his first campaigns. Praise him, and tell him I am pleased."

Yes, David smiled upon Amnon and Tamar—then. And where King David smiled, so did all his household. We all watched, and spoke of the girl's sweet nature and her brother's kindness, and were blind. Yes, even I.

I think even Amnon himself was blind at first; she was his father's daughter, after all. And he had known her since she was new-born, and he a boy of six. Oh, he was fond enough, but careless, as a man might be with a child.

But Tamar was a child no longer; she had put on her veil, and thought herself a woman. She had round breasts and soft dark doe's eyes, and she was as full of warm love as a ripe pomegranate of seeds. And she was only his half-sister, when all was said.

I counted myself clever, and even I did not see how it truly was between Tamar and Amnon. Not until the day that I came upon them in my garden, hidden away behind the lilies that banked the pool, did I see clearly. And then I saw too much, and too little.

~

That day I had gone with Bathsheba into the upper town, as I sometimes did, to see the wares a new merchant offered David's court. Many merchants passed through Jerusalem, now; this one brought small treasures from a land far to the east: silver boxes shaped like pomegranates, scarves embroidered with sky-bright feathers, sandalwood combs to scent the hair. Veils woven of gold and silver. Gems that flashed cat's-eyes.

The merchant's wares were strange and fine enough for any queen. But the day was hot, and I had lain half the night awake, listening to David tell what he would do now that the sea-cities of Philistia were open to him, and the price of Philistine iron was something less than blood. And I had seen gold and silver and gems before. So I smiled upon the merchant and told Bathsheba I was tired, and would leave her to make purchases for me.

"For you always know what pleases me. And do not forget to buy for yourself as well. King David can afford to be generous." And I kissed Bathsheba, and went back to the king's palace, and to the queen's courtyard.

And to my garden. And there I found Amnon, and Tamar. Together, among the lilies by the little pool.

They lay close-pressed as if bound together; Tamar's braids chained Amnon with living copper, fire-hot in the sun. They did not hear me. They would not have heard the king's guard in full armor. They were beautiful against the lilies.

I watched them as they kissed. It was not a sister's lips that Tamar offered Amnon. And it was not a brother's kiss that he gave her in return. It was not a brother's hands that stroked her yielding body.

I clapped my hands together and called out Tamar's name, making my voice sharp and hard. They fell apart and struggled to their feet; Tamar's long braids tangled in her brother's bracelets, trapping them together. Amnon would have freed them, but Tamar gripped him hard, staring at me with eyes still soft from passion. I saw white on his arm, framing her clinging fingers.

For a moment we all stood there, frozen in the sunlight like bees in amber. Then I spoke as I must. "Is this how you care for your sister, Prince Amnon? This is not well done."

Amnon bowed his head. "I know, Queen Michal." Amnon's voice was steady, strong as the sun-hot stones of the garden wall behind him. "I am sorry; I thought we would be gone before you returned. We came only to talk where we might be truly alone. A quiet place is hard to find in the king's house."

"Yes," I said. "I know."

"And then—we did not know, until we kissed. And then—well, you saw."

Tamar's face was hot and red as hearth-coals. She stared at me, and bit her lip hard, but did not speak. I thought she was wise to keep silent; I remembered the follies I had spoken, when I was as young as she.

"Yes, I saw. You have mistaken a brother's—a sister's—fondness for more. I had heard that it happens; such lust will pass, if you do not trespass again. So I will say nothing, and forgive the harm you have done my lilies."

"No! It is not like that!" Tamar's voice trembled. "Oh, please—" She did not say what she pled for; perhaps she did not know herself.

Amnon put his hand over Tamar's and gently urged her fingers from his flesh. Then his hands worked softly, unweaving Tamar's braid from his golden bracelet. "It is all right, sister. There is nothing to fear."

"Not from me." I could not be cruel to them; they were so young. "But Prince Amnon, is this wise?"

"No," Amnon said. "It is not wise. But we share one heart, Tamar and I." He looked straight into my eyes. His own were hero's eyes; eyes to obey.

"And now?" I asked.

Amnon looked down at his little sister and smiled. "Well, Tamar?"

She blushed poppy-bright. "I—it is not for me to say."

"Then I will." Amnon put his arm about her shoulders and hugged her to him. "I will ask the king for her; she will be my wife. I would never dishonor my sister."

"Oh, Amnon!" Tamar melted against him, molded to him. Yes, she was his, heart and blood.

Amnon smiled at her once more; a man's smile for the woman he finds most fair under all the sky. My own heart ached; a small pang only, as an old wound might pain an aging warrior.

"I wish you well," I said, and smiled, and the little pain was gone again.

"The queen is kind." Amnon caught up Tamar's hand in his; their fingers twined together, a lover's knot to flesh. "Come, beloved—we have trespassed in the queen's garden long enough."

"Yes—the queen is kind—I am sorry—" Tamar stammered, and blushed, and Amnon drew her away.

I laughed, and watched them go, walking slowly down the path to my garden gate. Tamar pressed close against Amnon, as if she could no longer walk alone. The sun struck flame and fire from their shining hair.

When they were gone, I looked at the lily-bed. The stems were crushed and flat to the ground where Tamar and Amnon had lain twined together. Fairer than lilies.

And with all their future spread like a new-woven carpet before their feet. There was no good reason Amnon might not have Tamar; they shared only a father, after all. In other lands royal brothers and sisters wed as a matter of course.

And for that reason, if for no other, I knew that David would smile upon them, and bless their union. *What other kings possess, that too must King David have.*

I smiled again, and bent to see what I might save, out of all my ruined lilies.

⁓

The next morning I spoke to my maid Narkis as she combed my hair. "Prince Amnon and Princess Tamar—tell me what men say of them."

"Nothing, until yesterday." Narkis combed on, steady; in her skilled hands the ivory comb never caught on tangles, never pulled too sharp.

"And then?"

"And then Prince Amnon went to King David and asked if he might wed his sister the Princess Tamar."

Well, and why should he not? "And King David said?"

"The king laughed, and said the princess was too young to think of marriage yet."

"She is near fourteen."

"So Prince Amnon said."

"And the king answered?"

"That there was time and to spare to think of futures, and that he would not be tormented by his own children." Narkis set aside the comb and rubbed my hair with a perfumed cloth, long stroke on stroke, to make it shine. "Prince Absalom too was there."

"Did he too speak?"

Narkis finished polishing my hair and gathered up the comb again. She lifted my lily-scented hair. "He did. Will the queen have two braids upon each side, or three?"

"Three, and thread the new coral beads upon them. And Prince Absalom spoke of?"

Narkis wove coral and hair together. "A sister who loves too free. A brother who desires too much."

I did not think that Absalom cared one drop of sweat if Tamar lay with Amnon. As for desires—

"Did Prince Absalom say more?"

"No, for he spoke in heat and anger, and King David would not hear him. The king said that it was only right a sister love her brothers. And that all his children should love one another and bring him peace and joy."

Narkis held my silver mirror up before my face. "Is the queen pleased with her servant's handiwork?"

Triple braids looped back from my face, smooth and rich with carven coral. "Yes, the queen is pleased. What else?"

Narkis laid the mirror down. "Prince Amnon begged again that the king grant what he asked. And Prince Absalom swore his brother would never wed Princess Tamar. What earrings will the queen wear today?"

"Those the Lady Bathsheba gave me at harvest—the ones shaped like wheat-sheaves. And when Prince Absalom had spoken?"

"The king said that Prince Absalom was not yet king, and that only the king might say who a prince or princess should wed." Narkis fastened the circles of golden wheat into my ears. "And then the king said that who was he to deny what Yahweh put into a man's heart, or a maid's?"

"And then King David told Prince Amnon *'perhaps'*." It was not a question; I heard it all as clear as if I had stood there between king and princes. Set Amnon in one balance, and Absalom in another; weigh them against each other. Now smile upon Amnon, now upon Absalom. *Perhaps* and *if* and *maybe*.

'You are not yet king, Absalom—' And Absalom would think that he someday would be.

'Who can deny love, Amnon—?' And Amnon would think that Tamar would be his to cherish always.

And then it would be, later, *'Did I say so?'* and a smile.

Oh, yes, I heard it all clear. And I heard another thing, too, an echo from long ago, when I was still a girl in my father's house. An echo ringing now in David's words like the tolling of a faraway bell. *'Who is king here, you or I?'*

Almost I forgot Narkis was there, until she murmured "The queen is wise. Yes, the king said *'perhaps'*."

~

The seeds of disaster were sown; Absalom tended them until they were ripe for harvest.

For David's kingdom was only two kings old. In most lands, the oldest son living would follow his father on the throne; here, no one yet knew how the power would pass from one hand to the next. Had David been the son of King Saul?

And so Absalom saw Amnon's love as ambition. For Amnon was the eldest son; wed to Tamar, Amnon's claim to David's crown would be better than any other's.

Better than Absalom's.

~

It did not rest there, of course. Absalom would not let it, though David had warned him in plain words: peace and love in David's house. Absalom did not heed.

"Everyone heard them, Michal—quarreling in the banquet hall, and before the king's guests." Bathsheba was pink with anger; she still cherished David's image in her heart, and would not see him hurt.

"Yes, I know. Six others have been before you with the tale."

An ugly tale. Absalom had challenged Amnon's choice of seat, close by the king, demanding he relinquish his place to Absalom. King David had not chided Absalom, but only turned away, so that he need not see. It was Amnon who acted well; he kept his temper leashed, and gave soft words for harsh.

So I added, "But you cannot say they quarreled, Bathsheba. It takes two to quarrel."

She smiled at that. "Yes, and Amnon will not. Oh, he is such a fine boy—well, he is a man now—they grow so *fast*! But—Oh, *why* is Absalom the king's favorite son? Amnon is worth forty of him!"

"The gatekeeper's dog is worth forty of Absalom." I did not wonder that Absalom was the favored child; David always swore Absalom was himself when young.

"And Amnon would be a fine king, like his father—" Bathsheba stopped, and reddened. "I know that does not sound well, Michal—but—but King David—"

"Is not a god. All men die, even kings. We all think of the future, if we are wise. Is it disloyal to think of the kingdom's welfare?"

Yes, Amnon would be a fine king—but Amnon did not care whether he became king or not.

And Absalom cared too much.

~

So there was no open quarrel then, but Absalom was bitter against his brother, and all knew it. Amnon tried to make peace, but Absalom turned his face from Amnon, and so at last Amnon abandoned the useless effort.

For Absalom thought himself injured, and he himself kept his
wound open and sore. And Amnon was a young man new in love.
There were better ways for Amnon to pass the time than in striv-
ing to please Absalom.

And there were better ways for Absalom to pass the time than
in quarreling with his brother. While Amnon walked with Tamar
among the palace gardens, Absalom walked with King David among
the palace halls. While Amnon played love-tunes to Tamar upon
his harp, Absalom poured venom into David's ear.

Behind David's throne, Amnon kissed Tamar in the secret room
that was no secret.

And beside David's throne, Absalom warned of a prince who
would be king.

But for a time there was peace again in David's house. An
uneasy peace, fragile as cobweb.

A peace that could not last.

"The king quarreled with his sons today." Narkis freed my hair
from its woven and jeweled braids. She would comb it smooth
before braiding it down my back against the night.

"That is no new thing." I reached up and ran my hands through
my loosened hair. "What have you heard?"

"That Prince Absalom spent all the day with King David."

"That too is no new thing." I sat quiet under Narkis's skilled
hands.

"That Prince Amnon again asked the king for the Princess
Tamar." Narkis set the comb aside and began plaiting my hair.
"And that the king did not wish to hear him, but Prince Amnon
would speak."

"And? Not so tight; my head aches tonight."

"I will tell Saya to bring cool water to bathe your face. Prince
Amnon said that he had waited a month, and that King David
must answer. Prince Amnon said, 'Your daughter Tamar is four-

teen—is she never to be a wife?' And Prince Absalom laughed, and said, 'Not yours, brother!'"

Narkis knotted gilded leather about the braid's end. "Is it as the queen would have it now?"

"Yes, that will do. And the king said?"

"That Prince Absalom held himself too high. That Prince Amnon must not speak of this again. That Princess Tamar would wed where her father bid. And then the king said, 'Do you think, my sons, that you are cleverer than I?'"

~

After that, Amnon left the king's house and took a house for his own, in the city beyond the king's wall. I was not surprised, though David seemed to be, and did not like it.

"The boy thinks himself too fine to live in his father's house. But he will have his way, and I am only his father; what can I do?" So David said, and smiled. But I knew David; he was not pleased.

Now Amnon had his own house; master under his own roof. Amnon had no wife, and so Tamar went often to her brother, to keep his house in order for him. At first she went only by day. Then she went by night as well—and stayed.

It was no secret; too many knew, and told. I called Tamar to me, once, to warn her. "Be careful," I told her. "They say you go too often to Amnon's house—and not as a sister. Oh, do not stare at me cow-eyed, child—once I loved as hot and hard as you. And do not stammer lies at me."

Tamar stood there silent; under my hand her skin was hot as sand at noonday. Her eyes were oil-bright.

"Listen to me, Tamar. King David has forbidden your marriage to Amnon—now. So wait; be patient."

"But I am fourteen now, Queen Michal!"

"Yes, I know. But do as I say, Tamar. Wait. I know the king, and his mind will change with the moon. But you must be patient, and not defy him. Let no one say you are more to Amnon than a good sister."

"It is not my father," Tamar burst out, "it is Absalom! Everyone knows that! My father does not care for me, only for Absalom! And Absalom—"

"Is a fool," I said. "Listen to me, Tamar—"

"Oh, you do not understand!" she cried, and fled before I could say more. At fourteen, now is all there is, and tomorrow is endless years away.

Amnon was half a dozen years older than Tamar; he did not despair of happiness so easily. He sought an ally against King David. Amnon was not a fool; he thought of me.

Of Queen Michal, the woman to whom King David denied nothing.

I was walking through my courtyard when I heard the voices beyond my gate. Some quiet words, a laugh; I was not sure whose. A voice raised in anger; Absalom's. I walked cat-footed over to the ebony gate and stood quiet in its shadow so that I might see and hear.

It was Tamar, and Amnon, and Absalom. They did not see me; they heeded only each other. Absalom had caught Amnon's sleeve, as if to hold him back from my gate.

"Our father is blind, Amnon, but I am not. Marry Tamar—yes, and set yourselves up as king and queen! Well, you will not have her—and you will not be named king, either! What right have you, more than I?"

Amnon laughed, and flung an arm around Absalom. "Any right I have I will give you gladly as Tamar's bride-price! Come, brother, will you not help me in this? Perhaps if you add your words to mine, our father will heed—"

Absalom flung Amnon's arm off. "Never!"

"Oh, brother, please—" Tamar caught at Absalom's hand. "I shall die if I may not wed Amnon—I care for nothing else, nothing, I swear it—"

"Liar." Absalom hurled words harsh as stones. "Harlot. You are no sister of mine—"

Tamar's eyes widened; she, too, was a king's proud child. "Then I may do as I please, and as my father pleases! And Queen Michal will help us, if you will not! You are a beast, Absalom, and wish to see no one happy but yourself!"

Absalom answered her with a blow. Not a slap, as any brother might strike his sister in heat and anger—or she him. Absalom struck Tamar with a warrior's clenched fist. The blow swept her off her feet; Tamar cried out as she fell.

Amnon sprang forward; he grabbed Absalom's shining hair and smashed his fist into Absalom's proud face. Once only, as Absalom had struck Tamar. Then Amnon let Absalom go.

"Never do that, brother," Amnon said. "The next time I shall beat you as you like to beat others."

Then Amnon knelt beside Tamar, who sat weeping, her hand pressed against her cheek. "Hush, my sister, my dove. Let me see— there, it is only a bruise. It will heal." Amnon bent over her, gentle as a shepherd with a frightened lamb. Tamar clung to him, and wept.

Absalom stood back from them, all hot arrogance. His mouth curled, as if he would spit venom. Amnon's blow already darkened his smooth cheek; Absalom could not bear marring. For Absalom, it was perfection or it was nothing, and so he found life hard.

"My rings scarred her," Absalom told Amnon now. "See, she bleeds."

Tamar sobbed louder; Amnon pulled her hands away from her face, and laughed. Amnon made it sound an easy thing, to laugh. "A scratch only," he said to Tamar. And to Absalom, "Do you think I would care? I do not love Tamar only for her pretty face. You're a fool, brother."

"No," said Absalom. "It is you who are the fool."

I came forward then, out of the shadows of the ebony gate. "You are both fools to quarrel so loudly. King David likes peace in his house."

Absalom glared at me, then bowed his head. Amnon met my eyes straight. "I do not wish to quarrel, Queen Michal. I will beg Absalom's pardon, if he will beg Tamar's."

Absalom's head came up. "Never. She is what I say she is. And you—"

I clapped my hands together, sharp. "Prince Absalom! No, do not speak; I heard it all—yes, and saw it, too. You had no cause to strike her, and your father would not like to hear of it."

Tamar looked up, then. She smiled at me, though her cheek was crimson and her eyes wet. So young, and so loving—as Bathsheba was. As I once had been.

And Amnon, cradling her in his arms—strong and wise, and gentle too. A true prince.

Amnon rose to his feet, and lifted Tamar to stand close beside him. "If the queen heard it all, then the queen knows what—"

"What all the world knows," Absalom cut across Amnon's measured words. "That you and my sister—"

"Be silent!" My voice cut keener than Absalom's. "Is King David dead, that you talk so under his own roof?"

That silenced Absalom, who stood sullen as Amnon drew Tamar toward me. "O Queen, you know what we wish." Amnon hesitated then, looking at me with his clear beautiful eyes.

"You wish to marry your half-sister Tamar," I said. "And she you."

"Oh, yes," said Tamar. "Yes. I will die if I do not."

"No," I said, smiling. "But you will be unhappy if you do not."

Amnon too smiled, and hugged Tamar to him. "I care nothing for the crown, though Absalom here will not believe it—"

"I am not a fool!" Absalom spat out.

"Nor am I, brother. Care rests heavier upon our father's head than does that pretty golden crown. There is more to being king than having all about you kiss your sandals."

"And say how fine and handsome you are!" Tamar said, safe under Amnon's arm.

Absalom glared at his sister, but did not move, or speak. He was not a total fool, or so I thought that day. I did not know, then, how very unwise Absalom was, or how cruel. Or how much he coveted the band of gold that circled his father David's head.

"We came to beg the queen's help." Amnon stroked Tamar's arm and bade her be still. "If the queen knows so much, then she knows what boon I would ask of her."

I laughed, then. "Oh, yes, Prince Amnon, even I can guess that!"

"The queen is the wisest of women." Amnon grinned at me; his smile sent an arrow of pain through my heart. If only David had ever been what I thought him, when I was as young and hot as Tamar—

But if he had, there would be no Bathsheba, no Solomon. Perhaps there would be no kingdom; for the first time I wondered what Israel and Judah would be now, without King David. Squabbling tribes, or Philistine slaves? Or nothing?

But there *was* a kingdom; Judah and Israel united from Dan to Beersheba. One kingdom, and one king. And peace within that kingdom's borders. The next king must take what David had forged from blood and grief and hold it safe.

Absalom was no king. Absalom thought kingship a bauble, a toy to play with.

But Amnon—Amnon was the eldest, as well as the best; a strong claim that would be made stronger still by marriage to his half-sister Tamar. A family's inheritance was often kept whole by such marriages—to cousin or to half-sister. That David's property was a kingdom only made its passage to the next generation, safe and whole, more vital.

Amnon, I thought. *Yes, the next king should be Amnon. Even David must see that, and say it, too. King David is not so young as he was; it is time he spoke, and named his heir.* Amnon. And the first step would be Amnon and Tamar's marriage.

So I thought, and so I spoke. "Since you both wish it so, I will speak to King David and plead your cause. Does that please you?"

Tamar's eyes widened and she squeaked like an excited kitten. "Oh—Queen Michal—you *will*?"

"Yes," I said, smiling. "I will speak to King David for you. I see no reason you should not marry Amnon."

I looked at Absalom as I spoke; he glared dark and sullen as a storm-cloud. *No,* I thought. *Not Absalom.*

Amnon caught up my hands and kissed them. "Then we are as good as wed, for surely my father will grant whatever you ask."

"Perhaps," I said. "He may not. But I will ask."

"Love can deny love nothing," Amnon said, and smiled down at Tamar, and touched his finger to her reddened cheek.

That was how last I saw them—Amnon smiling at Tamar as she gazed up at him, her eyes hot as stars—and the mark of Absalom's hand scarlet upon her face.

CHAPTER 22

". . . for Absalom hated Amnon. . . ."
—II Samuel 13:22

But I could not see David that day, for he was out of the city, not to return until the morrow. So I left word with his servants that Queen Michal wished to speak with him. Then I went to sit with Bathsheba and sort Solomon's clothes with an eye to making and mending.

It was pleasant enough work; women's work, over which we could sit and chatter. See how much Solomon has grown—remember how he fell into the mud in this tunic—think, shall he have blue or yellow for his new cloak—

And as we talked idly of this, and of that, I told Bathsheba what I had seen and heard that morning in the long gallery.

"Oh, poor girl!" Bathsheba's heart had never hardened; she was still as soft and sweet as she had been on the day I first saw her, when I stood upon my balcony and watched her combing out her dusky hair. "It is being talked of, you know, among the women. They say Amnon would wed her, would King David only agree. I do not see why he will not—they are so very much in love—"

"Yes, they are. In another of David's sons, I would call that love ambition—but I have seen Amnon look upon Tamar. He thinks only of her." All unbidden I thought of them in sunlight among lilies, of Amnon's hands on Tamar's hair.

"Oh, yes—but they say Prince Amnon has already spoken to the king, and—"

"The king has refused to speak of it. Yes, I know."

Bathsheba brooded over Solomon's tunics. Then she smiled, bright as dawn over the hills. "Oh, Michal! *You* must ask him! There is little the king refuses you."

"Because there is little I ask." I kept my mouth straight and my voice low; Bathsheba was so earnest I could not help teasing.

"Oh, but everyone knows—Michal! You are laughing at me again!"

I shook my head and swore I was not. "But I too see no reason Amnon and Tamar should not marry—and every reason they must."

Bathsheba's eyes grew very round. "Must? Oh, dear—Tamar is not with child?"

"That I do not know, but it will not matter—once I have spoken to King David and they are wed."

Bathsheba stared at me, then cried out with joy. "Oh, Michal— I knew you would. You are so kind, always!"

You would think that love had never clawed her own heart or caused her a moment's pain. I let her hug me, and kissed her, and smiled.

"Yes, I have promised to speak for them. I told them so this morning." I thought of telling Bathsheba my reasons. Love was not all.

But love was all to Bathsheba, even now. So once more I chose words I thought suited to her ears, and heart. "They are of one heart only," I said. "Who could bear to see them live apart?"

"When will you speak to King David? Surely—oh, he must grant their marriage when *you* ask it, Michal."

"The king returns tomorrow," I said. "I will ask him then. Tell me, Bathsheba, how does a *good* boy put such rents into his clothing? You would think he fought wolves barehanded!"

~

But I never spoke for Amnon and Tamar to their father the king. For that very night Absalom went to Amnon's house in the city, and there found Amnon and Tamar together. Gossip claimed

Absalom dragged Tamar naked from Amnon's bed; it might even have been truth.

But I think it would have made no difference how Absalom had found them. For Absalom was jealous of Amnon, and jealousy is cruel as the grave. It was for that, and that alone, that Absalom slew his brother.

In a fair fight, and in hot blood over his sister's dishonor, so Absalom said. But Amnon's servants said there had been no noise, until Tamar's screams. And Absalom was always sly, and Amnon trusting.

The only one who knew the truth now was Absalom. For when she saw Amnon dead, Tamar caught up a knife and plunged its blade into her own heart.

Or so the tale ran. I did not believe it.

It is not so easy to kill one's self, when one is fourteen and hot for life. And if Tamar had indeed been dragged naked from Amnon's arms, from Amnon's bed, where had she found the knife that Absalom swore she'd turned upon herself?

But whoever struck Tamar to the heart did not strike true. She lived long enough to suffer—and to name Absalom.

~

All the king's household gathered in the painted throne room to see King David give justice; half the city crowded the outer court. Amnon had been well-loved among the people. Absalom was not; he was young and strong and beautiful, but he was too proud to win easy hearts.

I sat on my padded and gilded stool beside King David's throne, and was thankful for the paint that made my face a bright mask. All David's wives were there that day, clustered around his throne. Ahinoam wept; she had not painted her face, and her gown was torn and ash-smeared. She was Amnon's mother; he had been her only son.

Maachah did not weep, as if her daughter Tamar were not

worth tears. Maachah would plead with David for her son
Absalom's life; she saved her tears for that.

Neither woman was my friend, but still I pitied both Ahinoam
and Maachah. There is no pain as deep as that of losing a child; I
looked upon the two women and thought of Caleb. But at least
Caleb still lived, although he was dead to me. I think Maachah
suffered more than Ahinoam, although she wept less. Maachah
must endure the waiting, and the judging.

And so we all waited to hear the words King David must speak.
The only sound was Ahinoam's weeping, muffled behind her hands.

Then Absalom came before King David, walking proud the
long path to the throne. There he stood, all a prince, and stared
into his father's eyes.

"I slew my brother Amnon." Absalom spoke before David even
raised his hand. "I do not deny it, Father. But hear me—do not
condemn me before you know the truth."

What truth? I thought. *Amnon was good and loving and Absalom
is neither. What more is there than that?* I looked at David, motionless upon his throne, his face blank and hard as polished stone.
And for a moment, I almost pitied David, too.

But only for a moment. For then Absalom flung himself to his
knees before David, and swore his only care had been to his sister's
honor and safety. "That was all, Father—I swear it! Was I to stand
by and see my sister Tamar stolen away and dishonored? I loved
her well, and Amnon forced her to his will—"

And King David caught this up like a man finding pure water
in the desert. "Amnon forced her, you say? Have you any proof of
this, my son?"

"The best proof of all—does not her own deed speak for her?
She could not live with the shame of her rape." Absalom bent his
head and covered his eyes, and seemed to weep.

It was true; Absalom was his father born again. I thought of
Tamar's bright eyes and Amnon's kind hands. I thought of how
they had been together, among the lilies in my garden.

Almost I rose up crying out against Absalom's lie.

But I did not. I looked at David's eager face, and was silent. I would not risk all I had only to call Absalom what he was. Amnon and Tamar were dead; they needed nothing from me now. Let King David judge as he pleased.

Absalom flung himself down and kissed his father's feet; David wept and came down from his throne to lift up Absalom and embrace him. "It is a brother's right to defend his sister." There was a murmur from those who watched, like the low growl of a bear deep within a cave.

King David looked, and listened, and turned away from Absalom. "But a brother's death must be truly mourned. You must go from this house and this city."

Absalom bowed his head, as if David's words were too great a weight to carry. "Yes, Father. I understand."

There was more, of course, all well-wrapped in stern words and weeping. But such a banishment meant nothing. Absalom owned fine lands beyond the city where he could dwell in comfort. And David must mean to forgive him all, or he would have forgiven him nothing. Absalom would go free, unpunished.

So David wept, and Absalom spoke meek enough, as if truly penitent and grieved. Absalom's sullen eyes told another tale. David had never schooled Absalom, taught him to curb his desires or his temper. It was too late now. Absalom had no wish to learn.

That was when I knew that David was not wise. Clever—oh, yes, David was always that. But it was shallow, that cleverness. Scales glittering upon a serpent, ripples flashing across a river— that was David's cleverness. Of a serpent's patience or a river's slow power he knew nothing.

I folded this knowledge away to lay beside my other hard-won wisdoms. And then I rose to my feet and went to where Bathsheba stood, behind all the other wives. She stared at me, round-eyed; neither of us spoke. I put my arm around her, and led her away.

~

Banishment was not a high price to pay for a brother's murder, a sister's death. But King David thought it harsh enough.

"It will teach the boy a lesson," he told me that night. "It will steady him."

I thought of Absalom's brooding eyes and angry mouth. "Perhaps it will, David. But what will he learn from it? Absalom—"

"Is high-mettled, like a young colt. Well, it is time to curb him, break him to harness. Then he'll run sweet and fleet under the rein." David laid a careless hand upon my breast; I did not move. I no longer need pretend I craved his touch; David had other lusts I alone could satisfy.

"And where will he run?"

David laughed. "Where I bid him, where else? He's the oldest prince now; he needs his course set for him."

I pushed myself up; David's hand fell away. "You do not mean to name Absalom heir?"

"All my sons shall share my inheritance." David's eyes were sly, glittering in the lamplight like a fox's.

"But king?" I said. "Absalom?"

"Only Yahweh can make a king, Michal." Now David's voice reproved a woman's folly. Nor would he say more, although I coaxed and flattered.

~

When I left the king's rooms I did not go to my own bed. I was restless as a cat in springtime; I did not wish to wake my maids, or Bathsheba, and so I prowled my garden.

The queen's garden changed by night. At first all was blackness, flat and heavy; then I saw shapes, darker and paler. Bushes, benches, fountain. Shadow-flowers and ghost-water.

My feet found the path, and I walked it up and down, from the fountain to the wall. Twenty paces up and twenty back. Up and back, my steps sure and quiet as passing years.

Absalom. David's favorite son. David's heir?

David had not said so. Oh, no—well, and I knew that trick! A hint, a promise—

A plea. *'Ah, Michal, if only WE had a son—'*

But I had borne no son to David, and now I was well past thirty. Too late. And now that love and not hatred warmed my blood, I would have changed that if I could. *My* son, trained up to be all that David was not; Saul's grandson, to take back what David had stolen from him . . . .

Too late, and too late wise. And even if I had been wiser than owl and serpent both, I could not grow a child within my womb. That had been denied; I had been glad of it, once.

Up the path and back again. If not Absalom, then who? David should choose, and he would not.

A laugh, a jest. *'Ah, Michal, is King David yet dead? There is time enough, and to spare—'*

I told over David's sons, looking for a king among them. Amnon—but he was dead and cold, and of the rest—out of a whole litter of fine hounds, which to choose?

None, for not one could hold what David had gathered. His sons were soft, as David was not. King David had made them so, with gifts and ease and granted whims. For David would not raise a son up to take his place. The shepherd would not train another to tend his sheep.

Did he not see that he must? Or did he not care what would happen to the country and the people once great David was dead?

So I asked as I walked the dim path between shadow and shadow.

At last I stopped by the fountain and scooped black water up to cool my hands and face. I was tired, now, weary of questions without answers. The sky was lighter; deep clear blue instead of black.

I washed my face, and went in to my own bed. There were no answers there, either. I thought I would lie awake all the night, as I had often done when troubled.

But I slept deep and quiet. And I did not wake until long past dawn.

Absalom did not pine long in exile. David called him back to Jerusalem less than half a year later.

"He has learned his lesson, Michal," David told me, when he had already sent word to Absalom that he might return. "He has steadied, as I told you he would; men speak well of him now."

That was true; Absalom had put his exile to good use. He had tended his own lands, and given charity to all who passed by and asked it of him. He cared for friends now, and sought the good opinion of others.

Men who had seen Absalom during that half-year and spoken with him, praised him to King David. No longer a heedless boy, they said. Absalom walked meek and soft before the Law now, they said. Absalom had repented of his arrogant ways.

They said. I did not believe it.

And they said, now, that young Absalom was the next David.

That, I believed.

The first spring moon waned as Absalom returned to Jerusalem. Before the new moon held the old in her arms again, Absalom rose up and led an army against his father.

It was David's fault, as well as Absalom's. For David still played the game he had begun long ago. *"Who shall be next king?"* *"Why, that is not for me to say—"* Oh, David was coy as a fair maid with a fine dowry.

But it was no game to Absalom, who resembled his father so much—and so little.

David twisted all to his own advantage—time and over he had coaxed victory from denial and defeat. I remembered how young

David had waited and bowed aside, and always come back in the end to claim what he would have. Princess Merab was not to be his?—well then, had not King Saul another daughter? King Saul loved him not?—well then, had not Philistia a king as well? Nabal the farmer would not grant food and shelter?—well, then, had not Nabal a comely wife who would?

Absalom could not endure an obstacle. If the road did not run straight beneath his chariot wheels, he thought that path forever barred to him. King David would not name him heir to the kingdom?—well, then, King David would never say the only words Absalom wished to hear.

The last time I saw Absalom was in the king's own garden. David had called me there; I was always his chosen witness. Well, of all his great household, I was the only one he could trust. Only before Queen Michal could great David ever speak freely, say what was truly in his heart and mind. We owned each other, now.

That day we sat on a marble bench beneath an arch of roses; shade and sweetness, when the crimson roses bloomed. And Absalom came, at his father's bidding, to speak with him—

"On matters of great import to the kingdom," David said.

Absalom leapt agile to that lure. "Of course, Father. I am your eldest son; you know I will serve you and advise you."

Advice, from Absalom? I looked him up and down; weighing him against a crown. Oh, Absalom was handsome, that I would grant him. All David's children were fair of face; a royal heritage. But that was not enough.

Shining curls and broad shoulders, hot eyes and sullen mouth— that was Prince Absalom. I already knew what lay beneath that gleaming surface: ambition and greed—and murder.

Stupid murder; senseless murder. Amnon had offered to step aside, in exchange for Absalom's aid. *'And will you barter away a crown for Tamar's sake?' 'Of course, brother—my birthright for your*

sister. Come, if you will stand our friend, I will always stand yours—'
In Absalom's sandals, David would have known that Amnon's love,
and Tamar's, were all the weapon that he needed to remove Amnon
from the pathway to the throne. To have Tamar, Amnon would
cheerfully have sworn his rights away before the priests and the
people. Yes, David would have seen that cunning would serve better than a blade. Absalom was not even as clever as David.

So I thought as I sat and watched, and listened as David toyed
with Absalom's hopes. King Cat and Prince Mouse, David thought.

"I have heard much good of you, Absalom."

"That pleases me, Father. I wish to show you what I can do; I
am no longer a boy."

David smiled and held out his hand. "To me you will always
be my son—the child I held in my arms and rocked in the wilderness when I fled from King Saul."

"That was long ago, Father." Absalom answered quickly, plainly
fearing to hear one of David's tales yet again.

"Sometimes it seems so, when I look upon my sons—you,
Absalom, grown into so fine a prince."

So fine a prince, who slew his brother. And his sister too, I
thought, although that vile deed Absalom had never admitted.
But once he had slain Amnon before her eyes, Absalom could not
let Tamar live to speak.

"King David has been granted the sons he deserves." I smiled,
and folded my hands in my lap. "All the land rejoices with him."

Absalom looked at me, slantwise; a prince of David's city, all
oiled curls and painted eyes. David's court copied Egypt's, and
Tyre's; I thought suddenly of my father's face, all leathered by sun
and wind, creased by laugh lines and scars.

David laid his hand over mine. "The queen is right, Absalom.
I have heard you have a care for the people now, that you sit in the
courtyard and advise those who come to the king for justice?"

"Yes, Father. It is a small thing—they are simple men, and the
king is so far above them—I try to help them, when I can." Absalom
suddenly knelt before David, graceful as a dancer. "And to lift even

small burdens from you. Let me help you, Father. Let me learn to rule men, as you do. I am the eldest prince."

Even Absalom did not quite dare demand that King David promise him the throne, but we all three knew that was what was meant by Absalom's plea. There was a moment's silence as David seemed to think upon Absalom's words. A moment in which all the sound was spring breeze through rose-leaves.

Then David laughed, loud, as if he himself were a boy again. "What, have I worked hard as any servant only to set my sons to drudgery? No, no, Absalom—you are young yet. You must not think of me. A father's joy is in his children's happiness."

Absalom's face hardened; in that breath's instant he did not look young at all. "I will try to bring you joy, then, Father."

"You do, my son. The best of my sons." David placed his own necklace about Absalom's neck. "Take this, with my love—a king's gift to a fine prince." David would bestow turquoise and gold, but he would not say Absalom was his choice as next king. Without that, the rest meant nothing to Absalom.

So Absalom thanked his father for his gift, and then asked yet another boon of David. "I am an unworthy wretch, Father, vile in my own sight. Grant me one thing more—that I may fulfill a vow I swore when I was an exile from your house and your love."

"Never from my love," King David told Absalom, smiling at him, fond as a fool. "What is this vow you swore, my son?"

"To go to Hebron, to the priests there," Absalom said; his head was bowed and his eyes hidden. "Will you give me your blessing, Father?"

"To Hebron? What have you sworn, Absalom?" I kept my words soft, a woman's idle curiosity. No more than that.

Absalom smiled; he was all the shining prince, that day. The gold and turquoise David had set upon him were sun and sky about his throat. "I have sworn not to tell it, O Queen."

"The vow does not matter. You know I care only for my children's happiness and peace." David rose and took Absalom in his arms, and kissed him. "Go to Hebron, Absalom my son, and may you find there what you seek."

~

So Absalom went to Hebron, to the priests there. And he went with his father's blessing.

~

CHAPTER 23

"And David said . . .
Arise, and let us flee . . . ."
—II Samuel 15:14

It was a sweet spring morning, and so Bathsheba and I sat upon my balcony to enjoy the warm sun. Bathsheba stitched a leaf-and-berry border on Solomon's new linen tunic; I spun. In a dozen years as King David's queen, I had never learned to sit happily with idle hands.

Once David's wives and concubines had laughed at me; as time had passed, and the king's house became a true palace, and peace and simple pleasure were lost, the king began to praise the old womanly virtues. Now it was the fashion for the palace women to do a housewife's work—or to seem to. I knew many embroidered girdles whose stitches had been being set since Solomon had lain in his swaddling bands. I said as much to Bathsheba, who laughed.

"Like Eglah and her endless border! And even if she ever knots the last stitch upon it, what use will it be?" Bathsheba inspected her own work, and frowned. "Do you know, Michal, I think I shall use blue wool to work the berries, instead of red. Do you think it will look well?"

I considered the matter, and cast my lot for blue. "Unusual, but then our Solomon is an unusual little boy. Yes, I think blue will look very well, Bathsheba."

"Then I have only this here, and here—today's work should see it finished." Bathsheba looked pleased, and with good reason.

She had clever fingers for embroidery, which I did not. I did the good plain work on Solomon's clothes; Bathsheba made them beautiful.

But Solomon's tunic was not finished that day, nor did Bathsheba pick it up again to set another stitch until the spring was gone and the summer over. For even as we sat, and sewed, and chattered, news had come fleet to Jerusalem from Hebron. Absalom had indeed fulfilled a vow there.

He had had himself anointed and proclaimed as king.

Bathsheba had just set her needle once more into the linen, and I had just begun to wonder why the city-noise beyond the palace wall had grown suddenly harsh, when one of my maidservants ran out onto the balcony. The girl was young and silly and breathless—but not too breathless to shriek out her news.

"Rise up, for we must all flee, O Queen—word has just come from Hebron—Prince Absalom is calling himself king! And he even now marches upon Jerusalem with many mighty men! We must all flee lest we be raped and put to the sword!" The maid had plainly run all the way to tell us this great news at once; now she was flushed, panting and rolling her eyes like an eager mare.

"Well, do not sound so pleased about it!" I set my spindle aside and put my arms around Bathsheba, who had uttered a cry of alarm and dropped Solomon's tunic to the floor. The embroidery threads would be a fine tangle to unravel later. "Be silent, Bathsheba—and you, Orit, tell me what has happened. And tell it plain, before I slap sense into your foolish head."

Orit was sullen, then, but spoke plain, as I had bidden her. "Prince Absalom has made himself king. The messenger said so. And he marches with a fine army against Jerusalem."

"Is that all?" I said, and laughed. "Well, and what if he does? Jerusalem has fine walls, and King David has an army of his own. And this time the well will be watched!" David's men had taken the city by climbing up a forgotten tunnel to the city well, and so had come within Jerusalem's walls. Absalom could not do the same. That trick could not be worked twice.

"The army is all for the prince, O Queen. And so the king—King David—says we are all to flee into the hills. At once!"

Bathsheba leaped up. "Solomon! I must find him! Oh, Michal!"

I saw Bathsheba was truly frightened, and I grew angry at Orit. "Nonsense!" I leaped up too, and slapped Orit, hard. She did not look so eager after that. Then I turned to Bathsheba, and smiled.

"We will go nowhere, Bathsheba—what, leave the king's stronghold because Absalom has a pack of boys at his heels! They may come and bay at the walls as they like, and much good will it do them! Flee into the hills—I never heard such folly, and surely King David never uttered it!"

"But he did, O Queen! I swear it!" To hear Orit's excited words, you would think the silly girl *wished* to flee before mighty armies.

"Be silent until you can speak calmly," I said. I must speak to Narkis; if Orit were truly so foolish she might suit another, but she would not serve me. I walked past Orit and went to the edge of my balcony.

There I set my hands upon the wall and I looked down over Jerusalem. The streets were as crowded as if it were market-day. The noise that rose to my ears rang with the clash of metal; the morning sun flashed sparks from spearhead and shield.

The streets full of the king's armed men; a sight to alarm the timid. I lifted my eyes and looked farther. The city gates were shut—both the inner doors and the great brass-bound outer gates.

I smiled. Let Absalom fling himself at Jerusalem's mighty walls. We inside would be safe enough. And soon Absalom's men would tire of following a foolish boy, and go home. David need do nothing, save set a guard upon Jerusalem's famous well-shaft.

"Michal?" Bathsheba was worried still. She came to stand beside me; on the way she trod upon Solomon's tunic and did not even notice. She too looked down at the warriors, and out at the city walls. And then she looked at me.

"He will forgive him again," said Bathsheba.

Her voice was almost despairing; this, from Bathsheba! For a moment I could not speak. Then I smiled again, and took her hand firm in mine. "No. If Absalom has truly done what Orit says he has, then David will not forgive him." He could not.

I squeezed Bathsheba's hand. "Do not worry—it is only Absalom's folly, if indeed it is anything at all. Come, we will go and speak with King David and set your mind at ease."

~

And so we left our women's work lying there on the balcony and went to the king. I was not pleased by what I saw as we walked through the palace. Servants running this way and that, women wailing and clutching their children, clothing and jewelry piled in the corridors—as great a tumult as if invaders already plundered within the gate.

Soldiers stood at the door of David's hall, and they did not wish to let me pass.

"I am the queen," I said. "Let me in to the king, or you will spend the rest of your days guarding the palace midden!" I walked past, taking Bathsheba with me; the soldiers shuffled their feet and shifted their spears, but they plainly could think of no way to stop me. If they had truly been told to keep me out, they deserved flogging for incompetence.

David was with Joab. I did not like speaking with Joab there, but there was no help for it. "I have just heard a tale, O King, and I would know its truth."

"If it's about Prince Absalom, you may believe it, O Queen." Joab's face was as sour as an unripe lemon. "I told you not to trust him, David, and you would not heed me, and now see what has come of it. Well, there has been peace too long in the land, I suppose. Young men grow bored with it."

Bathsheba flung herself upon her knees before David. "O my lord, what is to be done? How could Absalom treat you so, when you have been so kind to him?"

Joab looked down at Bathsheba and laughed; a lion's cough.

"Because he thinks the throne will be kinder, my lady. Well, he is wrong there, and I will prove it to him."

David looked at Bathsheba, and smiled wide. "Absalom is young and his spirit runs high—well, he is a true prince, my son—"

"Have you heard what the king wishes to do?" demanded Joab, his words slashing across David's. "He wishes us to leave Jerusalem—with all his household, mind—"

I did not heed the rest of Joab's words; I stood there and looked upon David as if I had never before seen his face. So silly Orit had been right. I could not believe it. Leave Jerusalem and lay ourselves down before Absalom's knife? This was no boy's prank; this was rebellion. Was David mad?

Joab made a rude noise and looked at me. "Speak sense to him, Queen Michal. He thinks Absalom plays some silly boy's game with him. Look you, David—this game you played with King Saul, and where is great Saul now?"

"It is true." Once it would have torn my heart to give good counsel to David. But now if David went down, so did Prince Solomon, and Lady Bathsheba, and Queen Michal. "Joab is right, David. Absalom would play David to your Saul. And he will not be merciful, as you were."

As merciful as David had been when he had made my father look a fool in all men's eyes. As merciful as David had been when he abandoned my father to his demons, and lured the men of Israel to take glory at his hands. As merciful as David had been to the House of Saul—only so merciful would Absalom be to David.

But Absalom would not write songs to David's glory, afterwards. I had known Absalom since he was a boy; Absalom would not be generous to even a fallen enemy, no, even though that charity cost him nothing.

"Ah, but I am still David, and Absalom shall learn that!" David laughed, and took Bathsheba's hands and lifted her to her feet. "Go, find your women and pack what you would keep with you. We will be gone from Jerusalem by nightfall."

I stared; Bathsheba gasped; Joab swore. David held up his

hand, all the king. "No, I will hear no more, Joab—do as I command. Now go, all of you, and make ready for the journey. And Joab—send Hushai to me."

"David—you cannot mean this. Why should we leave Jerusalem and give ourselves into Absalom's hands?" I could not believe David meant this; it was sheer folly, and even a woman could see that.

"Just so have I told him. Queen Michal, and he will no more listen than the stones in the wall." Joab glared at David. "Well, you are the king, David, and so I will follow you. But you are a fool, uncle, and so I tell you!"

David laughed. "I am sly as the fox in the vineyard—do you think I know not what Absalom thinks, and how? Well, I shall humble him and teach him, and he will be all the better for the lesson."

His eyes shone and he made his voice ring valiant; he was as hot for action as a stallion seeing the war-chariot. Not King David, but David-giant-slayer, David-hero. David the young beloved was what he would have men see. And I looked, and what I saw was a man looking to the past, not to the future. A man who was growing old.

When he was young he had humbled King Saul, calling like a dove of the rocks from the high places, taunting my father, flaunting youth and power before the mad king. So, now, would he treat his rebellious son Absalom. So thought David.

But who, this time, would learn the harsh lesson? The young warrior, or the aging king?

~

Yes, who would learn, and who teach? That question rang endless inside my head as Bathsheba and I walked away from King David's chamber. David—or Absalom? Young David, some men called him. . . .

"I do not understand." Bathsheba's voice echoed plaintive in the tiled hallway.

"What is there to understand? David is—"

"I know King David is the greatest warrior in all the land, and the wisest man." Bathsheba did not let me finish; when she was nervous or worried she chattered on like a sparrow, hardly hearing her own words. "If he says we must leave Jerusalem, then I know it is the only way. I am sorry, Michal—I know you must think I am a fool to fear where the king does not. Only—"

"No, I do not think you a fool," I said, and took her hand. She clung to my fingers as if she were a child.

"Who is mightier than the king? Did he not defeat the Philistines, and—and the Ammonites, and—"

"And King Saul." My words dropped clear into the air between us.

"Oh, Michal—I did not mean—"

"No," I said. "Of course you did not. But it is true. Truth is truth whether I like it or do not." But David had never learned that, or would not admit it if he had.

"And now he will defeat Absalom. Of course he will. But still I do not see why we must all leave Jerusalem—well, of course I do not, for I am only a woman, but—" She stopped, and looked at me hopefully. Bathsheba thought me wise.

I thought of all I might say to her—that David sought his lost youth upon this battlefield, that David had won his great victories by guile and by treachery, that David would not know truth if Yahweh himself came in all his glory and laid it plain at David's feet. But if I said all this, what then? Such words would only hurt and frighten her.

So I only squeezed her hand, and said nothing of all that. "Oh, there is a reason we must leave Jerusalem," I said. "But it is a man's reason, and I do not think you would understand. Leave the reasons to the king, and turn your mind to what we must do before nightfall."

I should have spoken plainly with her then. But dearly as I loved Bathsheba, I thought of her as a little sister, younger and less wise than Solomon; I did her less than justice. And to spare her a moment's pain, I too twisted truth to my own ends, just as David did.

For a few paces we did not speak. Then Bathsheba said, "I have never gone to war before. What shall we pack?"

A foolish woman's question, some would call that. I knew better; what we chose to take with us now might be all we would ever have. "Nor have I. You must help me choose wisely, Bathsheba."

And let us hope that David has.

~

And so all the king's household was packed in haste and in panic, and bundled out of Jerusalem like a maidservant in disgrace. Bathsheba and I did better than many, for we thought a little before we made our choices. And so Bathsheba and Solomon and I had good plain clothing and sandals that could be long walked in. And we gathered together bread and dried fruits and waterskins to keep close by us.

And I did another thing. I took some of our necklaces and bracelets and hid them within two loaves of bread. Then I knotted the loaves into one of my veils.

I was not David, to know Yahweh's mind. But I did know Absalom's. If Absalom became king indeed—well, that would be as Yahweh willed. But Solomon's future was my care and my will.

And I did not trust Absalom's devotion to his brothers.

~

But if King David thought to soar like the falcon and strike like the viper as he had in his shining youth, he soon found out his mistake. David the Hero had moved with a band of warriors; David the King moved with wives, and concubines, and their children and their servants and their baggage, and their pack-animals, and their heavy wooden litters. David the King moved neither swift nor silent; I had not heard so much noise even at sheep-shearing time in Gallim.

And as for weeping and wailing and moaning—well, I had never heard the like. You would not guess, to hear them now, that any of David's wives had once been farmers' and merchants' daughters. The only one who did not complain from morning until night was Maachah, who had been the King of Geshur's daughter, and who was Absalom's mother. Either pride or grief, or both, kept her silent.

I was too busy to look back and weep for the loss of Jerusalem. In truth, I did not think of the city at all. And so when we came to the top of the hill and I turned, I was unprepared.

The last time I had seen its walls from the free hillside, Jerusalem had shone golden in morning light. Then I had been a farmer's wife, brought unwilling to be a queen. Since that day I had not once passed beyond the inner wall of the upper city.

Now Jerusalem lay sullen under slanting afternoon sun. Perhaps I would never again pass through the brass-bound gates into the city that had been my home and my prison for so many years.

"Mother? Mother-the-queen? Why are you staring? Do you see soldiers?" Afire with excitement, Solomon tugged at my girdle. Well, he was only a boy; this was all a wild game to him, one he never before had played.

I touched his soft hair. "No, I see no soldiers. And if Yahweh smiles upon us, we will see none."

"None save my father's, you mean."

"As my little owl says, none save King David's." I looked from Solomon back to the city behind us. For myself, I cared nothing if I never set eyes upon Jerusalem's walls again. It is not the walls that are important, but what they enclose safe within; I would be happy in any house I shared with Solomon and Bathsheba.

But Bathsheba and I were only two women who were no longer young; Solomon was our life. And Solomon was a true prince. He belonged under a palace roof—

For the next king of Israel will not be chosen out of a flock of sheep upon a hillside. The thought slid into my mind from nowhere; from long ago. *Do you wish to serve the future or the past?*

I am blind, I thought. *Solomon is the future. Oh, yes. Solomon. My son. The son Yahweh gave to me. To me, not to David....*

I had curved my hand about Solomon's head, stroking his hair; my fingers caught in a tangle. He was all wide eager eyes and tousled hair, his tunic embroidered with dust and stains. *Say nothing. Not to Solomon, not to Bathsheba. He is only a boy.*

But boys grew into men; I knew that, even if David did not. Solomon would be a man, one day—

"Michal! Michal, you should be in a litter—you will tire yourself—" Bathsheba leaned out of her own litter, pushing aside the painted leather curtains. "Solomon, come here at once!"

Solomon looked up at me hopefully, deaf to Bathsheba's call. "May I run alongside the soldiers? All the other boys are."

My glittering dreams fled; later I might summon them back again. Now I looked, not at a future king, but at a small boy who did not wish to be denied a treat.

"No," I said. "You must go to your mother, Solomon, and do as she bids you."

Solomon set his jaw. "Men don't ride in litters."

I knelt beside Solomon and put my arms around him. "Perhaps they do not, my heart—but men are kind to women. Your mother is nervous and afraid. You are not, so you must stay with her and protect her. Now go to her; she will feel safe with you there to hold her hand."

Solomon smiled at me then, and ran over to clamber into the litter with Bathsheba. She beckoned to me again and I shook my head.

"No," I called. "Yes, of course they have brought the queen's litter! I would rather walk—and so should you. We have grown fat and lazy in the king's house!"

Before I followed them I looked back, once, at Jerusalem. I hoped now for some sign that we would return. *The next king. . . .*

In the dying light the palace walls flamed red as blood.

CHAPTER 24

*"And the king, and all the people
that were with him, came weary . . . . "*
—II Samuel 16:14

We crossed the Jordan by night, in haste. All the next day we traveled, until even my bones were weary. I walked as much as I could, but I was palace-soft. When my heels blistered, I too must ride donkey-back, or retreat to the queen's gilded litter.

At last we stopped, and the tents were set up and fires lit.

I kept Bathsheba and Solomon with me, and had no patience with those who called Solomon too old to share a woman's tent. I would have him nowhere but under my eye. He slept at the foot of our bed; I could hear him breathing, slow and safe. I was glad Solomon could sleep, though I could not. For all my weary bones, my mind could find no rest.

"Michal? Are you asleep?"

"No—but you should be, Bathsheba. Tomorrow we march again."

"I cannot sleep. I am so sore—and the camp is so noisy--"

"And you are so troubled. Well, and so am I." We spoke soft as sighs; Solomon must not be wakened.

"You, Michal? You seem always so strong and sure. So—so calm, as if you know always what to do."

"No more sure than you. I am older, and have seen more. That is all." That was not all, of course. But there were some things I could never tell gentle Bathsheba. "But I too am sore weary and afraid. Now promise you will not tell the maidservants—I have worked too many years teaching them to tremble at my glance."

Bathsheba's hand sought mine, and clung. "I will never tell, I swear it."

"That is a great burden eased." I squeezed her fingers, willing her to rest. But she could rest no more than I, and for the same reason.

"You say we march again tomorrow—but where are we going? And what will happen if—" Bathsheba stopped. She was a good wife; she did not wish to sound disloyal.

I spoke the words for her. "If King David does not defeat Absalom?"

"Oh, Michal—I try not to think of it, and I know it will never happen, for the king is the greatest warrior in the land, but—"

"Hush, you will wake our boy. Do not worry. I will never let harm come to you or to Solomon. Trust me for that." No, no matter what I had to do to keep them safe, the sister and son of my heart. "This folly will soon be over, and we will go home. Now you must sleep, for tomorrow will be no easier."

"I will sleep when you do."

And so I put my arms around her, and we lay there and watched shadows dance dark upon the tent walls, forced there by the watchfires. The night was not silent. Footsteps went past; leather creaked and metal clinked; men called out to one another. Beyond those noises were coughings and stampings from the donkeys and camels, low complaining moans from the cattle, wailing bleats from the sheep.

And under and through all other sounds the night wind sang against the tent ropes, as restless as my thoughts.

We lay, and listened, and at last, unwilling, slept.

King David thought Absalom would be tempted and follow him, hoping to take all while David and his men were heavy-laden with women and children and treasure. An enticing, easy target for a rash young warrior-prince—Absalom would pursue, and strike— and find that King David's foreign mercenaries had not deserted a failing king, but waited only to close a deadly iron ring about Absalom's men.

But Absalom was no bull-headed Saul, to grasp after morning mist. Absalom struck straight and true for the walled city of Jerusalem. With that fortress safe under his hand, he could afford to wait.

And so Absalom took King David's city. It was easy enough. King David had fled; the city was undefended as a virgin alone in her house.

I was there in the king's tent when David heard the news, brought by a weary messenger who trembled so hard he could scarcely speak the words.

"Jerusalem is taken. Prince Absalom sits there upon your throne, O King."

David looked upon the messenger's bowed head; David stroked his beard, and then he laughed, and clapped his hands together. "Does he, now? I wish him joy of it—foolish boy!"

And David raised the man up, and embraced him, and sent him away with the king's thanks ringing in his ears. The man looked only puzzled, as well he might. He had brought tidings of disaster, and had the ill news flung aside as a fine jest.

I looked past David to Joab, who had come in behind the messenger. Joab, at least, did not laugh.

"Now you see what comes of giving that boy even so much as one handful of dust. He is slick as an oiled weasel." Joab spoke as plain as if I were not also in the king's tent. "And you stand there and laugh! Do you want men calling you as mad as King Saul?"

David looked at me, and smiled. "Do not mind what Joab says, my queen. He does not mean to cause you pain." David set his hand upon my shoulder; it lay heavy there, as if I were a staff to hold him upright.

"I do not mind what Joab says, and truth does not cause me

pain," I said. I did not look again at Joab. "And he is right, David. Why will you listen to no one? Now Absalom holds Jerusalem—and who holds that city holds all." Had not David himself told me that many times?

David laughed again, and squeezed my shoulder. His fingers pressed upon one of the pins that fastened my gown; the point bit sharp into my skin. I do not think David noticed that, or that I drew away from his hand.

"Absalom thinks himself more than his father now, and his entry into Jerusalem a great victory. But he must take the king, to take all—and that he will never do." David's face was alight, as if he were a young man again, new-come to King Saul's house; he saw only his own glory. "Ah, my son is clever—but he is only a boy still, and not yet wise. Do not stand there with sour faces—oh, come, Michal, did you ever know me to have only one string to my bow? Only one stone to my sling?"

"You can't use a sling against Jerusalem," Joab told him.

"No, not a sling, nor yet a bow—but a snare. Come close, and listen, and I will tell you what no other yet knows." David set his hands upon our arms and drew us near to him. "Now hear me well—"

He spoke low and soft, and suddenly I was a girl again. A girl in a dark tower room, listening to that voice spin a glittering web of words, a trap for fools.

Ah, yes, King David had left Jerusalem, with the way broad and the gates open. And King David had left ten concubines there to welcome Absalom. A king's women were always claimed by a new king.

But the royal women were only bait in the trap. For David also left a man called Hushai.

"I know Absalom," David said. "But he does not know me. I tell you again I am cunning as the fox in the vineyard." And David smiled a fox's smile, all sly wicked pleasure.

Clever once, I thought, *and clever still*. Too clever?

I looked at Joab again. His face was set like stone.

~

Hushai had been long with David, and knew the king's mind better than the king. So Hushai told Absalom. Hushai was tired of serving an old king who did not reward him as he deserved. Hushai wished to serve the new, who would treat him better.

Any man of sense would have sent Hushai's head as gift to David. But Absalom was as vain as his father, without his father's cunning. Absalom believed Hushai.

He took David's city; he took David's women. He thought he had taken David's place.

He was wrong. As David had said, there was a trick left to the old fox yet.

~

But at first it seemed as if David were in truth the aging fool Absalom plainly thought him. Absalom laired safe within Jerusalem's walls, and toyed with David's abandoned concubines, and sent men to spy after David.

David led those spies a hard chase; once before David had fled through these hills for his life, and he still knew each track and turn and hollow. David left his pursuers a tangled thread to un-ravel, if they would follow him. So I was told by David. I knew only that for a time we set up our camp anew each sunset. Always moving, aimless as sand shifting across desert, or so it seemed to me.

It was not an easy way to live; a warrior's camp is no place for women and children. The priests and the laws say so; women and warriors agree.

Children do not. Even Solomon, who was a good obedient boy, grew wild as spring ended and summer began, and still we lived in camps and caves. Bathsheba and I tried always to have him under our eyes, but still he spent much time with the soldiers, and with the grooms and herders.

Bathsheba begged and scolded; I told him plain that he must not. "They have their own work to do, Solomon. That is trouble enough, even without a prince underfoot."

"And why should you wish to talk with them?" Bathsheba demanded. "They are only rough men, after all."

"Yes, I know, Mother, but I want to hear what men say." The line of Solomon's jaw was square and stubborn. "They do not talk as women do, you know," he added kindly, as one instructing the young.

I bit my lip so that I would not laugh. "That is all very fine, Solomon, but—"

But then Bathsheba spoiled my firmness by flinging her arms about Solomon and clutching him to her plump bosom. "Of course they do not, my clever darling, but you must *not* run about underfoot. You will not, will you?" But she was smiling at him, and so of course he paid her little heed.

"I promise I will not make you worry, Mother," Solomon said earnestly, and kissed her upon the cheek as if sealing a solemn vow. He did not look at me; he knew I was not so easy cozened. Then he wriggled out of Bathsheba's soft arms and dashed off before I could lay my hands upon even the hem of his tunic.

"Solomon!" It was no good; he was away. To scold Bathsheba for sweet-hearted folly was to scold a dove for cooing. I did not waste my breath, but only sighed.

Bathsheba took my hand in hers. "Oh, yes—but at least he is happy—although how he *can* be, I do not know!"

"Because he is a boy," I said. "Boys have no thought for anything but the moment—and it is not Solomon who must pack our beds or cook our food or raise our tents."

"Or clean our clothing!" Bathsheba added. "Do you know, Michal, when I think of how our ancestors wandered in the wilderness for forty years—well, I do not know how they bore it! I would have stopped at the first village that would take me in!"

That made me laugh, and agree. And then I went back to my own tent, to rest before we again moved on. The sun beat hard upon the tent-roof; I lay half-asleep in the dim heat, and wondered how long this wandering would be my life.

Did David think to retrace each step he had taken long ago when he had danced away before King Saul? Perhaps, but why? The lure had failed; Absalom would not leave Jerusalem to attack King David.

And if Absalom would not challenge David upon the battlefield—and I would not, were I Absalom—well, once again there were two kings in the land. Which would men follow now?

So I asked, and found no answer in the shadows that fled across the walls of my tent as clouds above hid the high sun's face. Then there was a nearer, darker shadow; my maid Narkis set the curtain aside and slid into the tent.

"There are men who would speak with you, O Queen. What shall I say to them?"

"How do I know that, until I know their names?" I was drowsy with heat, and so did not move.

"It is Joab," Narkis told me. "And Abishai, and Ittai also."

I turned my head and stared at Narkis. Joab, and Abishai, and Ittai—David's finest war-captains, the men who commanded David's host of fighting men. "What do they want of me?"

"How do I know that?" Narkis asked, and her voice was sharp.

No one spoke so to me; was I not the queen, after all? Anger sprang up hot and quick, so that I nearly answered as sharply. But when I looked at her I was ashamed, and kept my temper to myself. Narkis was as weary as I, her hair just as full of dust. And no one ran to do *her* bidding, or to bring *her* the first jug of water from a stream.

"You do not, of course." I lay there a moment, and thought of Joab. Joab, David's sword-blade. . . .

"Shall I tell them the queen sleeps?"

"No," I said. "Tell them I will see Joab. Bid him enter."

Narkis bowed, with the flicker of her eyelids that meant she disapproved. But I did not care. I must know what it was that Joab wished to say to me now. And I did not want it said before witnesses, nor yet where anyone who passed by might listen.

When I rose to await Joab I swayed and brightness flared before my eyes. I fought dizziness; I had risen too quickly to my feet. That was all it was. I told myself so as Joab entered my tent and I faced him at last.

Never before had I seen Joab alone; I held my chin high, all the proud queen, and waited for him to speak first. I would give nothing away.

But Joab only bowed, and thanked me for granting him leave to speak. His words were quick, impatient; Joab spoke in angry haste. "For I will tell you plain, we are all at wit's end; David will listen to none of us. But he will heed you."

Ah, it was only David, again. "If the king will not heed his own men, will he heed a woman?"

"Yes, if that woman is you. And if that woman tells him what he already wishes to hear. Now will you listen to us or not?" Joab never oiled words.

"I do not need to hear the others. Joab's word is enough. Will you sit?"

"No need. All I ask is that you tell David he must stop this folly."

"Which folly? There are so many now." To speak truth for once, even to Joab—ah, that was delight.

"This war-camp—*war-camp*, he calls it, with women and children screeching and running underfoot!" Joab looked as if he would spit upon the floor; he looked at my striped carpets spread upon the dirt, and did not.

"Do you think we like it any better than you? Tell me what you would have me say, Joab, and I swear I shall tell it to the king, each word—yes, even if I must bind him fast with my own hair to make him listen when I speak!"

Joab grinned. "You're a match for him, Queen Michal; he should give his other wives to Absalom!"

"Poor Absalom!"

"No man needs more than one wife, if she's the right one," Joab said. Fine talk; Joab had no wife at all save his sword.

"Perhaps," I said. "Now tell me."

What Joab spoke was only common sense; the army could not move swiftly burdened with all the king's household. The women, the children, the beasts, the baggage—all must be locked safe away so the army was free to fight.

"And David too must stay safe away from battle—oh, he will not like it, but it is folly to risk him. And to speak plain, Queen Michal, in this I do not care what David likes."

"Should the king not lead his men?" To stay behind, with the women—ah, David would not like that. It would sting the hero's pride.

"The king should lead his men to victory," Joab said, and his eyes were flat, like a viper's.

"Do you think he would not?"

"You're a clever woman. Tell me."

"King David thinks too little of Prince Absalom. And too much of himself. He schooled Absalom, after all."

"And David is getting old," Joab said. "Prancing about the hills like a partridge—" Again he looked about my tent-floor; again he gave it up. "So tell him, Queen Michal."

"Yes, I will tell him. Now I ask you to tell me a thing, and truly. Will Absalom defeat us?"

"Not if *I* lead the host against him. That I swear to." Joab grinned like a wolf. "David's always been too damn soft with that boy."

⁓

It was not easy to catch the king; David seemed never to rest quiet for more than a few moments. I was fortunate, for chance brought David past my tent at the very moment I was scolding Solomon—again.

"—and I have told you before, Solomon, that you must stay away from the cattle-pens! Do you think the oxen will not kick you because you are a prince? Well, they will, and you will deserve it—but your mother and I are the ones who must tend you, and—"

Solomon stood with his head down, kicking the pebbles in the dirt. He looked as sullen as any boy being brought to task for willfulness—save that Solomon was clever enough to hold his tongue and not make silly excuses when he knew I was angry.

In truth, I suppose I was not truly angry with him—well, I knew what boys were, after all! But the long days and longer nights while we marched and waited and marched again had honed tempers and tongues.

"Now what can my little peacemaker have done to deserve a shrew's welcome, Michal?" It was David, dressed in a short warrior's tunic, playing at being the simple fighting man. Now he smiled at Solomon and ruffled the boy's hair.

It was David who had dragged us all into this life of dirt and danger, and for no good reason save his own pride. Yes, my anger was for David. But I must not let David know that. And so I spoke as any cross woman might.

"What has he done? He has disobeyed his mother and me and runs about the camp like a wild beast! That is what he has done, O King."

"A wild beast!" King David was in a mood to be amused. He swung Solomon up and held him high. "Have you disobeyed your mother, boy?"

"Oh, no, Father. She said I mustn't let the cattle kick me, and I won't."

"No, Solomon, that is *not*—"

"There, you see, Michal? Leave the boy alone—he'll come to no harm, and camp life will toughen him." David set Solomon down, all fatherly indulgence. Well, it cost David nothing, after all. David did not have to care for Solomon and for his clothes. "Now run along, boy—you can learn much in camp, if you're willing to work and listen. I did, once, and look at me now."

Solomon did not stay to look, but bowed and ran off as King David had bidden him. David would have gone striding on, then, but I put my hand upon his arm. "Wait, David—I would speak with you, if you will grant me so great a boon."

Those few words were carefully chosen; I knew they would remind David of the great boon I had once asked when I had begged for Bathsheba's life. David would always listen to me when I invoked that memory.

And so David smiled, and bade me speak, as I had known that he would. And I said the words Joab and Abishai and Ittai, the war-captains of David's host, had begged of me. I said them well, for they were words I truly meant.

"See, O King, how this life turns your children wild and your women shrewish—well, who can stay sweet-oiled and pleasant in a warrior's camp?"

"You are always fair and pleasant to my eyes, my queen. And as for the children—why, they are soft and eager to be hardened. They are a warrior's sons, after all."

"And are your daughters to take up sword and spear as well? No, do not turn from me, David—I speak only for the good of us all. We slow your army, lord. The soldiers fear for our safety, when they should be bold. Find a place for us, that we may rest, and make you welcome when you return victorious."

David looked hard at me. "I have heard these same words—or their brothers—from my war-chief and my captains."

I smiled and spread my hands wide. "Who can hide anything from the king? He sees even the pebble at the bottom of the well. Yes, I had these words from Joab, and from Ittai and Abishai too. Since you would not heed them, they asked me to speak. And my lord the king knows that I would speak no words of Joab's if they were not my own as well."

I folded my hands before me, and waited. David had heard. Now he would do as he wished. I hoped it would be as his captains wished—and as I wished. I had had my fill and more of war-camp life. I tasted dust in my food, and in my dreams. I could not remember when last I had bathed. All our perfumes were gone.

"Well, well," David said at last. "Perhaps I have been too

stiff-necked—there, never let men say King David cannot admit a fault. Behind thick walls you would be safer, and then the army could move freely and fast." His eyes gleamed; I thought once more of an aging stallion being led to the war-chariot.

"As the king says. And should not David be in the forefront of the army—with the men?" And I smiled inwardly, for I knew what Joab and the others would say to that!

~

CHAPTER 25

"O Absalom, my son, my son!"
—II Samuel 19:33

And so reason prevailed at last. We traveled one more weary road, north to a city loyal to David. The king's household stayed there, safe within the walls of Mahanaim.

And there, to his great anger, the king remained as well. For when David would ride out in his fine chariot at the head of the host a cry of protest arose from the people, who would not see King David risk his own throat to enemy blades. And Joab, who had started the outcry, stood beside David's chariot and told him bluntly that the king was too precious to chance in battle.

"Nay, not that you are too old—did any say so? But does a man set a jewel in the road for robbers? If you fall, we all fall. I have led your men against your enemies without you before. This is no different."

For David it was. This enemy was his own son—David wished to be the one to teach the lesson. And I do not think he trusted Joab to know the king's mind in this. David knew Joab well, after all.

"They would not let me go," David said loudly, as we stood upon Mahanaim's walls and watched the army march. "You see how I am loved! But Joab is right, he knows his job—I taught him, didn't I? And I bade him treat Absalom soft, and bring the boy safe to me."

Did David think Absalom would draw back and treat *him* soft? I thought of that, and of Joab, and then I smiled. *Yes, David,*

Joab knows his job. You taught Joab well, O King. It was you who gave him his taste for murder.

~

Mahanaim had been a king's city once. My brother Ishbaal had ruled there, in the days when he had been king over Israel. There had been two kings in the land then, too; Israel's king, and Judah's. That had been a dozen years ago.

Those days rose up, clear again in my mind, as I watched the army stride away from Mahanaim. Days when King Ishbaal sat in Mahanaim, and Abner ruled for him—and King David sat in Hebron, and ruled for himself. Always for himself. Days in which I sat placid in Phaltiel's house, and spun my thread and wove my cloth, and thought the village of Gallim all the world I should ever see.

I would have thought Mahanaim a great city, had I seen it then. Now I weighed it against Jerusalem; balanced against that, Mahanaim was little more than Gallim had been. A market town, that was all—and a crowded one, now that King David had come and demanded houses for his wives, and his daughters, and his servants.

A merchant had given up his house to the king's wives; the merchant was a wealthy man, and his dwelling was a large, good house. Of course it was still too small for a dozen women and their servants and young children; they must huddle together in it like sheep in a crowded fold. But that was not the merchant's fault, and he had done his best to make us welcome there. Walls had been newly lime-washed. The courtyard had been swept and all the rooms cleared for us. Above us, on the housetop, vines curled over a high-arched arbor. It would be pleasant to sit there in cool breeze and shade.

"How kind," Bathsheba said. "How kind of him to give up his own home for us. We must thank him and his family, Michal."

"Yes. Yes, we will do that—perhaps tomorrow, when I am not

so tired—and so dusty!" I smiled, for at last we had come to a place where we might once more know comfort. "Perhaps there is a full cistern, and a basin—"

"A bath." Bathsheba sighed the words; dreaming of water as of a lover.

"Yes," I said, and my voice held the same longing. "Yes, a bath. For us, and for Solomon too, if we can catch him!"

Bathsheba laughed, then, and I put my arm about her. "Come, let us find rooms for ourselves in this fine, fine house."

"This is not what I am used to," I overheard Abigail say. "Is this a way to house the king's wives? Why, we are all pushed in here together like—"

Abigail's voice rasped in my ears; I stepped forward and spoke to them all. "No, this is not what we are used to." My voice rang out clear, smooth and chill. I do not know why I troubled myself over the matter, save that it was Abigail who had spoken. But once I began, I realized that if this were not stopped now, David's women would do nothing but quarrel and squabble until those of us with sense were driven mad.

"We are used to eating dust and washing with our tears; we are used to following the king's army until our sandals are worn from our feet and our skin burned from our faces." I looked at them all—Abigail, Haggith, Eglah, and all the rest. "That is what you are used to, Abigail, and what I am used to. And since you prefer that to this, go and tell King David so, and see how you are housed then!"

I looked past Abigail then, to the others crowded there. Some were haughty, some puzzled. All were sore weary, wishing only to pause somewhere, and rest. "As for me, I am not so proud, but then, I am only the queen," I said. "I will take this place, and gladly. Any of you who wish to dwell in peace in the queen's house may rest welcome here. The rest of you may do as you please."

Of course the queen's house I had claimed was not quiet; I did not hope for that. But there were no quarrels where I could hear them, and that was all I asked. And I did not spend all my days trapped under that roof. Mahanaim was not Jerusalem and the war had made new manners; here I owned freedom such as Queen Michal could never have in King David's great city.

~

Many years had passed since I had walked with other women to the village well, had joined in their talk. Idle chatter, men call such talk—well, and so it is, if it is idle to talk of birth, and death, and food and clothing and marriage.

Mahanaim's women were shy of me at first, and silent. They stared at me round-eyed, and turned their faces away to whisper to each other, but they would not speak freely before me. Then, as I walked every day to the well, and to the market, and smiled and laughed with Bathsheba, and praised their children, the women began to smile back, and then to greet me. And then they began to speak to me, when they learned that I would listen.

What women say at the well today, all the world will say tomorrow. I listened.

"I have heard that Prince Absalom swore to slay all his brothers that he might be king. Is it true?"

"They say Prince Absalom has lain with the king's concubines—they say the king left his women in Jerusalem as a sign Prince Absalom was king indeed. Is it true, O Queen?"

"Is it true the king promised Prince Absalom half the kingdom if he would lay down his sword?"

"Who is heir, now that Prince Amnon lies dead?"

The foolish questions of women.

~

A quiet life, waiting in Mahanaim. And then one day I saw a woman at the well.

A woman at the well, like any other. But she moved with a smooth rise of hip, a lazy sway of veil over her back, rippling like waves over sand. . . . She dipped her jug and drew it up again, water dripping from the spout, flashing crystal in the sun. Someone spoke to her; a jest, it seemed, for the woman flung back her head, and laughed.

I knew her then. It was Zhurleen.

Zhurleen, once my truest friend, though I had not known that until too late. Zhurleen, who had been sold into a shameful life, through my folly. Zhurleen—neither memory nor ghost, but a living woman who must hate me. . . .

I thought Zhurleen did not see me. She settled her jug upon her hip and began to walk away.

I moved, then, and hurried after her. "Wait!"

She stopped, and set her water-jug down at her feet. Then she waited until I was close to her, and smiled. "The queen is kind, to trouble herself with a humble Moabite woman. How may I serve the queen?"

There was so much I had always wished to tell Zhurleen, if only I were ever granted speech with her. And now all I could think of to say was, "So now you are a Moabite?"

"Was not great David's grandfather's mother a Moabite woman?" She smiled again. Her hair was no longer crimson curls down her back; it was braided, neat and simple, and covered with a blue veil.

"Ruth," I said. "Her name was Ruth."

"Yes, the wife of Boaz. Well, what is good enough for the king is good enough for me. Besides, Moab is greater now than Philistia—and a far safer land to be from!"

"Zhurleen—"

"I am Zilpah now. We all change, O Queen."

"I have not changed," I said, and thought I spoke the truth. "I have never forgotten you and your kindness."

"Nor did I forget you—no, no, I never thought you had asked the king to sell me, so do not look so at me. Whatever faults you may have, you are not small-hearted."

"Perhaps not. But I am a fool and a coward." It was sweet to speak plainly to one who would believe what I said.

"And if you are, what is that? Has wisdom and courage brought King David happiness? But you—you are happy now, are you not?"

"I have a boy to care for, and a sister to love. Yes, I am happy."

"I am glad—and gladder still that you have learned again to be happy."

I smiled. "It was a hard lesson, but I have learned it. And I am queen besides; I can do much for you!" I could have Zhurleen once again at my side, with her laughter and her wisdom. She would serve me, as she had once sworn she would—Bathsheba would love Zhurleen as I did—

"Can you? I would kiss you if I dared, Michal—so often the great ones have short memories for favors! But if you would do much for me, leave me in peace with my husband."

The sun's harsh white light beat upon my head; the stones beneath my feet were hard and fire-hot. For a dozen heartbeats I could not move. I do not think I breathed. Perhaps I made a sound, for Zhurleen touched my arm, quick and light, with her fingertips.

"No, I do not mean to be cruel. You think of the old days— and that is kind of you. But the old days are gone, and the new will be as we make them."

"Another lesson?" My blood beat as hard as if I had just stepped back from a ravine's edge, unseen until the breath before.

"Who am I to teach the queen? Who knows better than the queen that we all learn, and change, if we live—why see, even I have learned what you once tried to teach me—that a good man is better than a wealthy one. Of course, a good wealthy man is still best of all!"

"Are you happy, then? I—I would have you be happy, Zhurleen. You were kind to me, and more than once. I have always remembered that—I never forgot you, never."

"Oh, I knew that, when I heard that you took in the king's harlot Bathsheba—no, do not frown at me, for I say only what everyone said at the time."

"And what do they say now?"

"Why, that the Lady Bathsheba is a good mother to a fine son, and must be a worthy woman if the queen loves her so well." Zhurleen tilted her head and looked at me cat-wise. "And it is said that Queen Michal loves the Prince Solomon as if he were her own."

"Yes," I said. "But he is not mine, save by love. I shall never have a child of my own body, Zhurleen. Not once, in all these years—and now I am too old."

"Do you doubt your god Yahweh's powers, then? Did he not give the worthy Sarah a child when she was all but dead of old age?"

"I know how my prayers have been answered." Once I had demanded David of Yahweh; well, and so I had David. Then I had demanded vengeance of Yahweh; the stone had been set into my hand that would bring down David—and Bathsheba. "There is nothing I now dare ask, lest it be granted."

"Then whose son is to be king after great David? Men already ask—and now Prince Amnon is dead, which is a great sorrow, and Prince Absalom—"

"Is not dead, which is also a great sorrow."

"Ah," said Zhurleen, and lowered her lashes. "The prince who slays his brothers—and the little sister—I remember her; she was a pretty child. Modest and loving—not like her brother Absalom. Now, if King David had only wed Princess Tamar to Prince Amnon—that is the way to found a dynasty of kings! And Prince Amnon was well-loved."

"Yes," I said. "Too well loved. That is why Absalom slew him."

Zhurleen shrugged; her veil rippled. "Men say the king should choose an heir. Men say it is a thousand sorrows that Queen Michal is childless."

Later I knew that was the moment I first took the step that led from past to future. It was a simple thing; a few words only. I raised my hand to my hair, touched the silver cord that bound my braids smooth to my head.

"I think of Prince Solomon as my true son. He calls me 'Mother'—do men say that?"

"Not yet," said Zhurleen. "But they will." And we smiled at each other across the clay water-jug. Then she lifted the jug to rest upon her round hip. "Now I must go, and so must you. And I shall make all the good-wives jealous with tales of how I spoke with you, and you were all that was gracious to me, as if I were your good friend. Perhaps I shall even say I knew you long ago—then no one will truly heed a word I tell them!"

"Wait—" I did not know what I could say, save that I did not wish to see Zhurleen go. "You must come to me, you must let me help you. You once helped me; I have never forgotten that—"

"If you would be kind to me, then do not know me," Zhurleen said. "I am no longer the palace woman; I have a husband, now, and a child—a little daughter to raise to wisdom. I thank you— oh, a thousand times! But it would be no kindness to do me honor now."

And so I watched her go: a respectable matron with a child to tend and a man to cook for. A woman with a veil upon her head and a full water-jug upon her hip. A woman like all the others.

Like all others who were happy and content. And so it did not matter that her hair was woven now with grey; that her bracelets and anklets were only of brass, and not of silver and gold. Zhurleen still walked like a cat well-pleased with herself. Like a cat who lands always upon her feet, no matter how far the fall. Her hips swayed; the stout cloth of her gown shifted restlessly with each step she took.

That was the last I saw of her: a hand balancing a water-jug as it rose and fell to the easy lift of her hip; a sky-blue veil. Below the edge of her veil the tasseled ends of Zhurleen's braids slowly danced, like leaves in the wind.

~

Later I told over the jewelry I had brought secret out of Jerusalem. Bracelets, and necklaces too; true gold. Untarnished, unchanging, like Zhurleen's good heart.

I wished to do something for her, to give what I had to make her life easy. This gold would buy much—

Yes, envy and malice and spite—and robbers in the night! Zhurleen's voice was clear and laughing as if she stood before me. I must have learned wisdom from her, after all.

Zhurleen was happy. If I wished her well, I would not meddle in her life.

But I wished to do something for her; she had done much for me and it had cost her dear. I knew that, no matter how light she spoke of it.

And so, in the end, I called Narkis to me and gave the jewelry into her keeping. "For the good women of this city," I told her. "Take it and have the goldsmith melt it down; each woman in the lower town is to have one piece—so big. Or two, if there is enough gold. Each woman, mind. Not one is to be left out."

~

In the end, the war was lost and won in one battle. For Absalom had heeded Hushai's advice, and so Absalom waited. Waited when all his other men pressed him to attack King David at once, while David was on the march with all his household.

"Let the old man tire himself out," was Hushai's counsel. "Attack later, when his men are weary, and all can see he fails."

Hushai's words were heeded; Absalom waited. And as the summer waned, so did the eagerness of Absalom's men. Many who had come for battle and glory went home again; some came to King David's camp instead.

And so, as David had planned, Absalom did not bring his host against David's until the summer ended. Until Joab was ready.

With the king and all the king's household sealed safe in Mahanaim, Joab took the king's army further north, to the forest of Ephraim. Absalom's army finally came forth from Jerusalem; I was told later that it made a fine show.

But battles are not won by fine shows, but by fine deeds; not by bluster, but by cunning. King David's men were seasoned warriors, not young men dreaming of glory. And when the two armies met, Joab enticed Absalom's soldiers into the tangled, pathless forest.

And once into the forest they were lost, and all Absalom's ambitions with them.

Joab's men had scouted the woods; they hunted Absalom's men deep into the trees, and slew many. Many more were lost to the forest itself, escaping men's swords only to fall prey to lions or bears.

Absalom saw how the battle went against him, and fled. He was not one to stay and die with his loyal men. Perhaps he thought he could reach David and plead for his life once more.

Joab knew better than to give Absalom that chance. Joab marked when Absalom fled, and followed, and forced him into an oak grove where the branches grew thick and laced too close for Absalom to break through before Joab caught him up. As David had told me, Joab knew his job. Joab struck hard and true, and brought Absalom safely to the grave.

~

Runners brought the news swift to Mahanaim: *Rejoice, King David's men have won a great victory! Forty times forty of the enemy lie dead upon the roads, and forty times forty more in the forest. Praise for the warriors, and twice praise for Joab, who avenged the king's honor!*

David stood tall in the midst of the singing shouting people; the two men who had run all the way from the battlefield to bring the king first word knelt smiling at his feet.

"What news?" asked King David. "What news of my son Absalom?"

"He is dead, lord. Joab slew him in the wood. Praise be to Yahweh, the traitor Absalom is dead, and many of his men with him. A great victory, lord!"

David stared down at them and then put his hands over his face. "Oh, my son, my son!" And then he turned and walked back through all the jubilant people, back into his house.

There was a strange silence; the men who had run so far and so fast to bring him word rose slowly to their feet, looking like dogs that had been kicked.

What kings make, kings break. Who had said that? It did not matter; something must be done, and quickly. I could not let David risk the crown that would be Solomon's. So I stepped forward and clapped my hands, and called out as loudly as I could, "Rejoice, for Yahweh has brought us a great victory this day! Rejoice, for King David is king once more!"

It worked, for a time. There was dancing and singing and much rejoicing as David's men returned and were claimed by those who loved them. Most came safely back from that battle in the forest of Ephraim.

It was Absalom's men who lay cold beneath the clear night sky.

⁓

But David would not come down and show himself to the people; David would not rejoice. David kept within a small room and would do nothing but wail and moan for his lost son Absalom.

And soon the rejoicing grew quieter, and then ceased, and men walked low-voiced and sullen. Well, and who could blame them, with all their glory tarnished and the king for whom they had fought so well treating them like dogs?

I thought David had gone mad, and I told him so. "You are David—would you be Saul? Go to your men and smile upon their victory before it is too late!"

Even my harsh words did not stop his tears. Now I think he was weeping not so much for Absalom, as for David. Perhaps he knew then that the glorious youth that had been his was now lost to him, lost with Absalom, who had been David come again. That David was gone forever. Was that why he wept, and would not be comforted?

I do not know what would have happened if Joab had not come when he did. For David would not heed me, or Nathan, or any of his counselors. He would only wail and mourn for Absalom, until the soldiers who had returned expecting praise began to look mutinous. No man likes his great deeds flung back in his face as if they were dirt.

But at the end of the second day Joab returned from the battle-field. And when he came and saw what was happening, he spoke to David such words that David never after forgave him.

"In Yahweh's name, David, what is this noise? They can hear you in the marketplace! Wailing like a woman, and over what? A false son who would have killed you if he could!"

"You have slain my son, my beloved son." David turned away slowly, as if he were already old.

Bathsheba put her arms around him. "My lord, my lord, you have other sons—loving sons!" It did no good; David brushed her aside as if she were nothing.

Joab stood there and stared at David. Then he looked at me, and I knew that I must once more ally myself with Joab. Blind hate does not summon futures.

"Speak sense into his ears, Joab," I said. "He will listen to no one, and will not even speak to his brave soldiers. Oh, be silent, Bathsheba! He will not listen to you, or me, or anyone else. But

Absalom is dead now, and I am tired of being dragged from Dan to Beersheba. I wish to return home to Jerusalem."

"Leave me," cried David. "All of you—leave me to my grief."

"No, by Yahweh!" Joab drew his sword and flung it down to crash upon the stones of the floor. "Do you see this sword, David? It has fought for you and killed for you, and kept you on that pretty gilded throne and called 'my lord king'! It has just won you back your crown and saved your life, and the lives of all your wives and sons and daughters too—and all you do is whimper because a worthless boy is dead. The Lady Bathsheba is right—you have other sons, and better, too!"

David held up his hand, but Joab would not be stopped now.

"Do your men mean nothing? They have followed you and fought for you when all others ran after Absalom. Well, now I see we should all have stayed at home in peace and let Absalom have his way, since you've been shouting to the housetops that if he were alive and we all lay dead you'd be pleased!" Joab strode forward and grabbed David's arm. "Are you as mad as King Saul? Will you throw away a year's hard fighting now? Come now and talk to your soldiers like a man and a king, or I swear not one man will be at your back by the morning!"

King David looked at Joab for a dozen heartbeats; I counted them. Then David turned and walked out. He did not speak to Joab, but I do not think that Joab cared.

When David had gone, I bent and picked up Joab's sword in both my hands. I held the weapon out to Joab, and he took it.

"Absalom, his son!" said Joab, and spat upon the floor.

I looked on Joab and smiled. "He can sing about it—later," I said.

~

That night King David gave a feast to welcome his brave men and to celebrate their victory over the traitor Absalom. Bathsheba and

I stood on the rooftop and watched great fires light the plain beyond the city wall.

"Rejoice," I said. "Rejoice, for now we return to Jerusalem."

"Yes, to Jerusalem and peace." Bathsheba sighed. "I am glad—I am so very tired of war!"

"The war is over," I said. "But the battle has just begun."

"Battle?" Bathsheba looked puzzled and worried; I laughed and hugged her close to my heart.

"Oh, do not worry, my love—in my battle no blood will be shed."

But I was wrong; the war was not over. Blood stains deep, and never fades away.

CHAPTER 26

*"Nevertheless the
king's word prevailed. . . .*

—I Chronicles 21:4

Women tire easily of war; men do not. What men were tiring of in that year was kingship. Long ago our people had asked for a king, and were warned what a king would be to them. Now they had learned for themselves what a king was. But it was too late now to go back; kings do not hand power away once they have grasped it.

Absalom's rebellion had failed, but his acts had given others courage. David's one kingdom had been made by joining two, Israel and Judah. Israel had been the stronger, but King David came from Judah, and so Judah was favored. Now Israel said that King David of Judah was nothing and less than nothing to the men of Israel, and rose up against David.

"I do not understand how they can dare," Bathsheba said, when we heard the news. "It is what all say, Michal—how can they dare raise their hands against the king? And when he has just won a great victory—why are they such fools—and ungrateful, too, for only think of what the king has done for them—"

So Bathsheba chattered on, while I sat and kept my face an ivory mask. How dare they indeed?

For Israel had only its tents; King David had his walled cities. Israel had its levies to summon up; King David had his army ready-summoned, waiting.

How dare they? I thought I knew, for I knew how David moved his playing-pieces. And I thought I knew how deep Absalom had cut David's heart. Now all would be punished for Absalom's rebellious folly.

And so I asked, when next I saw David. "All men ask a thing, great king."

"And what is that, my queen?" David liked to play such games; I let him win them.

"It is a riddle," I said, and touched his harp where it hung upon the wall. Another new one; a lion of gold guarded taut harp-strings, its beryl eyes unwinking.

"A gift," David said, his eyes as bright as the golden lion's. "From the king of Asshur."

"A kingly gift for a harper king. You should play more, David."

"A king has little time for such things." But he took down the lion-harp and ran his fingers across the strings. "I must tune this; music should not jar the ear. Now tell me your riddle."

I smiled. "It is this: 'How dare they?'"

"A strange riddle, my queen."

"Not so strange, O King. Your people are not fools."

"Some are." David plucked at the harp-strings, and frowned. "Fools, and worse. Traitors against Yahweh's anointed. But I will know them, and root them out. My kingdom goes whole and safe to my son." And David looked at me slantwise across the gilded harp.

So I was right; the men of Israel had been lured into a trap. See David, weak and cruel king. Rise against him, O Israel—and be crushed. Traitors, yes—but Israel's men would not have risen had they not been lured. There was no need to ask why; Israel had been Saul's kingdom, brother to Judah. A quarrelsome brother; now it would be nothing.

I was wiser than all the men of Israel; before my eyes David spread net and lure in vain. I did not ask 'which son, O King?' I only smiled, and listened as King David played harsh music on an untuned harp.

In the time it took the Israelites to talk and to agree and to summon their men, King David's army marched upon them. The king's army was seasoned and all well armed. The rebels were beaten back in a single battle.

The leader of the rebels fled to a city at the end of Israel. It did him no good; Joab and the army followed and camped outside the city walls. Joab demanded the traitor's head, and got it. That was the end of the war that David himself had started. King David had won—or so he thought.

For the year of Absalom's death was a year of blood, and it stained David forever. Too many men had risen against him and proved they loved him not. I think it was that knowledge, rather than a king's cold logic, that drove David to his next slaughter.

My sister Merab's sons. They, and my father's two sons by his concubine Rizpah, were slaughtered before the gates of Gibeah, the city where my father had once lived as king. Their bodies were hung upon the city wall, food for crows. David had a reason, of course; he called me to him so that he might tell it to me himself. "I weep for them, Michal—see, tears stand in my eyes even now. A king's lot is harsh, and Yahweh's will harsher—" And he held me in his arms and wept into my hair.

I stood cold in his arms. "Was it Yahweh's voice that gave the order, David?"

"Ah, my queen, you still do not understand. They were traitors; I know it is hard for you to believe. But they were not boys, Michal, but men. And the men of Israel rallied to them—"

David spoke on and on into my ear, but I heard instead words he had spoken long ago. *'—I swore that King Saul and his house would take no harm from my hands—'*

And now all that was left of the House of Saul was Jonathan's crippled son Meribaal. And Michal, King David's queen.

My eyes were dry; I felt nothing then. Pain would come later. David fell to his knees before me and wept upon my hands; I looked on, heartless as an idol.

David's tears were real enough. But they were not for Saul's sons or grandsons. *They are for himself.*

David wept for David. I understood that much, even then. Now I know that David was never again the same, after that year.

That year that some men loved him not.

＿

That year was also a year of changes. King David had always had an army; Joab commanded that. But now David formed a palace guard, all foreigners; command of the guard was given to a man called Benaiah. And Benaiah took his orders only from the king himself.

Joab did not like this, of course. Well, Joab had worked hard enough for his place, after all, and come to it over the bodies of many good men. I spent much time that year watching the king's great court; I stood hidden behind the grille above the king's throne when Joab protested.

"There can be only one commander of the host, David. I lead your army, and have these dozen years! Who is this man? He has never served with me."

David smiled; I could sense it. "He has served me, Joab. And you are still commander of the host; these men are only guards for the palace."

"What need has the palace for guards? It's in the middle of Jerusalem! And cannot my men guard a palace, my men who have slain your enemies in their thousands?"

"Your warriors are too valuable to waste idling about the court," David told him, and would hear no more from Joab. "Benaiah commands the palace guard; the king decrees it."

I watched Joab's face, and thought if Benaiah were wise he would never let Joab too near his back. And I thought, too, that if David no longer trusted Joab, then David was a fool to let Joab know it and live.

Joab was given a present of the king's own cloak, all fine blue wool embroidered with scarlet. A great honor for Joab: the king's own cloak, embroidered by the queen's own hands. David gave all the army an extra wine ration and a special feast of fine meats to prove in what regard he held his good men.

And Benaiah's guard stood in the gateways and walked the rooftops of the king's palace.

David sat quiet in Jerusalem until the next planting. And then he called for Joab and told him the king had a new use for the army. Joab was to take his soldiers and count all the people of the kingdom, from Dan to Beersheba, and was to take care to number all the able-bodied men.

"Now we shall know how many dwell in my land, and where they dwell. I will know who can spare sons to the king's army, and who cannot. And I will know who pays their tithes and taxes, and who does not."

"Numbering the people goes against the Law," Joab told him.

"The king is the Law."

"Do the priests know that?"

But Joab did not care greatly about priestly laws; what King David ordered, that Joab did, now as always.

Others cared more. Many of the people feared Yahweh's wrath, and this fear was fostered by the priests, who feared King David's power. The Law had lain in the priests' hands in the days before a king sat upon a throne in Jerusalem. But since the time that Solomon had been born, men had heeded the priests and prophets less, and the king more.

As the king had given the priests more honor, the king had taken more power. And now, at last, even the priests could see the net in which they had been snared. A net woven of gold, and fine meats, and sweet words.

~

"A great sin, the priests are calling it; I had it from Eglah, who had it from her handmaid Leah, whose cousin Tirzah heard it at the silver-smith's."

"To count all the people—the greatest crime a man can commit against Yahweh—the high priest Abiathar said so in the main gate today. I heard him myself."

"Shall the people be numbered? Does not the Law say to us, number the sheep, and the goats, but not the people?"

"But does not the king make the laws?"

This was all the talk in the women's quarters of the palace. The king had climbed high and conquered much; would he now be brought down to crash upon the rocks waiting below? No one truly thought he would slip and fall, and so to think of it was exciting. This year was dull, after the last.

I sat in my own courtyard, and listened to all who came by. And when I was asked what I thought, I only smiled. I did not think that Yahweh would care more for this sin of David's than for any other.

~

But Nathan cared. Nathan saw his own chance to regain what he had let slip through his fingers long ago. He was wrong; it was too late. King David no longer needed the prophet Nathan.

But Queen Michal did. King David spurned Nathan as now worthless; Nathan had long since served David's purposes. But Nathan was still prophet. In the land beyond Jerusalem's thick walls, Nathan's word still weighed heavy, and was cherished.

So on the day that I sat behind the throne and saw David toss aside this old weapon, I reached out my hand and caught it up. I had thought it would be a hard thing; I was wrong. It was simple as spinning thread.

It was one of the days that King David sat in judgment and any man might stand before him. As Nathan had done before, the prophet came to the open court and foretold doom for the king, did he not bow his head to Yahweh's will—and that of the priests.

"For you sin against Yahweh! His people must not be numbered—so says the Law. It is a wicked thing, and you will be punished for it if you do not repent."

And men shuffled, and murmured to one another—but as if they grew restless, and not as if they feared Yahweh's wrath. Perhaps Nathan had come too often to this well; much he had prophesied had not come to pass. For all the prophet's talk of destruction and vengeance, David still sat upon the throne in Jerusalem and ruled over all the land from Dan to Beersheba.

But David spoke to Nathan kindly enough. "My regard for Yahweh's Law is known to all the people. May I be struck down as I speak if I do anything against the Law." He paused, as if inviting the lightning bolts. "I have thought long upon this, Nathan—yes, and prayed to Yahweh, too. A king is as a shepherd to his people; he cares for them and guides them as a shepherd his flock. How can he guard them against evil if he does not know the least lamb among them?"

"Yahweh's people are not to be reckoned and counted over, as coins hoarded by a miser!"

"Are not the people more precious than coins? Should they not be cherished, each as a rare gem in Yahweh's treasure?"

"Yahweh is not mocked, lord king! There will be great harm from this evil deed!" Nathan drew himself up and thumped the floor hard with his staff—the staff that once had been the prophet Samuel's. The staff that David himself had given into Nathan's hands.

But Nathan was always too short and round for that fine gesture to be impressive. If he had not been a prophet, I think men would have laughed, then.

No one laughed, but David's voice said he smiled. "Yahweh's will be done, Nathan. But it will not be done if men are kept waiting for the king's justice. I will come and speak with Abiathar and Zadok when the court is over, and see what can be done to set their minds at rest. Now, will that content you?"

David spoke as one indulgent to an old man's folly. Nathan did not like the king's tone, but he kept his dignity.

"It is not I who must be content, but Yahweh." Nathan did not give David another chance to make him look foolish, but turned away and walked slowly out of the king's great court.

And I went swiftly to find a servant to bring the prophet Nathan to me. "Tell him in the queen's garden, and at once, if he will so honor me."

For I knew what I had seen, and I knew the time to grasp Nathan was now. Now, before Nathan brooded upon his wrongs, and emulated great Samuel—and walked away from the king in anger to anoint a new king in secret to bring down the old.

~

Of course Nathan came to me. Well, to hear a summons from the queen, who never summoned him? Any man would answer, in such a case; a man smarting from the king's dismissal would answer twice as quickly.

Nathan found me sitting by the fountain in my garden; I rose and knelt before him and begged for his blessing.

"Does the queen think an old man's blessing still has any worth?"

"Age brings wisdom. Give me your blessing, Nathan, and I will tell you why I asked you to come to me."

So he laid his hands upon my head and spoke the words. I do not know if his blessing aided me, but Nathan felt the better for it. No man likes to be made old and foolish in men's eyes. David had not been clever, there. Nathan was prophet still; if David's luck did not run true, men would remember that. And Nathan would remember David's mocking smooth words.

When Nathan had done, I rose and led him over to the carved bench beside the fountain. Water danced in the sunlight and sang against the marble basin—a good place to sit and talk. Six paces away nothing could be heard but fountain-song.

"Well, and what does the queen want with me?" Nathan was ready to be pleased, now. Zhurleen was right; it was easy to please any man. *'Only give him what he wants, and it is never much! Then you may take all he has and he will love you for it. . . .'*

I smiled, and gave Nathan what would please him: respect. "Nathan is wise, and kind, and I am much troubled in my mind on a matter."

Nathan took my hand and patted it. "Tell me, daughter. Any aid I can give, that you shall have."

"You are good, Nathan—and I have not always been kind to you. When King David took me from my husband Phaltiel and brought me here—you remember?" *Yes, remember when I asked your aid, and my husband Phaltiel was found dead by the roadside. And remember when I accused King David, and you did not believe me. Remember that, Nathan.*

Nathan remembered; I saw it in his face. "Queen Michal, once—"

I shook my head. "Do not say it; the fault was mine. Grief shaped my words too harshly." Whatever evil Nathan was now willing to believe of David must never be spoken. For King David must stay safe upon his gilded throne, so that Solomon might sit there after him.

There was a pause; we both listened to water fall on water. Then Nathan said, "You are a good daughter of Yahweh, O Queen. Tell me what troubles you. This time I will listen."

"It concerns a great matter, Nathan. The king, and his mind in a certain thing. He has grown strange, since Prince Absalom's death—have you seen it? Almost I think I see my father King Saul in him. A darkness in his eyes."

"Samuel once warned the people what a king would be to them. Now they see the truth of Samuel's words." Nathan sounded more pleased than grieved.

"And when I see King David begin to act as King Saul did, I am afraid. What will become of us all if King David goes the way of King Saul?"

Nathan shook his head, and sighed. "That is in the hand of Yahweh."

I bowed my head. "Has Yahweh turned his face from David, Nathan?"

The only sound was the water playing through the fountain. At last Nathan spoke, grudging the words.

"I do not know. He has sinned most grievously against the Law, yet Yahweh has not chastised him. Yahweh forgives him much." Plainly Nathan thought Yahweh forgave David too much. "Is that what troubled the queen's mind?"

I looked straight at Nathan and spoke plain. "No. What troubles the queen's mind is not this king, but the next."

"Adonijah is the oldest prince still living—"

I looked past the fountain. The sun shone white upon the lilies where once Amnon and Tamar had lain.

"Yes," I said. "But is Adonijah to be king, after David? Tell me, Nathan—is that how King David was chosen, and King Saul? Does Prince Adonijah find favor in the sight of Yahweh?"

Nathan looked at me, and his eyes were shrewd as an old fox's choosing a hen to carry away. "And who finds favor in the sight of Queen Michal? Prince Solomon? He is only a boy."

"Solomon will not be a boy forever, as David will not be king forever."

"Perhaps there have been too many kings in this land already."

I laughed. "Perhaps there have, but where there have been two, there will be a third. Now see, Nathan—I have thought much on this, and for a long time. A king need not scourge his people; David is right—the king should be the people's shepherd. But I think David himself has forgotten how to tend sheep." And I laughed again, inviting Nathan to laugh with me at David's folly.

When Nathan sobered, he patted my hand again. "The king has always called you a clever woman, and he is right, daughter. You are wise as Deborah herself. Have you spoken to the king of this?"

"No, and I do not wish to."

"But he will give you anything you ask; he has said so many times."

"Not this," I said. "Not so soon after Absalom. David trusts no one now—not even Joab."

"What is it you ask of me, then? That I ask the king to name Solomon? I do not think the king will listen to me now." Hard words to say; prophets are prideful men. Only Nathan would have been honest enough to admit such a thing. I could not imagine Samuel ever speaking so.

"I ask nothing, save that you think on this matter—and ask yourself who among David's sons would best be named king after him. That is all." I smiled, and touched Nathan's hand. "And that you speak with Prince Solomon, if you will. His mother and I would have him learn what you alone can teach."

"And would have me learn his virtues?" Nathan clasped his staff and hauled himself to his feet.

"Of course; it will spare you a mother's listing of them! They are many, I assure you!"

Nathan stood straight and round before me, all dignity again. "Since you ask it, O Queen, I will think carefully on this matter. But I can promise nothing. All happens as Yahweh wills."

It was a good beginning; I was content with that. And so I bade Nathan farewell, and watched him walk away from me. The prophet moved lighter now, as if walking were easier than it had been an hour before.

And then I sat and stared long at the dancing fountain. But I was no prophet or seer to gaze upon the future in crystal. All I saw was water falling clear through clear bright air.

~

"I talked with Nathan today; we spoke of Solomon. No, do not try to look at me, the comb will tangle in your hair." I liked to comb Bathsheba's hair in the evenings. It flowed about her like dark water; its thick waves caught the comb if I were not careful.

Bathsheba sat obedient. "What did you say—what did Nathan say of him? Will Nathan help us?"

"Perhaps," I said. "He will speak with Solomon, which is all I asked of him today."

"And tomorrow?" Bathsheba began to tilt her head back, recalled my warning, and stopped.

"Tomorrow, we shall see."

"Nathan will be pleased with him?"

"Of course; who could not be pleased with Solomon?"

Bathsheba was silent a moment as I combed. "Adonijah?"

"Perhaps," I said, and thought of Prince Adonijah. Absalom's full brother, and now the eldest prince. "But I do not think, my love, that the wishes of Absalom's brother will weigh heavy for a time."

"And Solomon is such a *good* boy! And clever—why, he can sing all of his father's songs—yes, and write his own, too!"

"And better!"

"No one sings a better song than King David." To the end of her days Bathsheba would not admit a fault in David. To her he was always a great king, and his words glorious. Well, she had Solomon of him; children pay for much.

"Oh, that I will grant you! Bathsheba, I beg of you, hold still!"

But she twisted under my hands and stared up at me. "I must ask—I know I am foolish, but—will you ask Nathan to anoint Solomon now?"

I shook my head. "No. Solomon is too young; life is too uncertain. And Nathan must not be goaded."

She sighed. "Oh, I am glad. Of course if you thought it wise, but—"

"But it would not be, and you are wise enough to see that!" I set my hands on her shoulders and turned her away again. "Now see, the comb is knotted into your hair. Be still while I work it free."

Bathsheba sat quiet once more. "It is the anointing that makes a man king—so I have heard the priests say."

"Yes." I smiled and smoothed her dark hair. "That may be what counts, in the end. The priests are closer than Yahweh, after all—and Nathan's voice is louder."

"And so now we wait?"

"And so now we wait, Bathsheba. And pray that David does nothing to offend the priests too grievously."

"Tell him he must not." Bathsheba tilted her head back so that her hair fell over my hands like heavy rain. "For all men know the king does just as the queen wishes!"

I laughed, and kissed her forehead. "I will tell him. Now hold yourself still, or your hair will be a nest for owls!"

I stroked her hair smooth again, and began to comb once more. And as I smoothed and combed, I thought of what Bathsheba had said. *'Tell him he must not!'*

He must not offend, lest he fall before the power of the priests. Jerusalem was not all the kingdom. . . .

"The priests," I said soft, staring into the shadows. The priests, who chose kings. The man the priests anointed had much to lose. What did the priests have at risk? "Nothing. They have nothing."

"Who, Michal?"

"Yahweh's priests. My father fell upon that blade, although it was a sword that slew his body."

"Michal?" Bathsheba's fingers curled about my wrist.

"Tell me, Bathsheba—what do the priests have?"

"Why—they have honor, and—and the king gives them many fine gifts—"

"And they take them, and eat at his table. . . ."

"Michal, are you all right? You sound so strange."

"I was thinking of a thing Solomon said to me." I gathered up

Bathsheba's hair and began to braid it loose, for night.

"He says such clever things—like his father."

"Yes, he is clever. It was after the Egyptians were here—you remember, speaking of their great temples? There, I am done— now you may move all you please."

Bathsheba rose and held out her hand for the comb. "Sit down—now it is my turn to scold you! And what did Solomon say that was so clever?"

I sat, as Bathsheba had ordered. "Solomon asked me why their gods had temples, and ours only a tent."

"To remind us of our fathers' wanderings in the desert." Bathsheba began pulling jasper pins from my hair. "Everyone knows that."

"Yes, everyone knows that. But I think, my love, that perhaps we have wandered long enough."

~

CHAPTER 27

". . . that she may be a snare to him . . . . "
—I Samuel 18:21

All that night and the next day too I turned thoughts over in my mind, like pebbles in a stream-bed.

It was a lean year; the harvest was small. Well, with two wars and few men to put a crop in the ground, that was not strange. And there was sickness, too; a fever ravaged the city and the villages beyond.

That, too, was no new thing; war years were bad years. But men do not long remember that, when they are ill and hungry. It is easier to blame than to endure.

And I knew they already blamed David. Narkis had whispered into my ear.

"The men say in the marketplace that Yahweh has withdrawn from the king because he numbered the people. They say that is what causes the sickness. And the women say it at the well-side, too."

That was bad; David had always been the women's darling.

But nothing was yet so bad that the damage might not be mended. And David must set his stitches now, before a small rent was a greater one, and the garment ruined.

So late the next day I smiled and asked a favor of Bathsheba. "Do this for me, Bathsheba—I would speak with King David. Go and send word, and tell him the matter cannot wait upon his pleasure." I could have done the thing myself, but it pleased

Bathsheba to be useful; she was never too proud to lift her hand to a task.

And so she kissed me, and hastened off, and I sat once more beside my garden fountain and watched the falling water. The day was cloud-dark, and so the water looked thick and sullen. The weather had not been kind this season; too many clouds, too little rain; another tally-mark against King David.

I too had a tally against King David, and I counted it over as I sat there and waited for him to come to me.

Once I had sworn to bring him down as he had brought down my father. I would have sold my body in Ashtoreth's temple to see him die as my father had—abandoned, humiliated, betrayed. I would have made no songs about it after, save those reviling David's name.

Once I had sworn to slay his happiness as he had slain mine. I would have slit my own throat as a thank-offering over the altar of any god who gave me vengeance for Phaltiel's death.

To have heard men call David truly what he was, to see his body broken and his eyes picked by the crows—yes, once that would have been all I wished to cherish through the years I would live.

But vengeance was a cold and empty thing to set in the balance against love. And so I had made my choice long ago, or so I thought. Yes, now I had Solomon and Bathsheba to love and care for. What did the great King David have to set in *his* scales?

A throne uneasily balanced between army and priests? A palace full of quarreling women? Sons counting the days until they could snatch at the heavy gold crown their father wore?

What did David have to make him happy? A crown?

He had given everything for that circlet of gold. *Rejoice in its weight upon your head, David, for it is all you will ever possess.*

And so when David came at last, it was easy to smile. Smile, and watch him walk down the crushed white shells paving the way to my fountain. He moved heavy now; an old bear, not a young lion; dull and thick as the day.

The clouds shifted and sunlight touched him; for an instant he shone bright. Then it was gone, and I looked at him in cool grey light. David was diminished without sun to make him dazzle and flash back from the mirrors he had always found in men's eyes—and in women's. And I knew it, and he did not.

'The sun for beauty and the moon for love, and king besides—' I heard Abigail's voice clear in my mind; a plaint from long ago. Now I watched David come to me old and tired, and I smiled and held out my hand. "Come, sit by me, David. Even a king must rest."

"Did you summon me here to play women's games, Michal? I have much awaiting my hand and eye."

"No, I summoned you here to speak of women's talk at the well—and of men's at the gate."

He sat, then. When he looked at me, I thought of my father Saul again. Suspicion lurked in David's eyes now, far back, like a serpent deep within a cave. "Did Nathan set you on to this, my queen?"

"No, nor Abiathar nor Zadok either, although I know what they say. These words are my own."

"Speak, then—your words are as pleasant to my ears as your face to my eyes."

"So much as that? You do me too much honor, lord."

David swore that impossible, but he was impatient and shifted upon the bench, and so I spoke before he grew too restive.

"You will not find these words pleasant, O King, but I beg you will hear them, for I have thought much upon this." I looked at David's eyes, and did not know if he would even listen, much less heed.

"Tell me, then—no one can say King David fears words."

"It is about the priests, as you thought, and about the sickness men are calling plague. No, do not look so angry; you swore you would hear my words."

"This matter is between the king and Yahweh, Michal—and

no other! And do you think I do not hear Nathan's voice in your words? I am not yet in my dotage!"

"Of course you are not; have I said so? David, we both know this is no plague sent by Yahweh. But the priests believe it—or choose to." I smiled, and set my hand upon his. "It is hard for a man to be troubled by priests, and for no fault of his own. But this is not a matter touching the king alone. All who love him are troubled by the king's quarrel with the priests."

David looked closely at me, but seemed satisfied enough with what he saw. I had long ago learned to show him a face smooth as cream. "Very well—speak, if you have words for my ear. But there is no quarrel—and remember that some things are between a man and his god alone." He sat silent a moment, brooding. "Nathan forgets that. I am king here, not he."

'Who is king here, you or I—?' I looked down at my folded hands; they revealed nothing. "Nathan is a good man, David."

"He may be as a good a man as Moses, but he is not king."

"No one says you are not king, David. Nathan says only that even the king must obey Yahweh's Laws."

"And so says that I do not!" David scowled, his face heavy and sullen as the water in my fountain.

"Oh, David—" For an instant I thought of a small spoiled boy; it must all be David's way, or no way at all. "No one says so. All the world knows how you serve Yahweh. But Nathan is a prophet, and a proud man—as Samuel was. But you are wiser than King Saul." That was truth; wiser was not better.

David smiled at me then, sly. "And you are clever, Michal. You were always clever, even as a girl."

"Was I? From great David that is praise indeed."

"Clever enough to lesson even a king. Speak, Michal. What is it you are thinking?"

"That even great David cannot openly defy the priests." I would not have spoken so to my father; Saul would have roared. David was not Saul. "That great David will bow to them, and make amends."

"What amends? I have committed no fault." David's eyes were

keen, now; seeking. He was not too proud to take a woman's thoughts and make them his own.

"They are jealous, David—oh, surely you knew that? Jealous of your greatness and power. Only be truly great, and see them come again to eat from your hand."

"And what would make the king truly great in the eyes of the priests?"

"I hardly dare ask so large a boon, even of great David."

David smiled, and spread his hands wide. "What can the king offer, only to have the queen smile upon him?"

Ah, yes—"*Ask and it shall be granted. All to please my gracious queen.*" We both understood.

"Go to Nathan, David. Be greathearted and generous, as befits a king." David must not war with the priests, no, not if I must crawl before him in the dust to stop it. David must hold his throne safe, so that Solomon might someday sit there. "Do not make the priests small in men's eyes."

David turned a ring about his finger. "Make them great instead?"

"See, the king knows it all already. Yes—let them take greatness from your hands."

"And not I forgiveness from theirs." David scowled again.

"We both know this sickness will soon pass from the land; why do you not go now to the priests? Yahweh loves you better than he loves them and they know it."

"And humble myself before them, and take the guilt upon myself?"

"As the shepherd of his people should, though guiltless? Ah, that is clever—but you have always been a serpent for wisdom, David." I smiled, and touched his hand.

"And the priests will set some price upon Yahweh's goodwill—"

"Which the king will pay—"

"And all men shall see how the king cares for them," David

said. "And how Yahweh favors the king above all others. You think as I do, Michal—have I not always said we were much alike?"

"My lord the king does me too much honor," I said, and smiled as if his words gave me great pleasure. "And when all has fallen out as the king has said, David the harper can make a song of it."

"To show all men the truth of the king's love for them." David took my hands and kissed me upon the mouth. "My clever queen! But I must not stay by your side as I wish; I spoke truth when I said I had much under my hand today."

"Wait," I said. "I would tell you a thing that Solomon said to me."

"Solomon? Well, if you must—"

"I must." I folded my hands in my lap, and smiled. "He asked me why the holy Ark dwells in a tent, when other gods dwell in fine temples among gold and silver. He is such a clever little boy, your son."

David laughed, thinking Solomon's question only a small jest. "A temple for the Ark? What will that boy think of next? This is not Moab or Philistia. Yahweh cannot be imprisoned in a temple."

"No," I said. "But his priests can."

David stopped smiling, then. And he was silent for a time. I sat quiet and said nothing. At last he stirred and rose to his feet. "You have indeed given me much to think on, Michal. Now I must go. Do not sit here overlong—you will grow cold."

And he patted my shoulder and went away. I sat and watched him go, as I had watched him come, and thought of the past, and David—and of the future, and Solomon.

~

But no temple was built that year, or for many years after. Nathan forbade it.

"Tell me what manner of temple would most please Yahweh," David said, smiling. "Tell me what you would have—yes, even to half the treasure in my house, for the glory of the Lord."

"So much as half—the king is too generous." And then Nathan smiled, too. "Has Yahweh asked for a fine house to be built for him? Does the Lord dwell in walls of wood and stone? Who are you to set the Ark within walls of cedar? Can Yahweh be kept closed beneath a roof?

"Yahweh has made you great, O King. He has given his people into your hand and delivered your enemies up to your sword. He asks only that you worship him and keep his laws. When Yahweh wants a great house of gold and cedar, he will tell us. Save your treasure, King David. It will not buy Yahweh's love."

This did not please David, though he swallowed the rebuke with good grace and praised Nathan's wisdom. It pleased the high priests still less; Abiathar spoke hard to Nathan, saying that the great gods of the world had fine temples, and the greatest of all should have the finest.

And it did not please me; I called Nathan to me and asked him why he had spoken as he had.

"I know what troubles you, my daughter. Be at peace: *this* king will build no temple to Yahweh's glory—and his own." And Nathan looked at Solomon, who played among the flowers in my garden, and smiled.

This king. I kept my face smooth; I would not grasp too quickly, for I might be wrong. I would be patient, I would wait. "Your words bring comfort, Nathan. I know I worry too much over our boy—but he is young, and waiting is hard."

"Even Yahweh's beloved cannot live forever, my queen. And there is much the prince must learn before then." Nathan drew himself up, leaning upon his staff. "I am old, but I still have the strength to wait and teach. We will hold the throne safe for Prince Solomon."

Safe for Prince Solomon. The boon I had asked, fallen into my hand like ripe fruit. Yes, and when Solomon was king, *he* would build a great temple, to Yahweh's glory and the king's safe reign....

For a moment I could not move for joy; then I caught Nathan's hands up and kissed them. "Yes; that we will do. Safe, for Solomon. You will never be sorry, Nathan. I swear it."

Nathan beamed upon me, and blessed me before he went away again. I stood in the dappled sunlight and watched as Solomon chased brightness through the garden. Butterflies eager for my roses; I laughed. "Come here to me, Solomon—you will never catch a butterfly."

He stopped, when I called. "I will; wait, Mother." And then he froze, like a statue, with his hand stretched out. After a moment, he smiled. "Come and see."

I walked over as I had been bidden, and Solomon held up his hand. A butterfly balanced shining bright upon his grubby finger. "Look, I *have* caught a butterfly!"

"Yes," I said, "I see. It is beautiful."

"You are beautiful," he said, and tried to set the small brilliant thing upon my hand. It would not come, of course; it fluttered off, up into the cooler air above my garden walls. Its wings flashed black and gold against the harvest blue sky.

Solomon jumped to catch it, and could not. But he did not scowl and stamp as most boys would have; Solomon laughed.

I smiled to see him happy, and then asked him why he laughed when he had lost his pretty living toy.

"Because its wings looked so bright in the sunlight, like your jewels. And butterflies do not come for calling, you know," he added kindly. "You cannot hold them, or they die."

"They do?"

"Oh, yes—I have seen it happen." Solomon tilted his head back and stared up. "Look, there it is—see, over by that tree."

I smiled. "You are a good boy, my heart—most would not care if the butterfly perished, if only they might hold it for their own."

"That is foolish," Solomon said. "What use is a dead butter-fly?"

"None, my heart. Only life is beautiful."

Solomon's eyes grew wide; I knew he was thinking. Then he looked up, and smiled, all sunshine and honey. "But I do like butterflies; I shall ask Mother to embroider some upon my tunic. They will stay with me always and not die. I will go and ask her now."

And then he ran off, seeking Bathsheba, calling, "Mother, Mother, where are you? I want you!"

I smiled after him, and then looked up. The butterfly had vanished into the endless blue arch of sky.

CHAPTER 28

"Now King David was old . . . . "

—I Kings 1:1

Time runs to greet tomorrow with welcoming arms while men still clutch empty-handed at yesterday. This is true for all men, even kings. And for King David it was truer than for most.

Time is woman's ally; mother, sister, daughter. Young and old and young again; sowing and tending and harvest. Time weaves past and future in an endless skein of love.

Time was King David's bitter enemy; the enemy that would bring him down in the end. He fought it, savage as an ailing lion beset by wild dogs. But time's fangs sank sharp into David's aging flesh. Even as he struggled against them, the years bled away.

Solomon was David's youngest son, born when David was at the height of his power as a man. When Solomon was nearing twenty, and tall enough to look down at me when he smiled, David was nearing sixty, an old man in truth.

And between one day and the next it seemed age struck a sudden blow to King David's heart. One day he lay in his bed, and would not rise. He would tell no one why; at last his servants sent for me. I went and looked down at David where he lay still upon his lion-bed.

"What ails you, David?" I spoke kindly enough, as one might to a chance-met stranger.

"Nothing ails me. Leave me be; let me rest." David turned his face from me, fretful. His burnished hair was silvered now; frost blighting its glory.

"Are you ill?" I bent and laid a hand upon his forehead. His skin was neither hot nor cold; was not fever-flushed or grey-shadowed.

David swore he was neither ill nor weak. But that was all he would say. He would not tell me what troubled him; to say truth, I did not care. I left him and went away, telling his servants not to trouble him.

"He is the king—may he not lie abed if he chooses? Let him be."

David did not arise from his bed all that day. But after that he walked and talked as an old man. No—an ancient man, seeing only the past; other men older than he still looked to the future. A man is allotted a given span to do with as he wills. Perhaps the glory of David's blazing youth had burned away too many years, leaving nothing for his age to feed upon.

The shining hero and the golden king were gone forever. And David had nothing, now that he was no longer young. He had never gleaned either love or wisdom from life. Wealth and power will not warm the heart against the chill of age and death, and they were all King David had, now.

I had everything. I knew it each time I looked at Solomon. Solomon was a man, now; tall and straight and beautiful. He was such a man as any mother would gladly call son. He had wisdom, and learning too, and a loving heart to warm those cool virtues.

And Solomon was well liked, and well spoken of, but men never forgot he was a prince. To see him, one would think even his father's father's father had been a great king.

"Who am I, that men should praise me?" David had often said. "Who am I, that Yahweh should honor me above all men?"

Solomon would never ask that, or need to. No man would ever wonder that Solomon was praised or honored. A prince always, but never proud; wise, but never arrogant; pious, but never priestly. Solomon never spoke for Yahweh, as David so often did.

"Yahweh can speak for himself," Solomon told me once; his face was solemn, his eyes danced light. Sometimes he reminded me of my brother Jonathan. But Solomon was no kin of Jonathan's, save by love. "If Yahweh does not like what I do, he will make it plain enough—or Nathan will!"

Oh, but he was the delight of our eyes and hearts; never did Solomon cause Bathsheba or me a moment's sorrow. All that Amnon had promised, Solomon was—and more.

Solomon was what David could have been.

"He will be the greatest king Israel has ever seen," Bathsheba said once, as we stood and watched behind the screen while Solomon greeted ambassadors from Egypt. King David often gave such tasks to his sons, now.

"As he will be only the third king Israel has ever seen, that will not be hard!" I said. And we smiled at each other, for the joy the sight of Solomon upon the king's throne gave us.

Someday, I thought. Someday, yes—and sooner than King David wished to think.

~

Someday was sooner than any thought, even I. Later in that year King David grew cold, and complained of it even at noon in midsummer. He could not get warm, he said; the sun loved him not and would grant him no heat, though he basked upon the rooftop like a lizard.

The wise men shook their heads, and tried this and that, until David roused up and roared that he was not yet dead, and bade them get out. They were glad enough to do his bidding; tending dying kings is a chancy business.

It was Solomon who brought King David comfort, of a sort. After David's last roar, Solomon sat with his father and spoke long with him. And then Solomon came to me.

"Mother, I would not say this to my mother—" Solomon smiled at me and touched my shoulder, "but my father the king is dying."

"Yes, I know." I did not care, either for joy or sorrow. Long years had passed since my hate had raged; love had quenched it. Love for Bathsheba, and for Solomon. Now that David at last lay dying, I found I could not care enough even to wish him sooner dead. *Poor David*, I thought, and smiled at Solomon. "What is it you wish to ask of me, my heart?"

"Do I come to you only to beg boons?"

"I know how you look when you wish favors for others, Solomon. Now what is it King David would have?"

"Surely the queen is the wisest of women!"

"Surely the prince is a monkey for jests!"

Solomon laughed and knelt before me, and held my hands in his. "I see it is useless to veil truth from you, O my mother-the-queen." Then he sobered. "You have known the king for many years."

"Oh, yes." I stroked Solomon's bright hair. "Since long before you were born, my heart. Since King David was younger than you are now."

"Then tell me, you who have known him so long—I had thought—" Solomon hesitated, and his cheeks reddened. "I could not ask this of my mother, but you—"

"You may ask me anything. You know that, my love."

"Yes—but you may not like to hear this either; you are the queen, after all. All the world knows how you and King David loved."

"Oh, yes. All the world knows. But that love is past, and long past. So ask."

"He is so cold, Mother. All the physicians do is pile more sheepskins upon him, but it does not help. I thought—perhaps something warmer than sheepskins to care for him? A fair maid to tend him, and sleep beside him under those sheepskins? Well—he has always liked women—"

"None better. Why Solomon, you are blushing like a maid yourself!" I looked at him sharp-eyed; mothers are careful of their sons. "Any maid?"

"Well—any pretty one." Solomon smiled, and did not quite meet my eyes. "The king's eye sees only beauty."

"And not worth," I said.

"Yes; and a king must see both. I remember that." Solomon rose to his feet. "He—the physicians only torment him; to what end? We all know he is dying—can they not ease his passage?"

"Not while he still breathes," I said. Then I sat and thought while Solomon waited. A fair young maid—David had always an eye for a pretty woman and had come to much grief thereby, and he was not yet blind. It would comfort him, perhaps; cheer him, if anything yet could. And there was another thing.

King David was dying—and still he would not name the prince to follow after him upon the throne. Oh, it was true that Solomon was much favored. Solomon was true gold in river sand. Some thought that enough; I knew David too well.

And there was another prince much favored by David, and by some of the people. Adonijah. Prince Adonijah was twenty-five that summer; even King David could call him 'boy' no longer. And Adonijah was Absalom's full brother, and much resembled him.

The other princes still living did not trouble me; they were nothing. I knew in my bones that the balance trembled between Adonijah and Solomon. Any weight set in that balance might tip the scale one way—or the other.

"Well, Mother?" Solomon said at last. "Is my idea good?"

"Yes," I said. "I think it very good. And I think it will prove more pleasing to your father than did Adonijah's gift of his own physician."

"The one who prescribed leeches to remove the chilly blood? By Yahweh, it would please any man better!" Then Solomon looked at me again, and I knew he was troubled.

So I laid my hand upon his, and said, "Tell me."

He caught up my hand and held it to his cheek. "I can hide nothing from you. But it is nothing, only thoughts that will not lie quiet when I bid them."

"What thoughts, Solomon?"

"Ill thoughts, when my father lies dying."

I waited, and he spoke on. "At first I thought, why should not my father have comfort? And then I thought, why should this girl not tell us what he says, and to whom? And then I thought—"

"And then you thought, 'if I take this young fair maid to wife after, it will strengthen my claim to David's crown'." I touched Solomon's hair. "But my heart, that is only sense."

"I know. But it seems heartless to use his weakness against him so."

"Will it be kinder to let Adonijah rule? You know him, Solomon—and I knew his brother. Remember what I told you of Absalom."

"And my brother Amnon, and my sister Tamar. I remember. I remember all you have taught me, Mother."

"Then do not trouble yourself over this. It was a kind thought first. That it is clever as well is a blessing, not a curse."

"And I also thought—it would be a hard thing to yoke a fawn to—" Solomon did not say it; David was his father, after all.

"An old bull? Twice do not trouble yourself over that, Solomon. If David touches a girl in lust now, I will myself walk naked through the streets of Jerusalem."

Solomon stared at me; I smiled and leaned to kiss his cheek. "Do not heed me overmuch, my love—this waiting is hard on us all. Now go, and seek out a pretty maid for your father the king."

"I?" Solomon looked startled as a stag brought face to face with men and dogs. You would think he had never set so much as his eyes upon a woman. "But Mother, I had hoped--"

"That I would choose her? Ah, no, my heart—it is not I who will take this girl to my bosom once David is dead. Please yourself, Solomon; what pleases you is sure to please King David."

"But where in all the land shall I find a maiden as clever and as beautiful as you and as my mother?"

I laughed. "I will not ask which of us is clever and which beautiful! Nor will I find her for you; go, and use your own eyes. And Solomon—remember it is a queen you seek."

"I will remember," he said, and raised my hands to his lips. "And when I choose, I will choose a girl like you."

~

"But he would do better," I said to Bathsheba later, when I told her what Solomon and I had decided that day, "to choose a girl like you."

It was evening before I spoke privately to Bathsheba; a queen's days, like a king's, are crowded with those seeking justice, mercy, favors. Sometimes it is a great favor asked—a life, perhaps. Sometimes it is a small one—a word, a smile. Always it is time. I treasured my quiet hours.

Now I sat before my window and looked out over Jerusalem. The sky gleamed iron-dark; soon it would rain. That would be pleasant, to lie here with Bathsheba beside me, and hear the soft rain fall.

"Oh, no," said Bathsheba. "Solomon is right; she should be like you, Michal."

I had almost forgotten what I had said to her; I remembered, and shook my head. "No, my love. Not like me."

"But Michal—you say this girl may be the next queen—and we both know I am weak and foolish! A queen should be good and clever, like you."

"It is possible for a woman to be too good—and I was never clever enough."

"And she should be beautiful, too—and you are beautiful, Michal—you know you are! You are like a girl still."

"All queens are beautiful." Of course I was like a girl still; my body had never ripened with a child. Once that had been a grief to me. It was hard, now, to recall how sharp that pain had bitten.

That was long ago. Before Solomon. I turned away from the window and smiled at Bathsheba.

Bathsheba was plump as a tame partridge now that she was nearing forty, but she was still fair to look upon. A sweet heart makes a sweet face, even when a woman is no longer young. Now she smiled at me, and said, "But Michal—do you think it will work? Do you think the king will like this girl? And do you think Solomon—"

"Has a girl already in his eye? He swore not."

"Men," Bathsheba told me with great dignity, "are not always truthful, when they speak with women."

And then we looked into each other's eyes, and laughed. "No, I suppose they are not," I said. "As for the rest—of course the king will like her. And if he does not he will say he does, to prove himself still a man."

Bathsheba sobered and drew near to me. "The king is very ill." She took my hand, seeking comfort. Change drew nearer with each day that passed. The palace air pressed heavy with it.

"Yes, he is very ill."

"And Adonijah spends much time with him."

"As much as King David will allow."

Bathsheba laced her fingers tight through mine. "What does Nathan say?"

"What does Nathan ever say? Wait; Yahweh will speak in his own good time."

"I would rather hear King David speak," Bathsheba said, and her voice trembled with her own daring.

"So would we all, my love. Failing that, I would know what King David thinks. Perhaps Solomon's girl will be able to tell us."

"I do not think," Bathsheba said, "that Adonijah will like it."

"If he does, he is a bigger fool than even I think." And I thought Adonijah a bigger fool than Absalom had been. Now that King David lay dying, Adonijah gave himself a king's airs. Driving his chariot through the city to show himself, with men running be-

fore crying 'Long live Prince Adonijah!'—did he think no one from
the palace saw, or knew, or cared?

Absalom once had done as much. But unlike Absalom,
Adonijah did not court the people's minds and hearts. There was
no tending the poor, no granting justice. There was nothing but a
great show. Adonijah sought only to flash kingfisher-bright before
men's eyes.

Yes, Adonijah was a fool. That did not make him any less a
danger.

"Do you think Adonijah looks so very much like—like
Absalom?"

"Yes," I said. "He is very like."

"Perhaps the king will see that."

"Perhaps he will. Ah, listen—the rain has started." I rested my
cheek upon Bathsheba's hair, and for a time the only sound was
rain falling hard upon the city.

"But where is Solomon to find such a girl?" Bathsheba asked
at last.

"Bathsheba, my dearest sister—Solomon is a prince, and very
good to look upon, and gentle and kind as well. Somewhere in all
the land he will surely find *one* maiden willing to take him as he
is!"

~

"She is beautiful as the day," Solomon told me as we walked among
my lilies. "And modest, and well taught."

"And does this paragon among women have a name?"

"Her name is Abishag."

"And where is she from?"

"From Shunem."

"From Shunem. And how did you happen upon this maiden,
my heart?"

Solomon looked down at me, and smiled like a small boy who
has eaten a plate of honey-cakes and hopes to be forgiven. "I tried

to be wise, as you would be. I sent a trusted servant to seek out a fair maid to serve and please Queen Michal. It was he who found Abishag in Shunem."

"I heard nothing of this." I would speak to Narkis; I did not like secrets that I myself did not keep.

Solomon spread his hands wide. "I said it was to be a pleasing surprise for you. Well, I did not want my search gossipped of throughout the palace. Since it was for *your* pleasure, I knew my man would hold his tongue."

"Solomon—" It was no good; I laughed. At last I sobered and slid my arm through his. "Now, tell me of this girl Abishag. You have seen her yourself?"

"Yes." Solomon's eyes were bright. "I have seen her."

"And which day is she as lovely as?" I could not help teasing him; no mother could have.

Solomon smiled, himself fair as a summer day. "The hair of her head is like purple; thick and rich and dark as dusk. Her skin is apricots ripe in the sun. Her teeth are matched pearls. Her eyes are the night sky bright with stars." He paused, and added, as if it were a cherished secret, "And she smells of soap and cinnamon."

"So she pleased you?"

Solomon laughed, and turned to face me. He set his hands upon my shoulders and kissed my forehead. "Yes, Mother. I saw her for a short time only, but she pleased me."

"Well, that is good. Now bring her to me, and I will speak with her—and make all clear that you did not!"

~

Abishag was fair indeed; Solomon had not overpraised her. That was good, for David liked any pretty woman. And Abishag was comely in the fashion David favored above all others. Her slanting eyes were sloe-dark, her mouth moist and pink as a ripe peach, and she was round-breasted and round-hipped, and tied her scarlet girdle just tight enough to show this.

She was younger than I would have chosen—very young, and much impressed by the king's city and the king's house—and by the queen. She studied me as closely as I did her; I smiled, and bade her rise and sit beside me.

She rose up graceful as a willow in the wind, and spread her skirt carefully so that the embroidery was displayed to best advantage. A pleasing pattern; suns and moons worked in bright thread. I asked if it were the work of her own hands, and she said that it was.

"And the design is my own as well. I have been well schooled in all a woman's arts, O Queen." She spoke with a proper pride, neither too much nor too little.

"In *all* a woman's arts?" I asked, and smiled upon her.

"Oh, yes—I can do anything you ask of me!" She was all eagerness to please. All eagerness to live in the palace and serve the queen—or so it seemed.

"Then I ask an answer. How is it so fair a maid is unwed, and unspoken for? Tell me truly, Abishag—is there no man who makes your heart beat hard and fast?"

"I am unwed and unspoken for. For the rest, that is not for me to say." But she blushed hot as she spoke the words, and for the first time seemed as uncertain as any young girl.

"Then I will say it. It is Prince Solomon who has taken your heart. Oh, come, child—I am as a mother to him, and he has already spoken of you. Do you think I gossip with any maid chance brought to me as if she were my daughter?"

"What did the prince say of me?" Eager words, eager spoken, and cheeks red as poppies; yes, Abishag cared. Well, and how could she not? There was no prince like Solomon for wisdom and beauty in all the land. No, and no man either.

"Why, he said that he had met at last a sweet and clever maid, one fair as a queen." And I watched Abishag close as I spoke, and was satisfied with the wisdom of Solomon's choice.

For Abishag was a clever girl, and ambitious, which was not a bad thing. The queen's finery I wore, the hint of a crown for her brow, warmed her eyes. But Solomon's name was the spark that kindled fire there.

And so I smiled upon Abishag, and kissed her hot cheek, and lifted a twisted braid of pearls and coral from my own neck and hung it about hers. "So take this, with my love—it was brought by a trader from Tyre, and he said it had come farther yet. But traders cannot tell true to save their throats from slitting! And this jewel was meant for a young neck, child—yes, that is the setting it should have. Solomon was right to praise you so highly—it is long since I have seen a girl as lovely as you."

Abishag was flattered, of course, and blushed again, and stroked the necklace and coiled the sea-gems about her plump fingers. "The queen is too kind. There are many more beautiful than I. All men know that true beauty lies only under King David's roof, and that the queen outshines all others as the moon outshines the stars."

"Pretty words," I said, and smiled. "But I have a mirror, and a board to tally the years that have passed since I was born. Now tell me truly how you reckon your beauty."

Abishag looked at me, and her sloe-eyes were shrewd. "It has caught a prince," she said at last. "Or at least I am told it has. So either my beauty is great indeed or Prince Solomon has deceived me."

Solomon had made good use of the 'short time' he had spent with Abishag. And so, no doubt, had she. I pressed my lips together, firm, and did not laugh.

"Prince Solomon has not deceived you," I said, and took her hand. "So you have caught a prince, Abishag. Will you dare ensnare a king?"

~

Abishag would dare; of course she would dare. To care for an old man and bring me news of what he said—that seemed to her little enough. And the reward was great.

"I will *make* King David like me," Abishag told me, firm as a cat. "I tended my grandfather, when he was ill before he died. I shall tend the king as carefully and well, O Queen."

"Yes—but do not tell the king about your grandfather, Abishag!"

Abishag swore she would not, and listened close as I spoke to her of King David, and of what he liked, and did not. "And I know you go a maiden to the king, Abishag, and I think you will go to Prince Solomon still a maid. But I may be wrong; will that trouble you?"

Abishag looked down at her fingers; she touched a turquoise ring that I knew had been a gift from Solomon. "If it will not trouble Prince Solomon," she said at last, "then I will not let it trouble me." She lifted her head and looked at me straight. "Is that a queen's answer, O Queen?"

"Yes, Abishag," I said. I curled my fingers in the thin chains of the brass-and-crystal bracelet Bathsheba had given me so long ago. "I am very much afraid that it is."

~

Abishag was good to David. She stayed close by him always, and slept beside him in his bed, and tended to him most faithfully. But she lay with him chastely. So she said, and I believed her.

Still, David valued Abishag highly for her youth and warmth, and for the way she would listen for hours to his tales, sitting still as a cat while he rambled on about long-past battles and long-dead men. He thanked me often for my gift, and swore I was worth any dozen other women.

"Have I not always said so, and have you not proved it forty times over?"

"The king is too kind, and I cannot take praise that belongs to another. It was your son Solomon who thought a young maid would please you, and warm you in the night." I thought it time to show David how Solomon cared for him, before Adonijah came whining to him with the tale that Solomon had sought out Abishag and brought her to me.

"A kind thought," David said, and patted Abishag's hands as they lay folded and quiet in her lap. "Yes, a kind thought. Solomon has always been a good boy."

"He is a boy no longer, David. He is a man, and a good one. He is almost what you were, at his age."

David was never too proud or too old to lap up flattery like honey from the hand. "Well, if that is true, Michal, then he will be a fine man indeed. Yes, a fine man."

"A fine man," I said, "who would make a fine king, fit to follow the great King David."

But I had gone too far. David became sullen and suspicious, and said that I wished to see him dead.

"You have always wished it. You are a hard woman, Michal, and your heart is stone. You were always too proud—you never loved me truly, as your brother Jonathan did." And he began to weep, for his own words had always had the power to touch his heart. The old are frail, and David seemed very old, now.

He groped for Abishag, who came forward onto her knees and put her arms around the king's thin shoulders. "Jonathan—have I told you of Jonathan? King Saul's son, he was, and we loved each other well—have you heard the tale?"

"Tell it to me," Abishag said, and stroked his white hair. She gave no hint that she must have heard the tale a dozen times. As King David's life faded, that early friendship with my brother Jonathan grew stronger in his mind, truer with each telling of the tale and singing of the song, until even David thought their love outlasted time and death.

I knew that he no longer saw me sitting there; he lived again in his glorious youth, embraced in youth's arms. And so I rose, and smiled over his head at Abishag, and went quietly away. If anything was said that I should know, Abishag would come and tell it to me later.

~

Soon. All men knew it would be soon. King David could not outlast the year. So ran gossip in the city. I did not think he could outlast the summer.

Soon—and King David still would not say either *'It will be Adonijah'* or *'It will be Solomon'*.

Many thought Adonijah would be king after. Adonijah was the eldest prince, now that so many others lay dead; he was Absalom's full brother, and David had always loved him for that, if for nothing else. The high priest Abiathar favored Adonijah as well, and so Adonijah walked meek before him; Abiathar could anoint Adonijah truly as king. And many of the war-captains thought Adonijah a fine prince, who would make a finer king.

But the man whose support Adonijah desired above all other men's was Joab, for Joab could bring half the army as dower to the next king.

Prince Adonijah had always held his head too high to see Joab when he walked by—now Adonijah courted Joab, wooing for his favor. But Joab kept his face smooth as stone; Joab would say nothing, save that he served David and David's kingdom.

I knew better than to spread false coin before Joab; I was not his friend, nor he mine. I could only hope that when Joab looked at Adonijah, Joab remembered Absalom.

Solomon had his own supporters. Nathan, of course, and the high priest Zadok too. And Benaiah, the commander of the palace guard; perhaps that was why Joab would not yet smile upon Solomon.

An almost even match, the two princes, as the king's life ebbed. Either might gain the crown, and we all waited and hoped.

All save Adonijah. Like his brother Absalom, he was overproud and impatient. He grabbed too soon for the crown.

And so in the end, Solomon had only to stretch out his hand and catch it as it fell.

~

After all the watching, and the waiting, and the scheming, the end rushed upon us oddly sudden, like a long-threatened summer storm. The end began when Abishag came to me where I sat with Bathsheba in the queen's garden and told what Adonijah had done now. This time it was no mere matter of princely arrogance.

"Prince Adonijah gives a great banquet—he has asked all the princes, save only Prince Solomon. And he has said that his house will be open to all men as well, to feast as they will." Abishag knelt at my feet and spoke quick and clear. "And he asked King David to come and feast with them and the king would not, but he laid his hands on the prince's head and gave him his blessing. It is said that Prince Adonijah has asked Abiathar, and Joab, and all the other great men to this feast—but he has not asked Benaiah, nor yet Zadok, nor the prophet Nathan."

As all men knew, Benaiah and Zadok and Nathan favored Solomon. Bathsheba gasped and would have spoken, but I waved her to silence. I drew a deep breath before speaking. "Has Abiathar said he will go?"

Abishag nodded. "Indeed, he is there now, and has with him the sacred oil. I had that from one who saw it with his own eyes— or so he swore, for what that is worth in the market."

All the great men, and the princes, and Abiathar the high priest with the sacred oil—I knew what Adonijah must plan. Adonijah was risking all on one throw for the crown.

One more thing I must know. "And has Joab gone to this great feast as well?"

"Yes, O Queen. Joab sits beside Prince Adonijah even now."

And is Joab's sword drawn to strike? I drew Abishag up and kissed her. "You have done well and more than well. Now go back, before the king knows you are gone and wonders where. And make haste."

Abishag pulled her veil close and fled away; she was soft and quick as a shadow in the sun. I sat there in the queen's garden and looked at Bathsheba, whose eyes were wide.

"What does Adonijah mean by this?" She did not truly question; she too knew the answer.

"Adonijah means to be king," I said. "And he means to be king *now*. That is why Abiathar went as high priest with the sacred oil—Adonijah must have convinced him to anoint a new king while King David still lives."

David himself was the precedent for such an action; nothing but grief could come of it. For an instant I forgot all else in anger at Adonijah, as if I were his mother rather than Solomon's. "It is sheer folly; King David is all but dead—oh, why can none of his blood ever *wait*?"

Bathsheba clutched at my sleeve. "What are we to do? Adonijah king! Oh, Michal—what will he do to Solomon? You know what Adonijah is—"

"He will do nothing," I said. "I love you dearly, but you are sillier than a day-old rabbit! Now stop weeping and let us think."

Bathsheba dried her eyes as I bade her and looked at me hopefully. Bathsheba's eyes were as sweet and trusting as they had been the day I first had seen her sitting lonely upon her housetop; I had kept her safe all the years since then. I would not fail her now.

And so I thought—hard and fast. A man's weapons are sword and spear; a woman's her wits. I had learned to use my thoughts as David once used his warriors.

Adonijah wished to be king, and would not wait. He had Abiathar the high priest for his shield and it seemed he had Joab the war-chief for his sword as well; he had the people too—or at least he had those whose eye could be caught by gold's flash. But Adonijah did not have Benaiah, the captain of the king's guard. He did not have Zadok, who was also high priest. He did not have the prophet Nathan, and Nathan still counted for much.

Nor was I as certain as Adonijah must now be of where Joab's loyalty was given. So long as King David lived, I thought Joab would strike only at David's bidding—and King David was not yet dead. So Adonijah might not yet own Joab's sword.

And Adonijah did not have King David's pledge. I knew that

as surely as I knew my heart beat. If Adonijah were King David's choice, Adonijah would shout it from the housetops. There would be no need for hasty feasts and squandered gold.

"King David has not named Adonijah," I said.

"He has not named Solomon either. Oh, Adonijah is Prince Absalom all over again!"

"Yes, and look at Prince Absalom now. He was a fool and Adonijah is the same. And so is David, to let his sons act so."

"Oh, no—but—but he is—" Bathsheba was never one for flint-edged truths; now she wept, rather than utter them.

"King David is old," I said flatly. "He is old, and his mind wanders—even he does not know anymore what he has said, and what he has not."

"Yes," said Bathsheba. "And once he was so beautiful, and he made such beautiful songs, Michal!" She bowed her head; tears slid down her cheeks like rain down a wall.

"Yes, and believed them, too—" And then I stopped, on a gasp of breath so sharp and hard that Bathsheba put an arm about me and stopped weeping.

"Michal? Are you all right? Do you have a pain?" She put her hand over my heart.

I shook my head. "No. No pain." No pain, but instead a hard beat under my skin; triumph, hard and fierce, for I had the answer.

Many years ago David had told me that I must learn a king's ways. And so I had. David himself had taught me with his sweet lying songs. I had learned his lesson. And at last I held the future in my own hands.

"Michal?"

I put my arms around Bathsheba. "I am a fool," I said, and made myself laugh. "All this time and all this worry—when David himself swore Solomon would be king after him!"

Bathsheba stared, her eyes as round as full moons. "He did? But when? He never said so to me, or to Solomon—"

"But he did to me! Oh, it was long ago, when Solomon was

still sucking at your breast—David looked upon him and swore that Solomon would be king next, for the great love he bore you—and me. He had had a dream, David said, that the next king would—would be born twice, and have two mothers—and who else could that be but Solomon?" I spoke swiftly, clutching at Bathsheba's plump hands. The future would be what I desired; I would shape it myself with words and deeds as David so often had.

"King David said that? Truly?" Bathsheba's cheeks were pink as summer roses; I told her what she wished to hear, and so she believed.

"Truly, he said that. And see—it has lain hidden in my mind all these years—now Yahweh has let me know it again."

"But—why has not the king spoken?"

"He is old; he is tired. I will go and tell him what it is that Adonijah would do now. And I think that when King David hears that, he will remember what he once promised me."

CHAPTER 29

"Didst not thou, my lord, O King,
swear unto thine handmaid . . . ?"

—I Kings 1:13

I left Bathsheba there in the queen's garden and went to the king's rooms, where David lay. Abishag was there before me, as if she had never left; she sat beside David and rubbed his cold hands with her warm young fingers.

"Go," I said to Abishag. "Leave us." And when she had slipped past me and away, I walked across the room and stood looking down at David.

"Abishag? Where are you—I am cold." His voice quavered and wailed, winter-thin.

"Abishag is not here, David. I am Michal. You know me. I am your wife."

"King Saul's daughter." His hand crept over the blankets, searching. "Jonathan's sister."

"David's queen." I watched his hand move, seeking the comfort of other flesh. His hand was as thin as his voice; the ring he wore, the king's great seal-ring, weighed heavy against the bone.

"Michal."

"Yes, Michal. I have come to tell you a tale, David." As I thought of what I would tell him a fierce pleasure awoke, and I smiled. "It is only an old tale, oft told, but it made me laugh. Perhaps, when you have heard it, you too will laugh."

He looked up at me, then. He was dying; his body old, his voice and his hands thin and frail. But he was not yet dead, for his eyes still gleamed clear and cunning. King David still lived in his bright eyes.

An ancient serpent stirred against my bones; for the first time in many years I thought of my nephew Meribaal's eyes, and of my husband Phaltiel's. I had never seen Bathsheba's first husband; I had never seen Uriah's eyes. I had only seen David's on the day he had made me choose who should live and who die. . . .

"What tale?" David's voice was weak; fretful. The voice of a helpless old man.

"An old tale," I said again. "Your son Adonijah proclaims himself king, as his brother Absalom did before him. He gives a great feast, and the high priest Abiathar anoints him with the sacred oil."

"He dares—"

"Of course he dares; why should he not? What will you do to stop him?"

"I have not said Adonijah will be king!" A flash of the old lion; weak, but fierce still.

"No," I said. "You have said that Solomon will be king."

David stared up at me. "No. Never have I said that."

"Oh, but you have." Deep beneath my heart the serpent woke from years-long sleep. "You have sworn it on your knees before Yahweh. You had a dream that the next king would be a twice-born son with two mothers—who else but Solomon? He was born dead; I saved him. Now do you remember?"

"No," David said. "No." He shook his head, and coughed. I waited until he was quiet once more.

"That is what happened, David." The serpent shifted, coiled. "It is what happened because I say it did, and because no one can deny it."

"I can. I am king! Tell such a tale, and I will rise from this bed to tell all the court that you are mad. Mad Saul's daughter—" David struggled to raise himself up, but his body was too weak to obey him, and he could not rise even to his elbow. I smiled as he fell back, defeated by his own feeble body.

"Rise from your bed if you can," I said. "Go and tell all the court if it pleases you, O great king. And I will follow behind, shaking my head sadly and saying that King David is too old, too ill, to know what it is he says. That King David is mad."

He stared up at me, and something flickered behind his eyes. But he laughed, or tried to; truly he was very weak in body. "No one will believe you, Michal. You are only a woman, and I am the king."

"The old king," I said. "The ailing king. And I am Michal, the first lady of the palace, the queen of King David's heart, the woman who loves David better than she loves life itself. All men know those things, for you yourself told them they were true. So when I, Michal the queen, say David the king is half-mad with age, men will believe me, David."

Again he tried to rise up, to speak, but the effort made him choke and gasp for breath. All he could say was, "No—" and "I— king—"

I smiled down at him. "You see? You rave, David." The serpent danced; my blood throbbed hot at my throat and the taste of power was sharp as cinnamon upon my tongue. Ah, yes, this time it was Michal who would be believed—and David who was watched with pitying eyes.

"No." David lay very still, a rabbit before a serpent's gaze. "You are wrong. My people love me—they have always loved me— they will not believe—" He paused and his eyes narrowed, canny; I saw a ghost of David the fox. "My Bathsheba will not believe—"

"Bathsheba?" I laughed, and saw him flinch. "Bathsheba loves me better than she does you, David—and that by your own fault. Once she loved you well; if she does not love you now, it is through your own folly."

All David's women had loved him, and he had tossed their love aside. Just as once, long ago, he had tossed aside mine, as if love were no more than a pretty toy that he might scoop up to play with again whenever he wished.

But women's hearts are not trivial playthings, and it is never wise to throw love away—if only because its warmth may be needed in the cold future.

"As for your other women—who will they wish to see king, David? Solomon, whom they know to be both kind and clever, or Adonijah, who will see threats behind every brother's smile?" Now I shook my head, slowly, as if saddened by what I must next say. "No, David. If I speak against you, this time it is *I* who will be believed."

"I am the king," he said again. But his eyes shifted away from mine and I knew that I had won. Now, at last, I held in my grasp what I once had prayed for with every beat of my heart—power over David.

I smiled and shook my head again. "You are king, but I am queen. Your own well-loved queen, for whom you dared so much. All the world knows that truth—you remember your songs about us?"

"They were good songs, were they not?" David clutched at the golden past as if it could save him now. "Good songs. Men still sing them, Michal."

"Oh, yes, they were good songs. And now I too know how to sing. You cannot leave your bed; all men know your mind wanders where it wills. When I go from your room with the king's seal and the king's blessing on Solomon, who will not believe whatever tale I choose to spin? Whatever tale *I* choose, David."

The serpent within swayed to the hard slow beat of my heart. I bent low over David, to make sure he heard my words clear. "Do you remember a day when you took me from my husband Phaltiel—when you told me what I must learn, to be queen and happy both? Well, I have learned, King David. Harper David. Hero David."

"Ah, have you come for your revenge? Have you come to kill me at last?" David's voice quavered but his faded eyes gleamed with strange expectation. His hand reached up, shaking with the effort; his fingers closed bone-hard about my wrist. "Kill me, then, but you will never be free of me. Never, Michal. I was everything to you. Everything. As I was to Saul, and to Jonathan . . . . "

And suddenly I understood. I knew this was truth at last. And at last Michal understood what Saul's daughter, Phaltiel's wife, David's queen, never had. Oh, yes, David knew what lay behind my eyes—he always had. David did not care if it was all the world's love or all the world's hate, so long as all was his. So long as he and he alone was the lodestar of my existence.

Of all the world's existence. Even Yahweh must love or hate David more than all the world. Nothing less.

And so never would David be content. Never would anything be enough. Never, though he lived a thousand years. *'You see? Men like David will always make their own problems, little princess.'*

"Yes," I said. "I see. I see everything now." For I knew at last what I truly desired. And what I desired was not power, but freedom. Not to rule David as he had ruled me all these long years— but to be free of him.

A great stone seemed to roll away from my heart; a weight I had not known I carried lifted from my bones. For I looked at David's face, and listened to David's voice, and I felt neither love nor hate. There was only indifference, as if he were a stranger. I did not know when I had ceased to care or how long had it been since my hate was more than habit. I knew only that at last I saw clearly.

I saw that I was free and David chained, and he did not even know it. And I looked down into David's bright triumphant eyes, and I laughed; laughed until I felt tears splash upon my cheeks. I touched my fingers to my wet cheeks and tried to remember how many tears I had shed because of David. A river of them, I supposed; they no longer seemed important.

"No, David," I said, and I heard my voice kind to him—kind, but careless, as one speaks to a begging dog. Easy kindness to one for whom I cared nothing. "I have not come to kill you. Why should I? What are you to me that I should kill you?"

David stared up at me, his eyes narrow with a king's anger. "You—you—" But he was too weak to strike; his body began to shake, and for long breaths he was unable to force more words past his rage. At last he calmed, and said, "Do you think I loved you, Michal? You were never more to me than King Saul's daughter."

"You do not understand, David." I spoke patiently, without heat. "You are not important—hate me or love me, I do not care. The only thing I care for is that Solomon should be king. King *now*. King because I say he shall be."

I looked down at David and I smiled at him for the last time. "Give me the king's seal-ring, David."

As I spoke I put my hand on David's; his fingers closed over mine, as hard as the past we shared between us. He looked puzzled, like a small boy who does not know how he has erred.

And his eyes were bright no longer; they had clouded with years and memories, and with defeat. But still he tried to make his voice ring firm, as if he once more commanded warriors in the field. "Do you think you can take the king's ring, Saul's daughter?"

"Oh, David," I said, "I already have. I am no longer yours; you lost me long ago."

CHAPTER 30

". . . thy love to me was wonderful . . . ."
—II Samuel 1:26

When I went from King David's rooms I found Solomon waiting for me in the hall beyond. He was calm as always, even now, when all hung uneasy in the balance.

"Does my father know what Adonijah would do? Is Adonijah his choice?"

"He knows." I smiled and held out my hand flat; the king's great seal-ring lay coiled there. "This is his choice, Solomon. Use it wisely."

Solomon held out his hand and smiled at me; I slid the seal-ring onto his finger. The place beneath my heart was now warm with life, with love; never again could a poison serpent sleep there, cold and waiting.

Solomon stared at the ring for a moment. "The king does me great honor; I will try to be worthy."

"Yes, of course—but you need not say such things to me. Save them for those who do not know you as I do, my heart."

"Yes, I must move quickly now." Solomon smiled at me. "Did my father have any words of wisdom for me? Did he say, 'tell Solomon to show this ring to Benaiah and to Nathan'?"

"He did."

"And did he say that I should ride the king's own white mule to the marketplace, so that Nathan might pour the holy oil upon my head for all men to see?"

"Those were his very words," I said.

"I thought they were what he would say. I know they are what you would say, Mother, in his place." Solomon smiled at me, his eyes clear as sunlit pools. "Now I must do as my father bid me if I am to be king by sunset."

I held him only long enough to kiss his cheek. "Go with my love and blessing—and your father's."

Then I watched him stride away from me. Had David ever been so tall and straight and beautiful? I had thought so once, but long years stretched between then and now.

Long ago was gone. Now was Solomon.

"King Solomon," I said. I looked back, once, at the door to the room where King David lay, and smiled. And then I went to tell Bathsheba that our boy was truly king.

~

All went as smoothly as one of David's own songs, after that. As King David had decreed, Prince Solomon became King Solomon that day, to reign beside his father as equal.

Adonijah's friends proved as false as their master, and fled his side when they heard the trumpets and the shouting for Solomon. I later heard that Joab watched all this and only sat and drank his wine; Adonijah had wooed in vain.

Adonijah fled as well—to the nearest altar, to cling to its horns in hope of sanctuary there. He feared for his life, as well he might. Another than Solomon would have slain him out of hand.

But Solomon was always a man of peace, and so he had his brother brought from the altar to stand before him. Adonijah thought himself dead, then, until Solomon smiled and bade him rise.

"Our father has made his choice, and Yahweh has confirmed it," Solomon told Adonijah. "No, do not fear me, for I bear you no ill will. Kiss me, brother, and go live quiet in your own house, and we will stay friends, as we have been."

And so Adonijah kissed his brother and went away, and was

glad to do so. I thought there might be more trouble later, for there was bad blood in that line of David's sons. But now there was peace in the land once more—and Solomon was king at last.

The true king, for King David was all but dead. The crown, and the future, belonged to King Solomon.

And when I was summoned to the great court and saw the son of my heart seated upon the gilded throne, I knew this was worth even the pain I had once endured. The pain, too, was long ago.

Now I saw Solomon as the great king he was meant to be— and because I was a woman, I saw him as the father of children who would climb upon my lap, and call me 'grandmother' as if I were their own. And I would tell them tales of how it had been long ago, when I was young. How it had been when Saul was king, and David only a shepherd with a gift for song, and the great King Solomon not yet born.

But that was for tomorrow. Today I knelt before King Solomon in all his glory, and my heart was so full it ached. And Solomon rose, and came down to me, and lifted me to my feet.

"Never kneel to me, Queen Michal, any more than my mother does. I would have all men see in what honor King Solomon holds you." And he kissed me before all the court.

I kissed Solomon's hands, as subject, and his mouth, as mother. And I wept for pure joy, and the salt tears were sweet as love upon my lips.

～

Adonijah went into his house, not to live in peace and give thanks for doing so, but to plot against both kings, the old and the new. Less than a month had passed when he asked Solomon for Abishag when King David should no longer need her. And he was fool enough to do so in open court, before us all.

Adonijah might as well have asked for the crown outright as for one of King David's women. So all men knew, and so Solomon told him; being Solomon, the words of reproof were quiet, measured things. Being Solomon, he might even have pardoned Adonijah again. Adonijah was his brother, after all.

But Adonijah could not bow his head and leave well alone. He argued against Solomon; accused Solomon of plotting against him and against King David; accused Abishag of harlotry.

"Stop, brother. Do not let anger speak for you." So Solomon warned him; Solomon did not want his brother's blood on his hands.

But Adonijah would not stop; next he began accusing Bathsheba, and me—I do not know of what, for Adonijah did not live to finish his slanders. For Joab sprang forward and struck Adonijah down before Solomon's throne. To the end of his days Joab had a taste for murder in the king's name.

No one was surprised, save perhaps Adonijah himself. Certainly no one blamed Solomon—save Solomon.

"He was too quick to strike," he told me after. "I should have foreseen it—I know what Joab is. There was another way."

Perhaps there had been, but I would not say so—no, not even if I must swear Joab had done right, for I could not bear to see Solomon's eyes so troubled. I took his hand and laid it against my cheek. "No, Solomon; there was no other way."

"Adonijah was my brother; I should have treated him more gently."

"Did he treat you gently? No, my heart—and it was better quickly done. If Adonijah had risen up against you, many men would have been killed—many women left husbandless, and many children fatherless. It was cruel, yes—but kinder than what would have come after, had he been spared."

Solomon smiled, then, and kissed me. "I know you are right—you are the wisest of women."

"No," I said. "I was taught my lessons well, that is all. Do not grieve for Adonijah, Solomon—he would not have shed one tear for you."

"Or for those who followed him, to their cost. I know he would not; I knew my brother."

"And Adonijah did this for you—he showed you where Joab's loyalty now lies. With the anointed king."

"Joab is too quick to strike," Solomon said again. He embraced me, and then sighed. "Now I must go and tell my father—it is only right that he hear of this from me."

Once I would have rejoiced to give such news to David. It was hard, now, to remember how fierce such hatred burned. Now I was only glad that I was not the one who must go and tell David that his son Adonijah was dead.

~

And King David too died less than forty days after Solomon was seated upon his throne. The old king's clutch at life was feeble, almost uncaring, now; it was Adonijah's treachery and death, I think, that truly killed him.

When David heard of the death of his last rebellious son, he turned his face to the wall and would no longer eat or drink. He was dying fast, now; each sunset we thought he could not last the night.

And then one sunset it was true.

When Bathsheba was told the old king would be dead by morning she wept so hard I forbade her to enter David's room. For all David's faults, to Bathsheba he would always be the king who had once loved her hot through summer nights.

"No, Bathsheba, you must go and rest," I said. "David would not want to see you weeping here. He loved always to see you smiling; let him go remembering that. I will stay with him."

~

Men now sing of what King David said as he lay dying. They tell of sage words giving advice and wisdom to the living; of praise sung to Yahweh; of prophecies for the kingdom. Men say all this, and believe it, too; well, that is what David would have wished. It is a better tale, after all, than the truth. I sat beside David all that last night, and so I know.

David spoke—but of the past, not the future. He spoke of Saul, and of Jonathan; at the last, he spoke of me. Yahweh he did not speak of at all.

"Jonathan loved me dear. Dearer than life." His voice was already a slow whisper from beyond the grave; almost unheard unless one chose to listen. "I was everything to him. I was everything to Saul. More to him than his crown. More than his children."

Then David turned his head on the thin pillow, and looked at me. "You are wrong. I was everything to you, Michal. Everything." The voice was insubstantial as smoke in the darkened room.

I sat there with my back straight and my hands folded in my lap. I said nothing. After all the love and hate and years, there was nothing left to say between us. And so I sat, and watched as the lamps guttered low and David's thin-threaded voice spoke on and on against the coming dark.

"Everything," David said. *"I was everything—"*

No, David, I thought. *You were nothing; you have nothing. There is nothing without love, and that you never had. You yourself threw love away and trampled it into the dust beneath your feet.*

Everything; David demanded everything. But love was the only thing worth having, and love is giving, not taking. And that was something that David would never know.

"Come and sit beside me, daughter of Saul—sit, and I will sing for you—"

I sat and held his hand as he talked, and as the night ended, and as he died. And I wept for David, almost as much as if I loved him.

EPILOGUE

"the crown of the wise. . . ."
—Proverbs 14:24

Love is giving, not taking. I thought of this the day King Solomon's temple to Yahweh was dedicated. I stood upon the king's balcony with Solomon and Bathsheba, and watched as the priests bore the sacred Ark high through the streets of Jerusalem to its new home in the great temple.

The prophet Nathan walked before them; Nathan was very old now, and very fat, and leaned heavily on his staff. But he walked proudly. He was Yahweh's prophet, and today all men would see that King Solomon gave him due honor and reverence.

The streets were clean-swept; the watchers quiet, as if they feared to raise their voices even in praise on such a holy occasion.

"Oh, Michal—do you remember the last time the Ark was borne through the streets?" Bathsheba smiled, then sighed. "How different it was, and how long ago."

"Yes." That had been a joyous day, not a solemn one. The people had sung and danced along Jerusalem's streets, and thrown flowers down before the Ark. The sun had beat down hard that day, hard and golden as King David danced naked before them all. And I had watched his skin shining oil-slick in the sun, and wished so hard that Yahweh might strike him dead that my heart hurt with it. And later David had come to me, and there had been another dance, but there had been no watchers then. . . .

"Yes," I said again. "It was different, and it was long ago. King David danced."

"I know. They still talked about it at the well when I first came to Jerusalem. I always wished I had seen that. I never saw the king dance." Bathsheba's voice was wistful, but still she smiled at me; those days held only sweet memories for her. "The people loved him so."

"Yes." I turned to our boy; our king. "But they love King Solomon more."

"Yes, love is the greatest gift." Bathsheba sighed again; all content.

I thought of David, and of how he had thrown that gift away with both hands. "Love, and the wisdom to know it, Bathsheba."

Solomon regarded us seriously, as if such idle women's words were of great import to him. "It is not possible to love and be wise both—or so I have heard." His words were all solemn, like a king's; his eyes were all mischief, like a boy's. "If you could have but one, which would you choose?"

"Oh, love," Bathsheba said at once, and kissed her son upon the cheek. "What is wisdom, compared to that?"

"And you, O Queen?" Solomon smiled at me in the way that made my heart melt.

I thought of all I had and knew of both love and wisdom. I owned both, now. But if I could choose only one, which? Wisdom? Ah, yes, wisdom would have spared me much pain—and cheated me, in the end, of much joy.

I smiled upon Solomon and Bathsheba. "Love, O son of my heart. Oh, yes—love."

The Ark passed just below us; the noonday sun burnished its gold and made it flame.

"Look!" said Bathsheba. "See how the sun makes the Ark glow—like fire!"

We each put an arm around Solomon and watched as the Ark was carried slowly past the palace, up the hill toward the temple Solomon had built. I reached across Solomon to clasp Bathsheba's hand; we encircled our son with loving arms. Yes, love was better than wisdom, if that were the choice. But I knew, at last, that

there was no choice, for a woman—or for a man, either, if he would
be happy.

It was a simple secret, hard-learned.

To love is to be wise.

~ ~ ~

Discussion

1. Michal tells her story in the first person. What does the story gain by being told only through Michal's eyes? How would *Queenmaker* be different if it were told from another person's point of view or in the third person?

2. What are Michal's goals, and how does she achieve them? How and why do they change during the course of her life?

3. Although there are many men in Michal's life, eventually she learns that her relationships with other women are most important to her. How does Michal come to realize this? How do her bonds with other women help her? How do they hinder her?

4. The Philistine concubine Zhurleen embodies the traditional feminine path to power. What does Michal learn from her? How would the course of Michal's life have changed if she had followed Zhurleen's advice?

5. Bathsheba is used as a weapon by both David and Michal. Who do you think wins the struggle over Bathsheba? How does this affect Bathsheba's life?

6. Although she has no son of her own, Michal uses her power to train the next king. What does her raising of Solomon show about her knowledge of and use of power?

7. How does Michal's relationship with Abishag show the changes in Michal since she was a girl? How does it show the changes from King Saul's day in the way kings and courts are regarded?

8. Although Michal never likes David's general, Joab, she comes to an uneasy truce with him. How are Michal and Joab's goals similar? How are they different?

9. Michal learns about kingship and power from many people, including King Saul, Phaltiel, Nathan, and Zhurleen, as well as from David himself. How does what she learns differ in each case? How is it the same? What decisions does she make that lead to her becoming a true queen?

10. Spinning and weaving are used as motifs throughout the book. How do these traditionally female tasks mirror women's lives?

11. In the end, Michal thinks she has chosen love over wisdom and power. Is she right?

What to Read Next